THE
AMETHYST
CODE

A STEELE OPS NOVEL

ERIN MOIRA O'HARA

Editor: Juanita Kees
Cover design by Fiona Jayde Media
Interior formatting by Author E.M.S.

ISBN: 978-0-9944019-4-6 (Print)

To Simon, my best friend, partner in life and great love.
You are all of these things and so much more.
Thousands of hours have gone into researching, writing
and editing this book without one complaint from you.
I value and appreciate your advice, comments,
perseverance and never-ending support.

Books by Erin Moira O'Hara

The Knight of Castle Kildare

Conspiracy in Emilia Romagna

Beat of the Jungle

Steele Ops Series

The Kalista Diamond

Precious Gems

Jewel of the Kimberley

The Amethyst Code

Bindarra Creek

Tempting Fate

Date with Destiny

A Twist of Fate

ACKNOWLEDGMENTS

While researching The Amethyst Code, I learned so much about cyber fraud, internet privacy and the importance of having a secure computer system.

My appreciation and heartfelt thanks to the wonderful people who have helped me deliver a book that I am extremely proud of.

My critique partner, Suzanne Gilchrist, who is always available for a brainstorming session. You continue to motivate me with your enthusiasm.

A special thanks to my husband, Simon, for his critiquing, computer knowledge, advice and never-ending support.

The brilliant Juanita Kees for her exceptional editing skills, guidance and delightful sense of humor.

Fiona Jayde Media, for another stunning cover.

Amy Atwell of Author E.M.S for her patience and formatting expertise.

PROLOGUE

"It's bad enough you sold our family home. I can't believe you've replaced Dad too." Darius trembled with the fury consuming her as she glared insolently at her mother.

"Calm down, darling. I had no choice but to sell the house. We didn't have your father's income to support us."

"Maybe so, but you could have moved into Grandma's house, with me and Brianna. You didn't have to move to Port Stephens."

"I had to leave, Darius. I couldn't stand the nosy do-gooders who kept calling to offer empathy, when all they really wanted was my opinion of your father's deceit. Nor could I take the pity on my friends' faces, or in one case, a colleague of your father's who wanted to have an affair. My sister's hip replacement saved my sanity. She needed me."

"*I needed you!*" Darius marched to the kitchen window, unable to see her grandmother's back garden for the haze of wretchedness never far from the surface. "You abandoned us."

"No, darling. My heart was broken too. The memories here were crushing me. The loneliness insurmountable. Those first months nearly killed me. I'll never love another man like I loved your father."

Darius turned a disbelieving face to her mother. "Then why do you have a boyfriend?"

"Darius, your father has been gone five years. Darren is kind and caring. Please come to Hamilton Island and meet him. He used to sail with your father when they were young. Darren wants to take us all sailing round the Whitsundays."

"Not interested." Vibrating with anger, Darius crossed her arms, stuck her chin in the air and met her mother's pleading eyes. "I'm sorry, but I don't think I ever will be."

Francine Cortez sank onto a chair, her shoulders sagging. "Very well. Hopefully one day soon, you'll change your mind. In the meantime, I've brought you an early birthday present." She slid a red parcel across the table. "I love you, baby girl."

Darius' resentment slinked back into its box like a chastised puppy. Her mother had taken the brunt of her husband's betrayal. She'd lost the man she adored, and had to console her devastated daughters and mother-in-law, while weathering grueling questions from police and media. As a leading computer scientist, accused of cyber fraud on a massive scale, the authorities believed Professor Alexander Cortez had taken the easy way out. His death and the aftermath had torn Darius' world apart.

"I'm sorry, Mom. I love you too." She hugged her mother then ripped the parcel open, gasping at the deep blue bikini nestled on matching fabric. "They're the same color as my eyes." She lifted the bikini aside and held up a floor length dress with slits from ankle to thigh. "I love it." A small velvet pouch caught her eye. "What's this?"

"The atom charm you made for your father."

Darius' pleasure vanished in the blink of an eye. After her father's death, she'd given the charm to her mother, as it held traumatic memories.

"Here." Her mother tipped the silver chain and charm into Darius' hand. "I want you to have it."

Just holding the charm had her stomach roiling. She'd throw it in the bin as soon as her mother left for the airport. Her thumb traced a ridge on the back of the atom. Frowning she flipped it over, stunned to find a micro SD card. "What's this?"

Her mother's forehead wrinkled. "Isn't it the back of the atom?"

"No, it's an SD card."

"I don't know what that means, darling." Her mother glanced at the wall clock. "My cab will be here any minute and you need to get back to work. Please reconsider coming to the Whitsundays. It will be like old times."

Darius huffed. "No, it's not. Dad won't be there."

A horn tooted.

"Cab's here, Francine." Darius' grandmother called from the front porch.

"Coming, Sarah." With a tight hug, her mother kissed Darius' on the cheek. "I love you, baby girl. Ring me." Releasing her, Francine

Cortez grabbed her bag and hurried down the hall. "I'll be back in Sydney sometime in June. See you then."

Darius stared at the SD card. Had it been there for five years? Guilt swept her. She'd come home to see her mother off; driving back to work in this turbulent, preoccupied state would be idiotic. She reached for her bag, withdrawing the laptop and coin purse that held her spare SD cards and a micro SD adaptor.

Her hands shook as she booted up the computer, installed the SD card into the adaptor then into her laptop. With her heart in her mouth, she clicked on New Device. Instantly one file showed up. She clicked on it and frowned at the paragraph of incomprehensible symbols, numbers, and letters, both in upper and lower case. It had to be code.

Excitement and apprehension welled. Her father had left her an encrypted message. "Heavens." Grabbing a pen and paper, she jotted it down then closed the file and removed the card.

Darius could hear her grandmother talking to the neighbor, so she scribbled a quick note then ran to the garage, where she had a small workshop. This was her sanctuary, where she could work in solitude, as her grandmother and Brianna couldn't stand loud music or the smells that came with building robotic toys and silicon masks.

After a painstaking hour, she'd decrypted the cryptogram. The secret code had been one she and her father had used often. Tears streamed down her face as she read his heartfelt message. It listed a cell number and instructions to buy a pre-paid phone, before texting an ally called Phoenix. Their task...to expose a traitor. *Don't trust anyone.*

"Oh, Dad."

CHAPTER ONE

That was one lucky escape. He'd been wise to move out of his parents' granny flat. It had been convenient to bunk down there when he'd had leave to visit, but a man needed privacy. Simon Hawke ended the call with his *mamma* and breathed a sigh of relief. He'd narrowly dodged another dinner with his well-meaning family and the latest potential bride they wished him to meet.

Since he'd left the SASR and moved back to Sydney, the females in his family were making a concerted effort to get him shackled. Matchmaking had become their favorite hobby.

At almost twenty-eight, and hell-bent on avoiding the matrimonial noose, he'd taken the coward's way out and moved in with a mate until he bought a place of his own. Tonight's rendezvous with his team might be due to a cyber fraud hacker who had created panic within government offices, but it beat making small talk with a woman he didn't know, while his family pretended not to listen.

Running his eyes over the present love of his life, Simon smiled. She might have cost a small fortune, but here was one lady that gave him nothing but pleasure. Leaving his pride and joy parked safely on a side street, he strolled to the corner then turned left.

Shuffling along the path towards him, a shabbily dressed woman with frizzy orange hair and a large patchwork bag paused by a bench seat. She gave him a quick, almost dismissive inspection before foraging in her bag.

Conversation and mellow music drifted from the wine bar where Simon was to meet his team. The laid-back jazz and prime location always drew a crowd, especially on a warm evening like tonight.

4

No one paid particular interest to those around them, yet Simon couldn't shake the feeling of being watched. He looked around. Office and shop workers hurried along the footpath. Sydney Harbor Bridge flowed with bumper-to-bumper sunset traffic, like worker bees escaping the hive in search of the nectar of life.

A couple of backpackers sauntered down a crossroad toward Circular Quay, their packs bulging at the seams. Two corporate-types strode past, deep in conversation. Simon caught the word 'litigation'.

A familiar sleek Jaguar drew up alongside the curb. His boss climbed out from behind the wheel and gave him a nod. Jarred Steele had been one of the youngest colonels in the Army's Special Air Service Regiment. With the disbandment of his unit then the death of his grandfather, the Colonel had resigned to take up the reins of a multi-million-dollar security company. Jarred immediately added a special ops unit, offering his old team lucrative incentives they'd quickly accepted.

Jarred quirked an eyebrow. "Evening, Major."

"Evening, boss. I hear you have your house back to yourself, now that Nick's moved into his own place?"

"I do indeed."

"Jarred! Simon! Wait up."

The female voice drew Simon's attention to the other side of the road where a blonde in blue jeans and a short red jacket stood waving. "It's your favorite investigative reporter, Madeline Shaw."

"What the hell is she doing *here*?"

"Your guess is as good as mine." Simon shoved his hands into the pockets of his leather jacket as the journalist who routinely drove Jarred crazy, waited to cross the traffic-laden road.

Jarred exhaled. "Since stumbling across us in Vietnam, she's become a liability we can do without."

A slither of conscience twisted Simon's gut. "To be fair, Madeline's risked her life several times for us. I know she's headstrong, but she can be pretty damn awesome too." If she wasn't married, he'd have asked her out.

Jarred glowered, drawing a gasp from an attractive brunette who had been ogling him. She hastily gave them a wide birth.

Madeline stepped onto the road, pausing to allow a silver Mercedes to pass. It stopped and a man in black jumped out then grabbed her in a full body lock.

"What the fuck?" Jarred leaped off the footpath, Simon close on his heels.

Horns blasted as the driver of a van slammed on his brakes, missing Jarred by inches. Jarred swore and rolled over the van's hood, Simon followed.

The scruffy bag lady got there before them and trounced the would-be abductor with her carpet bag.

Spewing Chinese curses, the assailant shoved the pint-sized bag lady to the road. Madeline wrenched out of his grasp as the man pulled out a long-bladed knife from inside his jacket.

Madeline screamed and lurched back as her assailant slashed out, the knife narrowly missing her neck.

"Get the driver!" Jarred threw himself to the road and swept Madeline's attacker's legs out from under him.

Traffic had come to a standstill behind the Mercedes as Simon reefed the driver's door open. He jabbed the man in the nose, cracking bone, then hauled him out of the car and sent him sprawling onto the road in front of the van. Jarred and the other assailant circled each other.

Screaming, yelling and a barrage of honking horns turned the narrow street into a chaotic roadblock behind the van and Mercedes. The driver bounced to his feet, blood streaming from his nose as he launched a rapid hand and foot attack. It took all Simon's skill to block each strike, protecting the vulnerable parts of his body.

The whole street came to a standstill as Simon lashed out in defense and attack.

The man leaped back then pulled out a deadly blade.

"Holy shit." Simon backed up.

The knife-wielding Jackie Chan wannabe came at him.

Blocking the strike, Simon caught the guy's wrist and brought his knee up hard. The man twisted, taking the impact in his thigh without uttering a sound. *Professionals.*

Simon reefed the attacker's wrist back until his grip loosened and the knife fell. Instantly, the guy used his free hand to reach for a hand gun.

"Fuck." Simon dived behind the car.

When he came up, both attackers were inside the vehicle. Tires squealed, leaving the stench of burning rubber as they sped away, their path clear since they'd been the cause of the traffic jam.

Jarred had gone to check on Madeline, so Simon ran to the bag lady, sitting on the edge of the gutter. He reached for her thickly gloved hand and helped her stand. "Are you all right, ma'am?"

"I've had better days." Her croaky voice wobbled. "Are you hurt?"

"No, ma'am." They were surrounded by pedestrians, some gawking, others filming with their cell phones. "Show's over folks. Please move along."

As the onlookers dispersed, Jarred guided Madeline to Simon then pulled out his phone. "I'm sure the police have been notified by now, but as the Feds are handling Madeline's attacks, I'll ask Inspector Gibbs to run those plates."

Madeline exhaled a shaky breath and smiled at the bag lady. "Thank you. Those men would have taken me, if not for you."

The woman scratched her whiskered chin. "Don't know what the world's coming to." She pushed lank, frizzy hair off her face then leaned over to pick up the bulky bag.

"Ma'am?" Simon waited until the woman looked up. "You've had a fright. Do you have someone who can collect you, or can I buy you a coffee?

"That's very kind, son, but I'll take a cab home."

He pulled out his wallet. "Then let me give you the fare, in appreciation for coming to Madeline's rescue." He held out a fifty.

Ducking her head, she took his money. "Very kind of you, young man."

Simon watched her shuffle off around the corner. How she could walk under the weight of that coat and bag baffled him.

"You okay, Madeline?"

"A bit shaky." She shook her head. "Why is it that since meeting you guys, I routinely have someone trying to shoot me or stab me? It's murder on my clothes."

Jarred ended his call. "Don't blame this on us. If you'd stayed put in the Yarramalong Valley, we wouldn't be having this conversation."

Madeline straightened her jacket. "So, you're saying my attempted abduction has nothing to do with you or your latest mission?"

"Exactly." Jarred reached out and wrapped a golden curl around his finger. It was several inches shorter than the rest of her hair. "You're damn lucky he missed your throat."

She gave a shaky laugh. "My hairdresser won't be impressed." Stepping back, she flicked her hair behind her shoulders and narrowed her eyes at Simon. "I assume you're here to discuss the anonymous hacker and secret summit?"

"No idea what you're talking about." Simon kept his face blank as he wondered how the hell she knew about the hacker or summit. It warranted further investigation. "We're just meeting for a drink. You probably need one too." He urged her across the road to the wine bar, where patrons were filing back inside. Glancing back, he saw Jarred scoop up Madeline's missing lock of hair, fury radiating from him in waves.

"Here come the police. Take Madeline inside and I'll speak with them."

"No worries." Simon opened the wine bar door for Madeline. "With luck the Feds will trace those number plates, but it's likely the car is stolen."

She pursed her lips. "I trust Jarred is informing the local police that Zachary Gibbs and the Federal Police have jurisdiction over my attacks?"

"I'm sure he will."

"Good, I'll phone Zachary once I've gathered my wits and tidied up." She brushed past Simon to walk toward the rear of the bar in the direction of the powder room.

Once Jarred finished speaking to the four policemen, he joined Simon. "That was too damn close. How can one woman survive so many attempts on her life? We need to get these bastards before they succeed in killing Madeline."

Simon agreed. Over the last few months there had been four attempts on her life.

Walking through the bar to the outdoor beer garden, Simon scanned the patrons. His gaze settled on four men sprawled in armchairs around a low table. To the unseasoned eye, they looked relaxed, chilled, but few would realize they'd once been elite SAS soldiers. At the bar, he ordered six beers then pulled out his wallet.

Jarred waved it away. "You can get the next round."

"No worries." Picking up three beers, Simon sauntered over to join the others. "Hi, fellas. How's married life, Nick?"

"Better than you can ever imagine. What took you two so long? We could have died of thirst waiting for you to arrive."

"An attempted abduction."

"You're kidding." Nick raised an eyebrow. "I saw a blonde walk through who looked like Madeline Shaw."

"It *is*," snapped Jarred. He placed another three beers on the table. "She was the person almost abducted off the street."

"What?" Talos came to his feet so fast he jolted the table, spilling their beers. And being a six foot-five bear of a man, he drew attention.

"Relax." Simon sank into an armchair. "A bag lady prevented the abduction, but Madeline's attackers pulled knives. Another inch and one would have slit her throat. Both guys were skilled fighters."

Talos sank into his chair. "You got a good look at them?"

"Asian, early thirties, and driving a late model silver Mercedes. Jarred's spoken to the police and reported it to the Feds, who are running the plates."

A grim determination settled over Jarred's face. "They have to be tied up with one of the crime syndicates she's previously exposed. It's time she accepted our protection."

"I imagine she'll agree this time." Simon glanced over his shoulder as a stunning woman in a snug red dress and high heels entered the beer garden. She looked to have Spanish or Italian heritage. She hesitated, her dark eyes perusing the room then widening as her gaze locked with his.

For several heartbeats she looked like she wanted to turn tail and flee, but then she tossed a red shawl about her shoulders, lifted her ebony locks from under it, and sashayed to the bar.

"Looks like high maintenance," murmured Ryan. "Still, she might fancy a handsome chopper pilot who can surf."

Talos coughed. "You may have grown up on an island, Ryan, but that doesn't make you a surfer. Last time I heard, the Whitsundays Islands don't have big waves."

"Hey, big fella, I've surfed all over the world, and I'll give you a run for your money any day."

"No way. I have far better ways to spend my leisure time."

Simon returned his attention to the woman. She reminded him of an exotic flower, rare and fascinating. She hitched her fine backside onto a barstool, an effort even though she wore high red stiletto heels.

Jarred rapped the table. "You boys don't have time for distractions. We need to discuss a strategy to keep Madeline safe and out of our way."

Dragging his eyes from the exotic woman, Simon looked at each of his friends' grim faces. No one in the bar would guess they were experts in advanced weapons systems, and anti-counter-surveillance. As Colonel, Jarred had headed up their elite unit. Sam Locke was a logistics specialist. James Talarico or Talos, as he preferred, an expert in weapons and hand-to-hand combat. The fourth member of their team was Nick Flanagan, a top gun Blackhawk pilot, and until recently, a man who hadn't thought he had much to live for. Ryan Dutch doubled as medic and Blackhawk co-pilot.

As IT specialist and the sixth member of the team, Simon had developed software allowing him access to so-called secure databases. Alongside his Identiscan program, he could identify the general populace from a photo, or gather personal information on any person or company he wished. His talent carried immense responsibility and risk, which meant only a select few knew his true capability. A trait he'd like to keep concealed.

His gaze drifted back to the sexy woman at the bar. A guy in a suit had joined her, although by her body language, she was giving him the cold shoulder. Her brown eyes locked with Simon's in the mirror behind the bar. She appeared familiar, but he couldn't place her. This woman would tempt a man to the dark side.

"Simon, any progress with tracing our hacker?"

"No, boss. I'm working on it." He grimaced, surprised that his attention had wandered. Women were enjoyable to socialize with, but they never interfered in a mission. At least not for him. Over the last six months and several high-risk ops, three of the guys had been bewitched into marriage. Although the ladies in question were classy and extremely likeable, he hoped the epidemic wasn't catching. He had enough on his hands avoiding family interference.

It wasn't that he didn't love his mother and sisters, but surely their husbands deserved time off for good behavior. He couldn't remember when they'd last had a boys' night out. Golf had to be cut short to accommodate family time and taking off with mates for a week of fishing just didn't happen.

His gaze shifted to the intriguing woman again. She didn't look like she was in any hurry to settle down to marriage and the whole family thing.

"Is something on your mind, Simon?" Sam Locke's sharp tone drew Simon's attention back to the group. "More important than a hacker who gained access to the Defence Force's database? More important than the attacks on Madeline?"

"Hey, I'm doing everything I can. Madeline could be the target of a crime syndicate, or someone with a grudge. Damon Pearce hinted it might be a person within her inner circle."

Jarred's eyes narrowed. "My one regret over our last mission is that I never got to interrogate Pearce. He knew more than he let on."

Nick shrugged. "At least he did the right thing in the end. My wife would be dead if not for Pearce."

"That's true." Jarred leaned forward. "The bomb in Madeline's Melbourne apartment was rigged to blow when she answered the phone. She cheated death only because she didn't make it home that night and her answering machine picked up."

Sam leaned in too. "At least she's in Sydney. We've almost finished installing the alarm and cameras in her new apartment block, and it has secure parking."

"Her best protection is to discover who wants her dead," said Talos.

"Yes." Simon drummed the edge of the low table with his fingertips. "In regard to our hacker, he's still shadowing my emails, but I haven't traced him yet."

"That must be a first," mused Ryan.

"Tell me about it." It wasn't vanity. Simon had been seconded into the Joint Operation's Command Center because of his talent. That led to his recruitment to a covert unit within the SAS. His aptitude for developing software able to crack encrypted hard drives was a skill he'd developed at university.

"So, we keep sending bogus emails back and forth until you catch him," said Ryan.

"That's the plan."

Sam frowned at Simon. "Are you sure the hacker is responsible for the breach in the Defence Force's database?"

"I believe so." He leaned his forearms on his thighs. "Our hacker had to have read Nick's email to me requesting urgent extraction. The Defence Minister's refusal to aid us may be the catalyst that prompted the hacker to act. Accessing the Defence Force's database, then directing a Naval frigate to assist us, is no small feat."

He hated to admit it, but the hacker had done them a great service. Half the team and two innocents could have died otherwise. It had been a close call. "Our Chief of Defence and Prime Minister are putting pressure on me to catch the hacker."

Talos rubbed his chin. "No wonder. The PM has been bragging that Australia is a leading force in blocking cyber fraud, only to have this guy crack a secure military database, then slip details of a secret summit under your door."

"Exactly." Simon steepled his fingers. "The hacker came to our rescue for a reason. He wants me at that summit. Whether it's because of the sensitive programs I've written, or to set me up, is anyone's guess. As I'm not a senior analyst with the Secret Service or Federal Police, I wouldn't normally receive an invitation."

"I agree," said Jarred. "Gibbs is trying to swing it that the whole team is there, in case something big goes down."

Nick caught Simon's eye. "How's this summit different to the international conference on cyber security?"

"One sells the latest technology to an open audience. The other shows any major breaches that have occurred to a select few, so they can develop software to prevent it happening again. The summit's location and attendees are a closely guarded secret, and by invitation only. My old professor, Alexander Cortez, used to attend the summits. He often contacted me afterward to discuss ideas. The hacker could well be someone Professor Cortez knew."

Talos leaned back. "We'll know soon enough. The Chief of Defence has to be ruing the day he disbanded our unit. Now the government has to pay for our services."

"Indeed." Jarred glanced toward the restrooms. "Next on the agenda is our nosey journalist. Madeline knows about the Defence Force breach and summit. I'd like to stick her on an island without phone or Internet access."

Ryan laughed. "You won't get away with that twice."

"We could negotiate." Sam drained his beer and placed the glass on the table. "She wants the scoop, so if we get the job, Inspector Gibbs can negotiate with Madeline. It takes the heat off us."

"She gave us exceptional help in Broome," said Nick. "Along with a few gray hairs."

Talos grinned. "Yes, but when things got hairy, she didn't cave under pressure, and you've got to admit, she's a hell of a cook."

"Here she comes." Jarred pulled another chair into the circle. "Let's see how much she knows, and who is feeding her info."

"You'd have more luck milking a bull elephant," muttered Talos.

Jarred blew out a long breath. "If we're engaged to attend the summit, it will be as security for the delegates. Simon can run his Identiscan program on all attendees, and we can keep Madeline busy running background checks. If there's a story, she gets it on the proviso she toes the line and has the approval of the Feds."

They all glanced at Madeline, who had stopped to answer her phone. She was the polar opposite to the beauty at the bar, yet both women had a captivating presence.

Ryan laughed. "I've got it. We age Madeline, like we did with Jane in Vietnam. It's remarkably easy to deceive people with a prop or two."

Leaning back in his chair, Simon watched the fresh-faced lawyer type edge closer to the woman at the bar, touching her arm as he made some comment. She barely registered his presence before turning to the mirror, her eyes fixed on Madeline. Had she recognized the journalist?

Simon dragged his mind back to the issue at hand. "Depending on the summit's location, she may well need a disguise to gain entry."

Jarred grimaced. "I'll speak to Gibbs then decide how to proceed."

Glancing at Madeline's composed features, Simon's admiration for her grew. With her hair twisted up in a clip, there was no evidence of the severed curl, or trauma from her recent brush with her would-be abductors. He couldn't blame Jarred for wanting to stick her on an island. At least she'd be safe.

If not for the fact she was married, and a journalist, Jarred might have made a move on her by now. The magnetism between them was palpable, but crossing those lines was the last thing Jarred would ever do.

The woman slid off her stool then swayed. Simon tensed. She hadn't been tipsy when she'd walked in, and after one drink, she'd hardly be unsteady.

"I'll be back in a minute." He strode to the bar, where the young guy was offering to assist her outside.

She blinked at Simon. "*Hola, señor.*" Her soft Spanish accent curled around his senses.

"Is there a problem?"

"*Si.*" She stumbled into his arms. "I no feel so good."

Best not to make assumptions. Ignoring the impact of her feminine curves, he gave the man a questioning look. "What happened, she was fine two minutes ago?"

"Hey, I just said hello, and now I'm saying goodbye." In his haste to leave the beer garden, the guy fell over a chair.

Simon frowned. What the hell was he supposed to do with this intoxicating armful? Having her hands on him was stirring a part of him that would be hard to hide.

"I'm diabetic." Her voice wobbled. "I need to inject insulin."

"Should I stay with you?"

"*Non.*" She hitched the red shawl closer. "You let go of me now."

Her tantalizing scent teased him. There was definitely something familiar about her. Reluctantly, he released her.

"*Gracias.* I take insulin. Maybe you let me buy you dinner when I come back?"

"Sure." His gaze fixed on her shapely legs as she threaded her way between tables then entered the ladies' restroom. Grinning like a fool, he patted the pocket where he kept his keys and the lucky charm that never failed him.

"Hey, lover boy, you want to get the next round?" called Ryan.

"No worries." As he waited to be served, Simon wondered at his instant fixation with the Spanish girl. It had never happened before.

"What will it be, mate?" The barman waited expectantly.

"Six Toohey's New, thanks." He should get Madeline a drink too. "And a cabernet sauvignon." Simon reached for his wallet. It wasn't in his back pocket where it had been just before he... "That little fiend."

He strode to the ladies' toilets where his Spanish pickpocket had disappeared to and shoved the door open. All five cubicles were empty. Above the basins, a small window hung open, its hinges creaking in the evening breeze.

"You've got to be kidding." He leaped onto the vanity and poked his head through the window. An exterior floodlight beamed across a dumpster, but otherwise the narrow alley was empty. "Shit."

Jumping down, he noticed his wallet on the floor near the trash can. He flicked it open, unsurprised to see the notes missing. At least she'd left his cards and license, although they were in different slots. He pulled out a folded scrap of pink paper.

Señor Hawke, IOU $200.

"Yes, you do, sweet pea." She'd conned him well and truly with her huge brown eyes and mysterious allure.

The door opened and he looked over his shoulder to find Jarred leaning against the frame. "Care to explain your penchant for the ladies' restroom?"

"She stole my money and high-tailed it out the window." He shook his head. Disappointment and irritation warred. "I knew she was up to something."

Jarred looked up at the narrow window. "A pickpocket in stilettoes."

"At least she left my wallet and cards." He paced to the bar and paid for their drinks with his credit card. Madeline sat beside Jarred, and although pale, looked much calmer than he felt. Grim expressions all round. As for his little thief, Simon suspected she'd haunt his dreams tonight. Ryan's words taunted him. *It's remarkably easy to deceive people with a prop or two.*

He glanced around the beer garden, smiling when he noticed a surveillance camera. *I'll find you sweet pea. Count on it.*

CHAPTER TWO

He hadn't recognized her. Darius inhaled two deep breaths, her heart pounding as she stepped from behind the dumpster. Slipping into her flat court shoes and black trench coat, she ran to the end of the alley. After a quick peek at the front of the wine bar she clutched the carpet bag to her chest then hurried away in the opposite direction.

Adrenaline surged through her body as she ignored the interest in the eyes of men on the street, so different to the pedestrians who earlier had given her a wide birth. Most avoiding eye contact with the tatty woman in her stained coat and wrinkled woolen stockings.

Reaching the intersection, she ran for her car. Simon Hawke might be a necessary pawn, but if he discovered her identity, there was no telling what he would do.

She had what she'd come for and there wasn't much time to put the next phase into action. Reaching the car, she unlocked the door then threw in the bulging carpet bag that contained an entire persona created solely for tonight. It had worked better than she'd expected, and she now had Simon's new address, but what was his relationship with those men and the high-profile, glamorous journalist?

She climbed into the car and started the engine. Simon was still good-looking, but so different to the nineteen-year-old, skinny guy she'd adored. He'd morphed into a man who would draw women like moths to a bright light. The type of man she avoided.

Seeing him fight had taken her breath away. She couldn't equate his strength and skill with the guy he'd once been. That sort of training didn't happen overnight. Where had he learned to fight with such ferocity?

Five seconds in his arms had almost brought on a panic attack, but he'd shown no signs of recognition. She would have to be careful. The risk of exposure was too great.

According to the GPS, Simon didn't live far away. She hoped he'd stay at the wine bar for a while longer. Corey would make the next delivery with Bronte playing devil's advocate if needed. No one would question a smartass skateboarder, or a teenage punk with attitude.

Until she could be sure Simon hadn't betrayed her father and could be trusted, she would follow the plan.

∽❧

Simon stroked the glossy, red roof of his Mustang. She was an indulgence his brothers-in-law could only fantasize about. There were so many positives to bachelorhood. He glanced around the underground garage. Except for Ryan's Harley, all residents' vehicles were in their designated spots. As Mrs. Hudson didn't drive, Simon used her allotment.

There were six spacious, two-bedroom units in the *Art Déco* building, sought after for its prime views of Sydney Harbor. A great place to live if you could afford it.

Their night had ended earlier than expected after Jarred insisted on escorting Madeline home. The married guys opted out of dinner to return to their wives, and Ryan challenged a Swedish girl to a game of pool, so Simon left them to it. Not only was he anxious to catch the hacker, he couldn't stop thinking about the woman who had hoodwinked him with her seductive eyes and body. Tomorrow he'd view the bar's surveillance cameras.

Opening the fire door, Simon crossed the lobby then began the climb to the third floor. He reached the second landing as a teen in baggy jeans and a hooded jacket that hid his face, swung around the railing post. His skateboard clipped Simon's elbow.

"Sorry." The kid's high-pitched voice cracked, but he kept going. A small backpack bounced from side to side, his jeans slipping halfway down his backside, displaying black jocks.

The hair on the back of Simon's neck lifted. Mrs. Hudson and a gay couple had apartments on the ground level. The middle level apartments were owned by a retired couple and a headmistress. Ryan's place was on the top floor opposite an airline pilot and his physiotherapist wife. They didn't have children.

A teenage kid coming down from the top floor rang alarm bells. Simon ran up the last flight, making a mental note to check in with the other residents first thing in the morning.

A soft exotic fragrance lingered on the landing, bringing him to a standstill.

Music and a woman's laughter came from the pilots' apartment. It wasn't her. The tension dropped from Simon's shoulders. He inserted his key in the door then pushed it wide, almost stepping on a cream envelope. A replica of the one left at his parent's house three weeks ago, presumably by the hacker. Ripping it open, he pulled out a single sheet of paper. A quick glance showed a brief summary of planned topics for the summit.

"Blast." He tossed the papers on the nearest armchair and took off down the stairs. That kid might just be a delivery boy, but he had contact with the hacker.

With no sign of the kid on the dark street, Simon sprinted to the intersection. He spotted the boy on his skateboard, rolling awkwardly down the center line. "Hey!" Simon sprinted after him.

The boy lost his balance in his rush to push off faster. He bailed, leaving his skateboard to smash into the gutter as he rolled across the grass verge. Without a thought for his board the kid leaped over a railing, twisting like a gymnast, before landing smoothly to slide down the grass bank to the street below. The kid was fast, but so was Simon. Since his transfer into Jarred's elite squad, five years ago, his fitness had undergone a vast improvement.

As the chase continued through a park, Simon began to gain ground. He could tell the kid was tiring, but holy shit he could still move. The teenager's weakness came from being short and having to hold up his baggy pants.

They came to a small cluster of shops and the boy shot down a narrow alley.

Reaching the entrance, Simon hesitated. The brick walls on either side were covered in faded graffiti and barely wide enough to fit a small car through. It could be a trap. Darkness cloaked the space, except for a glow of light at the end.

No sound of running feet or any movement at all. The kid had found a place to hide or planned to launch a surprise attack. A suicide bombing in Afghanistan had taught Simon, children could be deadly.

He entered the alley, passing two barred doors and a shopping trolley crammed with flattened cardboard. Alert for the slightest shift in the air, he approached the end of the closed alley, wincing at the overpowering stench of cat pee.

The hair at the back of his neck bristled. His gaze found a slim figure inside a recessed entrance, leaning against a metal door.

Not the boy he'd been chasing, but a girl, plastered in heavy makeup. She wore black tights and a short leather jacket. His gaze skimmed her spiked hair, a nose ring and a butterfly tattooed below her right ear. The naked light bulb above her cast a circle of light as if she were on center stage. She didn't speak as she eyed him warily. Fast breathing gave away her apprehension.

"I'm no threat to you." His focus came to rest on her trembling lips.

She lifted her chin defiantly. "Why are you chasing that boy?"

"I need to talk to him. Where is he?"

"What's it worth?"

"Unbelievable." He dug two dollars out of his jeans. "That's all I've got."

"It all adds up." She took the money then pointed at a fire escape on the other side of the alley. "He went up that."

The bottom rung was too high for Simon to reach. "How?"

She shrugged. "Beats me and I saw him do it. You won't catch the monkey now. He went up on the roof."

"Do you know him?"

"No, I don't." She fiddled with a dangly earring.

Simon glanced about the dirty alley. "What are you doing down here?"

"Not that it's any of your business, but I'm squatting with friends." She nodded at the door behind her. "If I scream, they'll be here in seconds."

Her pale blue eyes were clear, so not an addict. She might be living in a squat, but her speech indicated an educated background, and she had a vulnerability he couldn't ignore. "Are you in trouble? Can I do something to help you?"

Her eyes widened then she shook her head. "I'm fine. You'd better go before my friends think you're hitting on me."

She reminded him of a lost kitten with those big pale blue eyes and spiked hair. If not for the doorstep, she'd only reach his shoulders. "Look, I know of a refuge that takes in teenage girls." He pulled out his wallet and handed her a card. "They'll give you a safe place to sleep and help you work out what you want to do."

She read the card then brought her gaze back to his. "How old do you think I am?"

"Sixteen."

"I'm old enough to vote." Her tinkling laugh vibrated all the way to Simon's toes, which disturbed him, but he couldn't walk away.

"You can do better than this."

She lifted her chin defiantly. "What's it to you what I do?"

"Call it my good deed for the day."

A jolt of familiarity blasted Simon as the full impact of her smile hit. He cleared his throat and stepped back. "My sister, Jennifer, runs the refuge. If you forget her name, ask to speak to the pregnant lady and tell her Simon sent you.

He strode out of the alley, wondering what the fuck was wrong with him tonight.

CHAPTER THREE

Darius watched Simon Hawke stride out of the alley then sagged against the wall. "Heaven help me, that was way too close." She waited five minutes then grabbed her backpack from under a sheet of cardboard in the shopping trolley. After pulling the wig and reversible jacket off, she shoved them in the pack with the baggy jeans then shook out her hair. Resuming a semblance of her real persona was a necessary risk.

She ran along the alley, shivering when a rat darted across her path. There was no one about as she emerged from the claustrophobic passage, which should have eased her mind, instead the silence and close call unsettled her. A kickass alter ego wouldn't do any good if Simon lurked somewhere close.

Gathering her courage, she sprinted all the way to her car. Once inside she locked the doors then removed her fake nose ring. Arriving home looking like a street-wise punk would raise questions.

On the drive back to Warrawee, she reflected on Simon's words and his obvious concern for three females he didn't know. He'd shown respect and consideration to the homeless woman. He'd come to the *señorita's* aid in the wine bar, and then tried to help a runaway punk. She wanted to believe the chivalry was real, that the man behind it wasn't a deadly adversary, but rather the guy she'd once adored.

Her thoughts ran to the excited tremors she'd experienced in the bar. Not panic, but rather a revival of the attraction she'd once felt for him. Could Simon possibly vanquish her dating phobia? One bad egg didn't make the whole carton rotten. She needed to get that through her thick skull.

Without her disguises, she became a tongue-tied disaster. Even tonight, heavily disguised, her stomach had twisted into tight knots, from the moment he taken her hand, thinking her a homeless woman. In the bar, held within his arms, she'd almost confessed everything, which could have backfired. The kindness he'd shown a teenage runaway almost brought her to tears.

Turning into the driveway, she parked in front of the single garage then grabbed her carpet bag and jogged across the lawn. A sedan on the other side of the quiet street drew her attention. She'd noticed it several times this week, and as usual two men sat inside. Had the Federal Police decided to put a watch on her grandmother's house? And if so, did it have anything to do with her father or the secret summit?

Grandma had left the porch light on, believing Darius to be rehearsing at the local theatre. The truth would only distress her.

Once inside her bedroom, Darius dropped the carpet bag then pulled out the dry-cleaning receipt she'd taken from Simon's wallet. She fell back on the bed and stared at the ceiling. A web of spidery cracks ran out from the center rose, invisible to the casual observer, but evident if you took the time to look closer, which is exactly what she should have done with her father's atom charm. If not for her mother giving it back, she never would have found it.

Staring at the ceiling, she considered her progress. Without knowing Simon's movements, it had been necessary to approach his parents' home. Her intention had been to slide another envelope under their front door, as she had three weeks ago. It had been a shock to have the door opened by his mother.

Thankfully Mrs. Hawke, a lady of Italian heritage, had been too delighted to find a young woman on her doorstep to notice the envelope. They'd never met, yet Darius hadn't expected to be dragged inside and grilled about her personal life. She'd escaped after promising to attend Simon's birthday barbecue.

A lot could happen in two weeks.

At least the afternoon hadn't been wasted. She'd found out Simon had skipped a family dinner to attend that meeting with his colleagues. Colleagues who looked like mercenaries. And, she had his new address.

He had the expertise she needed but could double-cross her in this web of deception. There were other colleagues who could have betrayed her father, and in six days they would all be gathered in one place.

She held up the dry-cleaning receipt. "Did you betray your friend and mentor, Simon?" She chewed her bottom lip. "Who were those other men?"

She remembered her father saying Simon had been recruited into the Defence Force's Command Center, in Canberra, but the physical change in him was palpable, and his friends didn't look like computer scientists. They looked like trouble. Big trouble.

She needed more information. What was the old saying? *Keep your friends close—keep your enemies closer.* Much closer in the bar and he might have kissed her. Perhaps if she picked up his dry-cleaning then made sure he wasn't home, she could search his apartment. It might give her an insight into his personal life.

Sliding off the bed, she removed the pale-blue lenses from her eyes and dropped them into a vial. Reaching into the carpet bag, she retrieved another vial of brown lenses and slotted them in with the others into a small zip-lock bag. She had every color necessary for her disguises, along with an assortment of wigs, masks, eyebrows, props and spray tans. She could change her appearance so convincingly that not even her mother would recognize her. The other actors in her amateur theatre group considered her flair for crafting life-like silicon facemasks uncanny.

Picking up a cotton pad, she poured makeup remover over it then cleansed her face. The fake tan and butterfly tattoo would take a bit more work.

Her pre-paid phone vibrated inside the carpet bag. "Hi, Phoenix. I've delivered the envelope to Simon Hawke's new apartment."

"Hello, Dragonfly. I hadn't realized he'd moved. Still, you shouldn't have gone there, my dear." The distorted computerized voice sounded agitated. A first in the two months they'd been collaborating to clear her father.

They were partners, for better or worse, and she refused to be treated like a child. "I attempted to deliver the envelope to his parent's house as you requested, but his mother caught me. Don't worry, she has no idea who I am. Mrs. Hawke mentioned Simon had moved but was meeting friends this evening at a wine bar in The Rocks. It wasn't difficult to lift his wallet and get the new address."

"I'm not sure that was wise."

"He didn't catch me." Perhaps it was a safety net, or self-preservation, but she didn't want Phoenix to know about her talent for disguises. "I went to the bar and discovered Simon Hawke hangs out with five intimidating men and Madeline Shaw."

"Ah yes, the journalist."

An uneasy shiver rippled down Darius' spine. "What's her connection to Simon Hawke?"

"Not long ago, Madeline Shaw broke a story on major crime syndicates operating between Australia and Vietnam. They were trading in human trafficking and slavery. More recently she exposed a people smuggling racket in Western Australia. I assume she got the stories through her association with a firm by the name of Steele Security and Special Operations."

Darius shivered. "There was a man with gray eyes and a commanding presence. I wouldn't like to mess with him."

"Never mind Jarred Steele. I'm keeping tabs on him and his men."

His men? "Am I to understand Jarred Steele runs this security firm?"

"Yes. Anything else to report?"

She hesitated, still coming to terms with that interesting snippet of information. "Two Asian men tried to snatch Madeline Shaw off the street. Simon and Jarred Steele did some fancy fighting to save her, but one of the Asian men almost cut her throat."

"That *is* interesting. It's probably someone she's exposed or about to expose for illegal activities."

"What do we do next?"

"I have booked you on a flight for the second of May."

"The second?" Darius hadn't realized it would be so soon. "That's only three days away. I will need to apply for leave and think of something to tell my grandmother?"

"Tell her it's a spur of the moment holiday to Fiji. You will be gone eight days."

"So, the cyber summit is in Fiji?"

"Not exactly. You will stay in Suva for two nights before taking a flight to Lakeba Island. It's one of the larger southern islands in the Lau Archipelago, east of Fiji. From there a seaplane will fly you to a private island. I believe you do a little amateur theatre, so your cover will be an actress after some relaxation and solitude, staying as a guest of the resort's owner."

"And?" A nervous excitement consumed Darius.

"The summit attendees will arrive Thursday. That gives you one day to discreetly acquaint yourself with the resort's layout."

"I appreciate you including me."

"As it was one of your conditions, I had little choice. Your air tickets and details of your accommodation in Suva will be couriered to you early tomorrow morning. I'm also sending spyware, USB's to download the delegates hard-drives, miniature eavesdropping discs and a vial of sleeping elixir."

That seemed a bit weird. "Why do I need sleeping elixir?"

"Two drops in a glass of water will knock a person out for an hour or two. Enough time for you to do whatever is required."

Darius worried her bottom lip. "Security will be tight."

"If you're caught within the resort grounds, say you're taking an evening stroll. You will be staying in a private villa in the next cove. The kitchen is fully stocked, so there is no need to bother the resort staff."

She squirmed. Phoenix may have engineered their plot to expose a traitor and a terrorist group, but she was taking all the risks. "Tell me about the delegates' accommodation?"

"They're being housed in small private villas called bures, which are dotted about the larger cove. There will be room in the staff quarters for most of the security guards, with one of the larger bures taking the overflow. Once you arrive at the villa, you will find an envelope with a master key to all the bures."

"I assume my pre-paid phone won't work there, so how do I reach you?"

"You don't. If something goes wrong, swim out to a catamaran anchored in the cove below your villa."

"Is that where you're staying?"

"No. The less you know about me the better. The catamaran is to be used *only* if you are facing imminent danger. I believe you know how to sail."

"Yes." It bugged her, that Phoenix knew so much about her life and interests. She didn't even know if she was speaking to a man or woman. Darius drew a deep breath. "Don't worry, I'm good at flying below radar." She'd need a bigger suitcase.

"Wear a hat and sunglasses at all times. Under no circumstances are you to give your real name to any of the delegates or get too close to anyone who might recognize you. Our success depends on you being discreet."

"I understand." A grin spread over Darius' face. No one would recognize her.

"Hide the spyware on your first evening in the resort. Once the delegates arrive, wait until they're enjoying the evening entertainment then download their data. Interpreting it is my specialty. I will leave the concealment of spyware to your imagination."

"What will you be doing?"

"I'm convinced someone working for a terrorist organization will approach several delegates with an offer they can't or won't refuse. The same person who may have contacted your father and then betrayed him. I intend to record those conversations."

Darius bit her lip. "Do you want me to deliver anything else to Simon?"

"One more envelope. It will be in the parcel arriving tomorrow. If all goes smoothly, the next time we speak will be face to face. I will hand you a black gambling chip, so you know it's me. Good night, Dragonfly."

"Goodnight, Phoenix." Darius placed the pre-paid phone in her drawer then stared at the mirror. In this particular light, her eyes appeared purple. A color scientists claimed didn't exist. She'd met skeptics who insisted her eyes were the result of a genetic mutation called Alexandria's Genesis. In her father's words, they were a deep ocean blue. She smiled sadly and brushed out her crown of golden gossamer, another of her father's imaginative terms. At the moment, it looked more like crinkled spaghetti. Her thoughts returned to her impasse.

It might have come five years late, but her father's encrypted message had led her to Phoenix, so she had little choice but to trust this unknown ally.

ের্জ

Drenched in perspiration, Simon billowed his T-shirt to cool the sweat trickling down his chest. A morning run usually took care of pent up energy, but it didn't seem to be working today. He'd changed his route to drop in on Jarred and bring him up to date. Whoever their hacker was, he or she now sat at the top of the Fed's most wanted list.

His phone chimed with an incoming call. Slowing to a walk, he checked the ID then answered. "Hey, Jen. Did you check up on that girl for me?"

His sister gave an exasperated sigh. "A complete waste of time. I took a cop with me in case of trouble, but there are no squatters there. It's a second-hand bookshop. Every nook is stuffed with dust-ridden tomes."

"Are you sure you went to the right place?"

"Yes. We even checked the premises on the other side of the alley. It's a bakery. I don't know what she was doing in that alley, but she certainly wasn't squatting."

Simon scratched his head. "She could have seen me chasing the kid down the street, then panicked and ran into the alley to hide."

"That's more likely. Did you find the skateboarder you where after?"

"No, he's long gone. How's the pod?"

Jen laughed. "Getting so big I look like a whale. Hey, don't forget mamma and papà are putting on a barbecue for your birthday. You'd better be there."

He cringed. "I'll come as long as you and my other two scheming sisters don't invite any prospective brides to throw in my path."

"Yes, yes, we got your texts threatening to boycott."

"What about our meddling mother and Nonna?"

"You're safe. Kirsty sent a family email. Everyone has been told not to invite any single, unattached females who are not related by blood. Happy?"

"Are you sure, Jen? Mama seemed overly excited about the party when I spoke to her last night."

"That's because she worships the ground her only son walks on. You can't blame her for making a big thing of your birthday. For the last few years we were all terrified you'd be killed in one of those awful places the military sent you."

"All right. I'll be off the grid for about a week, but I promise to be at my party."

"Great. Talk to you soon."

Ending the call, Simon sprinted around the corner, barging straight into a woman in sunglasses, a pink cap, white top and brightly striped Spandex pants. "Whoops." He caught her in his arms. A sizable baby-bump slammed into him. "Are you all right?"

"Yes, I'm...fine." Her fingernails dug into his arms as she stared up at him. "No damage done." She snatched her hands away, as if suddenly realizing she had him in a death grip. "All good." She pulled back, side-stepped him, then power-walked away.

Simon stood transfixed, watching her long, blonde ponytail swish from side to side. His gaze dropped to her hips and butt, reminding him of the thieving *señorita*, which must be why his senses were suddenly assailed by that exotic scent.

"Get a grip, dude." His gaze rose to find the woman looking over her shoulder at him. She gave him a hesitant wave before taking the steps to the park below. For a pregnant lady, she had a great figure.

Simon shook his head then jogged up the middle of the road until he reached the *Art Déco* apartment block. As he entered the foyer, Mrs. Hudson opened her door.

"Simon! I was hoping to catch you."

"Mrs. H, what can I do for you?"

"Your sister stopped by not that long ago. I told her you'd gone running and she was disappointed to miss you, but said she'd catch up with you at your birthday."

"Kirsty?" He shuddered to think his older sister had resorted to dropping by; no doubt eager to burn his ears about a female he had to meet.

"Not Kirsty." Mrs. Hudson tapped her lips. "Um... Jennifer. I was a little concerned with her climbing all those stairs, being in the family way, but she insisted she'd be fine."

"Jennifer?" He frowned. "I just spoke to her on the phone, and she never said a word about calling here."

"She had your dry-cleaning and a letter, so I lent her Ryan's sister's key to the apartment. What a lovely girl."

"My dry-cleaning?" He flipped open his wallet and searched for the receipt. It wasn't there. He must have left it in the granny flat.

"Thanks, Mrs. H." He started up the stairs.

"I must say you're nothing like your sister. She's so petite, and that lovely blonde hair. She hardly looked old enough to be having a baby."

"Blonde?" He turned back to Mrs. Hudson as a nasty suspicion churned his gut. "What was my sister wearing?"

"A white tank top, pink cap and multi-colored tights."

Simon stiffened as the puzzle pieces began to click into place, disquiet snaking up his spine. Questions raced through his mind. At the top of the list—why the power-walker would be posing as his pregnant sister and dropping off his dry-cleaning. How did she know about his party?

This went beyond a case of his sisters sending their friends around on trumped-up errands in the hope of catching him at home.

The kid with the skateboard. He'd been in the building when Simon found the letter. The girl in the alley. Damn it, he'd referred her to the shelter where his sister worked. The gorgeous thieving *señorita* in the bar who'd lifted his wallet *and* his dry-cleaning receipt. He thumped his hand against the wall. Christ, he should have seen it sooner. All three of them were likely in cahoots. This had nothing to do with his sisters' matchmaking efforts. This had hacker written all over it.

He ran up the stairs. Entering the apartment, his gaze searched the lounge and dining area for anything out of place. His dry-cleaning had been laid over an armchair. His car keys were on the bookcase, instead of where he'd left them on the hook by the door. Ryan wasn't home as he'd been called out to a VIP event. Even so, the blonde had taken a huge risk coming here, and by moving his keys, she had to be sending him a message.

Unsettled, Simon paced across the room. The keys lay between two framed photos of his days in the SAS. One depicted him and another seven soldiers in camouflage gear, each holding an assault rifle. The other had been taken on a deep-sea fishing trip. It depicted eight men, unshaven, and without shirts, their muscles straining as they each proudly held up their catch of the day.

Over the last five years, he and the boys had been on many such trips. After their last mission in Afghanistan, one was dead and another had suffered a breakdown, but they were hopeful, Jack would join them later in the year for another fishing trip.

Looking at the photos, Simon grimaced. They looked to be an intimidating bunch.

Picking up the keys, he noticed his lucky charm missing. That pissed him off big time. He searched the carpet then paced into the kitchen, halting when he spied a large cream envelope on the bench.

"Shit."

Slitting the seal, he pulled out two sheets of paper. The first was a map displaying the Lau Archipelago, a group of islands in the Koro Sea. He knew the region, having fished and dived there with the boys three years ago. A red cross had been drawn over a miniscule dot, obviously a small island.

The next sheet scheduled two days of forums, kicking off in six days, and the names of speakers and delegates attending the summit. As he read through the list, he couldn't help but be impressed. An advisor to the United Nations, the head of an international intelligence and data investigation company, computer scientists from financial institutions, secret service agencies, military and government bodies within Australia and her closest allies.

"Holy shit, that's a lot of analytical minds in one location." He paced the lounge area, back and forth. The blonde had left him sensitive information because she worked for the hacker or she was the hacker. Why?

He rang the dry-cleaner who confirmed Mrs. Hudson's description of a pretty blonde expecting a baby. Unfortunately, she'd paid with cash, so he couldn't trace her that way. He rang his mother who admitted a blonde lady had come to the house a few days ago, looking for him, but she hadn't been pregnant.

He surmised the expectant mother, skateboarder, punk and the light-fingered *señorita*, had to be tied in with the hacker, but to what end?

Simon ran a hand through his hair. The hacker would have pulled Simon's old address from the Roads and Maritime Authority, so his mother must have told the blonde he'd moved, which is why the *señorita* stole his wallet.

He clenched his fists, forcing the *señorita's* delicate face and sensual body to the back of his mind. "I will catch you, sweet pea, and all your little friends."

CHAPTER FOUR

Selecting Jarred's number, Simon checked out the rest of the apartment. His boss needed to be aware that the hacker wasn't working alone. It could be a syndicate.

"I was about to call you," came Jarred's even tone. "I've spoken to Gibbs. He's picking up the envelope but doesn't hold much hope of getting fingerprints. Multiple people could have handled it."

"I know. In the meantime, I've had another delivery. A pregnant power-walker pretended to be one of my sisters. A neighbor let her into the apartment to drop off my dry-cleaning."

"Dry-cleaning?"

"She used the receipt stolen from my wallet by the Spanish woman."

"That's a noteworthy tactic—using credible and inconspicuous citizens to make deliveries." Jarred sounded more intrigued than annoyed.

The thought had merit. "I'm thinking the *señorita* pulled that stunt to get my address, then the skateboarder was hired to deliver an envelope. And, I think he led me down the alley, where a female posing as a squatter, could side-track me. I mentioned my pregnant sister and the teenage refuge where she works, which resulted in a pregnant power-walker collecting my dry-cleaning so she could deliver this last envelope."

"I wouldn't discount it. What was in your latest delivery?"

"More info on the summit attendees, and a map of the Lau Archipelago." He brought Jarred up to date then waited as his boss absorbed the information. Jarred never made hasty decisions.

"With the threat of cyber fraud hanging over our heads, I'm concerned about all that specialized brain power in one location," mused Jarred. "For instance, these delegates would make desirable hostages."

"The same thought crossed my mind."

"Set up a surveillance camera in your stairwell and sweep the unit. Is anything missing?"

"A sentimental charm I carry for good luck. It's not valuable, just a gift from a girl who—" Simon broke off as his gaze locked on the window sill, locating the missing atom charm.

"Simon, what's up?"

"I found the charm." He inhaled deeply and let out a long breath, relieved to have found it. "It was a present from Professor Cortez's youngest daughter when she was about fifteen."

"Your old university professor?" Jarred's voice sharpened with interest.

Picking up the atom, Simon rolled it in his fingers. "Professor Cortez had the capability to hack into the Defense Force database." Ice-cold fingers of unease curled around his gut. "The only problem is...he's dead."

"Didn't you work with Professor Cortez on software to fight cyber fraud?"

"Yes, and about five years ago he was accused of using the program to steal millions of dollars. The allegations were never proven, but there are many who believe it's why he jumped to his death in Nepal."

"Are you one of them?"

"No." Simon tapped his thigh. "Alexander could have slipped, had a heart attack, or collapsed from altitude sickness, but I can't see him taking his life. He wasn't the type."

"Tell me more about the professor?"

"Where to start?" Simon dropped into the armchair, uncaring that he'd crush his dry-cleaning. "During my degree, I worked closely with him to develop a program that would prevent hackers breaking encryptions protecting sensitive data. Our aim was to provide military, financial institutions and other high-risk utilities with an impregnable barrier against online espionage. A failsafe firewall to stop hackers. In doing so, we needed to first write a program that, through social engineering, could access any database. Employees can't help but open links. It's every company's nightmare."

"Did Professor Cortez have a jealous colleague or disgruntled student that you know of?"

"There may have been, but to my knowledge, he was respected by his colleagues and students."

"What about family?"

Simon thought back to his university days. "Alexander loved his wife and two daughters. They regularly went away hiking or sailing. I just can't see him jumping into that crevice. If he did steal the money, he could have used the program to invent new identities for his whole family before disappearing without a trace."

"Are you suggesting he was murdered?"

"No, but it might have been an accident, and the Sherpa guiding him could have lied to save his own reputation. We will never know because after the mayday call, there was an avalanche, which buried both bodies."

Jarred exhaled. "Professor Cortez may have been guilty and knew the police were closing in. The humiliation and censure would have been extensive for a man with his reputation. Jumping to his death could have been his way of protecting his family. It doesn't explain why the hacker wants you at the summit."

Simon's skin crawled. "Perhaps to access a deeper level of the program or make changes to it. The fact remains, I'm the person receiving confidential information, and I worked with Professor Cortez on that program."

"I assume there are safeguards?"

"We installed a suicide code in case the program was stolen."

"What sort of suicide code?"

Simon fisted his fingers around the atom. "One that locks you out, if the incorrect password is applied more than three times within twelve hours. That's why a brute-force attack won't work. A first-rate hacker could instigate millions of passwords combinations, but he'd be locked out after three attempts. I use the same lock out on all my confidential files."

"We must assume our hacker has obtained the professor's program and recently gained access. Your thoughts?"

"There are three levels, each requiring its own secret key. Our hacker must have accessed the first and second level, which means he—or she—has both the Professor's password and mine. It's unlikely, but Alexander could have written them down. To break through the firewalls of banks and major utilities, the hacker would need admission to the third level, which requires another secret key."

"Which is why he needs you," murmured Jarred.

"Not quite. Professor Cortez considered it unsafe for either of us to have that much power, so a third person was used. I don't know who, but Alexander told me a cryptogram had been used to hide the third secret key."

"Damn. I'll ask Gibbs to get us a copy of the police file, including the Sherpa's mayday call," said Jarred. "In the meantime, I want you to pay a visit to the Cortez family. It's been five years since the professor's death. Ask if they remember anything."

"Like the Amethyst Code."

"Exactly." Jarred exhaled. "Call on Mrs. Cortez this evening. I'll schedule a team conference for tomorrow. If Gibbs gets approval to send us to the summit, I'm intrigued enough now to accept the job."

Simon smiled. "I was hoping you'd say that, but how will you schedule a team meeting while we're supposed to be guarding Madeline?"

Jarred chuckled. "I'll organize a barbecue. Madeline will be too busy catching up with the ladies to worry about what we're talking about over a game of pool."

Simon shifted uneasily. "Madeline's a shrewd cookie."

"I can't very well ask her to leave my house while we meet," muttered Jarred. "She'd know we are up to something."

"She's staying at *your* place?" This wasn't good on so many levels.

"Yes," muttered Jarred. "I've had a call from her husband. Elliott claims he can't leave Vietnam, and we're the only people he trusts to keep her safe. He's prepared to triple our rate. My gut tells me he's on the level, but he may know who is behind her attacks."

"For a couple who spend so much time apart, Elliott's either incredibly confident of Madeline's fidelity, or couldn't give a damn that she spends so much time with you."

"Something you want to get off your chest?"

Simon drew a deep breath. His respect for Jarred prevented him stating the risk of having a beautiful, perhaps lonely, woman under the same roof. "It bothers me that Elliott appears amused by the sparks between you and his wife. It's almost like he encourages it. I haven't found any dirt on him or Madeline, but something is definitely off."

"Which is why she's staying with me for now. Keep digging. I'll see you tomorrow morning." Jarred ended the call.

Simon rang Ryan then set about sweeping the apartment. He didn't find anything. His next exercise was to buy a surveillance camera and set it up in the stairwell, running the wires to a monitor inside the apartment. He re-keyed the door lock. If any intruders came calling, Simon would at least have an image to run through his Identiscan database.

৯৵

Simon paced up the neat path outside the professor's sprawling two-story federation home. All looked as he remembered. Bordered by lush lawn and thick shrubbery, it brought back fond memories. He glanced up at the small Juliette balcony, almost hidden by a Tibouchina tree, heavy with purple flowers. The balcony held his last memory of the professor's youngest daughter. He'd been nineteen and the delicate teenager would have been fifteen. She had golden hair and incredibly deep blue eyes. She'd reminded him of the fairy, Tinker Bell. So much so that he'd called her Tink. The memory brought a smile to his face. He'd left the professor's study late, and as he'd stepped off the wide porch, a soft voice had called his name. Looking up, he'd found Tink leaning over the railing. "I have a present for you, Simon. It's a lucky charm I made in metalwork."

He'd caught the tiny package in his hand then opened it to find a beautifully crafted atom on an oval disk. "What did I do to deserve this?"

She'd given him a shy smile. "What you said at dinner made me think anything is possible. I've coated the atom in fairy dust so it will keep you safe."

For nine years he'd carried the atom, either on his key chain or in the shirt pocket of his uniform. And whether it was superstitious or not, the charm had been lucky for him.

35

As he knocked on the Cortez's front door, he tried to recall his words of wisdom that night. It was in response to something derogatory her sister had said. The only thing he could remember about the professor's eldest daughter was that she'd been a flirt. It was Tink's dazzling eyes and quirky nature that had always charmed him.

A matronly woman he didn't recognize opened the door. She had a baby in her arms and a toddler clinging to her leg. Taped cardboard boxes lined the hall.

"Can I help you?"

"I hope so, ma'am." He held out his security ID, which she barely skimmed. "I'm looking for Mrs. Cortez or either of her daughters."

"They don't live here anymore. Mrs. Cortez sold the house to my son four years ago, but I can give you their address. It's only a couple of streets away." The woman shifted the baby to her other hip then reached for a pen on the hall table. "I assume they're still there."

"Thanks for your help, ma'am. It's much appreciated." He hesitated. "I have good memories of this house."

"It's a lovely home. My son plans to sell it, if you're interested. He's accepted a promotion to Singapore. I'll give you his number." She wrote the Cortez's address and her son's number down then handed it to him.

"Thanks." He stepped off the porch, then after a considering glance at the Juliette balcony, slid the note in his shirt pocket and strolled down the path. It would have been tough on Tink losing the father she adored then having to move from her home.

He drove to the Cortez's new address and parked his Mustang in front of a neat little bungalow of whitewashed brick. As he climbed out, his gaze skimmed the picket fence and neat garden. It reminded him of a doll's house. Charming, but no comparison to their previous home.

He opened the gate then strolled up the path, noting the comfy cane chairs on the porch. A tiny white-haired lady answered his knock, her eyes widening as she looked up. "My, aren't you a handsome young man?"

He smiled. "Hello, ma'am. My name is Simon Hawke. I'm looking for Francine Cortez and her daughters."

"I'm Sarah Cortez. What do you want with my daughter-in-law and the girls?"

"I studied under Professor Cortez before joining the army, and unfortunately I was out of the country when he died. I'd like to pay my respects to his family."

"I see. Please, come in." She held the door wide and waved him into a cozy lounge off to the left. Crocheted blankets lay over the back of the cream couch and two matching armchairs. Lace doilies covered several side-tables dotted about the room, and an antique cabinet held an assortment of crystal glasses, china plates and cups. His gaze drifted over several vases crammed with vibrant-colored fresh roses, bestowing their heady fragrance throughout the room.

Sarah Cortez indicated the lounge. "Can I get you a cup of tea or coffee?"

"No, thank you, ma'am. I called at the old house and was directed here."

She nodded sadly. "Six months after my son died, Francine brought the girls to live here then moved up the coast to look after her sister. It's taken us a long time to recover from Alexander's death, but as they say, life goes on. Francine has a new man in her life now, and they're sailing around the Whitsundays."

That was a pity. He waited for the elderly lady to sit then claimed the lounge. "Do the girls still live here with you?"

"Brianna has an apartment close to the city, but she pops over for a few hours, every week. Darius lives here, the darling girl has been a great comfort to me."

"Darius." Simon smiled. "She must be about twenty-three now?"

"Almost twenty-four, and Brianna is twenty-six. They're both single. Are you married, dear?"

"No, ma'am." He glanced at a family photo he remembered from the professor's study. It showed Alexander and Francine posing with their two daughters, who looked about four and six. Brianna was a brunette with brown eyes like her father. Darius was blonde and smiling shyly at the photographer with her incredible eyes. He remembered them changing with her mood. A deep ocean-blue when she became animated or frustrated, and stormy purple when angry—which he'd only witnessed once—and most commonly, a sparkling blue when she teased or laughed. "I take it neither of the girls are here at the moment?"

"No, dear. Brianna is a talented ballerina and has a gala performance coming up in Paris, so I don't expect to see her tonight. Darius shouldn't be long though. She had to duck into work to test her latest robotic device."

He raised an eyebrow. "Robotic device?"

"Darius is a robotics engineer. We had thought she'd go into computer science, especially since Professor Chapman offered to mentor her, but she wouldn't consider it."

"If my memory serves me right, Professor Chapman was a friend and colleague of Alexander's?"

Sarah nodded. "Yes. He's been wonderful to Francine and the girls, sheltering them as best he could from the allegations. That was a terrible year, especially for Darius. She lost her father, was forced to move from the home she adored, then had her heart broken by a scoundrel. Thank God, she had her studies and amateur theatre group, otherwise I don't know how she would have coped."

Simon grimaced, remembering his advice to Darius, after Brianna had made fun of her for wanting to be an actress. He'd advised Darius to do drama as an elective. If nothing else, it would give her confidence. It seemed Brianna had become the sister who shone on stage, while Darius dabbled in amateur theatre.

He leaned back on the lounge, sinking into its comfortable cushions. "I recall Darius being shy with strangers. Has the theatre group helped with that?"

"Oh yes. She tends to play secondary characters but enjoys it immensely."

He shifted. "I'd like to come back and speak with you and the girls. I'm interested in anything Alexander might have said about his work before he died."

Sarah Cortez stiffened, her blue eyes losing their warmth. "That won't be possible. Brianna is flying to Paris tomorrow with her ballet company, and Darius is going on her first vacation since Alexander died." Sarah Cortez stood.

Simon came to his feet and followed her into the hall. "It's important I speak to Darius. Can I call back tonight?"

"No. I will not have you ruin her Fijian vacation by raking up lies about her father. Goodbye." She bustled to the front door. Once he was through, she closed it firmly behind him.

So Tink had become a robotics engineer. She'd always been bright. Alexander would have been proud. A Fijian holiday wasn't necessarily significant. The small island nation had always been popular with Australians. Still, it warranted further investigation. As did her association with Professor Chapman. His name was on the attendees list.

Simon looked ahead to see a slender brunette climbing out of a cab. Her low-cut jeans drew his gaze to her bare midriff. It wasn't Darius, but he remembered the sultry smirk.

Years had passed since he'd knocked back her flirtatious invitations. Brianna Cortez had never interested him.

"Hello," she called huskily, opening the gate. "And who might you be?"

"Simon Hawke. I studied under your father."

"My goodness." She smiled, showing perfect white teeth. "You've changed a lot." She gave him a thorough inspection, the interest in her brown eyes impossible to miss.

"Hello, Brianna. I recall you batting your eyelids, but back then I was more absorbed in gaining my degree than your father's displeasure."

She laughed. "I caught you looking more than once."

He couldn't help but grin. "You wore clothes that drew attention."

She sighed dramatically. "Yet you spoke to my sister more than me. Did you know Darius had a major crush on you back then? At least she did until I told her you and I were an item."

He stepped through the gateway unsure why Brianna's confession bothered him. Darius had always been around, until she wasn't. He'd figured she found better things to do than hang out with her father and a computer geek. Her teenage crush shouldn't concern him, yet he hated to think she'd been hurt.

"I want to ask about your father's movements up to his trip to Nepal, and if you know of anything that was bothering him."

Her smile faded. "That was five years ago. All I know is the Federal Police allege he hacked into a major bank and transferred millions to shell companies, and when it looked like he'd been caught, he jumped into a crevice. Because of that, Mom was refused my father's life insurance."

"Do you know anything about the Amethyst Code?"

"The what?"

"Amethyst Code. It's to do with a program your father and I wrote. Has anyone questioned you about it? Perhaps one of your father's acquaintances."

"I don't know what you're talking about. The police tore our house apart five years ago and questioned us for hours. I don't know anything about what my father was working on. Darius was the one who..." Brianna stepped past him. "Don't go there. It took my sister a long time to get over our father's death and the stuff that happened afterwards."

He nodded. "Who is your mother's new partner?"

"Darren Turner. I haven't met him yet, but he sounds like a nice guy. He sailed with my father when they were young. Why?"

He gave a light shrug as if it were of no consequence. "I'm curious. Your mother loved your father very much."

"My father is dead, and Mom is fifty-four. She deserves some happiness after what she's been through."

"How does Darius feel about the new guy?"

"She's not a fan." Brianna swept her tongue over her lower lip. "Look, I'm flying to Paris tomorrow, but we can hook up in a couple of weeks?"

"You're still not my type." Tonight, he intended to do a background check on Professor Chapman then find a way to speak with Tink before she flew to Fiji. Were Sarah and Brianna genuinely worried about her, or did they suspect Darius knew something? Why else would they warn him away?

"So why are you still standing here?" Brianna snapped, glaring at him sullenly.

Simon chuckled. "Don't take it personally. You're a beautiful woman, but I'd bore you in five minutes." The stunning *señorita* wasn't his type either, yet he couldn't get her out of his mind.

Brianna scoffed. "Your loss."

CHAPTER FIVE

Simon Hawke stood as large as life in her front garden. Darius drove past the house then parked in front of the neighbor's station wagon. She peeped through the rear window to see Simon salute Brianna then stride to a fire-engine-red, classic sedan.

His headlights lit up her interior, forcing her to duck for cover until he'd completed a U-turn and driven away.

"Now what?" Darius waited until her sister went into the house then did her own U-turn and parked in the driveway. In her rear vision mirror she saw a sedan pull up on the other side of the street. The two men were back. For the moment, she needed to keep a low profile, but if they were there when she arrived home from Fiji, she'd ring the police and demand an explanation.

Grabbing her carpet bag, she locked the car then ran down the side of her grandmother's house.

Through the kitchen window, she could see Brianna and Grandma at the table, having an animated conversation. They jumped as she burst into the kitchen. "Why was Simon Hawke here?" Darius dropped her bag on the floor. "What did he want?"

Grandma's shoulders sagged. "We were trying to spare you."

"From what?" She stared at her sister. "Tell me?"

"He asked about Dad's behavior before he went to Nepal, and if anyone else has been asking us or Mom questions."

Darius sank onto a chair. "Did you tell him Mom has a *boyfriend?*"

"Yes, and before you get antsy, Grandma told him we're both going away too. I must say, he's not your typical, nerdy computer geek."

Darius rolled her eyes. "That's because your antiquated perception of computer scientists is influenced by mediocre sitcoms and movies that portray men as all brawn and no brain."

"Wow, Dari, you're really bringing out the big guns tonight. Let me get a dictionary so we know what you're freaking talking about."

"Brianna, there is no need to be sarcastic or use uncouth language," countered Grandma. She smoothed her pure white hair then patted the neat bun. "I have the feeling Simon Hawke will be back with more questions. Perhaps we should book into a hotel near the airport tonight."

"No, I have too much to do here." Darius jumped up and began pacing the small kitchen. "Simon and Dad worked closely on classified software programs, which is why I expected him at the memorial service. What's he doing here now?"

Brianna drew in a deep breath. "Dari, you've spent five years brooding and speculating. You need to let go of the past and start living. When I get back, I'll hook up with Simon and find out what he's after."

Darius glared at her sister. "Dad did not jump into that crevice on purpose."

"Darlings, let's not talk about all this right now. You know how it upsets me when the past gets raked up again." Grandma handed Darius a bowl of green paste. "I've made you a face mask. Go put it on and have a relaxing bubble bath. Dinner won't be long, then we are going to spend a nice evening together."

Darius squelched a shiver of trepidation as she hugged her grandmother. They were peas in a pod, sharing everything from eye colour and height to their love of the theatre and concocting natural skin products. Was she putting this wonderful woman in danger?

"A bubble bath sounds perfect." She needed time alone to brood. She didn't want to think about her sister and Simon getting it on, but he would be no more able to resist Brianna's invitation than he had nine years ago.

She plugged the drain hole in the bath then flicked the taps on as her temper simmered. Men were forever making cakes of themselves over Brianna. Couldn't they see it was a power game to her?

Darius squirted lavender body wash below the faucet then twisted her hair up and secured it with an alligator hair clip. As the bath filled, she plastered her face with the avocado and honey mask. After using heavy face paint, this remedy always soothed and refreshed her skin. All she needed now was something to boost her self-esteem.

Would Simon have chosen her nine years ago, if she'd been more assertive? He'd always been nice to her, and in the bar last night, he'd definitely shown interest. How she wished she didn't need masks and props for confidence. Brianna didn't have a shy bone in her body.

Stripping off her clothes, Darius climbed into the bath and sank under the warm, soothing water. As she began to relax, she relived her recent encounters with Simon. Nothing had changed. He still captured her attention like no other man.

He wanted the sexy Spanish glamor puss, not an introverted homebody. And even if he was truly attracted to the real her, she'd eventually panic and retreat, pushing him away like all the others.

A light tap sounded at the door. "Dari, can I come in?"

"Sure." She sank lower beneath the frothy bubbles.

"Great look." Brianna pointed at Darius' face. "I hope it's not catching." She closed the door, then after a second's hesitation, sat on the footstool, chewing her fingernail.

A very un-Brianna thing to do.

Darius fought to keep her expression calm. Had Brie come to confess an attack of nerves over her Paris debut, or seek comfort after discovering her latest love interest was married, or to brag about another conquest? If it was to reminisce about Simon, Darius would have to drown her. "What's up?"

"He rejected me."

"Huh." To Darius' knowledge, no straight man had ever spurned the outgoing, talented and beautiful Brianna Cortez. "Is there a punch line coming?"

"Not funny, Dari. You think I'm a confident dancer who has the world at her feet, and that's true, but it's taken years of hard work and discipline."

The girl didn't have a humble bone in her body. "I know how hard you've worked, Brie, and kudos to you for achieving your dream. No one could be happier or prouder of you than me."

"I know, and that's why I've decided to come clean. Sometimes I say mean things to you, but you never hold a grudge. I even told you a blatant lie once, just to piss you off and make myself feel better."

"Why?"

Brianna took a deep breath. "Don't you ever repeat this, or I'll deny it. I was jealous. I still am sometimes."

"Of me?" She surged up, sending water gushing onto the tiles. Modesty be damned, this was unheard of. Briana was the outgoing sister who had it all together, and Darius the shy academic, which she preferred. She felt six feet tall. "Why would you be jealous of me?"

"Because people are drawn to you. You're clever and funny and have drop-dead gorgeous eyes. I'm especially jealous that you can eat anything you like without putting on weight."

Darius tried to assimilate her sister's hunched shoulders with the ultra-confident persona she usually portrayed. "I don't understand?"

"That's because you're so naïve, and loyal to people who don't deserve it."

"If you're talking about Dad, I'm loyal because I know he wouldn't desert us or commit suicide."

"This is about me," muttered Brianna. "I propositioned Simon Hawke tonight and he knocked me back."

"He did?" Her heart skipped a joyous beat. The thought of not having to witness them together calmed her ruffled feathers. "What has that to do with you being jealous?"

"It's not the first time he's rejected me. I lied about hooking up with him when we were teenagers. I practiced my flirting on him, but he barely noticed, preferring to speak to you, a painfully shy kid who played with a soldering iron and transforming gadgets."

Darius stared at her dumbstruck. "You lied, knowing how I felt about Simon? That's really low."

"Sorry, I was peeved by your friendship with him and your bond with Dad." Brianna laced her fingers in her lap. "I was jealous that they liked your company better than mine. Even now I'm envious of the stuff you do with Grandma, and the clever ways you hide your identity, to do some two-bit play."

"Hey!"

"Sorry, that was mean. I was even jealous when Dad gave you that cheap charm."

Tears filled Darius' eyes as her fingers instinctively reached for the atom. "I made this for Dad when I was fifteen. He gave it back to me in Nepal."

"I didn't know that."

Darius sank under the bubbles again. "Dad never missed an opening night whenever you performed, even when you had minor roles. He loved you, Brie. And you have no idea how much Grandma looks forward to your visits."

"I'm such a goose. You know I love you too, right?"

"You have a funny way of showing it sometimes." She reached for the towel then stood, wrapping it round her body as she stepped out of the bath. "Give me a hug."

"You're wet. Do I have to?" Brie's grin betrayed her objection.

"Yes." Fastening the towel, Darius stepped into her sister's arms, squeezing her tight. "I have a confession too."

"You?" Brianna dropped her arms and stepped back. "Do tell."

"I discovered an SD card fixed to the back of the charm."

Brianna narrowed her eyes. "Does it have anything to do with the Amethyst Code?"

"How do you—" Darius clutched her sister's hands. "What do you know about the Amethyst Code?"

"Nothing. Simon said it's something to do with a program he and Dad wrote. He wanted to know if anyone had asked about it."

"Heavens." Darius backed up to the wall and stared at the ceiling. Had Simon seen through her power-walker disguise?

"Dari, what is it?"

"The Amethyst Code is a cryptogram that hides a secret key."

"What does that even mean?"

"Text that's been replaced by letters and numbers, that have also been encrypted. Two layers of coding." She dropped her head into her hands.

"How do you know this stuff, Darius?"

"I spent a lot of time with Dad, and he sometimes showed me things. I came up with the name for him." She lifted her head to meet Brie's concerned gaze. "This isn't good."

"Shit, Dari. What was Dad involved in?"

"The Government gave him funding to write a program that would protect major utilities and institutions from cyber fraud, but in doing this, he created a program that could basically penetrate any security system, and in the wrong hands…"

"And Simon Hawke helped create this program?" Brianna leaned against the door, her hands on her hips.

"He and Dad worked closely on it until the Defence Force recruited Simon. I know they stayed in regular contact, but at Dad's memorial service, Professor Chapman mentioned Simon had moved on to a more lucrative career."

"He told Grandma he was overseas when Dad died." Brianna tapped one of her acrylic nails on her arm. "What do you hope to gain by digging all this up, Dari?"

"I believe Dad was murdered."

"But the Sherpa said—"

"Forget the Sherpa. With poor visibility and roaring winds, no one would hear a gunshot. The Sherpa might have thought Dad threw himself in the crevice, but a bullet could knock a man off his feet. And we can't ask the Sherpa, because he was lost in an avalanche the same day." She wouldn't endanger Brianna's life by mentioning the traitor or terrorist group.

Brianna sighed. "You're clutching at straws, and even if it was true, I don't know how you can prove any of this. "You're shivering. Let's go to your bedroom."

Securing her towel again, Darius led the way. She switched on the light then shut the bedroom door behind Brianna. Her room wasn't much warmer than the bathroom, but the carpet kept her toes from turning into icicles. She shut the curtains.

Brianna trounced across to the bed then perched on the edge beside Darius' half-packed suitcase. "I know there's more, so spill?"

"I've learned the government is planning a secret summit to discuss the program Dad wrote. It's been used to hack into the Defence Force's database. The hacker accessed encrypted codes to redirect a Navy frigate after Simon's request for assistance was denied. There was some sort of kidnapping off the coast of Broome."

Brianna's eyes widened. "Are you freaking kidding me? How do you know these things?"

"Calm down. A colleague of Dad's told me. The summit kicks off in six days. It's the best chance to catch the hacker and find out what really happened to Dad."

"You're not a secret agent, and *you* won't be at the summit." Brianna's eyes narrowed. "Wait, does this impulsive trip to Fiji have anything to do with the summit?"

"The summit's location is a secret. I'm going to a tropical island for a holiday." It wasn't a lie; she *would* be on a tropical island.

Brianna didn't look convinced. "What's your involvement?"

"I'm working on robotic aids that can be used to listen in and spy on the delegates."

"I don't like it, Dari. Can you trust this colleague of Dad's?"

Best if Brianna didn't know the *colleague* used a computerized voice and insisted on using code names. "It's the only way we'll discover the truth."

"This is beyond belief." Brianna fiddled with the frilly cushion beside her. "What else did this *colleague* tell you?"

"Not to trust anyone. He promised to protect us and make things right."

"You're kidding," whispered Brianna. "Is this colleague Professor Chapman?"

"What gave you that idea?"

"He rang last week, and I took the call. He said he'd received an invitation to a seminar and Dad's work was the main topic. He asked if we'd found any of Dad's notebooks or if anyone had been asking questions recently. I told him no."

"Wow." Darius considered this new info. "The Federal Police have all Dad's stuff and Professor Chapman would know that, so what's he up to?"

"The police can't pin this Navy frigate thing on Dad," snapped Brianna. "Entombed in a glacier is a pretty solid alibi."

"Exactly." Darius dropped the towel and donned her thick, powder blue robe.

"Promise me you'll keep your nose out of this?" Brianna stuck her hands on her hips. "Let Dad's colleague do the investigating."

A light knock at the door saved Darius from answering. "Girls, is everything all right?"

"Yes, Grandma." Brianna sent Darius a pointed look then opened the door. "I was giving Dari some tips on packing. I don't know why she needs such a big suitcase. It's Fiji, for heaven's sake." She slipped out the door then poked her head back in. "By the way, I hate gardening and cooking, so maybe I'll take Grandma and Mom shopping when I get home." She blew a kiss. "Have a great holiday, Dari, and get that goo off your face before you attract a swarm of bees. You'll never get laid if your face is swollen up like a baboon's bum."

"I don't want to get laid," she shouted at the closed door, then blew out a breath and leaned against it, considering her options. She'd love to know what Simon was up to, but she needed to work on her robotics and disguises, one of which was drying in the garage, hence the large suitcase.

Learning Simon had spurned Brianna buoyed her spirits. He'd never wanted Brianna, but he'd certainly wanted the girl in the bar. The girl Darius had pretended to be, not the girl she really was. The one he'd always called Tink.

The squeal of her sash window rising brought her back to earth with a heart-stopping thud. As mute and motionless as a fence post, she could only stare in stunned disbelief as a jean clad leg came through the divided curtains.

Where was kickass punk girl or skater-boy when she needed them? Even the *señorita* would have stabbed the intruder with her stiletto heel by now. She stared, paralyzed as a pair of wide shoulders then a head poked through. The man straightened, lifting a way-too familiar face toward her.

Golden-flecked green eyes widened then shone with humor. "Hello, Tink. What's with the green muck on your face."

"Nourishing mask," she whispered, her heart pounding so hard she risked permanent damage. "You scared me."

"So why didn't you scream or wallop me with something." He was such a handsome devil, she wanted to swoon, but that would mean bringing her paralyzed body back to life.

"I..."

"You don't seem surprised. Men often come through your window, do they? Or are you always this calm and collected."

If only he knew how far off the mark he was. Calm and collected? No way. "I don't believe in violence. Haven't you heard of front doors? They're what polite people use when visiting someone they haven't seen in *nine* years."

He chuckled then strolled across the room, stopping to tower over her diminutive five-foot-two by at least nine inches.

Simon touched a finger to her cheek, sending a sliver of fire to the tip of her cold toes. She watched, fascinated as he sniffed his finger then licked it. "Tastes like honey and lemon." He frowned. "That's not what I can smell though. A good thing, otherwise I'd be tempted to lick your face." He leaned close to her neck. His warm breath caressed her skin. "You smell like lavender and sunshine."

She opened her mouth to object, but only a strangled garble emerged.

He grinned and began ambling around the room, touching things he had no right to touch. "You've grown taller, but I'd know your eyes anywhere. How are you, Tink?"

"Confused." Her gaze snagged on the fluorescent pink cap in her suitcase, screaming to be spotted by the man sniffing her favorite perfume. Picking up the towel, she tossed it over her suitcase. "You didn't come to my father's memorial service."

"I was out of the country. I did phone your mother to offer my condolences and ask if she needed anything, but she said no." He sniffed her perfume and glanced at her. "Is this a popular brand? I've come across it a lot lately."

Heavens, he must have a nose like a bloodhound. "Yes, and expensive, so I only wear it on special occasions. How often do you climb into women's bedrooms and sniff them?"

"You're the first." He chuckled and replaced her perfume on the dresser then picked up her monstrous cat alarm. "Your grandmother said you were a robotics engineer. Is this one of your designs?"

"Yes. I made it a few years ago, but toys aren't my specialty. I work for a medical research company, developing robotic aids for non-invasive surgery." She licked her lips. "I heard you left the Joint Command Center for a more lucrative job."

He stilled. "Who told you that?"

"Um... I'm not sure. Is it true?"

"I accepted another position as a communications analyst, which I left last year. Now I'm working for a security firm here in Sydney."

"Do you believe my father was a criminal?"

He hesitated, carefully placing the heavy cat back on her desk. "Millions of dollars were stolen by someone using your father's program. Maybe they'd stolen it, or were standing over him, threatening your lives. Do you have the Amethyst Code?"

"No." She clutched the atom. "I mean, I don't know what that is."

He strolled back to her then took the atom out of her hand. The back of his fingers lightly brushed her skin, snatching her breath.

"This charm is almost identical to mine."

"I made it for Dad."

Simon turned the atom over. "Was something fixed to the back?"

"No." She avoided his eyes. "You still have the atom I made you."

He dropped the charm and lifted her chin, forcing her to meet his eyes. "How do you know that?" The golden flecks in his green eyes stood out as he watched her closely.

When she'd seen the atom on his keyring, she'd become angry then overwhelmed with sentimental memories. Simon had kept it for thirteen years. "I don't. I'm asking."

"Yes, I do, and thanks to your fairy dust, it's been lucky for me." He ambled over to her desk. "Do you think your father committed suicide?"

"He was murdered." To say the words opened old wounds but filled her with righteousness. No longer would she allow others to dismiss her beliefs.

Simon showed no reaction other than flicking a glance her way. "Leading up to that day, was your father depressed, acting strangely, protective, despondent, nervous?"

"He was worried about you." Darius shivered.

"Me?"

"Yes. Are you going to the summit?" Damn, she hadn't meant to blurt that out.

"Tink, you're full of surprises. How do you know about the summit?"

She licked her lips. "Professor Chapman mentioned it to Brianna." He said Dad's work is on the agenda, and he asked if we had any of Dad's notes."

Simon's gaze drilled into her. "Besides me and Professor Chapman, has there been anyone else hanging around or asking about your father's work?"

"There are two men parked across the street. They've been there every night for the last few days."

"I'll find out who they are." Simon reached for her sketchbook. It contained images of a homeless woman, punk, skateboarder and several disguises she hadn't used yet.

"Don't." She leaped forward, intending to snatch it, but tripped on her robe, and instead, smacked nose-first into his hard chest. "Ow." The alligator clip slid out of her hair, sending it cascading over her face. She stepped away, treading on the robe again, but no matter how hard she tried to keep her balance, she couldn't save herself.

Chapter Six

Simon dropped the sketchbook to catch her, twisting so he hit the floor first. She ended up sprawled across his torso. His mind emptied of all rational thought but the smooth skin under his hands. Silken hair of spun gold tickled his forearms. A delicate lavender fragrance invaded his nostrils. Every muscle in his body locked. He wanted to kiss her. Christ, he wanted to devour her. The minute he'd come through the window and smelled that delectable perfume, he knew he'd found his *señorita*, skateboarder and little runaway. He'd bet his last dollar she was the power-walker as well. How she'd devised such a believable baby bump was an intriguing thought. Now he needed to find out why she wanted him at the summit, and if she had a connection to the hacker.

Releasing Tink wasn't easy, especially as her beautiful wide eyes declared her own stunned awareness. Bits of green muck now stained his shirt, but he didn't give a damn. His gaze dropped to the open folds of her robe and her small, plump breasts. She was a goddess and he was in big trouble.

"Hell, for such a little thing you sure pack a punch."

"Sorry." Her voice shook. "This robe was Brianna's and she's taller than me. I'm always tripping on it."

The collision wasn't what he was referring to, but he figured that was better left unsaid. He rolled her onto the carpet then dropped a chaste kiss on her forehead. "I'm going to check on those guys in the car." He kept his eyes on her face as he helped her up.

"I'm coming to the summit." Her fingernails dug into his arms, reminding him again of the pregnant power-walker.

"No way, sweet pea. You're a distraction I don't need."

Her hands fluttered to his chest. "We used to be friends."

He groaned. They could never be platonic friends again. Not when he wanted to pick her up and take her somewhere private, where he could explore every inch of her. Which is exactly what had happened to his three mates when they first met the women who were now their wives. He waited for the expected tightening of his chest, the voice telling him to run.

Instead, both mind and body were focused on stealing a real kiss. He cleared his throat. Until he knew what she was up to, he couldn't consider a relationship with her. "Your grandmother said you were heading to Fiji? You're not thinking of gatecrashing the summit, are you?"

"Why, is it in Fiji?" Her heightened voice gave her away. She knew all right. Professor Chapman could have let the location slip. So much for secrecy.

"I imagine security will be tight." Her lips turned down in a pout that made his hormones roar for that kiss. Then as if it were no big deal, she shrugged. "I'm staying in Suva for a few days then who knows? I'd like to explore the Yasawa Islands. If you're interested, we could catch up after the summit." Her beautiful eyes told him she doubted he'd come.

"Give me your phone number, Tink."

"Okay." She picked up the sketchbook then ripped out a blank page and wrote down her number. "I'm flying out Monday morning."

"Dari! Dinner's ready." Brianna's voice bellowed down the hall.

Simon hot-footed it to the window. He didn't fancy a confrontation with Brianna. She might flirt her butt off, but she'd probably go for his jugular if she caught him with her sister.

"It's a date, Tink. Go have your dinner, I'll speak to the guys out front then come back and wait for you here. We need to have a chat regarding your fondness for disguises, stealing wallets and illegally entering other peoples' homes. Oh...and you might want to fix your robe...or you *will* get laid." He ducked through the window then shut it. The deep blush that blossomed amongst the green gunk as she clutched the robe was worth a thousand words.

She'd stolen from him, led him on a street chase, and gained access to his apartment. Finding out why suddenly took on an intriguing proposition. Only the hacker could have given her such confidential information on the summit. This unknown person could be using Professor Cortez's death to manipulate Darius.

Treading a narrow path at the side of the house, he was bombarded by memories of Darius hanging out in the professor's computer lab late at night and on weekends. She'd always bring sandwiches then badger them to stop working and eat. His lips twitched as he recalled the way she'd hassle her father to finish up and go home.

Between the house, high fence at the side and the dark sky, he almost missed seeing a large spider web. He ducked underneath then peered around the corner of the house. Despite the quiet, the hair at his nape bristled. A sudden spray of water splattered from an ancient sprinkler in the middle of the lawn. To stay dry, he'd have to time his run between the wave pattern.

Now that he had some distance, his thoughts returned to Darius. She believed her father was murdered and definitely knew something about the Amethyst Code.

The thought of Tink putting herself in danger sliced him to the bone. If for no other reason than to keep her safe, he would discover the truth behind her father's death and the hacker's identity, before Darius ended up on charges of treason. If she turned out to be the hacker, it would gut him.

Contemplating his dash across the lawn, Simon noticed a cigarette lighter flare to life across the street. As the spray arced away, he crept alongside the garden bed to a neatly pruned hedge, where he could watch the man strolling back and forth along the opposite path. Every ten seconds, a cigarette tip glowed then the exhaled smoke would drift away with the slight breeze. Another man sat in the car. If the Feds had the house under surveillance, they were making it obvious.

Cold pellets bombarding his back signaled the return of the sprinkler. *Damn.* He shivered as the full force of the freezing water hit. Dropping to his knees, he crawled to the far corner of the garden then memorized the number plate.

Good thing he'd seen the white Corolla veer in front of the station wagon next door, or he'd have gone home and tried to speak to Darius tomorrow. He'd parked his Mustang in the street behind and come over the back fence. Another smart move, or the watchers would have seen him. The white Corolla now sat in Sarah Cortez's driveway.

Simon pulled out his phone and swiped Jarred's number. It rang several times before a female voice answered.

"Steele residence. This is Madeline, how may I help you?"

He could hear female chatter in the background. Jarred had probably locked himself in his office or gym. "Hello, Madeline. It's Simon."

"Hi. Would you believe your caller ID is Bird Seed Supplies?"

"It's in case our phones are compromised."

"Good idea. I suppose you'd like to speak to Chief Steel Feather?"

"Yes please." Simon chuckled. Madeline had given Jarred the nick name after their mission in Vietnam and used it whenever he annoyed her. "Who else is with you?"

"Jarred's mother and sister. We're playing scrabble and he's cheating. Here, I'll put him on."

"Simon! I take it you have news?" Surprisingly Jarred sounded extremely upbeat for a guy who liked his solitude.

"I'm at the Cortez house. Do the Feds have it under surveillance?"

"I wouldn't be surprised, but Gibbs didn't mention it. What's the address and the vehicle's license plate."

Simon gave Jarred the info then told him what he'd learned. "The Professor's mother and eldest daughter are protective of Darius, but I don't believe they know what she's up to. Before you notify the Feds of Darius' involvement, I'd appreciate the chance to question her further."

"How long do you need?"

"Tonight and tomorrow." Simon glanced at the house. One of the lounge curtains twitched. "I'll need to convince her she can trust me. And I want to verify her flight then look into Professor Chapman. He could be our hacker."

"Very well. Anything you need me to do?"

"Not that I can—"

Glass shattered. Simon swung around to see Sarah Cortez's lounge window splintered over her front porch.

A black silhouette hurtled across the garden toward him. The sinewy man of average height wore a balaclava and carried a vicious looking knife.

"Fuck!" Simon dived sideways as the man lunged. "Under attack!" Simon dropped the phone and rolled across wet grass, springing to his feet as his attacker came at him again. Simon twisted away, but lost traction. The blade's tip slashed through his shirt, leaving a fiery sting in its wake.

"Police! Drop your weapon." A gun shot followed the shout from the street.

Without the protection of his Kevlar suit, Simon faced being slashed to pieces. A screech from the house distracted his attacker for a second. Slipping and scrabbling, Simon used the reprieve to yank the ancient sprinkler from the hose and swung to meet the next attack.

The clang of metal echoed around the small garden. The impact vibrated up Simon's arm, but he had bigger problems. All three Cortez women were on the front steps and he was being herded into a corner of soft mulch that kept sinking under his feet. It was only a matter of time before the blade made contact with his fingers then it was all over red rover.

The sound of running feet, the two policemen yelling, and another shot echoed through the quiet street. Lights lit up the front porch. A tiny dynamo in blue erupted off the porch and leaped onto the attacker's back.

"No, Tink!"

She ripped the man's mask off and yanked on his hair for all she was worth.

"Darius, no!" Brianna screamed.

More gunshots blasted. As he hadn't been hit, Simon suspected the shots were a warning from the policemen, but he couldn't take his eyes of the attacker and Darius. With a roar, he swung the sprinkler, whacking the guy's wrist and sending the knife, tip first, into the ground.

Desperate to land another blow, he could only watch in frustration as the fair-haired man spun around and around, trying to dislodge Darius from his shoulders.

Brianna and the policemen kept yelling. The guy got a good grip on Darius and hurled her at Simon. The impact sent them both crashing into a sodden bed of manure-laced mulch.

Simon rolled, keeping her under him as the man sprinted around the side of the house. Sarah and Brianna came running across the wet lawn, their eyes wide with shock.

"Are you two all right?" asked a gruff voice from the other side of the hedge.

"I think so." Simon scrambled to his feet then helped Darius up. Her sister and grandmother instantly enveloped her in their arms. He kept them behind him as he faced the man on the other side of the hedge, holding a standard police issue Glock.

"Keep your hands where I can see them." The balding man lifted his other hand, revealing his ID. "I'm Senior Constable Delaney, Federal Police. You want to show me some ID and tell me what's going on?"

Simon pulled out his wallet and passed over his security ID. "If you contact Inspector Zachary Gibbs, he'll verify my identity. I'm here tonight as a friend of the Cortez family. As for that lunatic with the knife, he came out of nowhere, and I have no idea who he is."

"My partner's gone after him and I've called for backup."

Darius wriggled free of her grandmother. "Why are the Federal Police watching our house?"

Brianna gasped. "What?"

Sarah Cortez glared up at Delaney. "Is this true?"

"We had a tip off there might be trouble brewing." Delaney shoved his Glock into its holster inside his jacket. "Something to do with a cybercrime committed five years ago."

Darius ruffled up like a broody hen. "Allegations. Nothing was ever proven."

"Leave it, darling." Sarah patted her shoulder. "We're lucky these guys were here."

Simon slung his arm around Darius' shoulders. "Constable, can we talk inside? I don't like the women out in the open."

"Yeah. I'll retrieve that knife for forensics, then check in with my partner and Inspector Gibbs. The street will be full of squad cars any minute, so I'll get the local lads to do a walk around. Please remain in the house."

Darius squealed. "Simon, you're bleeding."

"It's not serious." His gaze dropped to her bloodstained pajama shirt. "You're hurt!"

"No, it must be your blood. I'll drive you to the hospital."

"I'm fine." Simon nodded to Delaney then guided Darius and the other two women across the garden. "Luckily, I had my lucky charm backing me up." He looked down at Darius. "I assume it was you who smashed the window?"

"Yes, I was watching you from the lounge room when the Ninja came sneaking around the garage. I knew I'd never make it outside in time to warn you, so I threw the heavy vase at the window. She glanced at her grandmother. "Sorry."

"It's done now." Sarah Cortez glared daggers at Simon as she reached the top step. "The window and vase can be replaced, my granddaughters can't." She turned her attention to Darius. "What fool idea was that, jumping on his back?"

"I had to do something. He had a knife."

Simon wiped muck off his shoulder. "I might stick around tonight in case he comes back."

"Why? He attacked you, not us." Brianna crossed her arms and stood beside Sarah blocking the front door.

He sighed. "I didn't tell anyone I'd be here tonight. And if the tipoff is for real. The Ninja was here for you ladies."

Sarah glanced at the dark corners of her garden. "Simon might be right. Come on inside, girls."

"You two go in. We'll be there in a minute." Darius' posture brooked no argument. Still, Simon was surprised when Sarah and Brianna let it be and entered the house.

"Can we keep my disguises and the envelope deliveries between us?"

He nodded. "For now."

Her tense stance relaxed. "How badly are you hurt?"

"Some antiseptic and a little TLC should do the trick." He smiled. She had traces of green goo on her pale face. "I need a shower. Whatever we landed in is disgustingly rank."

"Chicken manure." She handed him his phone. "This was on the grass."

He held it to his ear as he followed her into the hall then shut the door. "You still there, Jarred?"

"You're on speaker," came Madeline's voice. "Jarred's driving. Are you all right?"

"Yes." Simon followed Darius into the lounge. "I was attacked by a guy with a knife. Fair, mid-twenties, five-eight, thin build. Two Feds came to the rescue. One has gone after my attacker."

"We'll be there as soon as we can," said Jarred. "I want to speak to Inspector Gibbs first."

"Can you pick up a pair of track pants and a T-shirt for me? My clothes took a beating."

"I've got some spare gym clothes in the boot," called Jarred. "Secure the ladies inside the house and inform the officers, Inspector Gibbs will speak to them shortly. It turns out they are there on his orders."

"No worries, see you soon." Simon ended the call.

Darius took hold of his hand. "Come into the kitchen. I need to get your shirt off."

"Wow, Tink, I'm not that sort of man."

She blinked at him for a couple of seconds then burst out laughing, the sound warming his cool skin. "You won't be so chirpy when I soak your chest in antiseptic."

He followed her along the hall to the kitchen where the other two women stood at the sink. They'd closed the blind on the window behind them. "Sorry about the smell, ladies, we fell in chook poo."

Sarah Cortez put her hands on her hips and glared at him. "Up until this evening, this has been a very safe street. You turn up asking questions, and suddenly my window is smashed and men with knives and guns are rampaging on the lawn. That hooligan could have killed Darius."

"Mrs. Cortez, you're lucky I was here. The guy in black was doubtless here to scare or hurt you ladies."

"What is the world coming to?" Her hands shook as she reached for the kettle.

Simon grimaced. "Do you have a piece of board large enough to cover the broken window?"

"There might be something in the garage—"

"No, there's not," cut in Darius. "I threw all the wood out when I made it my workshop."

"No matter." Simon walked past her to the rear door and tested the lock. "I'll call a glazier for an emergency replacement tonight and check all your windows. We don't want any unwelcome guests entering the house."

Brianna raised an eyebrow. "I would consider you unwelcome."

"I'm your bodyguard until we can move you all somewhere safe." He checked the kitchen window. "All good here. What about the bedrooms?"

"I've checked all of them." Sarah Cortez blocked his path. "You're soaked through, covered in blood and smell like a pig sty. Go have a shower then we can sit down to dinner, where you will explain how you're going to keep my granddaughters safe."

"Yes, ma'am." He searched his phone for the nearest glazier then organized an emergency call out.

"They'll be here within the hour."

"Thank you." Sarah Cortez glanced at Darius. "Darling, you smell ghastly too. Show this young man to the main bathroom then you use my ensuite. You'll need to rinse that blood and muck out of your pajamas too."

"Yes, Grandma."

Simon followed Darius along the hall and accepted the towel she pulled from a cupboard. "You sure you don't want to join me?"

She blushed rosy red. "I thought you weren't that sort of man?"

He laughed. "Me and my big mouth." He caught her hand as she turned away. "You saved my life, Darius, thank you. If there's anything I can ever do for you, you only need to ask."

She stepped closer. "Help me find out what happened to my father. I want to know why an honest man, determined to stamp out cyber fraud, is accused of stealing millions. Where is the money and who killed him? Help me clear my father's name and I'll be eternally grateful."

"Can I assume this is why you disguised yourself, stole my wallet then delivered the envelopes? Why you want me at the summit? You could have just asked me. I don't bite." Although the thought had merit.

"I didn't know if I could trust you. I still don't. You worked on secret programs with my father."

It was a fair call. Simon exhaled. "I'll look into your father's death, but you're going to need to tell me everything. How you got confidential information on a secret summit, who else knows what you're up to. Anything your father told you that might help." He cracked a smile. "And if you're dating anyone."

CHAPTER SEVEN

Smelling like a field of lavender in full bloom, Darius padded barefoot toward the kitchen with Simon's question still on her mind. Did he really want to know if she was dating anyone? Because, really, why would a guy like Simon be interested in someone as dull and boring as Darius Cortez, robotics engineer?

She tugged down on her bookworm tank top. Entertaining the police in pajamas would mortify Grandma, so she'd pulled on jeans and her favorite top. The chubby green caterpillar in his thick reading glasses usually had an uplifting effect on people, which they all needed tonight.

She could hear Grandma and Brianna giving their account of Simon's prior visit, and what they'd seen of the attack. Pausing, she cursed under her breath as Senior Constable Delaney probed into Simon's relationship with her father.

"What's up?" whispered Simon, his breath tickled her ear.

"Shush." She whirled and lost the capacity to think, breathe or speak. A bloody laceration crossed his naked chest. At one edge, just above the left nipple, a thin trail of blood drew her gaze down his torso to the purple towel, slung low around his hips.

Except for the nasty wound, he was magnificent, and by the cheeky twinkle in his eyes, he'd noticed her appreciation.

She swallowed the lump in her throat and concentrated on his cut. "We need to bathe that in antiseptic. You may need a stitch or two."

"A plaster strip will do the trick, Tink."

She blinked. "I still smell manure?"

"It's these." He held up his clothes and a pair of disgusting shoes. "Have you got a plastic bag I can seal these in? The shirt is beyond repair, but my jeans and shoes might be salvageable."

61

"Give them here. I'll soak them for you."

He gave her everything then grinned. "With your big blue eyes and hair up in that knob thing, you remind me of a very sexy Tinker Bell."

His light touch on her chin had her tingling all the way to her toes, not at all like the discomfort she usually experienced when a guy hit on her. Pulling back, she dropped her gaze to his chest again. "I'd like to have Tinker Bell's magic wand. With a twist of my wrist and a scattering of fairy dust, I could have my every desire granted."

"You don't need a wand, Tink. Most men would beat down the door to grant your every desire."

The smile dropped from her face. She saw the surprise in Simon's eyes, but was helpless to prevent it. Memories of her short, disastrous love affair clouded her vision. The humiliation and self-recrimination mocked her with such vengeance, she shrank against the wall.

"Darius, what is it?" He stepped closer, concern etched over every inch of his face.

"If I had that kind of power, I would use it to clear my father. Nothing else matters." She rushed into the kitchen where Grandma, Brianna and the policeman looked up. "I need to clean Simon's shoes and jeans then patch him up before he bleeds to death."

"There's no chance of that, Tink." He followed her onto an enclosed side verandah then through to the laundry, lounging against the door as she filled the plastic bucket with hot water and washing powder.

He frowned. "You want to tell me what upset you?"

"You're bleeding over the towel." She dropped his jeans and shoes in the bucket then washed her hands. After drying them, she grabbed a clean washer and dabbed at his belly. It was rock hard, smooth and warm. She shivered. "I don't think we should mention the summit to the police."

"Fine by me." He stilled her hand. "Darius, who hurt you?"

"What?" She shook her head. "I don't know what you're talking about." She scooted past him, careful not to make contact.

In the kitchen, she ignored her Grandmother's searching look and pulled out the first aid kit. "Sit down, Simon, so I can patch you up."

"I'd prefer to stand." He backed against the counter and winked. "I'm all yours."

She could feel the heat in her face as she filled a small bowl with water then added antiseptic.

Constable Delaney flipped his notebook closed then dropped it in his shirt pocket. "Right, I've spoken to Inspector Gibbs, but I still need your statements." His gaze shifted between Darius and Simon. "Unfortunately, your attacker got away, but we do have his balaclava and the knife, so there's a chance we'll get fingerprints or DNA. I'll get the boys to send your neighbors home and clear the street."

"What about protection for the ladies tonight? The security firm I work for could handle it."

"Inspector Gibbs informed me that it has been arranged. My officer will leave once the Steele Security guards turn up. Write out your statements then give them to one of my constables. Goodnight."

"Goodnight and thank you." Darius squeezed several cotton balls in antiseptic then dabbed Simon's angry wound.

He flinched. "Hell, Tink."

"Don't be a baby." She raised her eyes to his. "It's barely a scratch, remember?"

"That stuff stings worse than a wasp's bite. I think you're enjoying this." His intense gaze held hers captive as Grandma bustled about them, setting an extra place. Brianna had escorted Constable Delaney to the front door where Darius could hear them speaking in undertones. With luck her sister would convince the police to send Simon home, now that a security guard would be on watch. Darius' stomach churned at the idea of Simon's planned interrogation.

Simon couldn't think of anywhere he'd rather be than right here, being mollycoddled by his very own impish fairy. The antiseptic had a bitch of a sting, but he adored the soft blush that blossomed in Darius' cheeks each time her fingertips skimmed his skin. After the first three strips of surgical tape, he almost told her not to waste her energy, but her touch and absorption in the task enthralled him, so he indulged her as she painstakingly stuck little strips across his chest.

When she finished, Darius gave a satisfied huff. He glanced down at the picket fence of white strips, aligned across his chest and erupted into laughter, which hurt. "Heck, Tink, it's going to take forever to get these off. It's a good thing my mates can't see me or I'd never live it down."

He glanced at Sarah standing by the oven, watching them with unveiled anxiety. He needed to coax Darius into trusting him with her secrets, which meant professing a serious interest. That wouldn't be hard. He hadn't been this intrigued by a woman ever.

Surprise flared momentarily, along with an elevated pulse and anticipation. He wasn't into long term. He could do the friendship thing, like she wanted, but keeping it that way would be a problem.

Sarah Cortez cleared her throat, bringing him back to the here and now, only to realize he'd been staring at Darius as she cleaned up. Thankfully the doorbell pealed and rescued him from the older woman's perceptive gaze.

His reprieve was short-lived.

Brianna returned to the kitchen followed by Jarred and Madeline. Jarred's gaze dropped to Simon's chest then one brow rose. "I'm delighted to see you in one piece, but isn't that a little excessive?"

Darius clamped her hands on her slim hips and glowered. "Hold your tongue, Jarred. Simon was attacked by a knife-wielding ninja. He's lucky to be alive." She huffed then smiled. "Hello, Madeline."

Simon guessed his frown mirrored everyone else's in the room. "How do you know Jarred and Madeline?"

Her mouth opened then she shrugged. "Who else could they be?"

Madeline continued to frown. "Have we met?"

Brianna gasped. "You're the journalist who broke that story about teenage Vietnamese girls being used for slave labor."

"So she is." Grandma shook Madeline's hand. "I'm Sarah Cortez and these are my granddaughters, Brianna and Darius."

Madeline shook hands with Darius then Brianna. "It's nice to meet you. As you've guessed, this is Jarred Steele. He comes across as fierce, and he growls a lot, but as far as I know he hasn't bitten anyone yet."

Simon failed to hide is grin. The incredulous look on Jarred's face was something to behold. Madeline had to be the only person in the world who could render the man speechless, yet his eyes held a wealth of promised retribution.

"You have no idea, how much I would like to bite *you*, right now, Madeline."

Sarah chuckled. "It takes a resilient woman to tame a wild man."

"Wild!" Jarred's astonishment brought another grin to Simon's lips.

Madeline gave Sarah a beaming smile. "You've made my day."

"Good, now what brings you and your husband to my home?"

"Oh, we're not married." Madeline flushed. "I was...meeting with Jarred on another matter when Simon rang. We heard the commotion and came as fast as we could."

"I see." Sarah gave Jarred a censorious glare. "Don't leave it too long, or some other man will snap up this lovely woman, right before your eyes."

"I don't know how I'd cope," muttered Jarred, raising an eyebrow at Madeline.

She laughed then strolled over to Simon and kissed his cheek. "I'm happy you're alive. You should swing by the hospital emergency though, that looks nasty."

Noticing Tink's gaze shoot between him and Madeline then the floor, Simon shifted to her side. After Brianna's confession, he didn't want Darius misinterpreting Madeline's concern. "Darius took care of me better than any emergency room nurse. I'm thinking of keeping her." He glanced at Jarred. "Did you manage to smooth things over with the Feds and local cops?"

"Yes. Write out your statements and one of the constables outside will see they get to Inspector Gibbs." Jarred handed Simon a sports bag. "My gym gear. It's a little more appropriate than what you're wearing."

"Thanks. It seems a shame to cover this work of art though." He winked at Darius, delighted when she returned his smile. He headed for the bathroom.

When he returned to the kitchen, Jarred and Madeline had left. Sara Cortez pointed at an empty chair. "You need fuel in your stomach, young man. We're having lamb casserole. Sit down beside Darius and eat. You may call me Sarah." She handed him a steaming plate of meat and vegetables.

"Thank you, Sarah, this smells delicious."

It was, and as he soaked up the last of his second helping gravy with freshly-baked bread, his mood lifted. Amazing what a full stomach could do.

Two men from Jarred's security guard branch had arrived to patrol the front and back gardens, and the glazier had turned up to fix the window.

Brianna plopped into her chair and met Simon's gaze. "As you're staying here tonight, one of the security guards is going to drive me and Grandma to my apartment and keep a watch outside. It makes sense to stay in the city as we have early flights tomorrow."

"I'm not sure that's a good idea," said Sarah.

"It's fine, Grandma." Darius kissed her grandmother's cheek. "You go and have a lovely holiday. I'll be fine. If it makes you feel better, I'll go to Charlotte's house tomorrow."

"It does, sweetheart. I will sleep better knowing you're well away from here." She squeezed Darius' hand. "After your holiday, why don't you reconsider coming to visit your mother and Darren?"

"Grandma, I'm not ready to meet him. I don't know if I ever will be."

"Darius, life can be lonely on your own. Don't begrudge your mother her happiness." Sarah glanced at Simon. "I need to finish packing. Promise me, you will keep this darling girl safe tonight?"

"You have my word, Sarah. No one will get anywhere near Darius tonight."

"You are to sleep in the front room. Leave the door open, that way you will hear the floorboards creak if anyone enters the house."

"Yes, ma'am."

"I don't want to forget anything. Come help me, Darius." Sarah patted Simon's shoulder then padded out of the kitchen. After an uneasy look at Simon, Darius followed.

He gathered dishes and cutlery then brought them to the counter, where Brianna had filled the sink. She eyed him warily. "You hurt Dari and I'll cut off your pecker."

"Ouch." He turned to face her. "I'm not out to hurt anyone, Brianna. I work for Jarred Steele as a security analyst, and I had the greatest respect for your father. I promise Darius is safe with me tonight."

As she washed the dishes, Simon dried, suspecting she had more to say.

She deposited the cutlery in the soapy water and turned to him. "I see the way you look at each other." She bit her lip. "Dari still cares for you, even after..."

"Why don't you tell me who hurt Darius?"

"I don't know all the facts, but she's always been naïve. She only ever saw the good in people. She was vulnerable, struggling with Dad's death. Our mother moved up the coast to look after her sister and I was dancing in London. Except for Grandma, Dari was pretty much on her own when she caught the eye of a has-been football jock."

"Didn't she have friends?"

"Yes, but Charlotte and Chloe had gone backpacking in Europe." Brianna scrubbed each fork and knife diligently then dropped them in the rack. "If I'd been here..."

He dried each implement and waited, until his patience ran out. "Did this guy physically hurt her?"

"I don't know what he did. She refused to talk about it."

The wooden spoon he held snapped in two. "You must know something?"

Brianna's eyes lifted from the broken spoon. "I asked around when I got back. The stuff I heard made my skin crawl. There were rumors he left a girl pregnant and several others with shredded reputations. I didn't hear anything about Darius, but it changed her."

He dropped the broken spoon in the trash can then looked at Brianna. "Has Darius dated anyone since?"

"Yes, but it's never more than one or two dates. She loses interest and tells them she only wants to be friends."

"No guy wants to hear that." He dried the casserole dish then folded the tea towel and hung it on the oven door. "It could be a protective mechanism. Dump the guy before he hurts her."

Brianna pulled the plug. "I did hear a huge Samoan or Maori beat him up pretty bad then warned him to get out of the state or he'd kill him."

"Give me this deadbeat's name. I'll do a little research myself."

"No. Darius would die of embarrassment if she ever found out you knew." Brianna lowered her voice to a whisper. "Recently, Darius went to dinner with a guy from work. Grandma seemed to think it went well, but then Darius saw him having lunch with a female colleague. See you later, alligator." Brianna sighed. "She definitely has trust issues."

He turned away from Brianna's gaze as Sarah and Darius emerged from a doorway down the hall. The thought of hurting her in any way didn't sit well. She was the kind of girl you brought home to meet the parents. The kind of girl you married and had a family with. Sam, Talos and Nick faced this dilemma when they first met the women who eventually stole their hearts. For them it had been the right decision.

Once the glazier left, he and Darius wrote their statements then gave them to the waiting cop. Simon carried Sarah's suitcase out to the Steele Security vehicle then returned to Darius on the porch as she waved them off.

She twisted the hem of her T-shirt. "I'm really tired. Can we talk in the morning?"

"Sure."

"I'll show you where you're sleeping and say goodnight."

"Thanks." He nodded to the guard sitting on one of the cane chairs. "We're turning in, Dean, do you need anything?"

"No, mate. I've got a flask of coffee with me. See you in the morning."

"Cheers." Simon held the door open for Darius then locked it and followed her along the hall to the first door on the right.

She turned the handle. "You're sleeping here, I'm next door. Tomorrow I'll take a cab to my friend Charlotte's house."

"Don't worry about a cab, I'll drive you."

"There's no need."

"I insist." He ran his fingertips down her silken cheek, pleased when her beautiful eyes flared and her breath hitched. Surprisingly, she returned his caress then came up on her toes and gently bussed her lips over his. The light, chaste kiss rocked his foundations.

"Goodnight. Sleep well." She entered her bedroom and closed the door.

So that's a fairy kiss. Standing motionless, his lips ablaze, pulse erratic and barely breathing. If Tink could render him senseless with a ghost of a kiss, what would a full-blown, tongue-tangling smooch do? He'd love to find out, but this wasn't the time. With a sigh, he flicked the light switch and stepped into the bedroom he'd been assigned.

"Bloody hell." Stunned, his gaze darted over the horrendously feminine room. Pink. It was everywhere in various shades. The walls, furniture, curtains, carpet. The bedspread had a pink background with darker pink roses all over it, which matched the pillows across the bedhead and in the chair by the window. As if that wasn't bad enough, two vases of pink and white silk roses stood on the mirrored dressing table, reflecting more pink at him. If this was Sarah Cortez's idea of punishment, she'd hit her mark, dead center. "Jesus, it's enough to give me nightmares."

A squeal then a thud snapped Simon into action. He ran to Darius' door and stormed in, hands fisted, ready to do serious harm. "What the...?" He froze as his brain attempted to comprehend the sight before his eyes.

Darius lay on the floor between an upturned chair and suitcase. She stared at him wide eyed and blushing profusely. Her fingers splayed over her breasts, vainly attempting to hide her delectable assets.

His gaze dropped to the jeans tangled about her knees, then slowly coasted up toned thighs to a triangle of white silk, speckled with tiny blue flowers. His breath hitched. A bumblebee hovered amongst the flowers as if searching for nectar. Heat consumed him. Hell, he wanted to be that bumblebee. He wanted to drown in her nectar.

"Tink?" The croak he made brought to mind a frog with laryngitis.

Her blush deepened. "My foot caught in the jeans. I reached for the back of the chair, but my suitcase was on it and it fell off. Can you please toss me my robe?"

"Your robe?" Covering her with anything but his body would be downright wrong.

"It's hanging behind the door that you almost lifted off the hinges."

He turned to the door, grateful for the chance to get his body under control. He needed something other than naked limbs, silk panties and nectar to focus on. Fat chance, it would take days—weeks—to get that image out of his head. He reached for the robe. "I thought we agreed to leave the doors open?"

"I forgot. Sorry I scared you."

He held the robe loosely in front of him and turned back to find her shielding her breasts with the bookworm top and struggling to get her jeans off. Ironically the caterpillar's eyes appeared to be boggling. As she attempted to push her jeans down with one foot, she slipped and kicked the dressing table's leg. "Ouch."

"Here, let me help." He squatted and with one good tug, divested her of the jeans.

Big mistake. "Damn it, Tink, you're like an oasis mirage in the middle of the desert. And I'm at risk of dying a slow, painful death." His body temperature rose steadily as he struggled to tear his gaze from her tantalizing mouth, which formed a perfect 'O' as she blinked at him.

The robotic cat fell off the chest, crashing to the floor behind Darius. She screamed and flung herself against his chest, knocking him flat on his back.

Now she'd be in no doubt of his state. "Don't move," he whispered.

Running feet sounded outside the window. "Everything all right in there?"

Simon wrapped his arms around Darius and rolled, taking them closer to the bed, him on top. "All good, Dean."

"Simon?" She wiggled, sending his blood hammering through his veins. She'd make a hell of a weapon in warfare.

"Don't move, Tink."

"I heard a scream," called Dean.

"Sorry about that. We got a bit carried away. Nothing to worry about."

Darius' eyes flared, a blush spreading across her face and neck. He didn't dare look any further.

"Oh, right," called Dean. "Try and keep the noise down, yeah?"

"Sorry." Simon groaned before rolling off Darius. Keeping his gaze averted, he passed her the robe then stood. "Goodnight, Tink."

"Goodnight."

Back in the pink room, he lay on top of the covers listening to Darius moving about. Even when all went quiet, sleep was the last thing on his mind. Holding her in his arms had left him hungry. This magnetism between them had him losing focus. The mission had to come first. He hoped she wasn't the hacker. An innocent like Darius would never survive prison. Which left the question, how far would he go to protect her? Professor Cortez would expect him to do whatever it took. He had a lot of work to do.

CHAPTER EIGHT

Secret cyber summits, ninja attacks, distorted voices and Simon's sudden appearance last night could mean only one thing. Darius had taken center stage in this highly dangerous melodrama, and it would take the performance of her life to pull it off. Especially with Simon and his five intimidating friends as part of the audience.

Not a fleck of white tainted the powder blue sky. A good omen perhaps. She closed her curtains then zipped up the suitcase. She'd cooked Simon and the security guard a huge breakfast to keep them out of her way while she packed. She appreciated Simon staying last night but had hoped to get rid of him early this morning. Not a chance. He cheerfully ignored all her hints, claiming he had nothing better to do.

Their heart-to-heart talk worried her. She couldn't betray Phoenix. If he'd stolen that confidential evidence, he might go to jail. Simon had offered to help but trusting him might come at too high a price.

She cringed. Lying on the floor, topless with her jeans around her knees did nothing to conjure a platonic friendship. The blatant desire in Simon's eyes and another part of his body were unmistakable, and his words about the desert oasis had stirred her soul. He'd had her in a vulnerable position and could have easily taken advantage of it, yet he'd backed off.

Now, he intended to drive her to Charlotte and Kyle's house, which meant he'd want answers before they arrived. Charlotte hadn't returned from her cruise yet, so Darius would have to pretend she was out somewhere. And, she'd have to tell Simon enough that he'd lose interest in her. Attending that summit had to take preference for the moment, and no way could she see Simon allowing that.

Opening her bedroom door, she rolled the suitcase into the hall. Two male voices conversed in the kitchen. Simon's smooth drawl curled round her senses. He didn't scare her. He never had, but his company made her antsy. Anticipation and anxiety warred.

Unwanted memories surfaced. She'd endured mortification at the hands of a first-class rat. He'd been a tradesman's assistant at the plant where she worked part time while studying. For weeks he'd made excuses to drop by the office and chat. When she'd agreed to spend a Saturday with him, he'd taken her to meet every member of his family, as if he wanted to show her off.

He'd been six years older, and according to the typist in the office, had a bad-boy reputation. But not once did he show her anything but polite respect. A week later he'd taken her to his friends' house for dinner. The wife had insisted Darius share a bottle of bubbly. Unused to alcohol and unable to escape the compact seating, she'd spewed the contents of her stomach into the rat's lap. A small consolation.

Several days later, he'd asked her to drive him into the city to get a cortisone injection for an old football injury. Afterwards, they'd walked through a park holding hands. She'd thought it so romantic. She'd been conned by an expert.

Their fourth date proved a fatal error in judgment. If she hadn't danced the night away, carefree for the first time since her father's death, she wouldn't have drunk the thirst-quenching drinks he'd persisted in buying. But that had been his plan all along. Once inebriated, he'd taken advantage, indifferent to her pathetic effort to stop him.

Bastard-Rat. His consumption of alcohol was no excuse. Nor was the fact he wasn't used to girls saying no to him, or that he hadn't expected her to be a virgin. Rumors suggested he'd been run out of town with some hefty injuries. He could burn in the fires of Hell for all she cared.

Four years later and it still pissed her off, but retribution wasn't an option. She couldn't bear the people she loved knowing her mortifying secret.

"Damn, I need to get past this."

"Past what, Tink?" Simon loomed in front of her, concern etched in his face.

"Erm...my fear of...flying." She brushed past him, the fleeting contact sending goosebumps racing up her arm. "I'm almost ready. I just need to put the washing away."

"Sure. I'll lock the back door and load your suitcase. Jarred's arrange for patrols to call by every morning and check nothing's been disturbed."

"Great." She tidied the kitchen then folded the clean towels and put them away. Her grandmother's bed didn't look as if Simon had slept in it. She wondered if the pink had been too much for him and he'd bunked down on the lounge.

He strolled in behind her. "I would have liked to spend the day with you, but I've got a meeting this morning, and I need to go home and change. Do you mind if I drop you at your friend's now then come back for our in-depth chat?"

There is a God. She still had so much to do before the flight tomorrow. "That's fine. I've washed and dried your jeans, but your shoes are still wet. Here's your jeans. The shoes are in in a plastic bag on the front porch."

"Thanks. Make sure you lock the front door."

"Shall do." Darius swung her small pack over one shoulder and followed. The attraction she felt for Simon left every other guy she'd dated for dead. Just being close to him had her pulse racing and a stupefying desire to hug him. The craving was so powerful, it scared her. What if she encouraged Simon, only to have him crush her heart or she got cold feet again? He'd call her a cock-tease. It wouldn't be the first time. She needed to be sure he hadn't betrayed her father and stolen all that money.

Pulling the heavy door shut, she picked up the bag containing Simon's shoes then crossed the porch, pausing to watch him. He'd parked his red car in the driveway and stood at the trunk, waiting.

What was it about him that called to her? She loved his soft drawl and dry sense of humor. Being wrapped in his arms, breathing in his cologne, the arousal in his beautiful eyes and body. She wanted so much more than friendship.

Razor-sharp barbs burrowed into her heart. If a thought could hurt this much, the actuality would be horrendous. Best to avoid that sort of damage.

"Hey, Tink, stop daydreaming. I'll be late for my meeting."

"Coming." She ran down the steps and across the lawn.

It was way too coincidental that her father's program had been used to access the Navy's database, to redirect a frigate in response to a request from Simon. According to Phoenix, Simon hadn't been with the people kidnapped, but coordinating a rescue from Broome. If Simon hacked into the Navy database, he'd broken the law. If he'd used the Amethyst Code, it would explain why Phoenix wanted Simon at the summit. That or to ask Simon for his help.

One thing was certain—to use her father's program, three passwords were needed. Simon Hawke should be the only person alive who knew the first and second passwords, but perhaps her father had given them to someone else he trusted.

Simon held the front passenger door wide. "Meet my pride and joy." He grinned. "I'm trusting you don't have sticky fingers."

"Sticky fingers?"

"My niece and nephews love cruising with me. Sticky fingers are a big problem with little people."

"No, I don't have sticky fingers." She settled into the body hugging, leather upholstery as he closed the door. Glancing about the interior, she wasn't surprised to find it as spotless as the outside.

He slid into the driver's seat. "I was captured by her beautiful lines and seductive power." His steady gaze fixed on Darius. "You have that in common."

She swallowed. He was good. Very good. As far as compliments went, it was the sexiest thing anyone had ever said to her and sent a roller coaster of thrills shooting throughout her body. It stung a little that he might have used these same words to seduce other women, yet the sincerity in his eyes made her wonder.

Reality had her stiffening. "I suspect Mustangs don't come cheap?"

His lips twitched. "When I want something, sweat pea, I pull out all stops to get it."

If she had any doubts he might be teasing, it was blown to smithereens by his intense regard. He was giving her fair warning. Whether it was for her secrets, her body, or a major cyber fraud hack, she could only guess.

She swallowed again. "We should go. Charlotte's prone to over-reacting. I told her about the ninja attack last night and that you were dropping me off this morning. She's likely to ring the police if we don't turn up soon."

A slow smile spread over his face. "Relax, Tink. I'll get you to Charlotte's. Key her address into my GPS." He started the engine then reversed out of the drive and smoothly accelerated. The V8 engine purring to life. For someone who might be tied up in illicit doings, he appeared very relaxed.

She concentrated on the GPS as her mind raced. Simon knew as much about the Amethyst Code as her father. It was possibly in a moment of pride, her father had told Simon who had the third password, but not probable. He'd insisted it had to be a secret, only known to one person. She had no choice but to clamp down her rising panic. Simon had a meeting this morning, possibly with Jarred Steele and those men from the bar. A scary lot to be sure. She'd love to eavesdrop, but she'd need a location to plant spyware and realistically, she didn't have the time.

Darius frowned at the blur of gardens they passed. The ninja attack couldn't have been staged. Simon had been slashed, resulting in a platoon of police converging on the quiet street. Then Jarred Steele had turned up and smoothed things over with the police. Jarred Steele had influence and he knew how to use it. If Simon hadn't been there, the ninja would have had her, Brianna and Grandma at his mercy.

Madeline Shaw was an entity Darius couldn't fathom. The journalist didn't hide criminal activity. She went in hard and exposed it to the world, which according to Phoenix, Steele Security had assisted with. Still, having a journalist raking over her father's past made Darius squeamish.

They stopped at a traffic light and Simon touched her clenched hand, making her jump. "Relax." His long fingers engulfed her fist, squeezing lightly. "You can trust me, Tink. I'd never hurt you in any way." His eyes softened, drifting over her face in a warm caress. "If there is anything you know about the Amethyst Code or the hacker, you need to tell me now. It might help us discover what happened to your father."

She so wanted to trust him. "The Amethyst Code... I..."

"Yes." His eyes drilled into her.

"I came up with it."

"Came up with what?" His sudden tension niggled at her misgivings.

She tugged her hand free. "The name. Dad had no imagination."

"Who gave you the envelopes that you delivered to me?"

"An anonymous friend of my father." She bit her lip. "The envelopes came by post or courier. That's all I can tell you."

He exhaled. "No, that's all you're willing to tell me. Darius, what you're involved in is treason. Let me help you."

"I need some time to think." And space. She needed a lot of space.

"All right. I've programmed my number into your cell phone, for when you change your mind or you need me."

"My cell phone?" A shiver ran down her spine.

"Yes. It was on your dresser." The lights changed to green and his attention returned to the road.

Her breakfast curdled in her stomach. "When and why were you in my room?"

"While you were in the shower. I wanted to check the lock on your window."

Had he seen her disguises and gadgets in the suitcase? She sneaked a glance at him. His fingers curled around the steering wheel lovingly. Jarred's singlet left nothing to the imagination. Cut so low under the arms, she could see Simon's chest and the sticky plasters above his nipple. The green shorts stopped halfway down solid thighs. His right leg bent slightly at the knee, his left sprawled carelessly wide, his feet bare. He was a man comfortable in his own skin.

In no time, they arrived at Charlotte's house and Simon carried her suitcase up the front path. "This thing weighs a ton. What's in it?"

"A smaller case for my holiday and books and clothes I borrowed from Charlotte." She laughed. "You didn't think I was taking a case that big to Fiji, did you?"

"That's a relief. It crossed my mind you might be doing a runner."

"I don't run from my problems, Simon. I tackle them head on." She unlocked the front door. The absolute silence in the spotless house made it obvious no one was home. "Charlotte is spending time with her boyfriend. She'll be back soon." Charlotte *was* with Kyle, on a Hawaiian cruise.

"That's cool. I'll just check the place out then be on my way." He did a walk through the house before stopping at the kitchen bench.

His gaze roved over the small immaculate kitchen and dining area. "Are you sure your friend hasn't ditched you and run off with her boyfriend?"

"Charlotte's a clean freak." Darius rung her hands, realized what she was doing, and crossed her arms. "She packs at the last minute."

"Where's the cat?" Simon pointed to the empty water and food bowls by the fridge.

"Um... Max must have gone to Charlotte's parents' house."

"Hmm." He strolled back to her. "No matter what you're involved in, I want to help you. I'll come back after my meeting. We'll go for lunch."

"You don't have to do that. I can grab something from the bakery around the corner." She came up on her toes to kiss his cheek, just as he twisted, catching her to him so their lips brushed. Warmth bloomed throughout her entire body. She attempted to pull away, to regroup, but his arm tightened, keeping her trapped against his hard chest, hard thighs, hard... "Oh!"

He captured her lips, whirling her into a realm of sensual bliss as he explored her mouth with his tongue and showed her just how thrilling a kiss could be.

Then he stepped away, steadied her and smiled. "I'll be back as soon as I can."

He closed the door behind him, leaving her staring at the red panels. She drew a shaky breath and reminded herself that she had work to do.

After checking the door had locked, she opened her suitcase, then removed the flattened cardboard box, bubble-wrapped feathered drone, her clothing and a silicon bodysuit. She lifted out the smaller suitcase which contained a robotic snake and a variety of Monarch butterflies ranging from small to very large. After assembling the box, she packed everything but the silicon body suit, her toiletries, underwear and a change of clothes, then laid the drone on top. It would be essential for monitoring the island and delegates.

Unclipping a plastic container, she emptied the contents onto the carpet to check she had everything. Plastic Jewel beetles, thirty miniature cameras disguised as a beaded necklace. A block of face putty, labelled as playdough, skin adhesive, three cans of spray tan, toners, two wigs and liquid latex. Not only could she alter the plastic insects to spying and listening devices, she had materials to transform her own face and body to such a degree she would be unrecognizable. It would be her biggest makeover yet.

Once everything was safely packed in the cardboard box, she taped it securely then labelled it Fragile Theatre Props. Now she just had to hope the FedEx courier wasn't delayed and pray Customs didn't flag the box. If it didn't arrive at her hotel in Suva before her next flight, her whole undercover operation would be a dismal failure.

After fitting everything else into her small suitcase, she zipped the lid closed then sat back on her heels. Once the courier took the box, she'd have to high-tail it to one of the airport hotels. She couldn't risk Simon discovering the truth just yet. This was her life on the line, and if she wanted to keep her family safe, clear her father's name and discover the truth, it would have to be alone for now. Trusting the wrong person could get her killed, which meant she needed to put Simon off.

She rummaged through her backpack for her phone. He'd be driving, so if she sent a text, he might not read it until later and by then she'd be gone.

Hi, it's Darius. Staying at a hotel tonight. I'm not good at relationships and I'd rather stay friends than lose your friendship. Good luck at the summit.

CHAPTER NINE

Simon listened to the text message, then slammed the steering wheel with his palm. "Fuck." He'd been expecting some sort of reaction, that's why he'd insisted on staying last night and then searching the garage while Darius slept. It's why he'd escorted her to her friend's house. Darius would not get rid of him that easily. Their mutual reaction to each other notwithstanding, she knew something.

The second he'd stepped inside the quaint shuttered house; he'd known the place was deserted. He should have taken Darius straight to Jarred. At least he'd had the foresight to ask Dean to follow them to Charlotte's. The security guard would watch the house until Ryan arrived. On that thought, he pulled to the side of the road and rang Ryan.

Half an hour later, Simon strode into Jarred's meeting room and dropped into a leather chair. Three of his mates sprawled in identical chairs around the large oval table, each cradling a coffee mug. The plate of half eaten chocolate cake was a new touch.

"Morning, boys. I thought we were having our meeting over a few games of pool?"

"Change of plans," said Sam. "I hear you had a close call last night?"

"You could say that." Simon lifted his T-shirt to show them his chest." He figured he was man enough to handle their sarcastic wit.

The stunned expressions spoke volumes. Their mouths dropped and eyes widened.

Talos was the first to crack a smile. "If the ninja had been a little more creative, he'd have added another slash and the kids could have used you as a train track."

"Alignment's out," called Nick. "You've got a larger gap between plaster twenty-six and twenty-seven. It would cause a derailment."

"Give him a break," said Sam. "It's his first war wound. Now he can compare scars with the rest of us."

Simon reached for a slice of cake. "It may be a scratch compared to your wounds, but it would have been a dagger through my heart, if not for my lucky charm."

"You referring to that atom you carry," asked Talos.

"Nope, I mean the professor's youngest daughter. Darius Cortez may have made me the atom years ago, but last night she jumped on the guy attacking me. It's a damn miracle she wasn't killed." He pointed to his chest. "This is her work."

Sam grinned. "Would that be the pretty little lady who told Jarred to hold his tongue?"

"Yes. I'm not being plagued by a bunch of little women, just one." Simon noted the sharp interest in each of his mate's faces. "Darius Cortez is the *señorita* who stole my wallet, and the skateboarder, and the runaway in the alley, and the pregnant power-walker who gained access to Ryan's apartment."

"You're shitting us." Nick leaned forward. "For what purpose?"

"She's trying to clear her father. I believe she knows a lot more about his work than she's saying. I don't think she's the hacker, but she could be working for him, and that puts her in danger."

Sam scowled. "Especially if the hacker doesn't need her anymore. Let's bring Darius Cortez in for questioning."

"Not yet." Simon tapped his fingers on the table edge. "I spoke to Jarred and he agreed to have Dean tail me this morning. He and Ryan will keep Darius under surveillance. She might lead us to the hacker. Tomorrow she's booked on a flight to Fiji. It's the first holiday she's had since her father's death."

"Unlike her mother," said Madeline from the doorway. "Francine Cortez travels extensively and has done for the last three years." She strolled over to Simon and placed a mug of coffee in front of him. "How's your chest?"

"Good, thanks, Madeline. The professor's mother told me Francine Cortez has been looking after her sister for the past four and a half years."

"Interesting. The sister, Janice Dewar, had a hip replacement six months after Professor Cortez died. She was back on her feet and as good as new within two months. According to the housekeeper, Francine spends months away at a time."

"When did you speak to the housekeeper?" Sam's questioning eyes mirrored Simon's thoughts. "How do you even know where the sister lives?"

Madeline shrugged. "I'm an investigative journalist. I looked up the Cortez's old neighbors in Warrawee, made a few calls early this morning, and one lovely old dear gave me Janice Dewar's phone number. It was answered by the housekeeper."

"No offence, but what did you wheedle out of her?" Talos grinned.

"I don't wheedle, James Talarico. The sister, Janice, is married to a retired property developer. They have an apartment in Portugal. Not that that's unusual. My parents have one in Italy. When at home, Janice and Francine take a morning walk along the beach."

Simon sipped his coffee. The Francine he remembered wouldn't desert her daughters to flit around the world. He stiffened. "The marina in Nelson Bay. That's where the Defense Force lost their trace on the hacker."

Sam straightened. "Could Mrs. Cortez be the hacker?"

"No, she's computer illiterate. However, she could be assisting Darius or passing on vital information from someone else. A lover perhaps. She's been seeing someone who once knew her husband."

Madeline slid into the chair beside Simon. "How's Darius?"

"Fine. I dropped her at her friend's apartment. She's flying to Fiji tomorrow."

"Fiji?" Madeline lifted an eyebrow. "Where in Fiji?"

"Not where we're going. I've checked her flights along with the sister's and grandmother's. Brianna is a ballerina and left for Paris this morning. Sarah is joining her daughter-in-law in the Whitsundays and left for Proserpine this morning. Darius flies out tomorrow, unless the Feds stop her."

"Morning all." Jarred strode into the room, pausing when he saw Madeline. "I don't remember inviting you to join us."

She smiled. "An oversight, I'm sure. Your mother and sister are entertaining the other ladies, so I've made you a coffee, just the way you like it."

Jarred's darkening scowl was a heads-up to duck, but Madeline ignored it and pushed the plate of cake across to him. "By the way,

I've organized for Fergie to plant a couple of Jacarandas. It will bring a soft touch to your garden."

"Soft touch." Jarred's deadly calm voice rivaled his cold stare for supremacy.

Along with the other boys, Simon held his breath. There was only going to be one winner here and Madeline didn't have a hope in hell. Not against a man known for his strategic, surprise attacks.

"Yes, Jarred." She settled more comfortably in her chair. "Fergie may have been an army sniper until his breakdown, but he loves pottering in your garden. He can't wait to add a bit of color to all that blandness. Good idea installing him in your boatshed. He's a perfect caretaker. Oh, and I've ordered some soft furnishings to give the house some vibrancy. Color lifts the spirit."

Simon could imagine Jarred silently counting as he carefully placed his folder and cell phone on the table then aligned them perfectly, before placing his hands on the table and glaring at Madeline.

"May I enquire how you know so much about my caretaker's past?"

Simon cleared his throat. "Fergie would thrive on bending Madeline's ear, especially as she's here with your mother and sis—"

Jarred held up one hand without taking his eyes off Madeline. "I assume this takeover of my home, family and staff is payback for sticking you on that island after the mission in Vietnam?"

"Not at all. What I'm doing to your house and garden is giving them character. You will thank me in the end."

"*Thank* you?" Jarred shoved his folder aside, his incredulous snarl brought Talos and Sam to their feet.

"You're welcome." Madeline took a sip of her coffee then jumped as Jarred's cell rang beside her. Shrugging, she answered it. "Hello, Steele Intelligence and Security. This is Madeline, how may I help you?"

The low, feral growl emanating from Jarred was all it took for Talos to step between him and Madeline's chair.

They'd never witnessed Jarred lose his cool, and they'd been under his command in some harrowing situations, yet Madeline Shaw had a knack of getting under the man of steel's skin.

Her eyes widened as she glanced back at Jarred. "Prime Minister? I'm sorry, Mr. Steele is in a meeting at the moment."

"Give that to me." Jarred's bared teeth would send children screaming for their mothers.

Madeline shook her head. "I'm sure it is important, but as I said, Mr. Steele is in a meeting. I will have him call the PM back the minute he's free."

"Madeline!" Jarred pushed past Talos then Sam.

She bolted out of her chair and dashed round the table. "Can you tell me what it's in regard to?"

Jarred caught Madeline's free hand, but she leaned backward over the table beside Nick, who appeared frozen in awe.

"The upcoming summit."

"Madeline." Jarred pinned her to the table and stage whispered. "Give it to me."

"I'll be sure to tell him, goodbye." She ended the call and slid the phone along the table. "That was the Prime Minister's office."

"So. I. Heard." Jarred fingers imprisoned Madeline's wrists. "The PM wouldn't be calling me unless it was extremely, *fucking* important."

Except for a soft blush, Madeline showed no alarm whatsoever. She sighed. "Jarred, the PM would not be ringing you personally unless he's under a lot of pressure. Your team need time to discuss your options."

"Jesus, woman, we've worked for the PM on numerous occasions. It is not that unusual for him to ring me." Jarred released her, stood back then glared at Simon. "Pass me my phone?"

"No!" Madeline clutched Jarred's crisp white shirt. "This is your opportunity to use a little leverage."

The tick in Jarred's jaw was a sign of his waning patience. "My phone, *Major.*"

"Listen to me, you numbskull." Madeline snatched his outreached hand. "We need to talk about our covers for the summit and consider what the PM wants."

Jarred exhaled very slowly then carefully untwined Madeline's fingers from his hand. As he sank into the nearest chair, an audible sigh went around the room. Until then Simon hadn't realized they were all standing, ready to intervene.

Sam passed Jarred his coffee. "It wouldn't hurt to strategize. Why do you think the PM is ringing?"

"The JOC breach is a major blow and sure to have him pulling out what remains of his hair. We know the PM wants Simon at the summit. I assume he now wants the rest of our team there. It's what Gibbs has been pushing for."

Madeline turned her back on Jarred and glanced across the table at Simon. "Do you think the hacker will be at the summit?"

"It's possible. Whoever it is, has gone to a lot of trouble to make sure I'm there. It could be because he or she suspects I have the last secret key to The Amethyst Code."

"Amethyst Code?" Madeline pulled out a small notebook out of the back pocket of her jeans and picked up Jarred's pen.

Simon groaned. "Shit, Madeline, this is confidential. You can't comment on anything to do with the summit or Professor Cortez without clearance."

"Jarred had me sign a confidentiality statement before he'd let me go to the Cortez house. This is just my curiosity. Do you know the secret key?"

"No. Professor Cortez didn't even know it. He gave that privilege to an unknown party, who can't be the hacker, or we'd have seen much worse than the redirection of a Navy frigate." Simon rubbed the bristles on his chin. "Aside from knowing all three secret keys, to understand the coding, the hacker would need to be exceedingly proficient."

"Another computer scientist?" Madeline glanced at Jarred. "That narrows it down."

Jarred steepled his fingers. "What is our hacker up to?"

Madeline tapped a manicured fingernail on the mahogany table. "My research revealed Professor Cortez's body was never recovered. Could he have faked his own death and reactivated the program?"

"Why wait five years?" asked Sam. "And, according to Gibbs, the Sherpa who guided Professor Cortez, witnessed him jump into the crevice."

She screwed up her nose. "Did the AFP interview the Sherpa?"

Jarred shook his head. "No, he was lost in an avalanche the day after Professor Cortez died."

"Okay," said Sam. "What if the professor gave up the program and first two secret keys to protect his family, then knowing the Feds were closing in, he realized his reputation would be shot to pieces, so jumped to his death. Let's assume the blackmailer has been waiting for the right moment to showcase what the program is capable of. All that's needed is the secret key for the third level, then he can take the highest bid."

"There will be plenty of bidders," mused Jarred. "Imagine the ramifications of such a program in the wrong hands. They could infiltrate nuclear plants, utilities, military and domestic aircraft, banks. It would cause worldwide pandemonium. And, it would have happened by now, if they had the third password."

Simon shifted restlessly. "Blackmail makes sense. Professor Cortez was highly respected and as honest as they come. I can't tell you how many lectures I sat through, where he drummed integrity into us. His dream was to create a program to *fight* cyber fraud. Having said that, his family were everything to him."

Madeline flipped through her notebook. "I have a source who informed me Professor Cortez was suspected of syphoning millions from world banks into shell companies. But without hard evidence the Federal Police couldn't arrest him or prevent him leaving the country to go mountain climbing with his youngest daughter."

Simon choked, sending a mouth full of coffee spraying across the glossy table. "Tink...Darius was with her father in Nepal?"

Madeline nodded. "I tracked down the editorial. Professor Cortez was a regular mountaineer, respected by all the guides and climbing community. According to witnesses, the morning of Alexander Cortez's death, he appeared anxious about the weather, so insisted his daughter stay behind with a German family. The Sherpa who accompanied Alexander had done climbs with him before."

Jarred drained his coffee and zeroed in on Simon. "I want to know everything about the professor's wife, daughters and friends. Check bank accounts, travel destinations and phone accounts. I want to know if the professor was set up then murdered, or whether he was as guilty as sin and committed suicide. Darius Cortez may be a mistress of disguise, but is she the hacker?"

"I hope not." Simon opened his computer bag then pulled out his laptop. He still couldn't believe Darius had been in Nepal with her father.

He glanced up sharply as Madeline slapped her palm on the table beside him. "I knew I'd seen her before. Darius Cortez played a homeless woman in a who-dunnit play at Belvoir Street Theatre in December."

Simon frowned. "Are you saying that woman who came to your aid was..." He didn't bother finishing the sentence. The truth hit him over the head like a brick. "Damn it, she could have been killed."

Jarred eased back in his chair. "Darius Cortez is making a habit of coming to the rescue of others. We need to tread carefully. She may be as innocent as she appears, and the real hacker is manipulating her to make the deliveries. The question is, does he intend to use her in Fiji?"

"That's what worries me." Simon looked around the table. "What are we going to do about it?"

Talos sighed. "Give her some rope and let her run with it. We get Gibbs to organize a trace on her phone. With luck, she'll lead us to the hacker, one way or the other."

"I like it." Jarred turned to Simon. "The government can foot the bill to send us all to that island in the Lau Archipelago?"

Madeline raised an eyebrow. "That's east of Fiji, isn't it?" When no one answered, she shrugged lightly. "I guess that means you'll have to take me with you, chief."

Jarred stood, placed his hands on the table then glowered at Madeline. "You are not going anywhere near the summit."

"I can wear a disguise."

"Huh," scoffed Jarred. "A world-renowned investigative reporter, famous for exposing international criminals is the last person the hacker will accept at the summit. You would be in extreme danger, and you have your head in the clouds if you believe any man with a heartbeat won't notice you."

She turned to Simon, a soft blush blossoming over her cheeks. "What do you know about this island?"

Jarred threw up his hands. "Christ, she should be working on the God damn army's interrogation team." He exhaled. "Go ahead, she'll only dig it up some other way."

Simon hid his grin by flipping open his own notebook. "A European investment banker owns the island. From the satellite image, seventy percent is heavily foliaged. There's a golf course, small luxury resort and an airstrip. I tried booking for the coming week and was told they have no vacancies. I also sighted two stand-alone residences, one of which is huge. Reefs surround the island, so only flat bottom boats, barges or catamarans have access at high tide into one cove. I did notice a helipad at the larger residence."

"Could a seaplane land at high tide?" mused Talos.

Simon flipped to the next page. "There is a long wharf. I'll need to check."

Jarred cleared his throat. "All right, Madeline, as you like playing my personal assistant, please get me the PM's office."

"Can I come with you?"

"I will see if there is an island close by where you can do background research."

She narrowed her eyes. "If you stick me back on the Sheik's Garden of Eden, cut off from the world, I will take your steel feather and shove it so far up your..."

"I take your point," drawled Jarred. "I'm rather fond of my steel feather."

"Excellent."

Simon cringed. Madeline might think she'd won, but she didn't know Jarred like they did, and by the tight jaws around the table, every member of the team knew exactly where Jarred wanted to stick Madeline. Simon couldn't help wondering how she planned to follow through with her threat.

His phone chimed. "It's Ryan."

Madeline's fingers stilled over Jarred's phone as Simon answered.

"Hey, mate, we're all here and you're on speaker."

"Great. A FedEx courier has picked up a box from Darius Cortez. Dean is still here. You want me to follow the box or stay with the girl?"

"Grab the box at the first opportunity," ordered Jarred. "Try not to get caught, and then bring it here. If the contents don't interest us, we will let the box continue to its destination. Otherwise, I'll inform Gibbs and let him decide whether to put a tracking device on the box and bring Darius Cortez in for questioning or see where she leads us."

"No worries, see you soon."

Simon ended the call, apprehension thick in his gut. "I should have searched Darius' suitcase after I copied the contact list from her phone. I'll give her friend Charlotte a call and find out what she knows."

"One second!" Sam held up a finger. "We should wait until Darius is in custody or on the flight to Fiji. We don't want to alert the hacker."

Jarred looked around the table. "Assuming the PM wants our services, you should all prepare for a week in the Lau Islands. I'll speak to the PM now, Madeline."

She beamed at him. "Right away, Chief Steele Feather."

"Don't push your luck, honey."

Chapter Ten

The seaplane dipped to the left giving Darius a bird's eye view of a milky-blue lagoon dotted with miniature islands, each rising out of the ocean like giant mushrooms in need of a haircut.

Her pilot pointed. "Very popular for snorkeling and scuba divers."

"I haven't been diving in years."

He grinned. "I could take you on a day trip."

"Maybe some other time. This is a working vacation." Her spray tan wouldn't last if she spent time relishing the underwater world, and the changes would only get worse. He picks up a Polynesian girl and brings back a pale imitation. The salt water would wash the black henna out of her hair, and then her face would start peeling off. If that didn't freak him out, then silicone breast-fillets floating past certainly would.

He gave her a considering look. "I heard the resort was down a waitress, who usually doubles as a dancer and masseuse. I'm guessing you're here to fill the position?"

"No." Although this information was perhaps something she could use to her advantage. "I do have experience in all three. I suppose I could help out if they need someone." Not exactly a lie. She'd done tap and Jazz ballet in her younger years. Waitressing was a piece of cake at the local theatre shows, and Grandma enjoyed her head and foot massages.

His gaze drifted to her legs. The golden spray-on tan, a sharp contrast against her white shorts. "You will fit right in, especially with the wealthy guests. Very big tippers." He winked. "Speak to Alisi, she is my cousin."

"Sure." She turned back to the view, blinking rapidly as one contact lens shifted slightly.

The Lau Archipelago was a chain of islands and inlets. She could easily spend months sailing among them, exploring, snorkeling and diving to her heart's content. The city of Suva wasn't the ideal place to holiday, but as there were few flights to Lakeba, she'd used the time to assemble and paint her beetles, frogs and butterflies, color her hair and get a professional spray tan.

During her brief stopover at Lakeba, she'd learned few tourists flew to these islands. Visitors usually arrived by private yacht or cruise boat. Tourism obviously wasn't their main income.

"So, tell me about the Lau Archipelago?"

He grinned. "It's made up of sixty islands, of which only thirty are inhabited. We lie between Melanesian Fiji and Polynesian Tonga. It is an ancient meeting point for the two cultural spheres."

Darius frowned. "How do the people make a living?"

"Fishing, farming and growing most of what they eat, but we are renowned for our woodcarvings and Masi paintings." He was obviously very proud of his ancestry.

"Look, we're approaching the island now." He pointed ahead to the left. "I will treat you to an aerial circuit."

"Thank you."

The island rose up fairly high, its shape reminding her of the number three, only backwards. As they drew close, she spotted rows of solar panels and an airstrip across the top of the southern end. The northern tip jutted out, almost concealing a small cove, where a catamaran listed gently on shimmering turquoise water.

"It's so restful."

He raised an eyebrow. "For the rich and famous."

"Uh-ha." Her gaze swept over the crystal-clear water of the small cove. On the hillside above sat two villas surrounded and separated by gardens and a high metal fence. Each residence was positioned to avoid strong winds. The smaller villa must be her home for the next few days.

Around the point, a large cove opened up. In center position, well above sea level, a sparkling pool surrounded by white daybeds beckoned. Overlooking the pool and beach stood a thatched roofed, open-sided restaurant, bordered by crimson bougainvillea and greenery. A wharf extended from the groomed sand out over a vast, closely-knit reef. She could see fish darting among the coral. If she weren't seeing it with her own eyes, she would swear the scene had been photo-shopped. She raised her camera and clicked away madly.

"That wharf is where you disembark. It's the only place deep enough for me to land," said the pilot.

They flew along a mangrove forest to the southern tip of the island then veered in over a cliff and lush golf course. A man on a ride-on mower gave them a wave as he motored up the fairway toward a single-story building.

"I bet a lot of golf balls end up in the ocean."

The pilot grinned. "The greenskeeper abseils off the cliff every Sunday, collects the balls then hires them out to guests again on Monday."

"I'm surprised he's allowed. Surely that's a health and safety issue?"

He shrugged and pointed at five giant tanks and a metal tower that supported a satellite dish. "That's the water supply and communication tower."

"How many guests can the resort hold?"

"Maybe thirty. Guests and supplies are flown in from either Suva or Nadi. Those departing take the return flights."

A steep range, dense with vegetation rose beyond the golf course. As they flew over the peak, she gasped at the sheer cliff dropping to a pile of boulders and another reef. "Glorious." She took more photos.

"Wait." He banked right, flew out over the ocean then turned back, sweeping in along the east coast.

"Wow." Darius leaned closer to the window. Frothy waves crashed over a vast reef extending the entire length of the east coast. A thin strip of white sand lay sandwiched between the turbulent sea and rugged cliffs. No way could anyone land a boat or seaplane on this side of the island. It really was the ideal place to host a secret summit, and a photographer's dream. She kept clicking then used her long lens to zoom in. A bright flash caught her eye, but when she looked closer, she couldn't see anything but thick vegetation.

She wished she could ask the name of the island, but who arrived at their holiday destination not knowing its name? She couldn't risk raising suspicion of any kind.

He banked left and flew out to sea, banking again to begin his descent. "I don't normally give flyovers, but as it's quiet, I'm sure Alisi won't mind."

"Your cousin?"

"Yes. She manages the resort. Her husband, Hans is the greenskeeper. My brother, Etera, is head porter. He's in charge of the bar and water activities too."

Darius chuckled. "A real family affair."

"Yes. The staff here are Fijian, except for Hans. I'm not sure what he is."

Darius frowned. "I don't see anyone?"

"The resort is closed for maintenance, in preparation for a private group arriving tomorrow. They've booked out the entire place. All hush-hush." He guided the seaplane down until it skimmed the ocean. "If you're to work here, everything you see and hear stays on this island."

"I have no problem with that."

"With your Polynesian looks and heritage, you will be welcomed with open arms."

Darius laughed. Her spray tan and disguise were working better than she'd hoped. If she could fool a local, then the summit attendees would be a piece of cake.

Stick to the script. "I'm actually an actress in need of a change of scenery and down time."

"An actress?" His gaze swept over her before returning to the approaching wharf. "You look more like one of those exotic dancers."

Darius bit her lip. She'd hoped for a convincing disguise, but maybe adding silicone fillets to her push-up bra hadn't been necessary.

The pilot cut the throttle and they coasted toward the wharf. The reef looked awfully close to the surface. She glanced around the cove and noticed narrow pathways winding amongst colorful hibiscus shrubs and swaying palm trees, all leading to private bures. Each dwelling overlooked the beach with its own hammock hanging between palm trees.

The seaplane jolted and her tummy did a cartwheel. She was here, no turning back now, yet it didn't hurt to plan ahead just in case things went skew-whiff.

"Thanks for a most enjoyable flight. How do I reach you, if I decide to take you up on that diving expedition, or if I need transport back to Lakeba Island?"

"Alisi has my number. I don't do scheduled flights, so you have to pay for my service." He grinned, "I could make an exception if you want my handsome company for a few days." He laughed. "I'll get your suitcase."

Darius swept her long, black tresses off her shoulder then opened the door and eased down onto the float. The pilot was a good-looking guy, but he didn't tilt her world.

A yell had her looking along the wharf to see a Fijian running toward the plane. His smiling face resembled the pilot's.

He came to an abrupt stop and scratched his head. "Are you the only passenger?"

"Yep, just me."

He held out his hand. "*Ni sa bula*, I am Etera. We were expecting an Australian."

"*Bula*, Etera." Darius took his hand and climbed onto the wharf. Phoenix had left it up to her to choose a name, once she arrived. A mischievous streak raced through her mind. "Thank you for your warm welcome, Etera, I'm... Bellini." She had almost gone with Belle, but best not to push her luck. "I am Australian, but my...mother is Polynesian."

Etera wore a shirt with a pink and white Frangipani print over a brown sulu that came half way down his calves. On his feet he wore leather sandals, and in his hand, he held a freshly woven palm-frond hat. A tall Fijian woman with short frizzy hair had followed him. She wore a long sulu, also covered in pink frangipanis, and behind her left ear was a genuine yellow and white frangipani.

She also looked past Darius. "*Bula*, miss, I am Alisi. Welcome to the island."

"*Vinaka*."

Alisi took the hat Etera held and placed it on Darius' head. "It is very hot today. Come, I have a cool drink waiting for you. Etera will bring your luggage."

"Thank you. I'm an actress and I have some props I need to trial, so please be gentle with the cardboard box." She'd invested a small fortune on the mechanics of the Goshawk drone and other bits and pieces, so she didn't want them dropped.

Darius strolled beside Alisi along the wharf then over the warm sand to a set of rock steps. "We flew around the island. It's quite spectacular."

"*Vinaka*. Thank you." Alisi pointed up the steps. "This way, please."

They followed a meandering path through the hibiscus trees then entered the large building Darius had seen from the air.

The cool interior was a welcome reprieve from the hot afternoon sun. In front of her stood a reception desk of inlaid polished wood, with a bowl of hibiscus flowers on the top. Clusters of cushioned cane chairs were placed around the spacious foyer.

Alisi turned left into a circular, open air restaurant. Six massive tree trunks braced the thatched, teepee-like roof on the open sides. Huge ceiling fans whirred overhead, directing a cooling waft of air onto Darius.

Removing the hat, she did a slow rotation of the beautiful room, crafted entirely from wood. A giant bar, shaped like a canoe, ran the length of the wall between the dining room and reception. Along from that, a low dais took up center stage with what looked like a partially hollowed out tree stump on it. It resembled a stumpy canoe on short legs.

"Alisi, what is that?"

The manageress smiled. "A *lali* drum. The men play it with *iuaua* sticks, which are a softer wood, so they don't damage the drum. Even so, you can see the wear from drumming. Traditionally, large *lali* drums are used to announce a birth, death or at one time, war. The smaller ones have always been used for music."

"I'd love to hear it."

"You will."

For such a big room, Darius was surprised at how few tables there were. All were covered in deep red tablecloths and spaced well apart. Intimate tables for two edged the open sides, either overlooking the pool or beach.

She couldn't help but admire the tranquil vista. It warranted a photo. Two red kayaks lay idle on the sand, protected from the sun by the overhanging coconut palms.

"Here you are." Alisi handed Darius a slim, cool glass of orange liquid.

"*Vinaka.*" Darius took a sip then another. "Hmm, I taste orange, mint and lime. Very refreshing."

"*Vinaka.* Etera has loaded your suitcase and the box on our golf cart. He will take you to your accommodation. We have been instructed not to disturb you, unless you require meals delivered."

Darius took another refreshing sip as she glanced around the inviting room. "I would prefer to come here for meals."

Alisi hesitated. "We have no guests until tomorrow, and then the entire resort has been booked by a private consortium. You are welcome to wander around the resort today and explore the island, but I would ask that you avoid the resort and enjoy the facilities of your own villa and beach from tomorrow. If you need anything, my staff will bring it to you."

One afternoon to do reconnaissance. Darius swallowed the rest of her drink and placed the glass on the bar. "*Vinaka*, Alisi. Please, call me Bellini."

"Bellini." Alisi smiled. "Etera will drive you to your villa now."

"Of course." Darius' mind began to churn. She needed an excuse to mingle with the guests, and Alisi was short of staff.

"This way, Bellini." Etera stood in the foyer smiling.

"*Vinaka vaka levu*, Etera."

"You speak Fijian?"

"No. It seemed only polite to learn how to say, thank you very much."

He smiled broadly then led the way past reception to a covered portico, its far side completely shaded by a wall of crimson bougainvillea so thick with flowers, it provided a cool breezeway.

Darius' gaze drifted to the two bright yellow golf carts. One was a short-based vehicle with black leather seats front and back. The other had an extended rear tray, holding her suitcase and the cardboard box.

"Cool." Darius slid into the passenger side. "Do guests get to drive these?"

"No, but you have a Vesper and your own golf cart at the villa."

"Very cool. Are there other vehicles on the island?"

Etera pressed a button and the quiet motor whirred to life. "We have golf carts for transporting guests and bicycles for the more active."

"I saw kayaks. What else do you have to keep guests occupied?"

"Most come here to relax, soak up the sun and be pampered." He released the brake and they cruised along a road enclosed by shrubbery. A lush tropical paradise.

Darius smiled to herself.

Etera came to an intersection and turned left, then steered them up the hill. He grinned at her. "For the more adventurous guests, we have tennis, surf skis, windsurfers and snorkels. Or, they can go scuba diving, fishing, para-sailing. We have two boats in the next cove."

"I only noticed a catamaran."

"It arrived several days ago. I suspect it is a new toy for the boss. We keep our boats in a green shed that isn't visible from the sky. I will point it out for you."

"You're fairly isolated. I suppose you need to be wary of pirates?"

"It has never happened, but you are right. There is a secure bunker under the owner's residence. Staff and guests can take refuge there if we are threatened by cyclone, tsunami or attack. We have been lucky so far."

"I saw the satellite dish. Is that how you communicate with the outside world?"

"Yes, but it is being disabled today for maintenance. So, for the next few days we truly are isolated. No phones, no internet, and no staff or guests in or out until Monday."

Maintenance on the satellite dish, during a secret summit. No one in, no one out. Completely cut off from the world. A shiver ran down Darius' spine. "If the island goes dark, isn't that putting lives at risk? What if there is an emergency?"

He quirked an eyebrow then chuckled. "It is nothing sinister. The group coming in requires privacy, and they have their own security. It is not unusual. We have catered to royalty, heads of state and movie stars." Etera grinned. "No paparazzi here."

"Where will you put the security people?"

"One group have their own safari tents and chemical toilets. The other is being housed in our biggest bure. The seminar organizers requested two thirds of our staff be given the week off. Alisi is stressed, as we've never operated with so few, and now we're down another waitress, who also works in reception, and belongs to our dance troupe."

"Yes, your brother mentioned that." Darius straightened. They were approaching a set of black gates. She caught a glimpse of a winding driveway lined with shrubs, but no house. "Ooh, is that the large villa I saw from the air?"

"Yes." He waved a finger at her. "No go zone for guests."

"How often is your boss in residence?"

"Whenever he needs a rest from making money." Etera laughed.

Darius craned her neck for a glimpse of the house. No luck, the shrubs were too thick and surrounded by high pool-like fencing. She would have to approach from the beach. "So, how does the boss make all his money?"

He shrugged. "We are almost to your villa."

It seemed Etera wasn't prepared to discuss the matter further. He veered off the asphalt road into a driveway that curved out of sight amidst the hibiscus shrubs, the ornamental gates were open and as the golf cart rounded the curve, Darius leaned forward. The small villa looked out over the horseshoe cove.

"Wow." She climbed out of the golf cart, grabbed her small pack and wandered to the edge of the terrace. Thick foliage obstructed her view of the main residence, but wide steps led down to the white sand and turquoise water.

Etera set her suitcase down and came to stand beside her. "This villa is not normally rented out to guests. It belongs to a close friend of the island's owner." He pointed across the reef. "Do you see the boatshed's slip rails leading out of the water?"

She searched the opposite shore several times before she saw two black lines disappearing up the bank, under overhanging palms. The shed's color blended so well with the vegetation she couldn't define its edges. "What about the reef? How do you get the boats in and out?"

"Extremely carefully. The reef in this bay is deep and has wide enough gaps, if you know where they are. It can be tricky. Come, I will show you through the villa."

"*Vinaka*, but I'd prefer to walk down to the beach."

"As you wish, Bellini."

"Oh and, Etera, please let Alisi know I have waitressing and dancing experience. I'm happy to help out if she needs me."

"*Vinaka*. I will tell her."

Once he'd taken the box and her suitcase inside and then driven away, Darius opened her pack and withdrew the newspaper clipping she'd brought to remind her of everything at stake. It quivered in her fingers. The photo had been taken two years before her father's death and placed in a picture frame on his study wall. A devious journalist had sneaked into the study and snapped the image of Darius with her father and a Sherpa in front of snowcapped mountains.

She traced a finger over the Sherpa's grainy face. Harnoop had been her father's favorite guide. After the allegations of treachery, no one had questioned his account of her father's death.

Darius straightened her shoulders. Someone set her father up and then shot him. That's the only thing that made sense. Harnoop wouldn't hear the gunshot in howling wind. He would only see her father propelled into the crevice. She folded the clipping and slipped it back in her pack. Someone at the summit must know something. All she had to do was mingle, listen and observe. And not even Phoenix could stop her.

The summit attendees were due tomorrow morning, so she had the rest of the day to familiarize herself with the resort and hide her devices. She would also offer her waitressing skills to Alisi at the first opportunity.

Taking her camera and the telescopic lens, she returned to the terrace and examined the catamaran. This was her means of escape in an emergency. Tonight, under cover of darkness, she would swim over to the cat and check it out.

In the meantime, she would send up the Goshawk for a closer look at the large villa and resort delegates. In particular, one Simon Hawke.

CHAPTER ELEVEN

Flexing tense muscles, Simon leaned against a palm tree and stared out over turquoise water to the horizon where deep blue ocean met clear blue sky. The gentle lap of an incoming tide should have calmed his mind. It didn't.

Other than the occasional squawk of a seagull, the rustle of palm fronds and tiny birds flitting between hibiscus trees, nothing stirred. The island's tranquility did nothing to settle his turbulent thoughts or frustration. Darius' friend, Charlotte had departed on a Hawaiian cruise, accompanied by her partner, seven days ago.

When he'd finally reached Charlotte Moore, she hadn't been able to hide her surprise or distress at Simon's call. She'd noticed Darius seemed pensive and preoccupied over the last couple of months but couldn't offer a plausible reason why Darius would go to Fiji on her own.

The box full of spyware, face makeup, an eagle drone and silicon bra fillers—that had sent Nick and Ryan into fits of laughter—had arrived at a hotel in Suva and hadn't moved until yesterday. Simon had tracked the box to Lakeba then to this island paradise yesterday.

Tink had definitely caught her flight to Suva on Monday and hadn't left the hotel until yesterday. He'd spent the last few days checking into her family's bank and phone records for the last five years. There didn't appear to be anything out of the ordinary. As for Francine Cortez's numerous travel costs, they'd come from her own account which contained money from the sale of the family home.

According to the French Press, Brianna Cortez had taken Paris by storm. Her performance at the *Opéra Bastille* had the public declaring her a Prima Ballerina.

To Simon's annoyance, Brianna wouldn't take his calls, leaving him no choice but to request Gibbs put her under surveillance. The French Police reported her returning to her hotel late last night, then checking out early this morning. Unfortunately, they lost her cab in peak hour traffic and hadn't been able to track her cell phone.

As for Sarah Cortez, she'd flown to Proserpine on Sunday. Then according to Gibbs, who had viewed airport footage, she'd collected her suitcase and left with a woman matching her daughter-in-law's description, destination unknown.

The three other women wished to protect Darius, but what if she was trying to protect them. The thought of some thug blackmailing her, or using force to extract information, drew forth a rage Simon had trouble controlling.

He might be leaping to the wrong conclusion. Francine and Sarah Cortez could be staying with friends. Brianna might be meeting a lover for a secret rendezvous. Meanwhile the French police and AFP would continue searching for them.

Facts he could deal with. Darius knew about the summit and she wanted to clear her father. Brianna and Sarah Cortez had conveniently vanished. Several of Professor Cortez's former colleagues would be attending the summit. A hacker had redirected a Navy frigate after Simon's request for help was denied. The incident guaranteed its inclusion in the summit. Nothing about this summit felt right.

After being transported to the island by two jets, all speakers, delegates and security personnel had been driven in golf carts to the resort's dining room. Each load of passengers had been treated to a refreshing drink and catalogue of the resort's amenities, then handed a program of planned topics over the next few days. They were then escorted to their luxury bures and invited to relax by the pool until twelve-thirty, when a smorgasbord lunch would be served.

Simon opted for time alone, too irritated to give his full attention to the job. As he'd been on the first flight to arrive, he'd requested the bure furthest from the restaurant. Passing by the other delegates' bures would provide ample opportunity to snoop. And, as Ryan and Nick were snorkeling in under cover of darkness, it made sense to snag the bure closest to the open sea. He just hoped they could navigate their way through the treacherous reef without being torn to shreds.

A hawk floating high on an updraft caught his attention. Its wingspan easily six-foot wide. He pitied the fish and small creatures destined to fill the magnificent bird's stomach. Without as much as a flutter, it drifted for several minutes until something caught its beady eyes. The predator went into free-fall, swooping beyond trees to the beach. He doubted a drone would dive like that.

Simon returned his attention to the glimmering ocean. Darius hadn't been at Suva airport, yet her box of spyware indicated she meant to crash the summit. The security guards would deny her access to the island, an outcome he favored wholeheartedly.

On the other hand, it was entirely possibly her family had been threatened, and she'd been coerced into criminal activities. "Shit." He strode to the hammock and dropped into it. Darius had his number, but she couldn't reach him.

With no internet and the confiscation of all satellite phones, he couldn't alert Gibbs or use his Identiscan program to do background checks on the delegates and speakers. To make matters worse, Madeline was in Suva, expecting to hear from Jarred. If she thought she'd been blind-sided, she'd be exceedingly pissed off.

Jarred, Talos and Sam had their hands full with summit security. It hadn't escaped Simon's notice that his mates shared his unease with the communication blackout and the unreceptive attitude of the other security team's six men.

Rubbing his forehead to ease the building tension, Simon accepted two certainties. The unknown hacker had lured him to this summit for a reason, and Alexander Cortez was most likely dead because Simon had sent the Fed's to see him.

At least the whole team would be on the island by midnight and, as security guards, Jarred, Talos and Sam would be armed. They might not have contact with the outside world, but they were a force to be reckoned with. He closed his eyes and drifted through a myriad of unsettling dreams.

"*Bula*, Mr. Hawke."

He cricked his neck with the sudden jerk. Every nerve ending in his body prickled. A stunning Polynesian girl stood beside him, smiling. He couldn't prevent his lips curving. "*Bula*."

"My name is Bellini. I have brought your lunch."

His sullen mood evaporated. He didn't know how she'd pulled it off, but here she stood, safe and as bold as a pick-pocket in a Persian Bazaar. The transformation had him so awestruck he decided to play along. "Oh, thanks." He watched transfixed as Darius set a tray of salad, grilled fish and fruit salad on the table beside his hammock.

"Do you not wish to eat with your colleagues?"

He looked around to check they were alone. "I had a headache."

"It is hot. You should wear a sunhat." She rearranged the tray, drawing his gaze to her dainty hands. The red-Hibiscus print *sulu* stretched over her bottom, filling his head with images of a bumble bee seeking nectar.

"Sir?"

He jumped at her light touch on his arm. "Do you not wish to eat?"

"I'll eat inside, I think."

Her thick, false eyelashes blinked several times, as she appeared to analyze him from a deep cognac gaze. "I can help with your headache?"

He doubted it, unless she was offering a sexual release. His anxiety had been swamped by a desperate need to hold her. That or strangle the little fool.

"I have a talent for relieving headaches." The slight quirk of her plump, pink lips had him itching to pull her onto the hammock. Not a great idea, out here in the open where anyone could come across them.

"I'm sure you've got plenty to do without me adding to your chores."

"It's no chore. Come." She flicked her long ebony hair behind and strolled toward his bure, her tight little butt swaying from side to side. "Five minutes is all I need."

If she touched him, he'd be lucky to last one.

As if reading his thoughts, her honeyed complexion darkened. "You don't need to worry. I will only massage your head."

Scrambling out of the hammock, he choked down a groan as his groin tightened. "Look, Bellina, I'm—"

"Bellini." She entered his bure, leaving him no choice but to follow. "First you need to drink a glass of water." Opening the small fridge, she withdrew a bottle of water and filled a glass. "You are probably dehydrated."

There was that. He might as well take advantage of her offer. He couldn't think properly with the tightness across his brow. Turning away, he glanced around the opulent room, wondering if she wanted him on a straight-backed chair or the couch. A head massage was as good a reason as any to get her into his bure.

She pointed to the king-sized bed in the upper section.

"Fine." He climbed the two steps, paced to the bed and sat on the edge.

She stepped between his spread thighs and handed him the glass. "Drink."

"You're a bossy little thing." Thankful for his loose shirt, he skulled the cool water, relishing its unusual tang. "Happy?"

She rolled her eyes as if he were a petulant child. If he hadn't seen through her disguise straight off, the eye roll would have given her away. She pressed closer, sinking her fingers into his hair.

A jolt racked his body. In this position, her much bigger chest filled his vision. For such a slim little thing, the added inches were a touch extreme. He fought back a chuckle.

Her fingers tightened, the slow, deep massage moving to the base of his skull. Raising his gaze, he fixed on her face. With the dark contact lenses, dyed black hair and deep tan, she reminded him of the *señorita*, although the wider nose, and rounder chin were a new addition. His head tingled at her touch and a compulsion to draw her close had him fisting his fingers. She may have sought him out to ask for help and needed to build up courage.

Her fingers spread and tightened over his scalp, in a sensual, soothing, hypnotic motion. He closed his eyes, relaxing, exhaling as a sense of wellbeing cloaked his whole body. Tink had a real knack at massaging. The tightness in his back and shoulders seeped away. All his concerns melted into the background as his senses came alive. Birdcalls and gently breaking waves filled his ears. Goosebumps covered his skin, along with a soft breeze teasing his neck. Sunshine and something floral invaded his airways. He'd never experienced such peace, such lethargy. He should bottle Tink and keep her to himself. Her fingers were amazing.

She shook his shoulder. Roughly.

"Wake up, lazy bastard."

That couldn't be right. She sounded like... Talos?

She slapped his face. Another thump. "Simo, what the hell is wrong with you?"

His eyes shot open. "Talos?"

The big man straightened to his full height of six-foot-five and scowled at him. "Hell, what's wrong with you?"

"What happened to Tink?"

"Who?"

"The Polynesian waitress. It's Darius. She was here a few seconds ago."

"I can assure you there is no one else here. You must have been dreaming, mate."

Simon rolled off the bed and examined his bure. The tray of food had been placed on a coffee table in the lower section. "Darius disguised as a waitress gave me a head massage. I must have zoned out."

Talos narrowed his eyes. "How'd she arrive on the island?

"Trust me, I'll find out when I catch up with her."

"You need to get over to the restaurant for pre-dinner cocktails and mingle."

"That's hours away." He stretched.

"Mate, it's eighteen hundred. You need to burn rubber."

"Eighteen hundred?" Simon checked his watch. "Holy shit. I've lost five hours."

Talos frowned. "You're not coming down with something are you?"

"No, but I haven't been sleeping well." He shook his head, rattled to have passed out for so long. It was unlike him. "Any news on the other Cortez women?"

"Not a whisper. Jarred is in a filthy mood. We have no way of communicating with anyone. Before we left Fiji, Gibbs confirmed a chopper would drop Nick and Ryan in the ocean, close to the island tonight, but we can't coordinate any changes or their passage through the fucking reef."

"I assume Gibbs is now aware our satellite phones have been confiscated." Simon grimaced. "What about transport?"

"I've searched the whole island." Talos ticked off his fingers. "One glass bottom skiff, several kayaks, a runabout, some paddleboards, a catamaran and one hang glider locked in a shed at the golf course. Nothing big enough to evacuate everyone in an emergency."

"Nothing?"

"No. Apparently they have a powerful launch for deep-sea fishing and water sports, but it's away for maintenance." Talos stalked to the open door. "Jarred said the same thing. It's a clusterfuck."

"You took a risk coming here, Talos."

"Anyone seeing me will assume I'm patrolling the area. You might want to hold off confronting Darius until we know more." After a quick check, he stepped outside.

A frog let loose with a deep throbbing warble as Talos disappeared along the path.

Simon headed for the food tray, his stomach grumbling with a fierce hunger. He needed lining on his stomach before he partook in pre-dinner drinks.

Once he'd emptied the plates, he took a cool shower, shaved then donned a fresh shirt, tailored pants and his crocodile-skin shoes. It was time to do some subtle interrogating and, thanks to Darius, he had a clear mind with which to work.

About to step out through the sliding glass door, he hesitated, an out of place impression compelling him to do a slow perusal of the luxury room. His gaze fell on his computer bag, exactly where he'd left it, but facing the wrong way. Strolling across the room, he unzipped both sides and checked the two compartments. Both computers were there. It was entirely possible Darius moved his bag when she brought the food inside. In reality, anyone could have entered the bure while he slept.

Turning the bag, so the heavier computer was nearest the table leg, he left the bure, locking the glass slider behind him.

Entering the dining room, Simon noted two professors he recognized. Phillip Nutlan, better known as the nutty professor. Sickly pale and thin as a rake, the gray-haired man's eyes darted frantically about the room. Rumor had it he lived with his elderly mother, didn't drink or smoke and disparaged anyone who did. He still wore a bow tie, black-rimmed glasses and a heavy scowl. Nutlan had never been close to Alexander Cortez. If anything, he'd despised Alexander's popularity and success.

The other man, Keith Heckle, beckoned Simon. Heckle had always been a happy soul and a little on the flabby side. His light-brown toupee didn't quite match the remaining hair underneath, but then it never had. He wore baggy cargo pants and a colorful Hawaiian shirt that did nothing to hide his much larger girth. This man had been a friend to Alexander and might know something of interest.

Simon wandered over. "Evening, gentlemen. It's been a long time." He held out his hand to Professor Heckle.

Shaking it firmly, Professor Heckle beamed. "Good to see you, Simon. We heard the Defense Force head-hunted you for their Joint Operations Center?"

"That's true, sir, although I'm no longer with JOC. I'm a consultant now." His cover would hold with everyone except the hacker. "Professor Nutlan." Simon offered his hand to the scowling man.

Phillip Nutlan twitched then lifted his hand, begrudgingly. "You must be with an impressive organization to be at this summit."

"I represent several organizations."

"I see." Phillip Nutlan's eyes narrowed. "Bad business about your old mentor."

"Let's not go there, Phillip." Keith Heckle patted his colleague's shoulder then turned back to Simon. "We'll be in each other's pockets over the next few days, so let's drop the formalities. Call me Keith and this here is Phillip. We Aussies should stick together in times of trouble."

"No worries."

"Good God! What the devil are you doing here?"

Simon swung round to see Professor Richard Chapman striding towards him. All conversation ceased as every person in the room turned their attention to the man with the booming voice.

Chapman halted barely a foot in front of Simon, glaring daggers. "You've got a bloody hide showing your face here."

Of similar height, Simon stood his ground and raised an eyebrow. "As an invited delegate, I have every right to be here, Professor."

"Not after what you did to Alexander. The man taught you everything. He worshipped you, and in return, you stabbed him in the back."

Ice filled Simons veins. "I beg your pardon?"

"I'd wager my career you know exactly what I'm referring to. You and your program destroyed Alexander." Richard Chapman's lip curled. "Do you deny sending the Federal Police to interview him?"

"No, I don't. In fact—" He would have elaborated but an explosion of glass drowned his words. Spinning around, he found Darius crouched on the floor, surrounded by broken glass and alcohol. Tear-filled eyes held his for several seconds before she bent her head and began placing shards of glass on the tray.

She had to have heard Chapman's accusation. Simon squatted to help. "Let me do that, you're shaking."

She pushed his hands away. "I don't want your help."

She'd definitely heard.

"Ladies and gentlemen, if I could have your attention." A male voice with a distinct British accent, called from a low dais against the back wall. "I am Alistair Finch. My job is to answer your questions and keep the summit running smoothly."

Simon wanted to take Darius aside and explain, but she wouldn't look at him, and he couldn't risk drawing attention, so he stood.

"What's with the communication embargo?" An American woman called.

"I understand your annoyance at having your devices confiscated, Judith, but for the security of all delegates, it is a necessary measure. I also have several requests. Under no circumstances are any of you to enter the next cove or approach the two residences there. They are strictly out of bounds." He gave a chuckle. "You do not want to tangle with security, believe me. Each day breakfast will be served between seven and eight. We kick off at nine. The speakers deserve your respect so don't dawdle. Morning tea is at ten, and we lunch at twelve-thirty. You have one hour to eat and stretch your legs. Afternoon tea is three-thirty and heralds the end of our workday."

"When do we enjoy the resort's facilities?" called a man with a New Zealand accent.

"You have three hours leisure time before dinner at seven o'clock. Each evening, Alisi and her staff will feed and entertain us. Tomorrow night you get to experience the traditional Meke dance, fire walking and local songs. Tonight Vijay, the resort's chef, and his staff have created a delicious buffet, so please relax while the staff entertain you."

Although listening, Simon's attention reverted to Darius the instant her hand stilled over the tray, a slither of glass suspended between her thumb and finger. She raised her hand toward a lone tear suspended on her cheek.

"Tink, be careful."

Her blank gaze bothered him, but a least she dropped the shard of glass.

He helped her stand. "Can we find somewhere private to talk?" When she didn't answer, he clasped his hands around her waist, and lifted her clear of the mess. She was light as a feather, her waist so tiny, his fingertips met.

Touching her was a major mistake. She recoiled. "Let me go."

He released her, stepping back to give her space. "I can explain."

"Don't." She turned tail and ran from the restaurant.

He made after her, until a brunette stepped across his path. "*Bonsoir, Monsieur* Hawke. I think the waitress is perhaps a little inexperienced for a man like you."

"My interest in the lady is none of your concern, ma'am." He raised an eyebrow.

Unabashed, her pale blue eyes held his invitingly. "I am Marguerite Lémaire."

"Nice to meet you, Ms. Lémaire. Now if you'll excuse me?" He turned to the manageress and large Fijian chef, approaching with a broom and dustpan.

The chef scowled. "What happened?"

He couldn't expose Darius. Simon held his hands wide. "I'm trying to figure that out myself. I think she got a fright."

The manageress smiled at Simon. "I am Alisi and this is Vijay. We are short on staff, so Bellini is helping out. She will be fine, please enjoy the rest of your evening."

Like that was even possible. Glancing about, he noticed the French woman in conversation with Phillip Nutlan and Keith Heckle.

"Hello, Simon. Mind if I join you?"

Yes, damn it, he wanted to chase after Darius. Simon had little choice but to acknowledge the interloper. A man with gray eyes held out his hand. "I'm Alistair Finch, an old friend of your late professor.

Alex and I go way back. He insisted you were the most brilliant student he'd ever encountered. Boasted of your achievements whenever our paths crossed."

Simon shook the Englishmen's hand, taking in the designer jeans and Italian shoes. "Strange, he never mentioned you, Mr. Finch."

"Call me Alistair. It's possible Alex didn't mention me, as I often teased him that you'd be better off with me at Cambridge University. We competed in a friendly rivalry where our students were concerned."

Simon swept his gaze over the lean man. He looked to be in his mid-fifties, and very comfortable in his own skin, if the ponytail and earring were anything to go by. "I assume you heard Richard Chapman's accusation?"

"Yes, the waitress' timely mishap diverted a potentially nasty encounter. I will speak with Richard. Just out of curiosity, what were you about to say, before she dropped the tray?"

"I did send the Federal Police to speak to Professor Cortez. I believed him the best person to track the thief. Not for one minute did I consider him guilty."

"We have much to discuss. I suggest we take a couple of kayaks out sometime over the next three days. I prefer we keep that particular conversation private."

"Suits me." Alistair could have vital information, possibly even the third secret key.

Conversations had resumed, although many eyes were directed at Simon and Alistair. "I look forward to our discussion."

Alistair raised a glass to his lips and lowered his voice. "Until then."

CHAPTER TWELVE

Dropping a tray of drinks wouldn't happen to a seasoned undercover agent, yet Simon hadn't denied Professor Chapman's accusation. He admitted to sending the police after her father.

Rage engulfed Darius at the humiliation her family endured after police pushed their way into her home then meticulously searched every room, before taking her father away. She'd laid in the dark for hours, too afraid to sleep.

Simon had called her Tink.

A wave of nausea threatened to bring up the contents of her stomach. She wiped her clammy forehead then drew in several deep breaths. She couldn't confront Simon—she couldn't even face him until she calmed down. That brought to mind Alistair Finch. Why would he warn everyone away from the next cove? He seemed vaguely familiar. It could be that he'd come to the house to see her father years ago, or she'd met him at one of the university functions she'd attended with her parents.

He'd politely taken a beer when she offered him a selection of drinks. To her shock, Professor Chapman had taken a glass of wine then pinched her bottom. It's a wonder she hadn't drop the tray then. If he'd come onto her mother, it would explain her aversion to him soon after the memorial service.

"Bellini, are you well?" Alisi stood at the top of the steps.

"Yes, just embarrassed. I'm fine now." Simon hadn't blown her cover, so she might as well see what else she could learn before he tracked her down.

"Are you able to help set out the buffet?"

"Sure." She jogged up the steps and paced alongside Alisi. "What about tonight's entertainment?"

"Etera and Vijay will play their guitars and sing with the other two waitresses. I would appreciate your help with breakfast in the morning and tidying the bures, if you can spare a few hours. Of course, you shall be paid, and after lunch you are invited to join the female staff. We will teach you our *Meke* dance for tomorrow evening. If the weather stays fine, the men will perform a fire dance ceremony."

"Great." Darius bit her lip. She'd have to put off searching the bures.

Parting at reception, Darius marched through to the kitchen then picked up a platter of oysters and returned to the dining room. Simon stood at the far end talking to Alistair Finch and a man she didn't know. With no exterior walls on two sides of the dining room, she could see Jarred Steele and another man she recognized from the bar in Sydney. Alisi had told her his name was Sam Locke.

The two men stood several feet apart, their gazes perpetually scouring the restaurant's occupants. Although their eyes skimmed over her, she detected no real interest. That would change once Simon informed them of her presence.

Yesterday she'd visited every bure, gluing jewel beetles on the ceiling side of the overhead beams. The lime-green striped bugs would pick up and transmit conversation within the bures. She'd also left sensor-activated frogs under shrubs at several junctions. If passed, they would emit a loud warbling, alerting her to a person's approach. Several times she'd met Jarred and Sam on pathways. Luckily, they hadn't questioned her. In fact, she got the impression each assumed her wariness was due to their intimidating bearing.

Tonight, while staff entertained the delegates, she would visit bures on the far side of the cove, install the spyware then download data from their computers. It was a very simple procedure all in all. Turn on the computer, insert a pre-programmed USB and after it installed the spyware, everything on the computer's hard-drive would be copied. Her drop location was the locked letterbox at her villa, which meant Phoenix had to be on the island to collect the data.

Placing the platter on the buffet table, she rearranged several other dishes of cold meats and salads. Her mind fixed on Alistair Finch. By insisting no delegates enter the next cove, he'd provided her with a great degree of privacy. It could be as simple as protecting the privacy of the actress staying in the small villa, or did he know her identity?

Early this morning, she'd clipped monarch butterflies as high as she could reach in shrubs surrounding the pool, main pathways and dining room. Each contained a sensor, transmitter and camera. Movement would trigger the devices, which meant Phoenix would need to be in close proximity to receive the transmissions.

Removing the lid of a steaming bowl of coconut rice, she took the long route round the room so as not to cross paths with Simon. As she reached the furthest table, she heard Professor Heckle challenge an American to a game of golf the next afternoon. Their bures were on the south side of the cove. She would search them while the men were on the fairway.

The thought of drugging anyone else made her queasy. She'd almost stopped breathing when Simon fell back on his bed. For several heartbeats she feared the two drops of elixir had killed him. After five minutes of checking his pulse and watching his chest rise and fall, she'd powered up his two lap top computers then plugged in USBs. It came as no surprise when neither USB overrode his password. As an expert in his field, Simon would have in-built safety measures to block anyone accessing his computers or downloading his data. It wouldn't surprise her if the other computer scientists had similar protection.

As Darius entered the kitchen, Alisi handed her another platter, piled high with shrimp. "Thank you, Bellini. If you see any empty glasses, would you please put them on the bar then it might be best if you return to your villa."

"Oh?"

"Some men have been asking the staff personal questions about you."

"Who?"

"Two delegates and a few of the security men. Etera said Professor Chapman hasn't taken his eyes off you either. Be careful."

"I will, thanks." Darius left the kitchen frowning. Of all her father's colleagues, Richard Chapman, along with his wife, had given her family the most support. After her father's death, the Professor had provided a shoulder to weep on. He'd been their defender against the persistent Federal investigator's allegations.

Professor Chapman could be Phoenix.

She should also consider Darren Turner, her mother's new partner. Supposedly his friendship with her father went back years and could be why he'd initially struck up a friendship with Darius' mother.

The thought had never crossed her mind, but in reality, it made sense.

Phoenix could be anyone.

Shuffling platters about the table, Darius studied and eavesdropped on those closest to her. There was a mixture of accents—Australian, New Zealand, Asian, English, American, Canadian and French. Of the nineteen delegates only two were women. One, a middle-aged American lady, had joined Alistair Finch at the bar. The other, a brunette, looked to be in her early thirties and spoke with a French accent. She oozed confidence and panache. At the moment, she stood extremely close to Simon, deep in conversation.

As if sensing Darius' scrutiny, he glanced her way.

Inwardly cursing, she picked up two empty glasses and, with a calm mask in place, gathered her mettle.

A half-smothered bark of laughter erupted from near the bar.

Frozen in place, Darius fought for breath as memories bombarded her mind. Summer vacations spent skimming across the ocean. Her father's unique laugh as they raced before the wind, the catamaran's sails billowing, salt water spray drenching them and not a care in the world.

Blinking furiously to ward off the threatening tears, she placed the glasses back on a table and did a slow three-sixty degree turn, her gaze devouring every male close to the bar. It made no sense— wasn't possible—absolute madness, but for the life of her, she couldn't hold back the flicker of hope that caught flame.

Dismissing men who were too short, too tall, too old, too young or too familiar, she focused on a man standing between Jarred Steel and Alistair Finch. Easily five-foot-six, the gray-haired, fair-complexioned man looked to be in his mid-fifties. She couldn't tell his eye color at this distance, but he wore silver-rimmed glasses just like her father's.

Alistair Finch patted the man's shoulder before heading for the buffet. Clutching a cane, the man followed at a much slower pace, his limp giving him a swaying gait.

"Oh, dear God." What if her father survived the fall and had come to the summit to expose his traitor? No one knew better than her how easy cosmetics could change a person's face. Her heart fit to explode, Darius moved to intercept him.

Professor Chapman blocked her path. "I need to speak with you, my dear."

"Huh." Had he seen through her disguise? The Professor's gaze dropped to her chest momentarily.

"I need a massage this evening. The other waitress informed me you're my woman. I'm happy to pay cash for your services."

His request sounded far too much like a proposition. She dredged up a smile, concentrating on the right inflection. "We are very busy tonight, but if you see Alisi, perhaps she can schedule you an appointment for tomorrow."

"No, no, I need you tonight. Meet me at my bure in one hour. Number ten. I have a full-bodied bottle of red. We can indulge in a glass or two after the massage."

"Sir, I—"

"Your skills will be rewarded, my dear." His lips curved in a sly smirk then he chuckled. "I envisaged this summit boring me to death, until I sighted you. Number ten, one hour."

With her mouth gaping, she watched him plod over to the buffet table. A married man, more than twice her age, had just hit on her. The sleazy creep. Had he been the man who hit on her mother?

She searched the dining room for the man with the cane. He carried a plate of food in one hand as he awkwardly trailed Alistair Finch to the table where Professors Heckle and Nutlan were seated. They'd surely recognize their old colleague and friend?

Grabbing a bottle of sparkling water, she worked her way to their table.

The man looked up. He had brown eyes, but not warm like her father's, and the bridge of his nose had a deeper curve. Unable to speak over the weird sense of disappointed relief, she placed the bottle in the middle of the table.

A presence behind sent a familiar thrill through her treacherous body.

"Bellini."

She couldn't face Simon, not after discovering his betrayal.

"Bellini?" Warmth flooded her arm as his fingers closed around her elbow, forcing her to turn and meet his enquiring eyes. "I wanted to thank you for ridding me of my headache."

"You're welcome. Excuse me, I am needed in the kitchen." Tugging her arm free, she stepped around him then sidestepped Professor Chapman, who had a monstrous scowl directed at Simon.

"Go chat up one of the other waitresses. This pretty little thing is spoken for. At least for the next few days."

The Professor's words brought Darius to a standstill. She whirled in a haze of contempt and disgust, set to haul the arrogant, sleazy toad over the coals. Simon's set jaw and chilling eyes drew her up short.

His lip curled with contempt as he stared down the professor. "If you think to intimidate me, Richard, you are sorely misguided. You are here to participate in an emergency summit, not indulge in extra-marital affairs. Alisi and her staff have enough to do without having to fend off randy old men like you."

Professor Chapman spluttered, his fist clenching at his sides as he returned Simon's glare. "You back-stabbing whelp. This summit's aim might be to prevent any more major utilities being hacked, but my money says it's you and your program behind the breaches, and I intend to prove it."

Simon sneered. "Knock yourself out."

Darius glanced about the room expecting to see every eye focused on the two men, but due to the music and buzz of conversation, only the four at the table closest were following the terse conversation.

Alistair Finch pushed back his chair and stepped between Simon and Professor Chapman. "That's enough, gentlemen. If either of you have some insight or know something pertinent, you may discuss it with me privately." Alistair Finch had a smooth British accent and gray eyes. Darius liked the earring and ponytail. They gave him a bohemian look.

Professor Chapman crossed his arms over his chest. "I've got plenty to say."

"Very well. Meet me on the beach in two hours. I find an evening stroll calms the mind and body."

"I'm busy tonight." Professor Chapman's smirk flicked to Darius.

Holding her tongue had never been so hard.

Alistair Finch's gray eyes narrowed. "I suggest you take Mr. Hawke's advice, Richard. The staff is off limits. I will see you by the wharf in two hours."

Professor Heckle cleared his throat. "I would also like to speak with you, Alistair."

"Very well. What time suits, Keith?"

"Tomorrow after lunch would be fine." He returned to his meal.

Darius studied Professor Heckle. She hadn't had much to do with him, although he'd sometimes dropped by their house to speak with her father. Her memories were of a jovial man with a hearty laugh and an odd haircut. It still looked odd. She bit her lip, repressing a giggle. It was a toupee, and not a good one.

Alistair Finch returned to his seat, giving her the chance to study him as she fussed with the buffet table. His stylish jacket, open-necked shirt, earring and tied back hair, seemed at odds with his serious nature. For a computer scientist in his fifties, he looked extremely fit.

Other than Simon, the two security teams and the French woman, everyone else appeared to be over forty and overweight, typical of people who spent their lives at a desk. All except Phillip Nutlan. A strong breeze would surely blow him off his feet.

Shuffling along the table, she picked up an empty platter and the two glasses, intent on making her escape. Professor Chapman obstructed her path, leaning across the table to pile his plate with shrimp. Without looking her way, he murmured. "Don't forget our appointment. Number ten, I'll be waiting."

Her stomach flipped. She wanted to smash the platter across his smug face, or at least stomp on his sandaled feet. This was sexual harassment, and somebody should teach him a lesson.

"Sir, we don't do massages in the bures?"

He huffed. "I'll make it well worth your while, my dear."

Pressing her lips together, Darius stepped around him and paced to the bar. For the next twenty minutes, she ferried food and empty plates between the dining room and kitchen until Alisi waved her away.

"We can manage now, Bellini. Thank you for your help."

"Okay. See you tomorrow morning." She took a step then hesitated. As a woman, it fell to her to alert Alisi and the other female staff to Professor Chapman's veiled proposition. Keeping her voice lowered, she repeated her conversation with him and what he'd said to Simon.

"Thank you, Bellini. I will inform my staff, so they can keep an eye on him."

"Great." Checking Professor Chapman hadn't departed, Darius grabbed her tote bag and left via reception. With no observers to witness her flight, she broke into a sprint.

To get to bure ten, she had to take the narrow, meandering path on the opposite cove to Simon's bure. Hearing approaching footsteps, she slowed to a walk in an attempt to look as if she had no particular destination, other than an evening stroll to the end of the cove. Coach lights illuminated the path and shrubs on either side, drawing a multitude of insects.

A giant rounded the path, his long strides eating up the distance. She recognized him from the wine bar in Sydney. Another of Simon's sharp-eyed, military-looking friends. That made three of them on the island.

"Evening." His dark gaze swept over her as he moved to one side, allowing room for her to pass. "Out for a stroll?"

"Ahh, yes." Good Lord, he was tall.

"Watch out for frogs. They're everywhere." With a friendly nod, he strode on toward the pool and dining room.

Quelling her skittish nerves, Darius focused on her errand. As she approached the first private path a frog launched into a throbbing warble. The frogs were going to draw unwanted attention, she'd have to turn them down.

Making a mental note to collect the frogs after she installed the spyware and downloaded the occupant's data, she increased her pace.

Pulling out her master key, she turned off the main path to number ten. Another frog burst into song, scaring her witless.

As with all the bures, this one had a glass slider at the front, louver windows on each side and an ensuite at the rear.

Once inside she closed the curtains, turned the bed down then opened a bottle of water. Filling a glass, she added two drops of sleeping elixir and placed it on the bedside table. Next, she tipped two more drops into the bottle's remaining water then put it in the bar fridge. Seeing an open bottle of red wine, she added five drops, just to be sure. That would teach Professor Chapman for playing up on his wife and harassing vulnerable young women.

A computer sat on the coffee table. Whipping out the slim USB, she quickly pushed it into the hub and powered up the computer. According to her instructions, she didn't need a password to install the spyware or access the hard-drive, as the USB had the technology to infiltrate and download data.

With the island in full blackout she had to wonder if Phoenix had some role in organizing the summit. Her instructions were to seal the USB's in the supplied waterproof bags then place them in the locked letterbox of her villa. She assumed he planned to collect them himself, possibly at night.

Tonight, she would download data from each of the delegates on this side of the cove then tomorrow evening she'd concentrate on the opposite cove.

Staring at the USB wasn't going to make the download run faster, so she began snooping. A folder of loose documents lay on the end of the bed. Nothing jumped out to indicate he was anything but a delegate. She found the professor's wallet under a pillow and in it, a photo with his wife and grandchildren. "You're married to a cheating slug, Mrs. Chapman."

Sliding the rear glass door open, she stepped down into the ensuite. His toiletry bag revealed Viagra and lots of condoms. "Dirt bag." Getting antsy, she returned to the bure. Perspiration caked her forehead as she willed the download to finish.

A frog's warble broke the silence. "Shit."

The light on the USB blinked green. Yanking it out she shut the computer lid, grabbed her tote bag and leaped through the rear door, closing the slider as a key turned in the front one. With her heart pounding under her ribs, she searched for an escape route. A high window ran horizontally along one wall, underneath stood an ornamental ladder holding two towels. Thankfully it took her weight. Pushing the wire screen out, she scrambled through the window and dropped to the ground, where she released a shaky breath. With luck mosquitos would eat him alive.

Her narrow escape thrilled her. She rather liked this covert operative stuff.

After ten minutes, she sneaked round the bure to a side window and peaked through the louvers. Professor Chapman lay sprawled on the flowery sofa, an upturned wineglass in his lap, and a large red stain soaking the crotch of his cream pants.

"Serves him right." Darius foraged under bromeliads for her frog, flicked the off switch then put it in her tote bag. Pushing through the shrubs bordering the paths, she darted toward the last bure. At each interlinking path a frog burst forth in song.

To save time, she booted up the computer in the furthest bure then inserted a USB before running on to the next bure and so on. Guitar music, drumming and men singing in harmony drifted from the dining room. She hoped all the delegates stayed to enjoy the evening's entertainment.

It took forty minutes and the last of her courage to visit the remaining seven bures, install the spyware, download the occupant's data, collect and tag each USB then collect the frogs. It wasn't until she reached her Vesper, she remembered the jewel beetle bug in Professor Chapman's bure. It would have recorded her opinion of the cheating slug. Not much she could do now. Phoenix had asked her to bug each bure and download the data from all delegates computers. If Professor Chapman were indeed Phoenix, he deserved to be drugged with his own elixir.

Starting the Vesper, she puttered out of the small courtyard behind reception and turned up the hill. Rustling foliage and distant crashing waves gave the dark winding road an isolated eeriness.

Although physically and mentally exhausted, she wanted to check out the big villa before Simon found her and demanded answers. The secure property provided a perfect habitat for Phoenix to hide out, especially as the owner wasn't in residence.

CHAPTER THIRTEEN

Darkness and a great hulking catamaran provided cover as Simon whiled away the minutes, waiting for the faintest light to indicate the chopper's arrival. He lay on the dark blue windsurfer he'd borrowed from the resort. Minus the sail, it offered the ideal means to meet the boys.

A ski mask, dive slippers, gloves and his black Kevlar suit, helped him blend with the dark water. Any delegates out for a midnight stroll on the ridge wouldn't notice him, and as Sam and Talos were patrolling this cove tonight, they were also keeping an eye on the small villa. If Darius left for any reason, they'd follow.

Keeping track of her reconnaissance tonight had been an eye opener. As Talos suggested, they'd given her plenty of rope and let her run. Sam had retrieved an envelope with ten USB's from her villa's letterbox which Simon uploaded to his own computer. Sam then returned them to the letterbox, along with a Federal Police tracker. Whoever pick up the envelope would be arrested once they reached the mainland.

The gentle current kept drawing his board away from the catamaran toward open sea, forcing him to hand-paddle back into position. Checking his watch, he figured it was close enough to midnight to let the current have its way.

As he drifted away, a lithe figure in black emerged on the beach below the small residence and dropped into a crouch.

"What the...?" Flattening his chest to the board, Simon kept his gaze on Darius. Once the lights in the villa went out, he hadn't really expected her to make a midnight dash. She could be meeting up with the hacker.

His gaze followed her as she sprinted barefoot along the beach.

Reaching the staircase of the large residence, she froze for several seconds, as if listening then raced up two steps at a time like a gazelle.

Grateful for his night vision goggles, Simon watched in fascination as she shimmied up and over a high, locked gate, much like Spider Girl.

Pulling out his flashlight, Simon signaled Sam and Talos.

A quick series of flashes came back from the beach and the terrace of the small villa. They'd seen her.

The hacker had to be on the island and, with luck, Darius would lead them to this supposed friend of her father's.

Simon checked his watch. Midnight. He clipped the flashlight to his belt then, using his hands, paddled toward to cove's opening, alert for sounds of a chopper flying low.

The faint throb came as he cleared the reef. Sitting up, he unclipped the flashlight. The second he saw a dot in the night sky, he sent the same message over and over.

Hazard. Execute deep ocean drop.

His team would trust him to guide them in through the deadly reef.

He continued sending the message until the chopper made a low sweep and two black shapes dropped into the black ocean with barely a splash.

The chopper whirled away to the north.

Unable to detect Nick and Ryan, Simon directed his flashlight out to sea, giving them occasional flashes to follow in.

Talos had made an earlier study of the reef from the top of the ridge, and discovered the boatshed had a narrow winding passage through the reef out to the open sea. It was a bit of a hodge-podge maze, but easily negotiated during high tide and daylight. Low tide, darkness and a dragging current would present problems. Tonight, the boys only had to battle with darkness. Once they entered the cove, their own underwater flashlights would make things easier.

Simon glanced up at the small residence. Jarred had been briefed on the lady staying there. An actress, here as a guest of the owner. As Darius appeared to be the only occupant of the villa, the owner would need looking into.

Seeing two heads, Simon signaled Nick and Ryan to the opening of the passage they had to traverse. Five minutes later they surfaced again, their snorkels and goggles just visible above the water. He directed them a little to the right. Another three minutes passed before two grinning faces appeared either side of the windsurfer.

"What's with the Morse code?" asked Nick, lifting his mask onto his forehead. "A text message would have done."

"No communication. We're in total blackout." Simon kept his voice low. "They've confiscated all cell phones and satellite toggles."

"What, even security?" Ryan's disbelief mirrored Nick's.

"Yes, and they disconnected the resort's satellite dish. Essentially, we are isolated without any form of communication."

"At least you have guns." Nick grinned. "I borrowed a couple of knives from the sheik's guards."

"That's good news." Simon eyed the packs on his mates' backs. "Jarred's worried Gibbs will send in the troops if he doesn't hear from us. And then there's Madeline."

"She's cool." Ryan's lips twitched. "Madeline threatened us with bodily harm if we didn't include her in the mission. We flew to Lakeba Island then refueled and came on here. The chopper pilot has taken Madeline back to Lakeba Island, and she'll pass on your message to Inspector Gibbs. What he'll do about it is anyone's guess."

Simon glanced across the dark water to the beach and large villa. No sign of movement. "Any news on Francine and Sarah Cortez?"

"Nothing." Ryan shook his head. "The Feds don't seem too concerned, but they're checking out Airlie Beach and Hamilton Island."

"Good." Simon stiffened as a slim figure plunged down the steep stairs. "Shit."

"What's up?" asked Ryan.

"Don't move, you might spook Darius." He held his breath as she descended the steps at break neck speed then leaped onto the sand.

"I'm impressed," whispered Ryan.

Breathing a sigh of relief, Simon dropped to his board. "Follow me onto the beach. We may be needed to cut off her escape. She's incredibly fast."

"Jarred should recruit her," murmured Nick.

Switching his gaze between Darius and the submerged reef, Simon paddled through the deep lagoon.

She stopped near the steps leading up to her villa, hands on knees, clearly breathing hard as she looked back along the beach.

Simon knew Sam and Talos would be close but could detect no sign of them. He nodded at Nick and Ryan as facemasks back in place, they indicated their intention to fan out. Only their snorkels showed above the water as they glided toward the beach.

Darius gripped a paddleboard on the sand and dragged it into the water.

A grin broke over Simon's face. They were on a collision course.

Although covered from head to ankle in black, the tights and skivvy clung lovingly to her svelte limbs and feminine curves. A familiar tightening stirred deep in his loins. Exhaling a long slow breath, Simon stayed absolutely still as she stretched out on the board then paddled furiously toward the catamaran and him.

Ryan popped out of the water on her far side. "What have we here?"

She gasped and pushed back to sit on her ankles. Her startled gaze locked on Simon dead ahead.

"Hello, Tink. What *have* you been up to?"

"I have nothing to say to you."

Nick surfaced on her left, his hand staying the board.

As quick as a flash, Darius dived into the depths.

Wary of the reef on either side, Simon paddled after her, relieved to see Sam and Talos hanging back in shadows cast by enormous boulders jutted along the cove.

Darius moved as quickly underwater as she did on land, emerging minus her beanie. Sleek black hair reached almost to her waist. After a furtive check over her shoulder, she waded and splashed through the waist deep water then ran through the shallows and across the sand.

Sam and Talos emerged from shadows, cutting off her escape.

Darius stumbled then sank to her knees. Her head and shoulders bowed, her breathing ragged.

Ryan waded out of the water beside Simon, his mask and snorkel dangling from a finger. "Simon, this girl has hidden talents."

"Yes, and I have a feeling we've only scratched the surface." Simon carried his board past the high tide mark then laid it on the sand. He pulled off his ski mask and looked down at Darius. "Like to explain what you're doing here?"

Arms crossed, she scowled. "You might have me surrounded, but it won't do any good. I have nothing to say to you or your friends." She shivered, reminding Simon her clothes were soaking wet and the boys had formed an intimidating circle around her.

"We need to get off this beach in case the other security team decide to expand their borders. Let's go up to your villa. Once you've had a warm shower, we'll talk. Unless you'd rather we lock you up for the duration of the summit then hand you over to the Federal Police?"

"Fine." She clambered to her feet then stomped up the sand.

Talos bounded up the steps ahead of her. Sam and Ryan followed.

"That's one gutsy lady." Nick dropped the board Darius had abandoned on the sand. "I think your bachelor days are over, mate." He grinned. "I'm thinking she'd fit right in with the other Steele Ops wives."

"Not if she's in prison for cyber fraud and God knows what else." Simon strode up the steps ahead of Nick. When he knew how many laws Darius had broken, he'd work out what to do next. Until then he couldn't consider a closer relationship.

Sam met them at the villa's terrace. "Darius is having a shower and Talos has gone to let Jarred know the boys have arrived. I'm on watch in this cove, so if you need me, signal. It might be wise if Nick and Ryan lay low here with Darius. They can keep her safe while you're at the summit."

"Yes." After firsthand experience at Darius' disguises, Simon had something else in mind, but he'd have to clear it with Jarred first thing in the morning.

"Find out what you can, then head back to your bure and get some sleep." Sam gave them a wave then jogged back down the steps.

Nick clapped Simon on the back. "Let's check the villa out, then you can talk to Darius while Ryan and I get out of our wetsuits and grab showers. She's more likely to open up to you if we're out of the way."

"Thanks, mate."

Once they'd done a walk through every room other than Darius', Ryan and Nick selected a bedroom and disappeared for showers.

Simon stripped off his Kevlar suit, had a quick shower in the downstairs bathroom then pulled on his board shorts again. He borrowed a T-shirt from Ryan before knocking on Darius' door.

"Can I come in, Tink?"

"You will anyway, so why ask?" She sounded so put out he fought back a laugh. Opening the door, he entered the room, unsurprised to find her standing with her arms crossed, covered from neck to toe in a thick dressing gown wearing a mutinous scowl she directed his way. "Say what you have to, then leave."

At least she planned to listen this time. "I didn't betray your father. In hindsight, I wished I'd spoken to him before I was deployed to the Middle East. He might have confided in me."

She narrowed her eyes. "You didn't deny Professor Chapman's allegations."

"That's because I did recommend the Federal Police speak to your father. They contacted me after a series of major cyber hacks, wanting my opinion on how the breaches could have occurred. At the time, I assumed the Defense Force must have put them on to me, so I mentioned Alexander Cortez's research and suggested they speak to him as he was an authority on cyber fraud. I honestly didn't know the Feds suspected him of using the program to perform the hacks."

Darius dropped her arms. "Was it you?"

"No. If it's any conciliation, I never questioned your father's integrity. If he hadn't died, I would have helped him hunt the culprit."

"When did you figure out my disguises?"

"I became suspicious after you assumed my sister's identity. I knew for sure the minute I came through your window." Simon ran a hand through his hair. "It's time to level with me. The Federal Police could arrest you on suspicion of cyber fraud, illegally obtaining secret documents, terrorism and any number of other things."

She swallowed then sank onto the bed. "I swear I didn't hack into the Defense Force data base."

Simon breathed a sigh of relief. Her clear, unwavering eyes spelled the truth "The fact you even know about that breach tells me you can identify the hacker, and that could put your life in danger."

"I'm really tired."

"That won't work this time, sweet pea."

126

She gave him a weak smile. "It was worth a try."

"Let's start with something easy." Simon squatted in front of her. "Explain tonight's expedition?"

"I drugged Professor Chapman because he's a jerk, and I needed..." She clamped a hand over her mouth.

"To download everything on his computer. Don't bother denying it. Did you drug me too?"

"Yes, I'm sorry." She hung her head. "It was a wasted effort."

He couldn't believe she'd drugged him, but it explained why he'd been out for so long. She looked so forlorn, he had to resist the temptation to hug her. "My computers have safeguards preventing anyone downloading my data. What did you use to knock me out?"

"A sleeping elixir."

Simon stood and began pacing. "Aiding the hacker is not worth the long prison sentence you're facing."

Her head jerked up. "I'm not helping the hacker."

He raised one eyebrow. "Don't play me for a fool, Darius. You were the bag lady who came to Madeline Shaw's assistance outside the wine bar. A judge might have taken that into consideration, except disguised as the *senorita*, you stole my wallet and cash."

She picked up a glass of water from the bedside table and gulped down several mouthfuls before meeting his gaze. "I used the money to pay for your dry-cleaning then put the change in an envelope addressed to you and left it in your mail box. Stealing your wallet was the only way I could get your new address."

"You could have asked. I would have taken you home with me."

She blushed. "That wasn't what I wanted."

"You delivered envelopes to my apartment dressed as a skateboarder and pregnant jogger. Envelopes originating from the hacker."

"No, it's a friend of my father's, helping me expose the truth. I made contact after I found an encrypted message on an SD card. It was fixed behind Dad's atom."

Simon stopped pacing. "Why did it take you so long to find it?"

"I gave the atom to my mother when I got back from Nepal. She gave it back to me in March. That's when I discovered the SD card."

"How could you read the encrypted message?"

By the stubborn set of her chin, she didn't plan on answering.

"If you want me to keep you out of prison, you have to trust me."

She exhaled. "Dad and I had an encryption game we used to play to send secret messages that no one else could read. When I opened the SD card, I found a file with an encrypted message from my father. It included a request for me to send a text message to an old ally, using a cheap pre-paid phone. Dad wanted me to ask this person to help me expose a traitor and...a terrorist group. I bought a pre-paid phone then sent the text, *five years late*." Her lips quivered. "I can't betray this person."

Simon tapped his fingers on the edge of the bed. "Did your father ever ask you to think up a password for the Amethyst Code?"

"It's possible." Her lips quivered and she lowered her gaze.

Hell, if she held the third key than she definitely needed protecting. He sighed. "I need a name. Help me and I'll do my best to get you out of this mess.

"This is my fault." She glanced at the door, as if searching for an escape.

"I don't believe that, Darius. The Defense Force hack occurred in February. You found the SD card in March."

She frowned. "Professor Chapman hinted *you* used Dad's program to steal the money. He said you were the true genius behind its development, and my father was a fool to protect you. I don't know who to trust, that's why I've been using disguises and planting listening devices. I have to see this through."

He smiled. "You've proven your worth as a spy. How do you feel about continuing your cover, but working for the good guys?"

She tilted her head. "You mean like a double agent?"

"Sort of. You can never meet with the hacker or any delegate alone and you'd have to keep in regular contact with me or the boys."

She straightened. "That reminds me. How did your friends end up on security detail at a secret cyber summit?"

He exhaled then looked at the ceiling, ordering his thoughts as he considered his reply. If he wanted Darius to trust him, he'd have to give her a little trust too. "Your father recommended me for the Joint Operating Command Center in Canberra. I'd been there a while when I was offered a position on a covert team within the SASR."

"What's that?"

"Special Air Service Regiment. Jarred Steele was my colonel, still is when we're called in as reservists once a year. Our logistics were handled by Lieutenant Colonel Sam Locke, who followed you up the steps earlier. James Talarico, the really big guy, is a weapons expert and held the rank of captain. Ryan Dutch and Nick Flanagan are the two guys who stopped you out in the water. Ryan was a major and Nick a Lieutenant. They're Blackhawk pilots when required. A chopper dropped them into the ocean tonight, so they're on hand if we need them."

"What rank did you hold?"

"Major. I'm in charge of telecommunications, compiling intelligence and gathering information we may need for whatever reason."

Her eyes widened. "Did you go on dangerous assignments?"

"Now and then. We entered hostile territory covertly, did reconnaissance and got out. Your father knew, as we kept in regular contact until about a month before I left for the mission I was on when he died."

"But you're not in the SASR now?"

"Only as a reservist for a couple of weeks a year. The Government disbanded our unit last year. I was to go back to the Joint Control Center and the other boys would have returned to their previous positions in the SASR. However, Jarred decided to take over his grandfather's security firm in Sydney."

She narrowed her eyes. "Steele Security & Special Operations."

His lips twitched. "Yes. The office staff had it running like a well-oiled machine. Jarred saw a need for a specialized unit, so he offered us contracts we couldn't refuse. He oversees our unit directly from his home."

"Doing what?" The look she threw him was skeptical at best.

"Personal security for VIP's and visiting dignitaries. Specialized work for government agencies and occasionally, a missing person retrieval."

"So, you were on a mission at the time of my father's memorial service?"

"Yes, holed up in a mountain village in Afghanistan. I didn't know about the allegations or that he'd died for several weeks."

She drew her knees up and hugged them. "My dad slipped or was murdered and someone framed him."

"Darius, please tell me who asked you to deliver those envelopes?"

"I don't know. We usually communicate by pre-paid phones, but he uses a voice distorter and we have code names. He's Phoenix and I'm Dragonfly. Sometimes I'm sent a package."

"What's in it?"

"Instructions, envelopes for you, a new pre-paid cell phone. The last package had miniature cameras, listening bugs, spyware on USB's and sleeping elixir. Phoenix didn't want me to approach you personally. You and your friends are the only people who know about my disguises."

And Inspector Gibbs, but Simon wouldn't mention that yet. "Who arranged for you to come to this island?"

"Phoenix."

"Did Phoenix ask you to plant the spyware?"

Her shoulders drooped. "Yes, but the insects and frogs were my idea."

He stilled. "Where did you put these insects and frogs?"

"In the bures and along pathways. The frogs were my warning system. I've collected the ones near the bures where I've downloaded data. There are another ten frogs on your side of the cove."

He rubbed his chin. "I'll have to warn Jarred. Phoenix has probably picked up conversations between him, Sam and Talos." He glanced around the room, only now appreciating its opulent, tasteful decor and the inviting bed. Tiredness dragged at him, but he really needed to speak to Jarred. "Get some sleep, Tink. I'll talk to you in the morning."

"If I agree to be a double agent, can I still help Alisi out in the morning?"

"I'll check with Jarred, but as long as you stay in disguise, it should be fine." She looked so crushed, he itched to give her a reassuring hug.

Gritting his teeth, he jogged along the hall then took the stairs down and paced into the kitchen.

Nick sat at the bench eating a large bowl of cereal. "How did it go?"

"She's not the hacker. It's someone calling himself Phoenix. Darius believes he's helping her expose a traitor and terrorist group."

"Bloody hell. Messing with terrorists will get her killed. It could explain the ninja."

"Yes." Simon grabbed an apple off the top of a basket of fruit. "I'm out of here. Do me a favor and keep Ryan away from Tinker Bell?" He grinned. "It's a nickname I gave Darius years ago."

Nick's lips curved. "Isn't Tinker Bell the fairy with a wicked streak?"

"She's also protective of those she loves." Darius stepped into the kitchen. "Why do you want to keep Ryan away from me, Simon?"

He'd been hoping she hadn't heard that. "Because he thinks he's God's gift to women."

"I am," called a voice from the lounge.

Nick laughed. "And a surfing legend in his own mind. You're safe with me, Darius. I've already found the only woman for me."

She grinned. "Good to know. You guys should get some sleep. The summit begins tomorrow, and I have a hunch it's going to be anything but boring."

Simon groaned. "That's what my gut's saying too."

CHAPTER FOURTEEN

Showing up early for breakfast, Simon haunted the dining and reception area. To his aggravation, Darius wasn't about, which left Alisi short staffed. Obvious by the way she and two waitresses ran back and forth while a chef and his plump Fijian off-sider worked in the kitchen.

Although the two waitresses had slim builds, they were taller than Darius, and they'd been about yesterday. As for the chef's off-sider, she'd make three of Darius and flaunted a magnificent, frizzy hairdo.

At least Jarred had agreed to Darius continuing as Bellini, where they could keep an eye on her. The fact his boss wouldn't be interrogating her relieved Simon. He'd witnessed Jarred build a rapport with insurgents then extract valuable information with little effort. He'd also seen him extract information through sleep deprivation and intimidation.

After finding the infrared sensor frog near his bure, Simon had to give Darius her due for their realistic appearance. The warbles were entirely believable, except for the fact frogs usually went quiet when disturbed.

Delegates had stopped filing into the dining room twenty minutes ago and were now growing restless. He glanced around, noting Professor Nutlan and Heckle speaking in lowered voices. The breakfast buffet had been cleared and replaced with water jugs and fruit. The doors to reception and the kitchen had been closed and two security guards stationed on the far side of the pool.

"So much for the lecture on punctuality," called one of the New Zealand delegates. "I could have swum a dozen more laps."

Coming to his feet, Alistair brought all conversation to a halt. "I apologize for the delay. Tragically, one of our American delegates, Lex Boyd, fell to his death this morning while jogging along a cliff top path. Mr. Boyd's body has been retrieved and placed in a freezer. Once communications are restored, we will notify the relevant authorities."

He rubbed a finger back and forth across his forehead. "I would insist from now on anyone looking to exercise, please stay clear of cliff faces, and don't swim on the east side of the island. The reef and current is far too dangerous."

After a quick glance at his watch he grimaced. "Another delegate appears to have slept in, so we will have to start without him."

Doing a slow perusal of the room, Simon noted somber expressions on all faces. He also noticed Professor Chapman missing. He hadn't been at breakfast either.

"Welcome," said Alistair. "Each of you are attending this summit with the sole purpose of preventing future breaches through international cyber fraud. Among you are computer scientists with extensive experience in many fields, representatives from intelligence agencies, and key personnel from the world's major financial institutions. I apologize for the secrecy and confiscation of your communication devices, but it is essential we keep this summit and its location secret."

"*Excusez-moi, monsieur*. Can you guarantee our safety?" asked Marguerite. "Are you sure the American wasn't pushed?" Her gaze drifted to Simon. "With all the rumors, I'm not so sure I feel safe alone in my bure at night." Her husky purr drew all eyes, as did her curvy figure.

While attempting another flirtation last night, Marguerite had informed Simon she worked for a bank in Paris and had an open relationship with her partner. Every lingering touch on his arm had been an invitation to indulge. He couldn't have been more disinterested.

Alistair smiled. "Marguerite, we have two security teams on the island. They are extremely capable and will be patrolling day and night."

"*Merci beaucoup*, Alistair."

He nodded then gripped his hands behind his back. "Five and a half years ago, at a summit similar to this, Professor Alexander

Cortez claimed he and an associate had inadvertently created a program that could infiltrate almost any institution. He vowed their initial aim had been to develop counter-measures to block such a program, and that would still be his priority."

Murmurs of disbelief and pointed stares reached Simon.

Alistair cleared his throat. "Unfortunately, Professor Cortez's announcement drew a lot of criticism. Soon after, we had major breaches, where millions disappeared from several world banks. Rumors surfaced that Professor Cortez orchestrated these criminal breaches in defiance, an act to show his critics how wrong they were."

His gaze lingered on Simon, drawing more unwanted attention. "As a fellow computer scientist and long-time acquaintance, I believed Alexander to be a hardworking and conscientious man. Would you agree, Simon?"

"Yes." Where this was going, Simon couldn't guess.

Alistair strolled to the other side of the room. "Professor Cortez's commitment in the fight against cyber fraud was well known. After the breach, he was interviewed by the Federal Police and released, yet he remained a person of interest. With his death, the police lost their best chance at apprehending the villain."

"Well, somebody must know something," called a Canadian.

Alistair grimaced. "Over the last five years, two highly respected computer scientists have died in hit-and-run accidents. Their deaths wouldn't necessarily have raised alarm bells, except five other senior computer scientists have been reported missing."

Raised voices and muttering broke out across the room.

Alistair waited until he had silence. "Specialists scoured each of the scientists' email accounts and found bizarre job offers from a respected international organization. Further investigation revealed the sender wasn't an employee of the company and the emails were fake. The Federal police found the same email on Professor Cortez's computer."

The noise level rose again.

Simon leaned back and stared at the thatched roof, his mind racing as he tried to join the dots.

Alistair clapped his hands and achieved instant silence. "The general consensus from our intelligence agencies, is that the emails were sent from a terrorist organization, to recruit scientists with the capability to hack into banks and major utility databases."

Professor Heckle gasped. "Are you saying Alexander worked for a terrorist group?"

"No. I'm saying there is a chance he met with someone, perhaps out of suspicion or curiosity, and when he refused their offer, his family could have been threatened. We will never know, but there are computer scientists, myself included, who believe Professor Cortez could have been murdered."

The room erupted as delegates loudly voiced their opinions, disbelief or anxiety.

Simon studied Alistair carefully. He appeared to be in charge of the summit, which would give him access to confidential documents.

Alistair strolled to a table at the front and picked up a notebook. "Several recent breaches are of deep concern to our governments." He looked to a man leaning on a walking stick. "Sir William, would you care to explicate?"

"I would. Thank you." The Englishman limped to the center of the room. "I work within Britain's National Cyber Crime Unit. Nine weeks ago, an unknown hacker redirected an Australian Naval frigate to rescue a group of people off the coast of Western Australia."

There were several gasps.

"It appears the hacker is in possession of Professor Cortez's program. He or she has accessed two levels. As you can all appreciate, governments and intelligence agencies throughout the world are extremely concerned."

"Why divert a Navy frigate?" asked Professor Nutlan.

Alistair shrugged. "We assume the hacker has a hidden agenda. Therefore, if any of you have been approached with an incredible job offer, or in connection with Alexander's program, or think you know something, please discuss it with me or Sir William privately. It is understood a third secret key is needed for the program to leverage its full potential, which could potentially allow the hacker access to any database in the world. At this stage, we can only guess the catastrophic damage this could do. That, ladies and gentlemen, is our number one worry."

Professor Heckle's erect posture and flushed face caught Simon's attention. He narrowed his eyes as the professor dabbed at his sweaty forehead and neck with a handkerchief. Was he struggling with the humidity or something Alistair had said?

"You mentioned several breaches," called a male voice at the back of the room.

Sir William nodded. "The money stolen five and a half years ago has been replaced, with interest."

"Holy shit." Simon leaned forward in his chair. "Did you trace the breach's origin?"

"Yes, which is surprising in itself. The money came from a shell company in the Bahamas. Further investigation suggests it has links to a terrorist group. We have intelligence that the terrorists did not instigate the transfers and are hell bent on retribution."

Simon rubbed his jaw. This was bad, very bad. Replacing stolen funds then leaving a footprint straight to a terrorist organization was suicidal, or the work of a cyber wizard with an agenda. Phoenix must have Alexander's program and had started making retribution, probably hoping to draw out the traitor and terrorist group. Or, he wanted to cause worldwide panic to attract the highest bidder for the program. Cold fingers of dread wrapped around Simon's throat. Darius had no idea of the danger she faced.

A commotion out in reception drew all eyes. Professor Chapman strode in scowling and agitated. He glared at Simon before taking a seat. "My apologies, I was inadvertently delayed."

Alistair's eyes narrowed. "Your attendance although late is appreciated, Professor. Did you also forget you had a meeting with me last night?"

"No, I did not. Circumstances prevented me attending."

"Perhaps you had too much to drink," called one of the Americans, sniggering.

"Poppy cock. I had one glass of red in my bure, whereby I passed out until two this morning. I then drank a glass of water. Next thing I know it's nine o'clock, and I've missed breakfast." He stomped to an empty seat. "I suspect I was drugged to prevent me voicing my suspicions." He scowled at Simon again. "Someone wants me out of the way."

Without a flicker of emotion, Simon took in Richard's accusing glare. After propositioning Darius, the professor deserved his humiliation. Simon made a mental note not to drink from any bottle he didn't personally open. He also needed to find Darius urgently, before the hacker put a bullet in her head or terrorists abducted her.

❦

Grinning like the village idiot, Darius piled a load of towels into the industrial-sized washing machine. Assuming her newest identity had been easier than she'd anticipated.

Being short-staffed and having witnessed Professor Chapman's unwelcome advances, it took little to convince the staff to help her. Explaining her idea and background in theatre costumes had intrigued them. Her disguise had astonished them. Best of all, after some thought, Alisi assigned Darius duties enabling her to move about easily. Unfortunately, she hadn't had an opportunity to reveal her disguise to Simon before the dining room had been closed off, and he'd been surrounded at the morning tea break.

Adding detergent to the machine, Darius pressed the start button then picked up a pile of fresh towels for the next bure on her list. It was the largest on the cove and where three of Simon's friends were staying. She waved to the chef, busy picking herbs from his kitchen garden. By the size of him, he sampled everything he cooked.

She'd met Sam earlier on his way through reception. Freshly showered and shaven, no one would guess he'd spent hours patrolling the island last night. He'd stopped to ask her name. Realizing he must have a list of all staff; she'd let him in on the secret. His stunned disbelief had boosted her confidence and brought on a fit of giggles.

Coming to the bure, she knocked on the glass slider. "Housekeeping."

Hearing no answer, she inserted her master key and pushed the door wide. Her housekeeping chores left her clammy but provided perfect cover to install spyware and download data while the delegates had breakfast.

Surprisingly the bure was extremely tidy. Beds made, towels hanging neatly, not a cup, wine glass or empty bottle lying about as she'd found in the other bures.

As she cleaned the bure, she searched every robe, cupboard and drawer. She looked under beds and couches but found no computers. Other than three duffle bags, containing neatly folded male clothing and three shaving bags, there was nothing to identify the occupants. Unlike Professor Chapman, these men didn't carry Viagra. Not that it surprised her. Each of them was healthy and virile looking.

Relocking the slider, she threw the used towels in her trolley then pushed it to the end of the private path, where a frog launched into its throaty warble. With a quick glance about, she ducked down, scrounged under a fern and retrieved the noisy amphibian.

The other cleaners had done the majority of bures, leaving her with only four, which worked out well, as the delegates would be breaking for lunch soon. She approached Simon's bure and knocked on the glass slider.

"Housekeeping!" Unlocking the slider, she peeped inside. The bure lay neat as a pin and empty. She changed the towels, wiped over the vanity and toilet, emptied the bin then restocked the fridge with bottled water. One of her green frogs sat in the middle of a shallow bowl of Frangipani flowers.

Grinning, she left the bure then trudged along the path to where she'd stationed a frog. Ducking behind her trolley, she lifted the fronds of a golden palm and reached under, unsurprised to find a pad of bare dirt. At least she knew where he'd found the frog.

Gripping the trolley's handle, she heaved herself up. For now, she had a load of washing to see to. After that she would find a way to speak to Simon.

Sweat trickled down her back and between her breasts as she lumbered along the path to the laundry, stopping along the way to silence the remaining frogs.

With four industrial-sized dryers going flat out, the humidity in the small room had become oppressive. Her silicon body suit was quickly becoming a stifling sauna.

The oppressive humidity sucked all Darius' remaining energy, leaving her struggling to load an empty washing machine. It was a relief to press the button and escape outside, where coconut palms shaded the staff courtyard and the only other occupant was changing a gas cylinder.

Not the slightest breeze stirred. "*Bula*, Etera, my goodness it's hot."

He grinned, looking her up and down. "*Bula*, Bellini. We expect a storm later. That will cool things down."

"Good, I'm melting inside this costume. Where's Alisi?"

"She's having an early lunch with her husband. He looks after the golf course."

"Oh, yes, your brother told me. Who else works up there?"

"At the moment, no one. On Sunday the rest of our staff come back and things will return to normal."

"I'm happy to help out." She longed to sit down but worried she wouldn't get up again. "Does Alisi need me for anything else?"

"You could watch reception until she gets back."

"No worries." Leaving him to his chores, she entered the kitchen, waved to the busy staff, who thanks to Alisi, Etera and Vijay, hadn't questioned her sudden change in appearance. Any delegate asking about Bellini would be stone-walled.

Stepping into reception, she was met with a blast of cool air, not that it reached her heated skin, but it was certainly better than the laundry or under the direct sun. Leaning on the high counter, she lifted her face to the giant overhead fan, relishing the breeze. Underneath her wig and bodysuit, she was a lather of sweat and incredibly itchy.

Intent on her newfound pleasure, it took a minute to realize footsteps were approaching. She straightened as the dining room doors opened. Two delegates walked out, their voices low and animated. They each pulled a packet of cigarettes from their shirt pockets then made for the end of the portico, where sand bins had been placed for ash and butts.

More footsteps and three scowling delegates strode past the desk. They stopped by the wall of bougainvillea then after a brief conversation took the path leading to the south side of the cove. It appeared the delegates were breaking for lunch early.

Simon and two men strolled out, stopping at the water cooler for a drink. They were joined by the French woman and Sir William, the man with the cane.

With the doors to the dining room wide open, Darius could see Etera and the two waitresses rushing to set up the buffet tables. Most of the delegates were out by the pool, chatting in small groups. She waited for Simon to look her way, but he seemed preoccupied, so she decided she might as well eavesdrop until Alisi returned.

The French woman squeezed in next to Simon. "*Monsieur* Hawke, do you have any idea of the hacker's identity?"

"I'm closing in. It's only a matter of time."

She pressed widespread fingers across generous breasts, perfectly showcased by the low-cut neckline of a fitted cream dress. "Your reputation precedes you, *mon cher*. You should consider coming to *Pari*, to work for *moi*."

Annoyance streaked through Darius. She didn't want Simon accepting a job in Paris, she wanted him to find out the truth behind the allegations and her father's death. She straightened a pamphlet display to give the appearance of actually doing something.

"Simon, have you ever considered joining a cyber fraud agency?" Sir William asked. "Once we've caught the hacker, we could use someone with your experience in our London office."

"Washington might be more to your taste," said a tall, dark skinned American. "You will appreciate the remuneration package we offer."

"His allegiance should be with Australia," stated a ruddy-faced, solid man. "The Australian Government can match anything you people offer."

"I will make it worth your while, *mon cher*." The French woman's husky voice dropped to a seductive purr. "You will find nowhere as agreeable as *Pari*."

"Except a tropical island in the South Pacific," volunteered Darius, irritated by the woman's flirty performance.

Simon glanced over, then did a double take, the warm humor in his eyes curling her toes. "I would have to agree. This is paradise after all."

"You there." Sweating heavily, Professor Chapman came barreling through reception, causing the group to shift so he could reach the counter. "There was a waitress here last night called Bellini. Where can I find her?"

"*Bula*, sir." Darius kept her voice high and bouncy. "Bellini is not one of our regular resort staff. She was only helping out yesterday."

"That's all very well, but where can I find her?"

"She is off duty somewhere with her husband."

"Blast, this summit is turning into one disappointment after another." With a surly grunt, Professor Chapman stomped out of reception.

Simon left his fan club and leisurely strolled over. "*Bula*. I couldn't help but hear what you told the gentleman. You said Bellini is with her husband?"

The other four were within hearing, foiling Darius' plan to reveal her identity. She frowned, knowing it would draw Simon's attention to her thick, black eyebrows. Tapping a pencil against her double chin, she pretended to ponder. "Yes, they were planning a walk along the beach after lunch. Can I help you, sir?"

"Not at the moment. *Vinaka.*" Simon turned away, nodded at the four delegates still waiting to collar him, then strode out to the pool area.

Only then did Darius notice Alistair Finch standing beside a potted palm watching her. He strolled across the foyer, his attention now on the four delegates. "I can't blame you for headhunting Simon Hawke. He is a genius and would work well in any of your intelligence agencies, or banking corporations, but accosting him like a pack of salivating hyenas will not gain his interest." Shaking his head, he wandered outside.

Darius slumped over the desk, her hands shaking as the four delegates followed him. She'd done it. Pulled off the biggest scam of her life. Enough people had seen her this morning that she could move freely about the island without raising suspicion. And she wouldn't draw unwanted male attention either.

"Phew." She plodded to the water cooler, filled a plastic cup with cold water and gulped it down her parched throat. Her feet were killing her. She ached from the weight of the silicon bodysuit, her head itched from the hot wig, and her face begged to be released from the tight mask.

Outside under the portico, a golf cart came to a jerky stop. Alisi jumped out and waved to the driver. He waved back, a huge grin spreading over his leathery Nepalese face. The cup dropped from Darius' nerveless fingers.

"Heaven help me." Five years had passed since she'd seen Harnoop escort her father up the well-worn track, but she would know his cheeky grin anywhere. Harnoop hadn't died in the avalanche.

Struggling for breath, she fought the rising fury. He knew the truth. He'd witnessed her father's death. He was supposed to have died in an avalanche, so what the blazes was he doing on this island?

A chilling intensity blasted through her like a glacial wind, leaving behind a calm, determined resolve. Harnoop would be about thirty now. His days of living incognito in paradise were at an end. Darius' award-winning performance was only just beginning. She picked up the cup as Alisi came through the main doors.

"Alisi. Who was that man?"

"*Bula*, Bellini. That is my husband, Hans. He looks after the golf course."

"The greenskeeper? I heard he abseils down the cliffs to reclaim golf balls."

"Yes, but don't worry. He spent many years mountain climbing in Nepal."

Under her heavy jowls, Darius clenched her teeth. Not that Alisi would see anything but a pleasant, chubby smile. "How long have you been married?"

Alisi's smile widened. "Three years, and we are expecting our first baby."

Darius glanced at Alisi's barely rounded stomach then back to her open face. "Where did you and Hans meet?"

"On this island. He came for a holiday five years ago and stayed. I will introduce you tonight after the show. Thank you for your help today. Remember we need a couple of hours to teach you the *Meke.* It would be better if you don't wear this costume." She giggled as she hurried through to the dining room.

Dumbstruck, Darius tried to fathom her next move. Why, of all the islands in the world, did Harnoop come here? Perhaps he worked for the person who set up her father. Perhaps he'd killed her father.

A web had many threads, but only one spider spun them. She closed her eyes as another thought struck. Harnoop had regarded her with mild curiosity. As Alisi's husband he would know it was a disguise, but only Phoenix knew Darius Cortez was staying in the small villa, so he couldn't be connected with Harnoop. Could he?

It was plain to see Alisi didn't know Darius' true identity or she would never mention her husband's Nepalese background. And Harnoop had been here five years, so whoever organized the summit must know, and had brought all the players to the one isolated location for a reason.

The Harnoop she remembered had been a gentle soul. He'd loved her father's stories of sailing to exotic locations, then dropping anchor to snorkel and scuba dive among colorful fish and incredible coral formations. The Lau Archipelago and Cook Islands had been favorites of her father's memories. Maybe Harnoop witnessed her father's murder then took off to hide here.

Leaving reception, she plodded round the building to the staff courtyard. It was empty so she sat at a table under two coconut palms. Her mind reeled.

She wanted to confront Harnoop, although that could put her own life in danger. It came down to trust and gut instinct. She needed to speak to Simon.

CHAPTER FIFTEEN

Simon checked he had no company before jogging along the winding path to the furthest point of the cove. Darius' latest disguise would have fooled him if she hadn't spoken in her normal, slightly aggrieved voice. Her shoulders and backside were triple the width of her usual slender frame, stretching the long Frangipani dress to the max. The untamed hair, enormous breasts and belly looked the real deal, as did the bronzed tone of her skin, chubby cheeks, broad nose, double chin and bushy eyebrows. She had to be sweltering under the extra weight.

Jarred stood looking out to sea, waiting for him.

"Hi, boss. I haven't got long as I've arranged to meet Darius after lunch."

"Anything to report?"

"We've been through all the major cyber breaches over the last twelve months and set a few strategies in place. Of concern is the fact a number of computer scientists have disappeared in the last five years, and two have died in hit and run accidents. It appears they all received astronomical job offers before their disappearance. Also, the money supposedly stolen by Professor Cortez, has been returned. The deposits came from accounts allegedly held by a terrorist group. That's a death wish in itself. I can only assume our hacker is attempting to draw in bigger players with much deeper pockets."

"Fucking hell." Jarred paced back and forth. "We should have been made aware of this sooner. Is there anything else I need to know?"

"Richard Chapman arrived late and grumpy after Darius drugged him with a sleeping elixir. He also made it clear he suspects I'm the hacker, but from the job offers I've been receiving all morning, few delegates care what he thinks."

"He could be trying to divert attention away from himself." Jarred rubbed his jaw. "Did you find anything suspicious on the data Darius downloaded?"

"Nothing that relates to our hacker. You know those croaking frogs that have been driving Talos crazy?"

"Yes."

"They're part of Darius' arsenal and have infrared sensors. Walk close enough, you set off a frog soundtrack. This morning I impounded one outside my bure and pulled it apart. She must have brought them with her."

Jarred raised an eyebrow. "A quirky alarm system. You might want to search your bure for bugs."

"Done. Darius admitted to planting listening devices in all the bures. I found one of the striped plastic beetles stuck to an overhead beam. Talos and Sam debugged your bure this morning."

"I'm not worried. After viewing the contents of that box, we've been careful what we say in our bure."

Simon glanced back along the path. "There's a large Fijian woman on reception. Have you seen her?"

"From a distance." Jarred's lips twitched. "Sam suggested I take a quick look after he met her pushing a housekeeping trolley."

Simon laughed. "If she hadn't spoken, I never would have twigged it was Darius. Then Richard Chapman stormed in, demanding to know where he could find Bellini. She told him Bellini was with her husband, whereby Richard left in a foul temper. Darius told me I could find Bellini on the beach after lunch. As we were surrounded by delegates, I reasoned it was her way of setting up a meeting with me."

Jarred's eyes narrowed. "At breakfast, I questioned Alisi. Apparently, several delegates and a security guard have been pursuing Bellini. Once I assured Alisi my interest lay in maintaining security, and I have to account for everyone, she told me Bellini is the guest staying in the small villa, which of course we know.

Jarred looked past Simon. "Here's Talos."

The big guy's long legs ate up the path. "What's up?"

"We've located Darius." Jarred chuckled. "Simon tells me those monotonous croaking frogs are an alarm system, set up by Darius to warn her when someone is approaching."

"No kidding." Talos placed his hands on his hips. "Very clever. It's a good thing she's decided to work with us, instead of against us."

Jarred looked out to sea. "If terrorists get wind of this summit and suspect the hacker is here, we may face a much larger problem."

"Wow." Talos looked from Simon to Jarred. "This summit could be a scam to get *everyone* who was close to Professor Cortez in one place."

"It's looking that way." Jarred tipped his head back and stared at the sky for a minute, then he met Simon's gaze. "You had a huge input in developing the program, which makes you a desirable commodity to any terrorist group."

"I know." Simon rolled his shoulders in an attempt to ease the building tension. "Darius said Professor Chapman mentioned the summit, which shows how seriously he takes its secrecy. And, he's been throwing about accusations from the minute he laid eyes on me. I suspect he's been badmouthing me to anyone who will listen."

Jarred's lips thinned. "Your reputation precedes you. One word of advice though."

"I'm listening."

"We've had one computer scientist fall off a cliff this morning, so be on your guard."

"I will. I need to meet Darius before the next session starts, but first I want to grab something to eat. I'll check in with you later." He strode along the path, aware Jarred and Talos watched until he rounded a curve. It wasn't hard to guess their thoughts. Becoming personally involved could affect his judgment.

Entering reception, he paused by a potted palm, noting Phillip Nutlan and the English woman seated at a cane setting. They were leaning forward, speaking in hushed voices, their expressions intent as they conversed.

Alisi hurried out of the dining room, carrying a tray of drinks. As she halted beside them all conversation ceased. Seemingly unaware of the hiatus, she picked up empty plates as she informed them a tropical storm was expected later tonight.

A male bellowing for help had Simon turning his back on reception and sprinting past the pool area. Other delegates poured out of the dining room, also making for the beach.

Heart pounding, Simon leaped the steps, landed on the sand and gave chase. He sighted the large chef comforting a sobbing waitress near an outcrop of rocks. Several feet away Sam and Talos were bent over a body on the sand.

A fist clenched Simon's heart, squeezing so tight, he could barely place one foot in front of the other as he skirted the crowd. He stopped beside Jarred and forced himself to look. Relief surged. It wasn't Tink.

Delegates surrounded them, calling out over the top of each other.

"Who is it?"

"Is there a heartbeat?"

"What happened?"

Confusion ruled as the crowd grew louder.

Sam and Talos were attempting to resuscitate Keith Heckle. The top of his bald crown shone stark white.

Several men from the other security team ushered the growing crowd back.

Jarred stood hands on hips, watching. "The waitress found him in knee deep water. With all the blood, she presumed he slipped on the rocks, whacked the back of his head then fell in the ocean and drowned."

Simon gave a low whistle. "Or he met with foul play."

"That's my take," murmured Jarred. "Besides the skull injury, there's bruising around his throat. I found his hair-piece near the wharf further along the beach. Whoever murdered Keith Heckle counted on the outgoing tide to dispose of the body."

"Did the waitress see anyone up this end of the beach?"

"She said it was empty."

"No!" The soft whisper came from behind, sending goose bumps rippling along Simon's arms and legs. Chubby fingers clutched his wrist. "What happened to him?"

Stealing himself, Simon glanced down into big brown eyes. "I don't know." He stared at her round face, unable to detect any familiarity, yet it was definitely Darius. "It's very hot out here, I'll walk you back."

Matching her slow awkward steps, Simon didn't speak until they were well away from the crowd. "We need to find somewhere private to talk."

She nodded, puffing way too harshly. "Your bure."

"It might be too far. I don't like the way you're breathing." The disguise was fabulous, but he needed to get her out of it.

As they reached the top of the steps, an Asian man carrying a medical box came running from reception. Seeing them, he paused, before dashing down the steps.

Simon wondered at Darius' stiffness as she stared after the man. Her eyes were troubled. "Are you all right?"

She blinked several times. "Yes—no. I..." She swayed. "Need to sit down."

"Here, lean on me." He helped her to a cane chair outside reception.

"Thank you." She fell into the chair and closed her eyes, oblivious to him taking off the heavy, high wedges. Her tiny feet were crisscrossed with angry red welts. She winced but didn't object when he massaged her feet.

"Zat man was murzured, wasn't he?" The slurred word worried Simon. She had to be melting under the wig and thick additional bits. She needed cooling, but how the heck he was going to carry her to his bure, he didn't know.

"Simo, what's happening?"

"Talos. I need help moving Darius."

The disbelief on the big guy's face was almost comical. "No way is this Darius."

"It is. We need to get her inside my bure, where I can cool her down."

Clearly unconvinced, Talos bent and lifted her in his arms. "Jesus, she's heavy." He staggered along the path. "You sure about this?"

"Yes." Simon scooped up her shoes and after a quick scan of the area, followed Talos along the meandering path. Hibiscus shrubs screened them from the crowd on the beach, which by the few glimpses Simon stole, had grown to include all the delegates and security. He noticed an enormous Monarch butterfly high on a Hibiscus branch. He'd seen several about, their orange and black wings dotted with white spots on the edges.

Darius lay limp in Talos' arms, which worried Simon. He would ring her neck when she recovered. That made no sense at all. Shaking his head, he overtook them to unlock his door then slide it open. "Lay her on the bed, I'll run a cool bath."

"With pleasure." Talos lowered her then stood back and arched his back. "If you're right, I'll eat my words, but until I see evidence, we are not undressing this woman."

"That's reasonable." Simon flicked on the cold-water faucet over the spa then paced back to the bed. "Lift up her sleeve."

Complying, Talos pushed the cotton material up her arm, revealing a banded overlay of spongy silicon below the thick elbow. "Christ." He peeled it back then pulled the silicon gloved arm and hand off Darius. Her own slim arm and tiny hand lay limp on the bed. "It's a wonder she can breathe in this heat."

Darius didn't stir as Simon eased off the frizzy wig. "Hell, Tink." Her head was completely bald, and bumpy. Lifting her head slightly he found a piece of Velcro. It was a facemask completely covering her head and extending down her thickened neck and under the dress. Relieved, he peeled it off.

Her golden hair, now a washed-out brown, stuck to her skull in a knotted mass, her delicate face, brick red. "Little idiot."

Talos pulled a knife from his boot and handed it to Simon. "Cut her out of that dress so we can get the sweat suit off before she suffocates."

"Thanks." Gripping the bodice of her dress, he made a slit then ripped it in two. A choked bark escaped Simon. He'd exposed a spandex bodysuit containing the biggest set of silicon breasts and belly he'd ever seen. The body cast reached her knees.

Talos shook his head. "It must undo at the back. Let's roll her over."

They found a zip which Simon opened all the way down over the broad back to voluptuous bum cheeks. A Velcro strip ran from the neck of the silicon body cast down to the base of her spine. Tearing the strips apart, Simon grimaced at the heat of her sweat-drenched skin. Seeing a black bra strap and bikini pants, he pushed the silicon sides further apart.

Talos gripped the edges and pulled. "I don't know how she managed to get into it on her own. He stripped the artificial bulk away. "Fuck, this thing weighs a ton. No wonder she collapsed."

The heat of her skin under Simon's fingers had him scowling. "I need to cool her down." He lifted her in his arms. Awareness flared, along with a sense of calm. "Thanks, Talos. I'll take it from here. Can you let the boss know she's safe?"

"No worries." Talos shoved the body cast in a wardrobe then left, closing the glass slider behind him.

Cradling Darius', Simon carried her to the bathroom then lowered her into the spa.

She jerked, gasping as her eyes sprang open. Brown contact lenses shielded her true eye color, but there was no mistaking their genuine shock. "Simon?" She shot up straight, covering her bikini bra with crossed arms. "I had nothing to do with Professor Heckle's death."

"No, that would take someone a lot bigger and stronger than you, sweet pea."

"My father's Nepalese Sherpa didn't die in an avalanche. He lives here on the island."

"Are you sure?"

"Yes, I recognized him straight away."

Simon stared into her worried eyes as he mentally ran down the list of resort staff. "Hans, the greenskeeper?"

"His real name is Harnoop." She closed her eyes and sank under the water, dunking her head completely. The brown dye leached from her hair as it drifted about her shoulders like ripples of Persian silk.

Captured by her delicate beauty and willowy curves, Simon felt a universal shift. He'd had a sincere affection for Darius as a teenager. In fact, if he were honest, he'd adored her and been genuinely disgruntled when she suddenly dropped out of his life.

It might explain why he'd been drawn to all her disguises, and his bizarre reaction to them, even now. She was messing with his normally clear thinking. He needed to keep her safe and in disguise until he could get her off the island.

CHAPTER SIXTEEN

Depriving her lungs of air wouldn't make Simon magically disappear. There were more important factors to consider than her own humiliation.

Darius surfaced, dragging in a deep breath. "I noticed Harnoop before you came into reception this morning. He's married to Alisi and they're expecting a baby."

"This gets more complicated by the minute." He filled a glass of water then handed it to her. "I want you in protective custody."

"No. If Harnoop wasn't directly involved in my father's death then he witnessed it and is hiding on the island. I need to speak with him."

"Darius, you're a liability. The hacker may well have killed Keith Heckle and the American. It's also possible he has deliberately antagonized a terrorist group to draw their attention to this summit. It's too dangerous to go wandering about. Leave the Sherpa to me and my friends."

"Simon, I have to be the one who speaks to Harnoop. If he's innocent, I'm risking his safety, but if he's involved, I need to know you've got my back."

A double knock sounded on the glass slider.

Simon glanced over his shoulder. "That's Jarred. I'll let him know about the Sherpa." He drew the door closed behind him.

Quick as a flash, she scrambled out of the bath, wrapped a towel around her torso then cracked the door open.

Simon stood aside for his boss to enter. "What's the verdict?"

Jarred Steele stepped inside, his gaze scanning the room then zooming in on the door she was hiding behind. "Keith Heckle was

151

definitely hit with a blunt object then strangled and dumped in the water. How's your mistress of disguise?"

"Recovering." Simon flicked a glance her way. "Two delegates dead within hours of each other. We have a problem."

"That's putting it mildly." Jarred strolled about, like a caged panther. "As Alistair Finch can't notify the relevant authorities, I advised him to have the satellite dish reconnected. Unfortunately, it's been sabotaged."

"Shit." Simon glanced her way again. "Ask Talos or Sam to take the runabout to the closest island. Then they can notify the mainland."

"Out of the question. According to Etera, the seas are too rough, and a storm is building. I'm hoping Madeline has got word to Gibbs." Jarred picked up Darius' wig. "I questioned Hans, the greenskeeper who found the American. He noticed a jogger stop and speak to a person on the bluff above the golf course. Twenty minutes later he discovered the twisted body of a man on rocks below the cliff. He saw no sign of the other person."

Unable to stay silent a moment longer, Darius threw open the door. "Hans is the Sherpa who was with my father when he died. He obviously didn't get buried in the avalanche." She hesitated. "He could be in hiding and recognized the murderer but doesn't want to get involved. I bet that's why he changed his name from Harnoop to Hans."

Jarred raised an eyebrow. "They're assumptions, Miss Cortez. I deal in facts."

"Call me Darius." She paced back and forth between the two men. "I assume you examined the area?"

"Of course. The track is several meters from the cliff edge, and I found no dislodged rocks or loose dirt to indicate Lex Boyd slipped. I did find trampled grass that suggests something heavy may have been dragged along the cliff top to a rock ledge."

"A body?"

"It looks that way."

Grimacing, Simon dropped a robe over her shoulders then turned to Jarred. "What's the mood among the delegates?"

"Most are howling for the satellite dish to be repaired. It did not go down well when Sam informed them it had been sabotaged. Professor Heckle must have seen or heard something."

Simon put out his hand to stop Darius as she was about to pass between them again. "Keith was agitated this morning. I suspect arranging to speak with Alistair might have something to do with his death."

"This will put you back in the hot seat." Jarred ran a hand through his short hair. "Richard Chapman wants all delegates interviewed to verify their whereabouts during the break. You were with me, which I can't verify without raising suspicion."

"At least Darius is safe."

Jarred's lips quirked as he looked at her. "You certainly have a knack for creating believable costumes. We may use your services in the future, if you're interested."

"Sure."

His eyes narrowed. "Simon mentioned this friend of your father's uses a voice distorter and only communicates on pre-paid phones. If you had to guess, would you say it's a man or a woman?"

"A man, I think. He sometimes calls me 'my dear', but most of the time it's Dragonfly." She shrugged. "He doesn't know I've been using costumes to carry out his instructions."

"He brought you to the island though." Simon opened the fridge and took out three bottles of water, checking the seals before he handed one to her and one to Jarred. "We could hide you on the catamaran with Ryan and Nick. Then, if there's trouble, they can get you away quickly."

"Please don't. I'm your best link to the hacker."

"It's too dangerous." Simon gripped her empty hand. "I don't want him anywhere near you, and we don't have the manpower to follow you about the resort."

"I'm safe while there are plenty of people around me and, at night, I will have Ryan and Nick to guard me."

"That won't work." Jarred rubbed his chin. "I've got them bunkered down on the highest points of the island. Nobody can approach or leave without being seen."

She lifted her chin defiantly. "What about Talos or Sam?"

"They've regular patrols that can't be rearranged to protect the daughter of Professor Cortez, who shouldn't even be on the island."

"Then I'll stay here with Simon."

153

Simon choked. "Not a good idea."

She adjusted her towel. "It's *brilliant*. I'm a guest, so there's nothing to stop me having a holiday romance with a handsome man I met on the beach."

He grinned. "You think I'm handsome?"

"That's beside the point. We're on an island paradise. The cool ocean breezes, sultry days and warm sand underfoot is the perfect setting for a holiday romance. I'm putting a huge amount of trust in you, so the least you can do is let me stay here at night, while I do a little reconnaissance through the day."

Jarred raised an eyebrow at Simon. "Your call."

"It seems I don't have a choice." He opened a drawer then pulled out a white T-shirt and threw it to her. "What about your hair? The color has leached out."

"Again." She sighed. "I'll need to borrow a hat. I've got more dye at the villa."

He passed her a cap then turned to Jarred. "The hacker has to be holed up somewhere. Have you searched the large villa?"

"Yes."

Darius gasped. "There's a bunker underneath it. I had a quick look last night, but I'm not very brave when it comes to dark, underground bunkers. I had planned to go back today and check it out."

"A bunker?" Jarred turned to Simon. "Go with her. Sir William has cancelled the rest of the day's program. I'll have Talos keep watch outside." He opened the slider then stepped through and strode back along the path.

Darius pulled on the large T-shirt and cap. "Let's go. I agreed to be part of the dance troupe tonight, and Alisi needs to teach me the moves."

Shaking his head, Simon followed her out of the bure. "We'll cut through the gardens to the road. If we meet anyone, let me do the talking."

"I have a Vesper behind the staff courtyard."

"Of course you do." He caught her hand in his. "How did you convince Alisi and her staff to go along with your charade?"

"They think I'm trying out that costume for a theatre production. And, it's a good way to avoid Professor Chapman."

"Good thinking. How exactly is this imaginary romance of ours going to play out?"

She couldn't hold in the giggle. "Trust me, I'm an amateur actress."

Still holding hands, they ran through the gardens, giving the portico a wide berth, then slipped through the gate to the staff courtyard. It wasn't empty.

The chef sat on an upturned crate, whittling a turtle from a sizeable chunk of wood. He looked up, his gaze snagging on their joined hands, before rising to give Simon a hard look. "Everything okay, Bellini?"

"Yes, Vijay. I'm taking my new friend for a ride on the Vesper."

He grunted, not taking his eyes off Simon. "If you're not back for your dancing lesson, I'll come looking for you."

Simon gave Vijay a nod. "She'll be back, safe and sound."

"Make sure she is." Vijay went back to whittling.

By the loud buzz inside the dining room, delegates and speakers had gathered, likely demanding answers.

Darius started the Vesper. As soon as Simon climbed on behind, she zoomed up the winding road. Her arms and legs glowed golden-brown, so she wouldn't need to apply another coat of tanning lotion.

"I rather like this espionage stuff." Uttering a laugh, she accelerated, leaning into the corner. She had four hours before Alisi needed to teach her the *Meke* dance. Four hours in which to search the bunker, recolor and crimp her hair, disguise the contours of her face, and show Simon what her Goshawk could do.

❧

The luxurious villa was monstrous. Having lifted the keys from Alisi's office yesterday, Darius had done a thorough inspection during the afternoon. The villa had provided a temporary safe haven last night when Talos and Sam were searching for her. Good thing as it turned out, or she wouldn't have found the entrance to the cyclone shelter.

Once Simon opened the gate, they coasted down the drive then she parked behind a golf cart near the kitchen. "This is the only door I have a key for."

"Did you set off an alarm yesterday?"

"No, why?"

He pointed above the door to a small black cylinder. "Surveillance camera. It could be just for show, or it's on a continuous loop. If we can find the hard drive, I'll wipe it."

Darius led the way through the kitchen and into the large butler's pantry. At the back wall, she pushed a wall hanging aside. "I never would have found this entrance if I hadn't felt a cool breeze on my ankles."

"Very observant." He dragged the door open then felt for a light switch. It flickered then came on, illuminating descending wooden stairs within the concrete tunnel. The steel door at the bottom remained slightly ajar.

Pinching her nose to block the dank, musty odor, she followed Simon down, stopping at the bottom as he searched for another light switch. They were in a massive storeroom. Shelves reached from floor to ceiling, filled with tinned food, bottled water, and other long-life rations that would see a large group of people through several weeks.

Simon picked up a battery-operated lantern, flicked it on then led the way through to a large kitchen and dining room. They found another storeroom with linen, camp beds, a generator, shovels and picks. The bunker also contained a shower and toilet block. The largest room hosted a billiards table, assorted sofas, armchairs, and several bookshelves. Only one door along a short hall wouldn't open.

Simon studied what looked like a credit card reader to the right of the door. "Could be where they store firearms, in case of a pirate attack.

A muffled scratching came from the end of the hall, then a loud clang, like solid metal hitting solid metal. Simon put a finger to his lips then the lantern went out. They were consumed in a shroud of dense blackness. She uttered a squeak as Simon's arms came around her and she was lifted off her feet.

A thin shaft of light crept along the floor at the end of the hall as a door creaked open.

Simon backed away, keeping Darius' locked against his chest, her heart hammering so hard, she feared it would pinpoint their location to whoever had entered the bunker.

A flashlight beam lit up the hall.

Simon stepped sideways behind a wall. They were in the bathroom.

She dared not breathe as the beam grew brighter then passed by. All she could make out was a huge black silhouette. The intruder stopped further along the corridor, reached out with one arm then she heard a soft whoosh before he entered the locked room.

Muted noises reached them as the person moved about the room. There was a good chance the intruder would notice them on the way out. Simon must have been thinking the same thing, as he lowered her to the floor then drew her through the darkness to the furthest cubicle. It turned out to be a shower with a wooden bench seat. Simon sat then drew her onto his lap.

An eternity seemed to pass before the intruder exited the room then passed by the bathroom with steady, well-paced steps. Definitely not a woman. Once Darius heard the external door creak then the heavy clunk, she deflated against Simon's chest. "I think there's more to that room than meets the eye."

"We could have set off a silent alarm and he came to view the cameras. Let's find the lantern then check out the end of the hall."

"Okay." She held Simon's hand as he felt his way forward. She sighed with relief when the lantern filled the bathroom and hall with a welcome glow.

They turned left, coming face-to-face with a ceiling to floor wall-hanging. Its faded ink depicting a village of bures and children playing by the ocean.

Raising the lantern, Simon eased the thin fabric aside, exposing a long bolt. "This is obviously the entrance used by resort staff. Whoever that was, he could have been returning or collecting something."

She shivered. "We should go. I'm hungry and need to get ready for my dance lesson. You can send up my Goshawk drone while I'm dying my hair."

"Great." He let the wall hanging fall into place. "I wonder if I can use it to drop a message off to Jarred?"

She blinked at him. "You don't seem surprised that I've got a Goshawk drone.

He smiled. "We intercepted your box of spyware shortly after the FedEx guy picked it up. Once we'd examined the contents, I installed a tracking device then we waited to see where it landed. Sorry, Tink, but you left us no choice."

"I guess not." She brightened. "Alisi is going to introduce me to her husband tonight. If I can get a few minutes alone with him—"

"Not without me." His rigid stance and clenched jaw confirmed his declaration. If she didn't agree, he'd most likely lock her up somewhere.

"Meet me after the show." Swiveling on her bare feet, she retraced her steps. The show tonight shouldn't be a problem. As a performer in the back row, she could copy the other dancers and mime the words. She'd need to keep her identity hidden, especially if Phoenix were indeed the hacker, and a murderer. She swallowed the lump in her throat. How had he known to use her secret code on the SD card, and when had he attached it to her father's atom charm?

They rode the Vesper to her villa, where she made them both chicken salad sandwiches. Then while Simon put the drone up, she headed upstairs to get ready.

Alisi had laid the elaborate costume and headdress on the bed. The intricate, woven bra and low-slung grass skirt were designed to draw attention. Tonight, she'd perform the *Meke* with the female staff, while the men sang, clapped and drummed. As if that wasn't enough to deal with, she'd gone and proposed a fictitious romance.

Darius opened her beauty case. It contained professional makeup, tanning lotion, wash-out dye, a bowl and color brush, hair crimper, false eyelashes and her contact lens vials. She quickly mixed up the black dye then coated her scalp, rubbing the creamy mixture through to the ends of her hair.

What on earth had she been thinking? A romantic liaison with Simon was a dreadful idea. Close proximity to him sparked reactions she hadn't anticipated. He'd seen her almost naked, and both times his heated gaze had glided over her like a flaming caress, drawing a bedeviling itch deep within her core that she couldn't scratch. His gentle kiss had ignited a curiosity to explore their connection further.

"This is ridiculous." She twisted her hair up under a disposable shower cap then laid out her creams, cosmetics and brushes across the vanity. They provided her with the capacity to alter the contours

158

of her face and shape of her eyes, an illusion enabling her to become another person. Simon had been the only person she hadn't fooled.

Recalling the awareness in his eyes, chaotic shivers of excitement and trepidation rippled across her skin. She longed to melt against his hard chest and seek his lips, but then what? The moment he pressed for more, she'd balk, push him away and run like the demon dogs of Hell were chasing her. She was destined to live out her life alone.

A tear trickled down her cheek. There were plenty of things to fill her life. Work, family, friends, travel.

୨୦୧

If the heavy humidity and thick purple clouds were anything to go by, the expected storm promised a thrilling show.

While learning the *Meke* in the staff courtyard, Darius couldn't help but notice the anxiety on Alisi's face each time she glanced at the sky. Eventually the other women ran off to secure the bures, main complex and staff accommodation, leaving only Alisi and the powerfully built, jovial chef, Vijay. From what Darius had observed, besides singing, cooking, clapping bamboo sticks and beating the *lali* drum, he spent his days tending the resort's kitchen garden, yet he struck her as the typical nightclub bouncer.

It had been an entertaining couple of hours. Alisi, singing and clapping her hands, and Vijay on the clap sticks, had patiently taught Darius the moves for the *Meke,* a very peaceful dance with mostly arm movements and hand clapping. Now it was time for their performance, which had butterflies tumbling about in Darius' stomach.

Flitting about reception, Alisi did some last-minute adjustments to one kitchen girl's grass skirt and the other's headdress. She smiled at Darius. "Ready?"

"Yes, although I find it hard to believe this is the traditional costume."

Alisi laughed. "It's not, but the guests love them. Now, don't forget, if any of the men bother you, signal Etera or Vijay. They will come to your rescue."

"I'll be fine. When can I meet your husband?"

"Hans is securing our bure and the other building on the golf course. Once the storm hits, everyone must stay inside until it passes."

"Of course."

Etera fidgeted by the closed dining room doors. Tall, muscled and bare-chested, he portrayed a tribal warrior to perfection, especially with his bronzed skin gleaming, wearing a grass skirt, armbands and anklets. With a grin he opened the doors then followed the other male dancers and musicians into the dining room. Several delegates had to move their chairs in to allow Vijay to pass by. With only the glow of candles, his huge frame reminded her of a grizzly.

Darius buzzed with excitement and anticipation. She'd heard the men's *Meke* differed greatly from the female version, being more dynamic and louder.

The delegates turned to watch the dancers. On every table, a candle flickered from within amber glasses, creating a soft, almost mysterious atmosphere. Evenly spaced about the perimeter of the dim room, she noticed security men, including Talos and Sam.

Jarred stood near the bar, deep in conversation with Sir William and Alistair Finch. One of the security guys from the other team leaned against a thick pole, his gaze locked on Simon and the French woman at a table in the middle of the room.

No sooner had Darius spotted Simon than he looked over his shoulder, staring straight at her shadowed position.

Frantic drumming reverberated across the room, drawing his attention back to the dancers on the low dais. Darius eased further into the shadows to watch the performance. It was enthralling. The men sang, stomped feet and waved woven fans about, using them as an integral part of the dance. They yelled, flexed their muscles and clapped the fans against their hands and thighs. As the drumming got louder and faster, so did the men.

Throughout the exhilarating performance, Darius stood transfixed. The men's enjoyment and pleasure shone through their expressive faces.

Once they finished, the men backed into a semi-circle, allowing room on the dais for the ladies. Darius fell into position between the kitchen girls, mimicking their confident sashay among the tables.

The French woman leaned closer to Simon, spreading her manicured nails across her chest as her pouty lips curved at something he said.

Darius clenched her fingers. Jealousy wasn't something she was accustomed to, but it wouldn't do to blow her cover by punching a delegate in the eye.

Just as the dancing troupe reached their table, the French flirt put her hand on Simon's arm, but *she* wasn't the lady he turned his intense gaze on. Oh no, that honor went to the newest member of the dance troupe.

Darius could almost feel the heat of his gaze drift down her spine and over her backside. Taking her position in the middle of the second row, protected on all sides by the other dancers, Darius plastered on a beaming smile. With her long, crimped hair and golden tan, the delegates would assume she had Polynesian heritage. The makeup ensured no one would see any trace of Darius Cortez.

Alisi looked over her shoulder. "Hans is in the kitchen eating his dinner." The relief on her face was plain to see.

Drumming and raucous cries filled the room.

Using Alisi as a shield, Darius danced the *Meke* as best she could, weaving her hands and hips in time to the music and other dancers. Vijay pounded the *lali* drum and Etera beat clap sticks. The other men sang, clapped their hands and stomped their feet.

Pretending to sing along with the other women, she studied each of the delegates. Some she knew, most she didn't. Thanks to her housekeeping duties, she now had a comprehensive list of all those attending and which bures they were housed in.

The gentle dance gave her ample opportunity to track Simon as he left his table to lean against the bar beside Jarred, his gaze never leaving her.

Others had noticed. Sir William and Alistair Finch wore identical frowns. The French woman scowled. Simon was making his interest very obvious, which she supposed made sense if they were going to fake a holiday romance.

The dance ended with a frenzied drumming. Amid the applause, a monstrous crack of thunder boomed overhead. Everyone ducked then the lights above the stage went out, leaving only the soft glow of candles. Thunder rumbled as lashing rain beat against the secured blinds. One tore free allowing wind to gust through, extinguishing every candle. Chaos broke out.

Someone knocked Darius onto her knees. She crawled off the dais, intent on reaching the kitchen and Harnoop. Feet stood on her grass skirt and she had to yank hard to get loose. Someone fell over the top of her, an elbow connecting with her cheek.

"Tink! Where are you?"

"Here." She stood and lunged for Simon, slamming into a wall of muscle.

"Gotcha." Familiar arms locked around her.

A clap of thunder shook the floor. Lightening illuminated the room for a couple of seconds. Harnoop stood next to them, his shocked gaze fixed beyond Darius.

A sharp crack blasted then something ripped into the thick pole between her and Harnoop, striking her with splintered shards of wood.

"Down!" Simon dragged her with him to the floor.

CHAPTER SEVENTEEN

Battling torrential rain, gusty winds and a hellcat at the same time hadn't been the best thought out plan. Yet, getting Darius to the safety of his bure had overruled all logic. She sat on the couch, wearing his bathrobe, her hair wrapped in a towel, and glaring daggers at him.

"Damn you to the fires of Hell, Simon. You stubborn, interfering, blasted man. Someone almost shot Harnoop. We need to find him before he's killed."

"Don't worry about Harnoop. The boys will keep tabs on him." Simon lit another ornamental candle. "It's more likely you were the intended victim."

"Me?" She started shaking her head then gasped. "It's *you*. The shooter was trying to kill *you*."

Simon grimaced. "It's possible, but I don't think so. I'm more valuable alive than dead. Unless it was Richard Chapman, he definitely has it in for me." Crossing his arms, he leaned against a wall desk. "Have you got anything else in your arsenal of spyware, other than frogs, beetle bugs and butterflies?"

The panic in her eyes slowly subsided, although her fingers remained clenched. "Only my Goshawk drone. It carries a high-performance video camera that I can zoom in close and will record the live stream if necessary. It also has night vision capabilities."

Simon glanced out at the torrential rain hammering the glass slider. "Maybe in the morning."

"We can't wait until morning." She twisted her hands together. "You or Harnoop could be dead by then."

"It's too dangerous to go out in that storm." He rolled his shoulders. "After what's just happened, Jarred will have one of the boys keeping this bure under surveillance."

"What if he doesn't know about the shooter?"

"He does. Relax, we're safe tonight."

"How can I relax? I'm terrified you're on someone's hit list, and I'm cold."

"Take off that wet costume and dry yourself. Then we're going to bed."

"Wh...what?" Her lovely eyes flared. "There's only one bed."

"It's a big bed. You can wear one of my T-shirts and a pair of boxer shorts. My only desire is to keep you safe." A lie, but she looked set to bolt if he made the slightest move. "Tink, if anything happened to you, I'd go out of my mind." At least that was true.

She swallowed. "I believe you, it's just that I panic when guys get close to me."

"Maybe other guys, but you practically melt in *my* arms."

She frowned. "Yes, but if it were to be a real romance, I'd lose my nerve and push you away. It always happens, even when I like a guy."

"Always, Tink, or only since that bastard broke your heart?"

She jumped up off the couch, her lips trembling. "My sister told you?"

"Breanna inferred some guy badly hurt you."

She turned her back on him. "I was warned the jerk had a bad reputation, but he seemed so nice. He never tried anything...not until...." A sob escaped.

"Damn." He lifted her into his arms then sank onto the sofa, cradling her against his chest. "Tell me, Tink. Get it off your chest."

"I can't. It's too humiliating. I was such an idiot."

"No one is perfect. Tell me?"

She sniffed. "I didn't realize the drinks he gave me had such a high alcohol content."

"Where were you?"

"A club with his mates and their girlfriends. I danced with the girls, only stopping to quench my thirst. If I'd stuck to water...it wouldn't have happened."

"Maybe that was his plan, sweetheart. To get you drunk then take advantage."

"When we left, he said I should drive, because he'd had too much to drink. I quickly realized I shouldn't be behind the wheel, so pulled off the road. I thought he just wanted to kiss me. Then he... I said no. I tried to stop him, but..."

She swiped at her tears. "After that night, he avoided me, and I realized what an idiot I'd been. I left my part-time job in case he was boasting about it behind my back."

"Bastard." Every muscle in Simon's body clenched with a need to pummel the creep. "Tell me his name, so I can belt the bastard to a pulp."

"He's not worth a jail sentence." Her gaze lifted to meet his. "If it makes you feel better, he didn't break my heart, just left me with trust and intimacy issues."

If anything, Simon's fury rose. "The creep is a predator. His sole purpose was to gain your trust, so he could take the worst kind of advantage. You wouldn't have been his first victim. Tell me his name?"

"No. If a furious father or brother doesn't get him, Karma will. As far as I'm concerned, the jerk is dead." She scrambled off his lap, dislodging the towel from her head. "I'm tired. Give me some clothes and I'll change in the bathroom."

"Fine." He wouldn't push. He stood then stepped up into the bedroom area. She followed him to the chest of drawers where he handed her a white T-shirt and red boxers. "No escaping out the window, Tink, or I'll tie you to a bed on the catamaran."

"I'd like to see you try. There are no posts." With a defiant flick of her mane, she picked up a candle and stalked into the bathroom, closing the door behind her.

Jaw clamped, Simon fisted his hands, determined to exact retribution from the bastard who'd crushed Darius' spirit. He'd have his work cut out but, somehow, he'd exact revenge for the girl who had once enchanted him. Still enchanted him.

"Holy heck." Where had that come from? He stripped off his wet clothes then grabbed a pair of boxers. If any of his family were privy to his thoughts, they'd be somersaulting with delight, breaking their necks to spread the news and plan a wedding.

His father's favorite motto came to mind. *Make the woman you love the center of your universe, and you'll never sleep in a cold bed.*

Another pearl of wisdom often came from Simon's maternal grandfather. *Una moglie felice é una vita felice.* A happy wife is a happy life. His grandparents still had a solid marriage, even though Nonna did most of the talking while Nonno rolled his eyes behind her back.

Simon rubbed his neck. When had he started thinking about love and a wife?

The bathroom door opened. Darius hesitated. She'd taken the brown contact lenses out. Her eyes widened. "What's wrong?"

He ran a hand through his hair. Tink had been hurt badly, but he might be the only man she trusted enough to get past her intimacy issues. They definitely shared a potent attraction. Now that he'd found her again, he wanted to at least explore the possibility of a future together, which meant a hell of a commitment, if it led to marriage.

Her eyes welled with tears. "I shouldn't have told you."

"No, it's not that, Tink. I missed you when you stopped coming to the lab. I missed your laugh and smiling eyes. Heck, I even missed your harassment."

"What?"

"You'd pester us to eat or finish up and come home. Sometimes you'd start turning lights off or threaten to shut down the computers. You'd taunt us with your mother's temper or bribe us with her cooking."

"Why didn't you come looking for me?" She crossed her arms under her chest, plumping up her breasts and drawing his gaze to erect nipples poking at his T-shirt.

Desire stirred. "I figured you'd discovered better things to do than hang out with your father and a computer geek. Plus, you were too young. Heck, I would have been arrested if we'd got involved. I did think about you. For a long time."

She reached for his hand. "I know I was young, Simon, but I was crazy about you. I've never felt that way about anyone else." Her lips twitched. "Who knows, if Brianna hadn't interfered, you might be my harassed husband now, maybe even a daddy."

"Tink." He moved without thought, gathering her in his arms, lifting her to his height. Her eyes flared briefly in surprise then she wrapped her arms around his neck and kissed him. It wasn't the experienced kisses he was used to, yet her enthusiasm fired something deep in his soul and released all qualms to what lay ahead. Tightening his arms, he fell onto the bed, intentionally keeping her on top, but to the side, away from his hardening erection. Her squeal brought a smile to his lips.

She spread her fingers over his naked chest then pushed back to frown at him. "For some reason kissing you doesn't freak me out. But if you touch me, it will shatter this fragile thing between us."

"I'm touching you now, Tink, and you're touching me."

"Yes, but that will change. Once I have time to think, I balk. I know it doesn't make sense, but that's what happens. I like a guy, and might even go on a date or two, but then I back off, and hurt their feelings. I can't help it."

The thought left him cold. "What if you push them away before they have a chance to hurt or humiliate you."

"Maybe, but I hate doing it, and I don't want to hurt you."

"I'm a tough guy, Tink, and I won't give up on you. Let's get some sleep." He rolled taking her with him, so they were lying facing each other. "We'll figure out what happened to your father together...as friends for now." It would kill him, but if he was to win her trust, he had no choice.

"What if I decide I do want a closer relationship with you?"

He couldn't help but grin. "I'd be a lucky guy, sweet pea. You want me to blow out the candles?"

"No." She frowned at her fingers as she drew lazy circles over his chest, oblivious to the reaction she was causing lower. "This is nice, lying here with you in the candlelight, while the rain pummels the roof. I feel..." She wriggled closer. "I feel... Oh!"

"Ignore it, Tink. I have no control over that body part with you this close."

Her giggle was the last thing he expected. "You sound so pained." She deepened her voice, mimicking him. "I have no control over that body part."

"Tease me, will you, Tink? I can't have that." He dug his fingers into her ribs, tickling until she was laughing and squirming, her eyes sparkling with delight.

"I'm sorry. I will not make fun of your body parts." She burst out laughing again, tears streaming down her face. "But it's so hard."

"You have no idea."

She blushed. "I meant it's so hard not to tease you."

He fell on his back, staring at the overhead beams with a pained expression. "Imagine the words on my headstone. Here lies Simon Hawke, frustrated and hard. Driven to an early death by a wicked fairy he adored."

She leaned on his chest; her smile lighting his heart. "You adore me?"

"I always have, Tink." Slowly he reached for the nape of her neck, drawing her down until their lips were almost touching. "I always will."

He kissed her, gently to start with then more deeply as she sank against him. He encouraged her to part her lips and claimed her mouth. By her surprised jerk, she wasn't expecting him to tongue kiss her, but then with a soft moan tentatively joined him in the intimate dance. This was clearly the way forward. He would seduce her slowly, drawing her to him day by day, and see where it took them.

Moving his hands to her hips, he leisurely skimmed his fingers up the curve of her waist, over her ribs, and under her arms then down again.

She sighed against his lips. "I like that." She shifted her weight to one side of his chest then traced her own pattern, her touch sending quivers skating under his heated skin.

"Me too." He kissed her again, gliding his fingers over the rounded globes of her backside then over her hips and ribs. She pressed closer, causing his fingers to skim the sides of her breast.

She gasped.

He froze. "You moved. I didn't mean…"

Instead of pulling away, she pressed against his palm. "Make love to me, Simon. Make love to me the way you kiss and touch me."

"No way, Tink. I'm not taking advantage of you. When you're sure you want to take the next step, we'll move on."

"I *am* sure. I like what you're doing, and I trust you. This is the way forward. I know it in my heart."

"Tink?"

"Simon, I want to make love with you." She whipped off the T-shirt and boxers so fast he was left blinking and completely adrift.

Then she straddled him in all her naked glory, her bottom pressed against his raging erection.

"Darius, this isn't what I intended. Damn, you're killing me."

She smiled gloriously, her incredible blue eyes taking on the violet hue he remembered so well. "Make love to me, Simon? Show me how it should be."

"Darius?" His body and brain were at war. "Let's wait until after the summit. I'll take you to one of the Fijian Islands, and we'll take things slowly."

"You can take me to a Fijian island after the summit, but I don't want to take it slowly." She fell on top of him, pressing her plump breasts against his chest, and her golden curls against his erection.

They both gasped as a bolt of sensual energy ignited between their bodies.

"Holy shit." He'd give her anything she wanted as long as she didn't move.

She wiggled her hips, nearly sending him over the edge.

"Darius, if you run from me after this, I will ring your neck."

"I won't run, Simon. I will never regret making love with you."

He rolled, pinning her under him, searching her eyes for any sign of panic. Not a glimmer. She glowed with excitement. He pressed her thighs wide.

She swallowed then cleared her throat. "Shouldn't you take off your boxers?" Her voice shook a little, but she didn't sound frightened.

"Why don't you take them off for me, Tink."

Her eyes flared. Her tongue darted out over her bottom lip. "You think I won't."

"I have no idea what you'll do. You're full of surprises tonight."

"Hmm." She shoved and he rolled onto his back, stretching his arms up to pillow his head in his hands, watching her closely for any sign of anxiety. If she changed her mind, he'd need to spend a week under a cold shower.

"I hadn't pegged you for a lazy-bones." She shuffled down the bed, grabbed his boxers at the waistband and yanked as he lifted his backside. They momentarily snagged on his erection then it sprang free like a flagpole reaching for the stars. Darius gasped, a deep blush spreading over every inch of her body. "It's...."

"Completely normal." He groaned. "I can make it go away with a cold shower." By her reaction, she hadn't seen a guy's erection, which spoke volumes. "Tink?"

"What?" Her gaze shot to his face. "This isn't panic, it's…curiosity."

"Are you sure?"

"Yes." She tugged his shorts down his legs then dropped them over the side of the bed and turned to him. By her finger twisting, she wasn't sure at all.

"Come here." He sat up, holding his arms wide. "If you're not sure, we can cuddle tonight and see how you feel in the morning."

She crawled into his arms. "I want *you* to kiss me and touch me. I want *you* to make love to me because we…care for each other."

"All right, but if you want to stop, we will."

"Deal."

He lifted her across his widened thighs, then cupped the globes of her bottom and drew her in until the only thing between them was his erection.

She blinked then tentatively placed her hands on his shoulders. "You're tense."

"That's because I'm about to combust, sweet pea. Want to join me in a cold shower?"

"Maybe later." She pressed closer, her nipples brushing his chest as she scattered butterfly kisses across his jaw.

With a groan, he edged her chin up to plant open-mouthed kisses down her delicate neck and along her right collarbone. She tilted her neck and arched, granting him access to her left side. Kissing, licking and lightly sucking, he worked his way down her throat, as he skimmed the sides of her breasts with his fingers.

She shuddered and arched further, so he cupped her right breast. She gasped and pressed into his palm, encouraging him to take it one step further. He caressed the soft flesh, running his thumb over her hard nipple.

"Yes." Her fingernails dug into his shoulders. "This is very pleasant."

Smiling, he palmed her left breast, closing his fingers as he bent to suckled on her right nipple.

She jolted and cried out. "Oh."

He devoted untold minutes to pleasuring each breast until she began rubbing against his erection. It wouldn't take much to tip her over. With luck that might be enough to satisfy her tonight.

Grasping her hips, he eased her away from his erection and claimed her lips, soothing her racing pulse to a steady beat. Only then did he slide a hand down her outer thigh, pause then trace his fingers up her inner thigh, closer and closer until they brushed her damp curls.

Her breath caught and she stilled.

"Are you okay?"

"Ye...s." She clung to his shoulders, her fingernails digging in sharply.

He cupped her, groaning at the slick dew coating his palm. She was so close he'd only have to circle her sweet spot and she'd reach heaven. She pressed against his hand, her back arched, her eyelids closed. "Simon, please."

Her whispered plea enthralled him. "Open your eyes, Tink."

Her lids fluttered apart, revealing passion hazed eyes as dark as the deepest ocean. Her supple body, blissful smile and graceful beauty had him captivated. Gently, he slid one finger inside her tight, honey-coated center, pausing when she jolted, then slowly withdrew, flicking her nub, before repeating his slow torment until she bucked again and again, her thighs spread wide.

Erotic little gasps spilled from her lips. Her body became taut with mounting tension as she moved in rhythm with his finger. He added another, almost coming himself when she uttered a husky moan.

"Fly for me, Tink." He dipped his head, rolling his tongue round a hard nipple as he dragged his thumb over her sweet spot, back and forth.

"Simon!" She went completely rigid, then a shudder racked her tiny frame and the sweetest of screeches left her lips. "I'm flying."

"Yes." Grinning, he hugged her close, loving the delight ringing in her voice, the soft flush covering her entire body, the amazement in her dark eyes.

"Only with you." She went limp, her face buried against his shoulder, her warm breath tickling his chest.

He held her gently, caressing silken skin from shoulder to hip in slow, lazy circles, ignoring the lust erupting from every cell within his body. He needed a few minutes alone or a damn ice bath to deal with this erection, but first he had to convince her they needed to slow things down.

It was the only way to earn her trust. The only way to deal with her phobia, but he needed words that wouldn't trigger anxiety. It was imperative she know he not only desired her, but wanted to spend quality time in her company, doing whatever couples did, when not eating or having sex. He couldn't allow her fears to surface or she'd bolt. Words were so complex when it came to women.

A grin spread over his face. She hadn't bolted after that cosmic orgasm. In fact, by the soft puffs against his chest, and even rise and fall of her chest, she'd completely relaxed. Not the operandi of a woman about to do a runner. More like...

He frowned, edging back to find thick, dark lashes fanning her cheeks and a half smile on her pillow-soft lips. Darius Cortez was sound asleep in his arms. No woman had ever fitted so well, and strangely he liked the sensation. Very much.

As for his rampant erection, it wouldn't be going away any time soon, as he had no intention of leaving her, even for a couple of minutes.

CHAPTER EIGHTEEN

The far-off rumble of thunder and steady downpour impinged on Darius' brain, but it was so cozy lying here in bed, she couldn't raise the energy to check the downstairs windows. Dad would beat her to it anyway.

Dad! She blinked, gulped down the familiar ache.

Cracking and eyelid, she scanned the dim room. Not hers.

A cane lounge took up most of the lower section, its familiar Frangipani print drawing a frown. Solid beams braced the ceiling, which had been cleverly carved to resemble palm fronds.

Fully awake, she registered the heat behind her.

With her heart pounding like a woodpecker on steroids, she inched onto her back, twisting her head as an avalanche of sensations raced through her body.

He'd made love to her, but not in the way she'd expected.

She swallowed, riveted by his male beauty. In slumber, Simon reminded her of a fallen angel, his thick lashes at rest, a dark shadow covering his normally clean-shaven jaw, full lips that held a wealth of temptation, especially with that hint of wicked smile.

Why had he held back? She wasn't blind, he'd wanted her. She reached out to stroke his short dark hair and froze. He'd said to ignore his erection, that he had no control over it with her so close. But that was before she threw off the T-shirt and boxers.

He'd been aroused, yet he'd stopped.

Was his shocked gasp, a reaction to her nakedness or small breasts? Had he been hoping for more? A groan nearly escaped. Her sister believed men preferred big breasts. Simon's gaze *had* dropped to *Bellini's* chest yesterday, the result of an extreme pushup bra. And his eyes had widened briefly at the sight of her massive breasts when she'd been in the silicon body suit, but so had the kitchen staff.

Last night he'd suckled and licked her nipples with something close to reverence.

Hadn't he?

Heat and humiliation engulfed her entire body. Other than her nipples, he'd barely touched her breasts. His main focus had been between her legs.

Dear God. It made sense. The football jerk had flirted with her for weeks. He'd taken her to meet his family and friends, but he hadn't touched her breasts, not until that fateful night. She'd been so skinny back then that the padded bra gave her confidence.

Biting her lip, she stared at Simon's handsome face, his wide chest, rising and falling as he breathed deeply, the scar she'd patched healing well. Simon could have any woman he desired.

Darius dashed away tears. She didn't know what he wanted. He'd given her a taste of pleasure and made her fly. He'd held her so protectively.

She needed to think.

This beautiful man had the power to crush her soul. He might say he adored her, and that he'd never hurt her, but his rejection would shatter her heart.

Better he never know the true depth of her feelings.

Best to beat a hasty retreat before he woke. A note would say what she couldn't.

For once 'I just wanna be friends' would be the biggest lie she'd ever told.

Easing out of bed, she rummaged through Simon's drawers, looking for anything dark. Alert to the slightest change in his breathing. Pointless, as the rain and crashing waves masked all sound. She pulled on jeans and a long-sleeved T-shirt, both too large, but with the cuffs rolled up they were better than his white T-shirt.

"Where do you think you're going, sweet pea?

She gasped. "Simon!"

He pushed up to lean on one elbow. "Running away again? Were you even going to leave me note?"

She nodded before realizing then silently cursed. "I thought it would be the best way to let you off the hook." Tears blurred her vision. "I should have realized your feelings for me are more brotherly than romantic. But it's okay, our interlude, although sweet, wasn't the amorous tryst I was anticipating."

Lies, all lies.

Smothering a sob, with a cough, Darius backed away. "The storm has eased, so I should let you get some sleep and go back to the villa." She sneaked one final, devouring peep at the man she wanted so badly her heart ached. He radiated with fury.

"You take one step out of this bure, and I'll drag you back inside, strip you naked and show you my attraction is anything but brotherly."

"But you didn't make love to me." She swallowed, determined to get this off her chest. "I can handle the truth, Simon. If you don't desire me than please be honest."

He leaped out of bed, to stand over her as naked as the day he was born. "Where the hell did you get the idea that I don't desire you?"

"Well, I woke up, and there you were, handsome and sexy, but then I thought about your reaction when I pulled off my T-shirt and... I realized you hadn't made love to me."

"Holy heck, Tink, that doesn't mean I don't desire you."

She blinked. "But you went all strange when I pulled the T-shirt off, and then you backed off, saying you wanted to wait until after the summit, and to take things slowly. Is it the size of my breasts?"

"What!" He ran both hands through his hair. "Darius, your breasts are beautiful. My reaction was the result of having you straddled over me, butt naked. It was better than any fantasy I could imagined."

"Then why did you back off?"

"Because this heat that ignites between us is extremely heady, and I didn't want to scare you with the strength of my desire."

"Oh."

He tilted her chin to the side and smothered her throat in gentle kisses. "I could have sworn you enjoyed everything I *did* do to you."

"Yes, but I figured you prefer certain parts of my body to others."

"Is that so?" He cupped her right breast, bringing a gasp to her lips. "Hmm." His warm breath against her throat sent a shiver skating across her skin. "Perhaps I should do a more thorough exploration, so we can discover if I do have a particularly favorite part."

"I suppose that's a...good idea."

He laughed then lifted her hands to his lips. "My research could take a while."

Giggling, she clung to his hand as he towed her into the bathroom. "It's almost dawn. Shouldn't we find your friends?"

"No, I have a point to prove, as long as you can live with a few bruises." His eyes held a wicked twinkle.

"Bruises?"

He chuckled. "Just a couple of little ones."

"You think taking a shower is more exciting than making out on a bed."

He closed the distance between them. "Trust me, Tink, you will enjoy taking a shower with *me*."

She shivered as Simon traced her nipple through the T-shirt with his thumb, making her knees weak and moisture pool between her thighs.

He lifted his other hand, cupping her chin and raising it until their eyes met. "If I had to choose what I love about you, Tink, it would have to be your mesmerizing eyes." He kissed each of her eyelids. "Or, it could be the curve of your neck, which tends to make me forget where I am." He placed one open-mouthed kiss after another from her ear to collarbone. "Although, your soft lips do command attention."

He took her mouth in a slow, deep exploration, his hands dropping to her waist to draw her against his hard body. "Hmm, now that I think about this, it could be how your tiny waist fits perfectly in my hands, but then so do your breasts." He edged back then slid his hands up her ribs, cupping both breasts then gently massaging.

"Simon." She clutched his forearms, arching to press against his hips, thrilled to find him hard, desperate to have his hands on her naked skin.

He smiled. "This T-shirt is hampering my research." He lifted it over her head and dropped it on the tiles. "That's better." He bent, capturing her right nipple between his lips.

"Yes." She clung to his hips, rubbing against his erection as he suckled, nipped, and used his tongue to toy with her engorged nipple, caressing and stroking her left breast, leaving her panting and crying out as he coiled her tighter and tighter, until she began to shake.

"Wait." He dropped to his knees. "It could be your legs I like best."

"What? No, it's okay, come back."

His chuckle vibrated against her rib-cage. "We need to be sure, Tink." He dragged the jeans and boxers down her legs then ran fingers over the backs of her calves, up her thighs, then down again, shooting delightful quivers throughout her body.

"That's so...so nice."

"Only nice? I must be losing my touch." He brought his fingers skating up the insides of her legs, brushing the center of her need, almost buckling her legs, before he reversed direction.

She clutched his bare shoulders. "Stop teasing me. I need you to touch me."

"Isn't that what I'm doing? Maybe you'd like this." He traced the back of her calves again, slowing as he reached her thighs, slowing further to circle the globes of her naked bottom. "Let's see what else I can find." His gaze lowered. "Hmm, I can smell your desire, and it's intoxicating, *Bella*."

The longer he stared, the hotter she became. Her face and body were on fire. "Simon, stop with the research and touch me."

His gaze lifted to her face and he sobered. "All right, but I want you to understand, I will never be your brother, and this magnetism between us isn't something one can fake. If you run, I *will* come after you."

Her heart blossomed like a rose in full flush, bursting with vitality. "I won't run."

"Good." He handed her a shower cap.

Gathering her courage, she stepped into him. If she were to play the part of Bellini, it made sense to wear a shower cap, but how Simon could think logically at a time like this was beyond her. She twisted her hair up under the cap then looked up to find him watching her hungrily. For the first time in her life, she experienced a surge of feminine power.

He flicked the lever, bringing water cascading down from two showerheads. Then lifted her into the shower, his hazel eyes darkening as he gazed into her eyes. "Tink, I desire every inch of you. I adore your infectious laugh. I'm blown away by your talent to totally transform yourself into someone else. I admire your determination and courage to clear your father. I respect the skill it takes to build a Goshawk drone and realistic animal bugs." He laughed. "But right now, I need to have my way with you."

Okay, that had her pulse ramping up. She melted into his arms, opening to him when he claimed her mouth, soft moans escaping as he rubbed his erection against her belly. He hiked her higher, his hands cupping her bottom, his chest hair rasping her sensitive nipples. "I want to kiss you, Tink. Explore your heat with my tongue."

"Isn't that what you've been doing?"

A slow smile covered his entire face. "Not quite." He let her slide down his body, then sank to his knees. "Tell me to stop, if you don't like it." He backed her against the tiled wall then lifted her left leg over his right shoulder and ducked his head.

"Oh!" Her body jolted at the touch of his lips on her sensitive skin. He flicked his tongue over the bud at her center, back and forth, over and over, drawing a moan from her very core. He thrust deep, causing her to buck against his mouth, and squeal when he sucked hard. Cool water dowsed them from both sides, doing little to stem the heat consuming her. She clutched his head for support, even though she was pinned to the wall.

He lifted her higher, supporting her with both hands as he maneuvered her right leg over his left shoulder, opening her wider to his mouth and tongue, devouring her like a starving wolf. She lost all control, bucking hard against his plunging tongue.

Her whole body began to tremble as she balanced on a precipice of ecstatic pleasure and torment.

"Come for me, Tink." He sucked hard and she exploded into a million pieces, shouting his name.

◦◦◦

The cool spray did nothing to diminish Simon's erection. A steel rod would have more chance of folding. He sat where Tink had pitched him, legs stretch out on the shower floor, holding her across his thighs and chest, his arms tightly wrapped around her slenderness.

After her wild orgasm, she'd gone limp as a rag doll, leaving him as tight as a spring. Every limb, every finger, every tendon had gone rigid, even his balls ached. She squirmed against his erection, fueling his lust-hazed craving to satisfy his ravenous hunger. To heck with the risk of impregnating her.

Don't be a bloody idiot. There'd be no coming back from that, and the last thing he wanted to be saddled with was a sticky-fingered kid. Unless she had deep blue eyes and golden hair. He closed his eyes and groaned.

"That was...intensely...magnificent." She squirmed again, rubbing against him suggestively, testing his resolve. Soft lips dusted his eyelids, fingertips skimmed his chest and ribs in wide, leisurely circles, narrowing until she flicked his nipples.

Her fingers closed round his erection, detonating his lust.

"Tink, you're killing me." He grabbed her hand, but kept his eyes closed. His memory and senses were bad enough, the real thing might bring on an aneurism.

She ran a finger along the dip between his lips, then rose on her knees to mimic the action with her tongue. He groaned again but couldn't resist her invitation. What harm could one kiss do?

Their kiss turned into two, then three, losing all rationality as he fell deeper under her spell. He'd only meant to tease her. He opened his eyes.

She drew back. "I want you, Simon." She wiggled higher, her inner thighs tightening around his waist as she gripped his shoulders. "All of you."

This had to be some sort of Karma. How could one tiny female morph into a whirlwind big enough to disorientate him so thoroughly?

"Tink, I..." He fought not to squeeze the perfect globes of her bottom, which had somehow found their way into his hands. "I don't have protection."

"You're kidding me?" She bit her lower lip. "What if you pull out before you..." She glanced down at his erection. "I know a guy who does it all the time."

"Sorry—what?" Her admission sent shock waves through his brain. Jealousy twisted his gut. He'd never experienced the emotion and didn't like it. "You said... What guy?"

"Charlotte's partner, Kyle. They've been doing it that way for two years."

The relief almost choked him. "Why would your friends take such a risk?"

"Charlotte can't take the pill and refuses to have anything foreign put inside her uterus, and Kyle's allergic to latex."

"It's a risk *I'm* not prepared to take."

"Fine, but if either of us die in the next few days, I will never forgive you."

"*Bella ragazza*, I am desperate to be inside you and I promise to carry a pocket full of condoms so we can go all the way the next chance we get."

"I'm beginning to think you're the one with an intimacy phobia."

He fought hard not to laugh, but then she relaxed her thighs and slipped, knocking against his erection.

They both gasped, frozen in time as they stared into each other's eyes, too stunned, or too aroused to move. Simon could barely breathe with the heat of her saturated folds coating the head of his erection in honey liquid. His control hung by a fine thread at risk of flowing down the drain with the water. He should have ignored her.

Who was he kidding? It had been a battle to keep Darius at arm's length since she tripped on her robe and ended up sprawled across his chest on her bedroom floor.

"Simon, I saw a condom in your wallet. Is it still there?"

"You're a life saver." He helped her up then stepped out of the shower and dashed into the bedroom to where he'd dropped his wet pants and wallet. "Bingo." He pulled out the packet then ripped it in two, sheathing his erection as he stepped back into the shower. "Where were we?"

She leaped at him, wrapping her arms around his shoulders and her legs around his waist, opening to his probing tongue and lips, taking them straight back into the inferno.

He slid his hands under her bottom, caressing her smooth skin, then ran two fingertips through her wet folds. Her thighs quivered, so he set her against the wall, supporting her with one hand, as he pushed his fingers into her hot haven, back and forth until she was panting and rocking against his hand, crying out. She was an erotic vision of sensuality, but he couldn't wait any longer.

Lifting her higher, he found her opening, then nudged inside, pushing a little deeper. He withdrew and pushed further. She was so tight he almost came then and there.

She tensed, her fingernails digging into his shoulders, her eyes wide as she held her breath, blinking at him in surprise. "You feel so thick inside me, but it doesn't hurt."

Words were beyond him. He held still as she relaxed her fingers then flexed her inner muscles, testing her position and his endurance.

Her smile was a thing of wonder. "Thank you."

"I haven't finished, *Bella ragazza*." He drove home, withdrew slowly then thrust again and again, reveling in her cries and gasps.

She came with a strangled cry, lifting her trembling pelvis to meet his thrusts, then stiffening, clinching him deep inside, taking him with her, in an exhilarating climax that left him lightheaded.

He sank to his knees, keeping her locked to his chest and hips, reluctant to put the smallest distance between them, as cool water flowed over their hot bodies.

She stirred, mumbling against his shoulder.

"Everything okay, Tink?"

"Oh, yes, more than okay. What does *Bella ragazza* mean?"

"Beautiful girl. My mother's parents are Italian, so I've picked up a few things over the years. How's your back?"

"I might have a tiny bruise or two, but it's worth it. How do I say beautiful man?"

"*Bell'uomo.*"

"What about, you are magnificent?"

He chuckled. "*Sei magnifico.*"

"How do I say, kiss me?"

"*Baciami.*"

"If you insist." She smiled gloriously, then kissed him, drawing him back into her web of intrigue. His mind might be in turmoil, but his senses were drowning in heavenly bliss.

CHAPTER NINETEEN

Dawn broke over the island as Darius watched Simon tape a flick knife to his belly. She followed him out of the bure, gasping at the onslaught of chill breeze and drenching rain.

Thankfully, the shower cap would keep the dye from leaching out of her hair, but there wasn't anything she could do about the rivulets of freezing water trickling down her neck.

Leaving the path, they picked their way through shrubbery to the beach then, sticking to the dark shadows, warily worked their way round the sandy cove. She hissed each time her bare feet made contact with a sharp shell. She wished they'd stopped by the staff courtyard to pick up her sandals.

Reaching the rocky point, Darius cautiously stepped over the dangerously slick boulders, stopping often as Simon scanned their surroundings. Once in the smaller cove, they took extra care, staying low and constantly searching for movement on the ocean, beach or above in the heavy foliage covering the mountain.

A guard from the other security team stood on her terrace, looking toward her villa. Simon signaled ahead then crouched and led the way along the beach, close to the boulders.

By the time she scrambled up the beach steps of the main residence's garden, her teeth were chattering, and shivers shook her whole body. It made climbing the locked gate awkward, but at least she had Simon to help her, and they hadn't encountered a patrol. Looking over her shoulder, she froze.

A light flicked on and off numerous times from the mountainside. "I think we've been seen."

Simon climbed up beside her. "It's Nick signaling us. I can't answer as I don't have a flashlight. Let's go before anyone else spots us."

Digging deep, Darius pulled her exhausted body over the gate then dropped to the soft earth on the other side. They needed to get into the bunker without leaving a trail. Impossible being soaked to the skin and covered in sand. "Tell me why we're coming here, instead of waiting for that guard to leave, so we can sneak into my villa?"

"Best we steer clear of your villa for now. Someone took a shot at us, and it could be because we were caught on camera. I want to see what's in that locked room."

He led the way under an arch of dripping bougainvillea. "See if you can find the metal door. I'll disable any cameras and join you."

"What if someone attacks you?"

He patted his stomach. "I have my knife." He kissed her then stepped between shrubs to run across the garden.

A warm shower and cup of hot chocolate would go down really well right now. Stepping off the path, she pushed aside dripping shrubs and stumbled over low plants and fallen fronds until she reached the far side of the villa, where a wall of clinging creeper concealed the metal door.

Her fingers were going numb as she groped among the creeper, searching for the lever that would grant her access. Its elusion had her silently cursing.

She was almost ready to collapse on the sodden mulch and bawl her eyes out, when her wrist connected with a knob.

"Ouch."

Relief surged as she yanked the lever sideways then dragged the metal door wide enough to slip through. Whoever used this entrance, made a point of pushing the mulch and clingy cover back into place when they left, giving no hint of the bunker's existence.

The rain had eased to a soft drizzle and pockets of blue sky poked through the white clouds. Staff and delegates would be moving about the resort soon. She eased the door almost closed, leaving her with a shaft of light to find her way down a steep set of steps. At the bottom she found a lantern and another metal door. Priority one was locating towels and dry clothes.

She found a stack of Frangipani print dresses in a storeroom. Fatigue, sore feet and aching muscles had her at a crossroad. She desperately wanted to sit down, take a short nap and refuel her drained battery, but Simon hadn't arrived and the locked room nagged at her conscience. She pulled on a dress then tip-toed back along the hall. What was taking Simon so long?

No prickle of unease or sound warned her she had company, until it was too late.

A massive hand covered her lower face from ear to ear. She was lifted way off the ground, locked within a colossal hairy arm, giving her no room for escape even if she could muster the courage to fight.

Terror had her frozen as the hulking giant carried her into the previously locked room where the ceilings, walls and floor had been painted dark blue and a high-backed chair sat in front of a wall of monitors. The door slid closed with a soft whoosh, a double click echoing as tumblers fell into place, cutting off any chance escape.

Her heart almost jumped out of her chest. Every screen streamed live footage from locations all over the island. Lanterns glowed outside buildings and along pathways within the resort. Her clandestine operations and abduction last night would have made fascinating viewing for her captors.

Darius skimmed each screen, relieved to see Talos and Sam at the front gate, talking to two men in wetsuits. Nick and Ryan.

Another monitor showed Simon, in black T-shirt and jeans, soaked to the skin, combing through the wall of creepers, his mouth moving as if he were calling her.

She tensed as a dark figure crash-tackled him into the shrubs, out of sight.

No! A sob rose in her throat, she elbowed, kicked, even tried head-butting the giant, to no avail. He held her secure, unable to budge his grip.

Simon needed help. He needed his friends.

She bit into a thick finger.

It made no difference.

"Release her."

The giant instantly obeyed the man in the chair's command and lowered her to the tiled floor then removed his hand from her mouth.

She whirled. "Vijay?" Her shock had her gaping as her brain registered the fact the chef, although as big as a grizzly, didn't look threatening.

He gave a light shrug. "Sorry I scared you."

The man at the panel tapped on a keyboard, shutting down the wall of monitors then he sighed. "Don't be alarmed, Dragonfly. I'm sure Simon Hawke will be fine. I must congratulate you on your ingenuity, but what did I tell you about keeping a low profile?"

He spun around and the man behind the smooth British accent smiled. "Welcome to our command center, my dear."

"Oh my God, you...*you're* Phoenix?"

৵৵

Rolling onto his knees, Simon ignored the dull ache in his shoulder and dragged in much needed air. He spat out bits of leaf matter and dirt. "Why the fuck did you do that?"

"Why the fuck do you think?" Jarred rose to his full height, brushed off clinging muck then held out his right hand and pulled Simon to his feet. "This job is possibly the most important we'll ever get. It will make or break us. If we fail, the implications are beyond comprehension. If we succeed, we will never look back. I don't need a love sick cowboy running about, chasing a slip of a girl who could well be our downfall."

They stood glowering at each other, both drenched, filthy and breathing hard.

"Give me some credit, Colonel." Simon blew out a long breath. "I believe Darius is the key to the Amethyst Code. Whether she's aware of it or not, I think she has the third password. The hacker needs Darius alive, and so does every terrorist group in the world. On the other hand, every government and intelligence agency would prefer she didn't exist."

"Shit." Jarred wiped his hands down his black pants then stared out to sea. "Let's look at the facts. The Sherpa is on this island. I will interrogate him. Professor Cortez's daughter is on this island, brought here by the hacker, which means he has to be here too. We don't have satellite access, so you can't run your Identiscan program.

185

Simon looked toward the villa. "There's a locked room in the underground bunker. I want to see what's inside. Darius is inside waiting for me."

A clatter drew their attention to the other side of the shrubs. "What was that?" Simon parted the branches and peered through. A black metal object lay in the center of the path. He squatted and reached out, plucking it up quickly.

"What is it?" Jarred stepped closer.

"A state of the art, wireless surveillance camera." Simon held his thumb over the lens then lifted his gaze to the swaying coconut palm above. "The wind must have dislodged it."

"Why is it blinking when the satellite dish has been destroyed?"

"Live feed, which means somewhere on the island is another dish."

"Then we need to act fast." Jarred rubbed his chin. "I can see a nail in the trunk. How the hell did Darius mount a camera that high?"

"She didn't. This device has been there a while, it's beginning to rust. Jarred, I need to get Darius off this island before…" His voice cracked.

"All right, I'll track down Sam and Talos." Jarred rubbed his chin. "We must assume there are other wireless cameras around the resort."

"And that we've been under surveillance all along. I'm going after Darius.

"Major! Use your fucking brain."

Jarred was right. They needed to treat this as any other military operation. "Once I know Darius is safe, I'll find the satellite dish and hook into it. I can do background checks on the delegates, speakers, security and staff on the island."

"Thank you, Major. Leave the camera on the path. If the owner comes looking for it, he won't realize we're onto him. We still have a few hours before breakfast. Use them wisely."

"Understood." Simon's attention caught on a yacht far out to sea. It was moving slowly, but on a direct course for the island. "We have company."

"So I see." Jarred narrowed his eyes. "I'd better get down to the wharf. We'll catch up after breakfast." He strode off around the side of the garden.

Keeping to the heavy foliage, Simon circled the villa. He'd already taken out the camera at the front entrance and over the kitchen door. He made his way back to the wall of clinging creeper and studied the area carefully, eventually finding the hidden camera. He searched the area below where a pile of leaves had been heaped.

A clunk had him dropping to his belly. Suddenly the creeper moved and an opening appeared. One of the waiters, Etera, stepped out. He glanced about quickly then shut the door, re-arranged the creeper and swept the piled leaves about, leaving no sign of disturbance. After another furtive look around, Etera ran toward the drive. A minute later, a golf cart motor whirled to life.

Using the shrubs as cover, Simon worked his way to the villa then slid along the side wall. He found a lever and pushed it sideways. The clunk had him silently cursing as he edged the door open. He slipped through and gingerly took the steps down.

Musty air filled his nostrils and throat. He stopped at the bottom to press his ear against another metal door to listen. Unable to detect any sound, he slid the lever across and pushed, cringing as the door creaked loudly.

Etera could have been checking the villa after the storm, but why the furtive looks? The hall was empty, so he made his way forward, hampered by the darkness.

A whoosh startled him. Spinning around, Simon's vision filled with a massive neck. "Jesus, you scared the crap out of me." He didn't see the fist, but he heard Darius scream as a fist ploughed into his forehead, slamming him into the wall behind.

❧

"No!" Darius hurled herself at the giant chef, snatching his mammoth fist in both her hands. Planting her feet, she dragged with all her might. One punch had knocked Simon senseless, two could kill him. "Vijay, leave him alone."

The chef shook her off. "He came looking for you."

"Yes, but only because he was worried. Someone fired a gun last night, and I was almost hit." The less these people knew the better. She fell to her knees, wrapping her arms around Simon's shoulders, shielding him from Vijay. "You have me and my Goshawk, what more do you want?"

Simon's eyelashes flickered against her cheek. *Thank God.* She had to play for time.

"Vijay! You've knocked him unconscious. He needs a doctor."

"That isn't possible." Alistair Finch spoke from behind her. "Check his pulse and pupils, Vijay."

"No, stay away, I'll do it." Darius laid her fingers against Simon's carotid artery. His pulse beat strongly, if a little rapid. She lifted one eyelid, again blocking the men's view. A green eye with flecks of hazel blinked at her. She squeezed his shoulder in warning. "Pupils are definitely dilated."

"Dragonfly—."

"Phoenix, if you want my co-operation, you will help me get Simon onto the bunk."

"Go ahead, Vijay, and then you'd better get back to the resort. Alisi won't be impressed if you're not there to cook the delegates' breakfast."

"You want me to check for weapons first, Professor?"

"Good idea. Who knows what those two divers brought in?"

A sharp pinch on her thigh brought Darius' attention back to Simon. Under a barely cracked lid, his eye shot back and forth.

She'd forgotten about the knife taped to his belly. "You're not touching him. I'll do it." She eased back, allowing the chef to fit his meaty arms under Simon, heft him off the tiled floor, carry him into the secret room then settle him on a bunk bed. Vijay held a card near a square on the wall and the door whooshed closed.

With two sets of eyes silently watching her every move, she ran her hands lightly over Simon's chest and down each arm. She placed one hand on his belly, over the knife then used her other hand to pat down each side from armpit to thigh, sliding her hand as close to his groin as she dared. She felt a slight quiver under her fingers. If Alistair Finch suspected an intimate relationship, he might use it against them.

Vijay removed Simon's runners then tied his feet and hands with rope, too tight for her liking. Seemingly satisfied, the two men shifted to the console and spoke in low whispers.

Simon cracked another eyelid, so she poked him and addressed their captor. "Phoenix, this crusade you're on isn't worth people getting hurt. It's not what my father would have wanted."

"I will be the judge of that, my dear." Alistair's gaze shifted to her. "As I was telling you before we were interrupted, I am an old friend of your father's. I respected his ethics and commitment to fighting cyber fraud. He wasn't a criminal."

"Then who set him up?" She kept her hand on Simon's stomach, glancing swiftly at his face when another ripple fluttered under her fingers. "Who caused his death?"

"Your father believed it to be someone he knew well, which is why he hid the SD card in the atom you made him. It's why, over the last five years, I've kept tabs on Professor Chapman, Simon Hawke, Phillip Nutlan and Keith Heckle—God rest his soul."

"But you're Phoenix. *You* had highly confidential information. How can I believe anything you say? How can I be sure *you* aren't setting me or Simon up?"

"We've gone over this already, my dear. I helped organize this summit, that's why I had all the information. Skills like your father's and Simon Hawke's are highly sort after, not just by professional companies and banks, but by governments, security agencies, and sadly, terrorist organizations. This young fellow you're protecting has a brilliant mind, and according to sources I can't divulge, he's developed other programs that boggle the mind. He is the prime suspect."

"Simon isn't the hacker and he wouldn't betray my father. His only interest is to prevent the program being used to create havoc throughout the world. And I don't see how I can help you any further."

"You can hide your hair under a sun hat and continue to be *Bellini*. Put that drone up again, so I can see who is on the yacht making its way here." He turned to Vijay, hovering by the door. "Yes, go. And cover any disturbance outside the bunker's entrance as you leave."

"Yes, Professor." The door whooshed open as Vijay lumbered out. It closed again and, seconds later, the chef appeared on one of the monitors. He closed the external door then shuffled leaf mulch about with his feet.

"What's Vijay's role in all this?"

Alistair sat back and crossed his arms. "He's a chef and security guard of sorts. He helps keep an eye on the monitors."

Those damn monitors had exposed Simon's friends, talking at the gate. The only one missing was Jarred, who must have been the person who tackled Simon.

His friends' whereabouts now were anyone's guess. They'd left the grounds then completely disappeared, which she could see had Alistair worried. "I'll put the Goshawk up, but first, I need to know if my family are really missing."

The professor narrowed his eyes. "I suppose Simon Hawke told you this?"

"Yes."

"To my knowledge they're not missing, but I will look into it. Anything else?"

"Do you know who killed Keith Heckle."

"If I did, for your own safety, I wouldn't tell you. Now…"

"Wait. I want your word you won't hurt Simon when he regains consciousness?"

"That won't be for a while, Dragonfly. In the meantime, he will remain secured here and no harm will come to him."

"Can I cover him with a blanket?"

"Certainly." Alistair ran his gaze over the wall of monitors. "Hurry, that yacht is getting closer and I should get back to the resort." He picked up a pen. "We need to discover where Simon Hawke's friends have gone."

She covered Simon then squeezed his shoulder. "I'll be back soon, don't…" So many thoughts assailed her. Don't do anything stupid, don't be a hero. What if he had a bleed on the brain? A large bruise was developing near his left temple. She leaned close to his ear. "Don't worry, I'll get help. I love you."

Picking up her Goshawk, she took a deep breath. Alistair had to be the hacker. How else had he set up such an elaborate operation or manipulated governments, foreign banks and intelligence agencies to send their best people to this particular island. An island without internet access to the outside world. Even if Simon fought free, he couldn't get out. Not unless he powered up the console, which meant keying in an extremely long combination of numbers and letters.

The door swooshed open and she had no choice but to proceed the professor through. It closed behind them and locks tumbled into place.

Alistair slid something flat into his shirt pocket. "Simon won't be going anywhere, not without this access card." He patted his pocket. "After you, Dragonfly. I took the opportunity of collecting your masquerade kit when I picked up the Goshawk drone. Everything you need to turn yourself into Bellini is in the bunker's bathroom."

"I feel weak." She swayed, clutching his arm as she fell against his chest. "I haven't had breakfast. If I don't eat, I'm likely to faint."

"I doubt that, Dragonfly." His lips quirked. "Once you've changed and eaten, we will commence the final act. Your father would be extremely proud of your ingenuity and courage, my dear. Do this last thing for me then I will make no more demands of you."

CHAPTER TWENTY

Trussed up like a turkey ready for the oven was a minor inconvenience, compared to how the hell he was going to get out of this sealed, pitch black vault. Being left alone with what looked like a mini supercomputer would normally have him frothing at the mouth with anticipation. Not today.

Having a hammer pounding inside his skull made it hard to concentrate, but knowing Alistair was Phoenix, responsible for endangering Darius, had Simon seething with rage. The man had to be deranged to pull off a conspiracy on this scale. As for murdering Keith Heckle and Lex Boyd, that would take a person with the strength of someone like Vijay, perhaps following Alistair's orders.

He figured enough time had passed for Darius and Alistair to have left the villa, so he worked his shorts down then tore the tape off his belly, taking a strip of hair with it. Carefully, he worked the flick knife between his fingers, then sprung the blade, working it back and forth against one tight coil. The second it gave, he unwound the rest then sliced through the rope at his ankles. It took a minute to get feeling back, then he slid the knife into his pocket and set about examining the room by touch. There had to be a light switch and door release somewhere.

In one drawer of the desk, he discovered a flashlight, in another a charger and satellite phone. He connected them then plugged the charger into a power socket.

He found a light switch on the wall beside the door and what looked like a credit card scanner, but no automatic release. Turning his attention to the room, his gaze skimmed over a small fridge, water cooler and kitchenette. A partially open door revealed a toilet.

His gaze snapped to a rack of servers, storage units, PCs and consoles. A water-cooling system had been set up to keep the cluster cool. Here was an advanced computing cluster with processing capacity years ahead of the most powerful desktop computers.

He moved to the curved panel, running his gaze over four keyboards aligned with desktop monitors. Another console sat dead center under a giant wall monitor. A large green button on the desk caught his eye. He pushed it. Nothing happened. It wouldn't be that easy.

Sliding into the chair, he rested his wrists on the desk and studied the console. Someone had gone to a lot of trouble and spent serious money to build this supercomputer technology. Surprisingly, the room had a coolness about it. Glancing up he found the reason. Four ducted vents blowing cool air in, which meant a generator running twenty-four hours around the clock, as the power for this setup would be immense.

It was easy enough to boot up the console, but he didn't have the time or software to break into the central server. His gaze fell on a line of black keys across the top of the console, numbered one to twenty.

"Here goes nothing." He pressed number one and the wall monitor above flickered to life, showing the reception area of the resort's foyer and Alisi at the desk. Pressing number two gave him a bird's eye view of the swimming pool where he could see the French woman, Marguerite speaking to one of the security men from the other team. She didn't look overly impressed.

Number three monitor showed inside the dining room where delegates had begun gathering for breakfast. Number four the golf course, where Hans—or rather Harnoop—was cutting grass. And so, it went. Alistair had eyes everywhere. One key showed an upside-down view of the base of a coconut tree. The surveillance camera that had fallen from the palm tree.

Other cameras showed staff, delegates and security personnel moving about the resort. He found Alistair having a conversation with Sir William. They both kept looking about, as if waiting for someone.

Simon located Darius, driving a golf cart past reception, heading toward the golf course. What worried him was the fact she had no protection, and he couldn't see Jarred or the boys anywhere.

By pressing the 'end' key, he brought up all the surveillance cameras, so leaned back to view the wall of images. Moving his finger across the touchpad, he clicked on the golf course. Instantly, it filled the whole screen.

Darius entered the far edge of the screen then disappeared behind a building. The greenskeeper was on his mower at the far side of the golf course.

"I've got to get out of here." He checked the charge on the phone. Too low.

With his head still pounding, Simon fell back in the chair and closed his eyes. The boys would come through, they always did. In the meantime, he had work to do.

He flexed his fingers. It would be a shame to waste the chance to test his skill. If he could install a RAT, then he could get administrative privilege and access the computer. He had nothing to lose.

Booting up all the computers, he almost cheered when the last one granted access without a password. Immediately, he sent off an email to Inspector Gibbs. It took ten minutes to download his Identiscan program. In the third drawer, he found a list of the delegates, speakers, security personnel and resort staff on a clipboard. This was his field. In thirty minutes, he had images matching delegates and speakers, their birth dates, addresses, occupations and infringement history. Things slowed up a little when he had to use his translation app for the Asian delegates and French woman, but everyone checked out.

An hour later, he had processed everyone on the island. A lot of data made interesting reading. Interestingly, Hans had been given a completely new identity thanks to Professor Cortez. Of concern, one of the security men on the other team didn't exist and, without a photo, Simon couldn't run him through Identiscan.

He made notes, checking deeper, back and forth between Australian and foreign intelligence agencies, immigration, defence, judicial records, electoral rolls and banking institutions. Simon needed a photo. If the guy had a record or a passport, or was on a terrorist watch list, he'd show up.

After stretching his aching back, Simon checked the time. Zero seven hundred, and not a word from Gibbs. There wasn't anything more he could do at the moment, except observe the island and do a thorough search of his prison cell.

As he searched each drawer, he scanned the wall of monitors. The rain had stopped. The tension left his shoulders when he saw a large bird of prey circling high in the sky, gliding on the updrafts. The distance was too great to tell if this was nature at her best or a mechanical drone. The odds were the hawk belonged to Darius, which eased his concern somewhat.

On another monitor, he noticed two joggers. They stopped at the villa gates and did a series of stretches. Looking up they spied the camera on top of a gate post giving Simon a clear view of their faces. Men from the other security team. They turned their backs and jogged down the hill.

Easing the bottom drawer back into its tracks, Simon absent-mindedly ran a hand under the counter, colliding with a slim, solid object. Excitement welled as he bent to examine it. "Yes." A hard drive had been taped to the underside. Ripping the tape off, he connected the hard-drive then opened it, only to gape in disbelief.

After verifying what he had, Simon closed the file then ejected the hard-drive. Flexing his fingers to ease the stiffness, Simon picked up the satellite phone. It was a stretch, but if Gibbs could afford a penthouse on Sydney Harbor and a prestigious Alfa Romeo, there was an even chance he had a satellite phone.

Simon keyed in the number and waited. It began ringing then clicked through. "Zachary Gibbs speaking."

"Inspector, this is Simon Hawke. Am I glad you picked up."

"That may change when you hear what I have to say."

"Go on." Simon sat forward. After this morning, nothing would surprise him.

"A terrorist threat has been intercepted. Something big is about to go down and your name, along with Darius Cortez's, was mentioned. Let me speak to Jarred."

A chill of apprehension ran through Simon. "I would, but I'm locked in an underground bunker and Jarred's not with me."

"Bring me up to date. Madeline said you have no communication."

"That's right. Our phones were confiscated in Fiji and the satellite dish on the island disabled. It's since been sabotaged. I've discovered the main villa has its own satellite dish, hidden from public view, which is how I reached you. There's a state-of-the-art control room set up in the bunker and Alistair Finch is Phoenix. It doesn't necessarily mean he's the hacker, but he does appear determined to clear Alexander Cortez. Also, I need to get Darius off the island. Someone took a shot at us last night."

"Damn. I've just been told the bureau of meteorology is forecasting a tropical cyclone, south-east of Fiji. It's due to hit later today."

"Shit." Simon scrubbed his face. "At least we have a bunker to shelter in. Any other good tidings you'd like to share?"

"Madeline Shaw left Lakeba Island yesterday. She's on a small yacht bringing your team guns, ammunition and several satellite phones. Two of my officers are on board as crewmen. A seaplane will pick them up well before the yacht is detected."

Simon frowned. "For what purpose?"

"Madeline is playing the part of a solo sailor, circumnavigating the world. My officers have orders to disable the yacht, so she can't be turned away from the island. I hope she makes it before the cyclone hits."

"You can relax, I saw a small yacht moving very slowly off the coast this morning."

"Thank God. Find a way out of that bunker and tell Jarred to call me." He hung up.

Simon fell back in the chair. "I'm not Houdini." He spun around to face the door and scanner beside it. His gaze dropped to something white poking under the steel door. He grinned. "But I do have a light-fingered fairy."

৵৹৻

Disguised as Bellini, Darius hid behind what she assumed was Alisi and Harnoop's house, situated with a clump of coconut palms between it and the golf course. Her gaze shot to the bluff where the jogger must have died. It fell well out of range for the surveillance camera to catch any foul play.

As it was just after seven o'clock, breakfast would be on, so she didn't expect to meet any delegates, and most security people would be down on the beach watching the yacht. She could only hope

Simon had got himself loose and found the exit card before Alistair realized it was missing.

Turning her attention back to the controller, she sent the Goshawk soaring into the blue sky for a panoramic view of the whole island. How she'd love to be up there, drifting on the breeze, not a worry in the world. Way out to sea, a fishing boat churned through the water, heading north, homeward bound after catching their morning haul.

On the golf course, two men were playing an early game of golf, so she zoomed in for a closer look.

Richard Chapman and Phillip Nutlan glanced up.

"Whoops." Sending the drone in a wide arc, she let it glide over the buff to Harnoop on his ride-on mower. The drone had a five-kilometer range, could fly at seventy-two kilometers an hour. Its optimized vision positioning and high-performance camera were state-of-the-art. The bird was a masterpiece of technology.

Almost too late, she saw Richard raise binoculars to his face. Quickly, she diverted the bird out over the tip of the island, to glide around the rocks to the resort. All looked quiet. She could see a man swimming in the pool and the French woman sitting on a daybed watching him.

Two security guys stood at the end of the wharf with Sir William.

Taking the Goshawk higher, she directed it over the ridge and her small villa. Nothing moved. Out of curiosity, she sent the bird cruising in a wide arc over the huge villa. The gardens weren't as immaculate as yesterday and the pool had palm fronds lying on the bottom. A small satellite dish glinted in the morning sun. She hadn't noticed it from the plane, but its existence had to be a plus. She couldn't see Simon.

Next, she directed the bird along the east coast of the island, where the coral reef prevented any hope of bringing a boat in that side. Waves smashed against jagged rocks either end, behind which grew vast clumps of mangroves.

A steep, heavily foliaged hill rose up from the long beach, where a reflection drew her attention. There one second, gone the next. She sent the drone in for a closer look, letting it cruise low over the trees.

Zilch.

Taking another circuit, she spied a green tent, almost invisible among the foliage. Were they camping illegally after canoeing in? Another thing to make Simon aware of. There'd been no sign of his Steele Ops friends.

So, onto the yacht.

A stab of pure satisfaction hit as the bird soared over the cliffs, the view on her controller spectacular. Watching her screen, she turned the bird west for a closer look at the yacht. Everything she filmed was also being transmitted to Alistair's iPad. She wondered if he had it on right now.

The yacht's mast looked to have broken off near the base. She could see a tanned woman in a cap standing at the helm. Her blonde braid reaching half way down her back. She wore short shorts and a skimpy bikini top. By the agitating water at the stern, the engine was working, but the sea was anything but calm.

"My goodness, she'll be smashed to smithereens if she hits the reef." Darius sent the Goshawk swooping over the water in an attempt to find a clear way through to the wharf. There wasn't one. Yachts had long keels to give them ballast, but the reef covered a vast area. If she lost the keel, she'd be at the mercy of the currents. The distant clouds didn't bode well either. Another storm was brewing.

"Damn." Sending the Goshawk in a wide arc, Darius brought it low over the ocean, on a collision course with the yacht.

The blonde woman screamed and dived sideways. As she scrambled back behind the wheel, Darius gasped. It was Madeline Shaw.

"Focus." She disconnected Alistair's feed then directed the drone in another wide sweep, bringing it in low again, this time flicking on the speaker. "You're on a collision course with a reef. Veer left and make for the smaller cove. Follow the drone."

Madeline stared at the bird, her mouth wide, as it hovered above. "Who are you?"

"That's not important. You must head for the next cove."

"Darius?"

"Yes, but don't blow my cover. I don't want to endanger my family."

"Your family are safe. They're under surveillance on a Whitsunday island."

Relief surged. "How do you know?"

"Because Zachary Gibbs located them. She swung the wheel hard as a gust of wind hit the yacht. "He's an inspector with the Australian Federal Police."

Hope filled Darius as she kept the drone slightly above and in front of the yacht's bow, leading Madeline through the narrow channel. Simon had mentioned Inspector Gibbs in the front yard of her grandmother's house.

Back to her immediate problem. Alistair would be furious she'd exposed the drone and disconnected the live stream. Sir William and the other security guards would want to know who controlled the drone. With luck they might think it belonged to Madeline. She could only hope.

Madeline might appreciate the help, but what was she doing here, and could she be trusted?

Darius jumped as gunfire rang out. "No!" Adjusting the dials, she brought the wharf into view. Two security guards were firing at her drone.

"Stop it."

The screen went crazy, flashes of sky, sea, and island spun past, then the camera and whatever was left of the Goshawk sank to the ocean bed. It settled beside a coral reef, abundant in colorful fish. The screen went black.

"Great. Just great." She hurled the useless controller into the thick canopy below. "Now what?" She couldn't see the yacht from here.

A chugging motor, growing closer had her catching her breath. She stepped back as a red ride-on mower skidded around the building, braking hard beside her and covering her in fine dirt. The driver lifted his huge straw hat and grinned. "*Bula*, Miss Darius."

She crossed her arms and glared. "*Bula*, Harnoop. Long time no see." Heavens, where was this newfound courage coming from? First Alistair Finch and now Harnoop. Maybe anger gave her the bravado she usually lacked.

He blushed. "I sorry about your *papà*. He... He always kind and generous to me."

"So why let everyone think you'd died in an avalanche?"

"With his death, I lose my standing. No work, no money. Your *papà*, he tell me stories about these islands many times. Before he...."

Harnoop's shoulders drooped. "On that last trek, he give me very big money and passport with different name. He tell me to come this island, to do job he arrange for me."

"So, he wasn't shot or pushed? He really did jump into the crevice?"

Harnoop hung his sweaty head. "I sorry, Miss Darius."

"Well that's that, I guess." She clamped her bottom lip between her teeth, fighting off the tears of disappointment and disillusionment. Her father had used his program to create a new identity and passport for Harnoop. He'd withdrawn money from somewhere other than his own accounts to give the Sherpa. But if he were guilty, why attach the SD card to the atom charm, asking her to expose a terrorist group. Questions she would never have the answer to.

Darius stared off over the roiling ocean, where white tips danced across the waves, giving no indication of the perilous reef below. A trap for unwary sailors. She could only hope Madeline stayed on course.

She didn't like loose ends. Simon could be right. Her father might not have attached the SD card. As his friend, Alistair Finch might have been aware of their coded game and used it to draw her into his web of espionage. She'd named it the Amethyst Code. Her father had liked the label and transferred it to the program he was working on. He'd never asked for a password.

She sagged against the golf cart and stared at her bare feet, going back to a time of laughter and silliness. Her father's teasing invitations to come up with combinations of characters, numerals and symbols to test his aptitude. He'd dare her to invent a code he couldn't break.

One day in particular came to mind. She'd been grouching about the house, clogged up with a head-cold, bored out of her brain, when he pestered her into playing. He'd suggested she use a piece of poetry, a passage from her latest book, the chorus of her favorite song, her first love's name.

She'd taken it one step further. Blocking his view as her fingers flew over the keyboard. He'd cackled and asked her to retype it, just to be sure.

"Heaven above, I know the password."

"What you say, Miss Darius, you speak so quiet, I not hear."

She straightened. "Nothing, I have to go. I'm glad you're safe, but *Hans,* there are bad people on the island. Be careful."

"Wait?" Harnoop looked over his shoulder then returned his serious eyes to her face. "I see two men arguing. One man knock the other down then throw him off cliff."

"What!" A chill ran down her spine, leaving her ice cold. "Why didn't you tell Jarred Steele what you saw?"

"Because it security man who throw jogger off cliff."

"Oh God."

Harnoop's gaze darted left and right. "I have message from Alisi. You should hide in boathouse Too many people looking for you. I bring food later."

She grimaced. The boathouse was far below at the other end of the island. "You don't have an invisibility cloak in your garden shed, do you?" The look he gave Darius, brought a smile to her face. "Never mind."

If she could make the cove and rescue Simon, they could sail the catamaran to Lakeba Island. She glanced at the distant purple clouds. Even if she could get Simon out of the bunker and escape, it would be treacherous sailing in a violent storm.

Harnoop whipped off his Frangipani shirt and brown *sulu,* leaving him wearing a pair of faded blue shorts. "You be me and drive the grass cutter to main villa, then run along track to boathouse." He passed her his clothes.

As plans went, it wasn't bad. "Thanks, Harnoop."

He wiped his eye. "I help you, like your *papà* help me."

She hesitated, torn between rescuing Simon and keeping Harnoop safe. Her heart decided. "I have a friend, Simon Hawke. He's hurt and locked in a secret room inside the emergency bunker. Please get word to Jarred Steele."

Harnoop's Adam's apple bobbled. "I not trust security guards."

"You can trust Jarred Steele." If they had a rogue security guard, he could be working for Alistair or a terrorist group. Something else Simon and his friends needed to know. "Okay, don't do anything."

Darius pulled Harnoop's shirt and *sulu* on over her dress as her mind raced. She'd passed on sensitive information to Phoenix and uploaded data from delegates computers. In good faith, she'd told

Simon about the SD card and her errands for Phoenix. She'd blown Harnoop's cover. "You should stay out of sight for a few days."

It appeared Simon had been right. She'd been manipulated by Phoenix, but he might not be her worst threat. If terrorist groups discovered she held the key to global domination, they would kidnap her without a second thought. She shuddered. If the world's governments realized what a threat she presented, they'd want her locked away.

Simon must know that but hadn't wanted to scare her. They needed to destroy the Amethyst Code urgently. If it didn't exist, she'd no longer be a target.

Harnoop scooped up her hair then jammed his sweaty hat down on her head. "You go now, Miss Darius. I hide under my house for a while."

She hugged him then climbed onto the mower. It had a key start, foot brake and forward or reverse foot lever. The only difficulty was keeping her speed to an unhurried pace as she hunched over the steering wheel.

At the entrance to the golf course, she got a panoramic view of the coast below. Delegates were following security personnel towards the rocks at the end of the main beach, eager to discover what had happened to the yacht, which Darius could see had dropped anchor inside the next cove.

Returning her attention to the road, she screeched, slamming hard on the brake as a security guard stepped out in front of her. His creepy leer sent a chill of terror through Darius. She leaped off the mower, but he caught her, clasped his hand over her mouth and hauled her behind the shrubbery.

Terror engulfed her. This couldn't be happening. She twisted, kicked, clawed at his hand. That didn't work, so she latched onto his finger, biting down hard.

"Bitch." He threw her to the ground. "You'll pay for that." His snarl matched the malice in his eyes.

CHAPTER TWENTY-ONE

Having accessed the computer, found the pot of gold at the end of the rainbow and escaped the villa, Simon wasn't yet ready to pat himself on the back. It had been too easy. He'd worry about that later. His first priority had to be Darius.

Halfway up the road to the golf course, laughter bubbled in his throat. Driving toward him on a grass cutter and viewing the scenery as if she had all the time in the world, came Darius, dressed as the greenskeeper. He raised his hand to wave when a security guard stepped out of the shrubbery. To Simon's shock, the guard dragged Darius, kicking and struggling into thick bush on the western side of the road.

"What the…" Simon broke into a sprint, panic rising like a torrent. If the guard intended to murder Darius, it wouldn't take much to snap her delicate neck or choke the life out of her. He could only hope the man had something else in mind. An appalling thought, but one that would give Simon time to save her.

"Get away from me." Darius screamed, terror inflicting every word.

Simon burst through the shrubs. His frantic gaze found Darius on the ground scrabbling backward, her eyes wild, her shirt torn. Fury radiated through every muscle as he spun to face her attacker, an ugly swine in the process of undoing his belt. With a roar, Simon charged, slamming the man into the undergrowth. Having the advantage of surprise, he leaped on the man's chest, hammering fast and furious punches.

Aware Darius had scrambled to her feet, Simon dragged the groggy guard to his feet. He smashed his fists into the man's bloodied face like a demon possessed.

203

The guard gurgled before crumpling like wet cardboard.

"Spineless bastard." Simon hauled the man up and threw him at a tree. Native bees immediately swarmed out of a low hive, rising to circle above them.

"Simon, stop." Darius clutched his rigid arm, pulling him away from the agitated bees, her face a mask of horror. "Please, stop before you kill him."

Simon heaved in huge breaths. She probably thought him a monster. His heart pounded as he glowered at the insensible man. "I need to teach him a lesson."

"You have. Let's get out of here." She dragged Simon along the bush track. "I know a shortcut to the boatshed."

He looked over his shoulder. The man had curled into a ball, his arms over his head, attempting to ward off the swarm of angry bees. "I'll demand he's sacked, and I'll make sure he never works in security again."

"Yes, darling." A gust of wind knocked Darius against Simon. "A storm is coming."

Adrenaline raced through his body. He pulled her into his arms, still coming to terms with what had almost happened. "When I saw him grab you, I didn't know if I'd make it in time. Hell, I wanted to rip him apart."

She raised a shaking hand to cup his cheek. "You saved me, that's all that matters."

He shuddered. "I never would have got to you without the key card." The thought had his stomach churning.

Her smile didn't reach her eyes, but by the tilt of her chin, she was determined to put the incident behind her. "We make a good team."

"Yes, we do, sweet pea." He hugged her closer, inhaling her scent, letting it calm his turmoil. For her sake, he'd forget about the guard for now. With luck, the bees would sting the bastard to death. "Let's make our way to the cove. A cyclone is on its way and I need to speak to Jarred."

As they scrambled down the steep bank, Simon told Darius about his phone call to Gibbs. "Whether he can send reinforcements will depend on the ferocity of the cyclone."

They came to a low trail. As they jogged around the cove, Darius told him about her conversation with Harnoop, Madeline's arrival and having the Goshawk shot down. Sir William and the security guards weren't taking any chances.

Anyone would think it just another day in paradise. Birds chirped, the incoming tide rippled over sun-bleached shattered coral and shells. Tiny fish darted through the shallows while a large lizard baked on a piece of driftwood. The small yacht had dropped anchor close to the boatshed and listed on the swells along with the catamaran.

Simon slowed to a walk. Out to sea, heavy clouds continued to gather. On the opposite side of the cove, delegates had congregated to watch as security guards dragged a row boat into the water. Two birds drowned out the other birds' chatter. Their whip-like whistles would wake the dead.

"That's Ryan and Nick." Simon put two fingers in his mouth and gave a short sharp whistle.

"Look." Darius pointed at the yacht. "That's exactly the sort of diversion we need."

Simon grimaced. Madeline stood on the starboard side of the yacht, feet apart, hands on hips and exuding unabashed confidence. She wore sunglasses, a bikini top, short shorts and her hair in a messy braid. She did not look anything like the sophisticated, not a hair out of place journalist he'd grown used to. "A diversion is putting it mildly. She'll have the delegates drooling like puppies."

Darius clutched Simon's hand. "The birds have gone quiet. Something's wrong."

A twig snapped. He squeezed her fingers as two fern fronds parted and a man stepped onto the track. "We've got company."

She whirled, shrieking at the fair-haired guy in army green T-shirt and pants behind her.

Ryan's amused eyes swept over Darius. "Hello, Mistress of Disguise. Who are you this time?"

She bristled. "No one. You didn't have to sneak up on us." She stiffened, obviously sensing the other presence now behind her. Simon grinned as Darius looked over her shoulder to where Nick slouched against a palm tree, his eyes dancing with merriment.

He raised an eyebrow. "What *have* you done to Simon?"

She darted a quick glance at Simon's forehead then raw knuckles and winced. "I didn't do it. Simon got hurt helping me."

Nick's lips twitched as he met Simon's gaze. "If you're not chasing Darius, you're rescuing her. Interesting relationship you've got going."

"You're telling me. It's like a carousel ride." Simon grinned. "Where's Jarred?"

"Here." The cool voice had them all glancing up the bank. By Jarred's rigid stance, he wasn't amused with their light-hearted banter. No spark of laughter lurked in his gray eyes as he jumped onto the track. He might be taller and heavier than Simon, but the man could move as silently and fast as a cheetah.

"Good morning, Miss Cortez, or is it *Bellini* today?"

She pursed her lips. "Bellini. I'm hiding my identity until we catch the hacker."

"I see." He looked at Simon. "Where's the entrance to the bunker?"

"There's one at the back of the pantry and another under a wall of creeping vines at the side of the villa. I've disabled two surveillance cameras, front and back, but there's another above the vine. A well-placed slingshot should do the trick." He quickly told them about the call to Gibbs, the looming cyclone, Alistair Finch, Vijay and the sealed room. "It's a command center with lots of high-tech computers and a wall of monitors hooked up to surveillance cameras all over the island."

Darius pulled out the chain holding her father's atom charm and unhooked a key "Jarred, this key will open the front or back doors. Once you're inside the villa, you'll find the secret door behind a long tapestry hanging in the pantry.

"How do we get into the sealed room?"

Simon passed him the key card Darius had lifted from Alistair. "Scan that."

Jarred handed the card to Ryan. "You two take out the camera then search the bunker. I want to speak to Alistair before I decide whether to inform Sir William. Keep the computer room sealed for now."

"On it." Nick took the key card then he and Ryan disappeared into the thick vegetation. There one second, gone the next, not a rustle or crunch to pinpoint their whereabouts.

Jarred's assessing gaze zeroed in on Darius again. "I take it that was your drone hovering over the yacht before security shot it down?"

"Yes." Darius narrowed her eyes. "An extremely expensive and effective spying device. I expect you to reimburse me."

He snorted. "Why would I do that?"

"Because my Goshawk saved Madeline and her yacht from being smashed to smithereens on that treacherous reef."

"The hell..." Jarred's gaze shifted to the yacht. "I'm going to strangle her."

Simon inwardly groaned. He'd put off mentioning Madeline, waiting for the right moment, if such a moment existed. "Gibbs allowed Madeline to bring us weapons and our satellite phones. He sent two officers with her, who were airlifted off the yacht once it was within easy reach of the island." Simon darted a glance at the opposite shore. "Look, Sir William and a security guard are rowing out to—"

"We need to get her off the yacht before they reach it." Jarred leaped down the lower bank then ducked under a canopy of spikey ferns growing out of black trunks.

Simon followed with Darius close on his heels. She squeezed between them. "Sir William won't hurt Madeline."

Jarred lowered a fern, giving them a clear view of the yacht. "What do you think will happen to a nosy journalist who shows up at a secret cyber summit?"

"I imagine under normal circumstances she'd get locked up." Darius grinned. "Luckily, Madeline is disguised as a freckled faced, teenage solo sailor. I almost didn't recognize her."

Jarred muttered something under his breath. "She'd be safer locked up. We have a hacker and a murderer on the loose. The last person they want anywhere near this island is an investigative journalist."

Darius peeked through the foliage. "What's our plan, Jarred?"

He sent Simon an irritated glare. "The row boat has a way to go yet, and the yacht's close to us." He looked at Darius. "Get Madeline's attention without using her name. Tell her to come ashore immediately. Keep the yacht between you and the approaching row boat. If I take Madeline into custody first, I can assume responsibility for her, thus keeping the bloody woman safe."

"Okay." Darius scrambled through the ferns then jumped to the sand.

Simon watched with concern as she hobbled over the broken shells and coral to the water's edge then waved her arms. "*Bula*, miss. Over here."

Madeline glanced over her shoulder then moved to the port side. "Yes?"

"I need you to come quick."

"Why?" Madeline leaned on the safety rail.

Darius pointed to the trees shielding Simon and Jarred. "He with the *steel* colored eyes wants you. Hurry."

"I'll just get my stuff." Madeline ran to the hatch then disappeared into the cabin.

Darius backed up to the bank, then ducked under a clingy fern and climbed up to Simon and Jarred. "She's coming."

Jarred scowled. "I can't believe Gibbs agreed to send Madeline."

Simon glanced back at the yacht where she'd reappeared on deck carrying a backpack. She grabbed a floatation ring then ran to the stern where she placed the pack on the ring in the ocean. Dropping her skimpy shorts, she threw them on top then slid into the water with barely a ripple. She swam breast stroke, pushing the flotation ring ahead until she reached the shallows.

Simon heard Jarred groan as Madeline emerged from the water. The skimpy white bikini enhanced her golden skin, long legs and full rounded breasts. The freckles dotted over her face were a clever addition and actually made her look eighteen.

Jarred swore. "Damn her to Hades, she's going to bring every man on the island running." He shoved ferns aside and jumped to the sand.

Simon and Darius followed.

Seeing them Madeline waved. "Hello, Darius, I figured it had to be you. Hi, Simon, what happened to your face?"

"A run in with the chef." The change in her appearance had him in awe. The immaculately dressed, stylish journalist had completely vanished. This near-naked girl looked like a teenage rebel out to experience everything life had to offer. No wonder Jarred had turned to stone.

Madeline raised a fine eyebrow. "Chief, you look hot and bothered. A dip will cool you down. The water is very refreshing."

He stood with hands on hips, glaring. "Is there a point to this nautical exhibition, or are you determined to blow my team's cover?"

She rummaged in her pack then tossed him a plastic wrapped bundle. "Your satellite phones, weapons and spare ammo. No thanks needed."

He tucked the bundle under his arm. "What happened to the yacht's mast?"

"Zachary's men sabotaged it. I'm hoping it's enough to stop the summit's organizers turning me away."

He sighed. "They won't. A cyclone is due to hit later today."

Madeline looked up at the heavy sky. "The last report I got suggests we will only get the edge of it, which is a plus." She turned her back to pick up the pack.

"Christ Almighty." Jarred ran a hand through his hair. "You might as well be naked."

Simon considered the triangular piece of material not quite covering Madeline's butt. It wasn't as skimpy as some he'd seen on Sydney's beaches.

The minute Madeline pulled on her shorts, and a loose T-shirt, Jarred's attention reverted to Simon. "The row boat is almost to the yacht. Climb up to the trail then stick close in case we meet anyone. Head for the main villa."

"Yes, boss." Simon held fronds aside. "After you, ladies."

Jarred muttered as he bound up the bank to Simon. "We should tie the two of them up and lock them in the bunker."

Darius looked over her shoulder. "Simon wouldn't let you tie me up."

"Don't mistake Simon's gallantry for something it's not."

Her gaze darted from Simon to Jarred. "Simon is a gallant knight."

"Fairytales." Jarred strode along the trail, leading the way.

Simon winked at Darius. She'd become the most important person in his life, but this wasn't the time to tell Jarred.

They came to the villa's perimeter fence and Jarred held up his hand. "We'll go over here." He didn't wait for an answer, instead stepped behind Madeline to place his hands on her waist.

She gasped.

"On the count of three. One—two—three." Jarred propelled her up the metal bars with such force, she only had to catch the horizontal rail, then shimmy over and drop to the soft earth on the other side.

Not to be outdone, Simon cupped his hands for Darius to step into. He hoisted her up and she sailed over the top then landed beside Madeline, grinning broadly.

He backed up then ran at the fence, latching onto two vertical bars with his hands and the rubber soles of his shoes. Once he landed beside Darius, Simon waited for Jarred, who indicated he'd circle round to the front of the villa with Madeline.

Simon and Darius crept alongside a hedge of red bristly flowers, reminding him of the bottlebrush trees in the front garden of Darius' old home. He dropped to a crouch and peered through the foliage. Ryan or Nick had tampered with the camera over the creeper. It now faced the sky. The ground outside the door looked undisturbed. "It might be best if we use the back door. I'll go first then signal you to follow if it's safe." He sprinted across the lawn then flattened his back against the rear wall. Nothing moved. He waved her over.

After a quick glance about, she sprinted through the garden, her breath coming fast as she glued herself to the wall beside him. "This undercover stuff is kind of fun when I'm not terrified out of my mind. We're not being followed, I checked."

He couldn't help but grin. "Good to know, Double-O-Seven. Stay close." He eased the door open then after a quick glance inside, motioned for her to follow.

They navigated the foyer and dining room without mishap, reaching the kitchen as the secret door scraped open. Simon thrust Darius into a corner, shielding her with his body.

"Wondered when you'd turn up." Nick's jovial voice was a balm to the tension building inside Simon.

Darius pushed against his back then squeezed around him. "It's my fault Vijay hit you, and that your knuckles are raw." Her beautiful eyes filled. "If I'd just accepted my father's guilt none of this would be happening."

He drew her into his arms then rubbed her back in soothing circles. "This isn't your doing, Tink. Whether you got involved or not, Alistair and the hacker have an agenda. We have to stop them before they do serious damage."

"Isn't Alistair the hacker?"

"Maybe, maybe not." At this stage, Simon didn't want anyone to know what he'd discovered on the hard-drive.

Jarred strode into the kitchen with Madeline on his heels. "Let's get Alistair and the chef in for questioning." He glanced at Simon. "Take Darius back to the resort."

"What? No way." Simon's heart thudded hard and fast. "I'm not letting her out of my sight."

"I understand your concern, Simon." Jarred ran a hand through his hair. "But Darius is our ears among the staff. We need her moving freely about the resort. Talos and Sam can keep an eye on her. Once the cyclone passes, I'll inform Sir William our shipwrecked guest will be staying in the small villa with Bellini. That should keep him happy and them safe.

Darius' fingers dug into Simon's waist as she addressed Jarred. "Alistair and Vijay know who I am."

"If they'd wanted to harm or expose you, they would have done it by now." Jarred looked to Simon. "Just to be sure, stick to the ladies during the cyclone."

A phone rang from within the bundle under Jarred's arm. He tore the plastic open and answered, pressing the speaker option. "Jarred Steele speaking."

"Zachary Gibbs, Jarred. I take it Madeline arrived safely?"

"Are you out of your mind, Inspector? We're expecting a cyclone and you drop a journalist into the middle of an undercover mission?"

Madeline glared at him.

Gibbs exhaled. "We can't get reinforcements onto the island until the cyclone passes. At least you now have communications and weapons that work."

Jarred touched the gun in his holster. "What do you know that I don't?"

"We intercepted a transmission. The weapons you've been issued with are loaded with blanks."

"Shit, this summit is the biggest clusterfuck I've ever had the misfortune to get involved in. Any news on the Cortez women?"

Simon felt Darius tense in his arms.

"All three are on Hamilton Island. We have them under twenty-four-hour surveillance. The house is bugged but, so far, they haven't said anything of importance. It appears they're having a holiday together."

Jarred frowned. "What about Francine Cortez's new man?"

Darius stretched up to Simon's ear. "The Federal Police have no right invading my mother's personal life."

Inspector Gibbs rustled paper. "No male has been seen, but Francine Cortez has spoken on the phone to a man called Darren. He's on a fishing trip and promised to celebrate his huge catch with her when he gets back."

"Lucky devil." Jarred tapped his thigh. "Any news on the hacker?"

"How far do you trust Simon Hawke?"

Everyone looked at Simon. He stilled. Within his arms, Darius' stiffened.

Jarred held a finger to his lips for quiet. "I'd trust Simon with my life, as I would with each member of my team."

"Is that wise? There are concerns Simon may have been involved in the disappearance of software he developed with Professor Cortez."

"I would stake my life that he's not."

"Then for your sake, I hope you're right."

"Is there anything else, Inspector?"

"Yes. Don't let anything happen to Madeline."

Jarred's gaze zeroed in on Madeline, who met it without a qualm. "My team are on a critical mission. I suggest you find a way to get her off this island and let us do our job."

"I can assure you that's my number one priority, however with this cyclone, I'm stuck on Lakeba Island. Ring me if and when you have news."

Jarred ended the call then narrowed his eyes. "As Alistair Finch knows who we are, I won't expose him yet, but I will have a chat with him."

It didn't diminish Simon's unease. "Where's Sam and Talos now?"

"They're checking out some buildings near the golf course. It seems two security guards have been sighted who can't be accounted for."

"I know where they might be." Darius' eyes sparkled. "When I had the Goshawk above the west coast, I noticed a green tent. The man who attacked me is probably sleeping in the tent and watching that side of the island."

"Attacked you?" Jarred and Madeline spoke in unison.

"A security guard I've never seen dragged Darius into bush up near the golf course, with the intention of raping her." Simon held up his raw knuckles. "You won't have any trouble identifying him. What do you plan to do about Alistair and the chef?"

"Interrogate them. If necessary, I'll lock them somewhere secure."

"The bunker downstairs would be ideal," offered Nick. "Some of the storerooms are lockable and we would have control of the surveillance cameras."

"Wait." Darius cleared her throat. "Don't forget Alistair can view the security footage on his iPad."

"Not anymore." Simon smiled at her. "I've severed the connection."

"What about the computers." Madeline passed Simon a phone. "I assume you gained access?"

"Yes, it was surprisingly easy, which makes me nervous. Alistair is either extremely confident I won't expose him, or he wanted me to see his elaborate set up, in the hope of enlisting my help. I don't think he's the hacker, but I'm struggling with the fact he insists he was a good friend of Alexander Cortez. I've never heard him mentioned in all the years I knew the professor."

Darius frowned. "The hacker could be Professor Chapman. He has a seedy side I didn't know about, and he's a computer scientist who worked at the same university as my father."

Simon drew her closer. "Stay well clear of Richard Chapman." He couldn't stomach the thought of the sleazy bastard anywhere near Darius.

Jarred rubbed his chin. "Simon, what can you tell me about Professor Nutlan?"

"He's respected by his students and the other academics, but he's an introvert and a bit odd. His nickname around campus is the Nutty Professor. He never married, lives alone, wears bow ties, only drinks herbal tea, likes cats, but has no tolerance for smokers or heavy drinkers."

"Hmm." Jarred glanced around the kitchen. "This villa and the bunker below *would* make an ideal base. Having the computers and monitors at our disposal is a bonus. Can we secure the bunker from inside?"

Nick nodded. "External doors are both made of steel and have sliding bolts which can be secured internally. There are also storerooms with weeks of food and water. It would be the best place to move everyone, if things go south."

"Excellent." Madeline tapped a finger against her chin. "Sam and Talos should bring the chef here, while Jarred interviews Alistair Finch."

Jarred scowled. "You are not to go anywhere near the chef."

"Of course not, chief." She smiled coyly. "I will, however, alert the resort staff to the approaching cyclone."

Nick stepped away from the wall. "What do you want me and Ryan to do, boss?"

"Clear out a couple of storerooms for any hostile guests, then monitor the surveillance cameras. As a courtesy, I'll take Madeline to meet Sir William and Alisi. That should suffice for now. Once everyone is directed to the bunker, I want the computer room sealed." He handed Nick two phones. "Text me if you need backup. And fix the villa cameras. We don't want anyone sneaking up on us."

"Will do." Nick stepped into the pantry. The bunker door scraped closed then the steel bolt clanged into place.

Jarred turned to Simon. "Stay away from the main hub until Talos and Sam have the chef. I will text you when it's safe for Darius to show her face and for you to join the other delegates."

"Suits me."

"Make sure you circulate. Let's see if anyone approaches you with an extraordinary job offer. With luck, the hacker isn't aware of your capture or Darius' presence. Any questions?"

"No." Simon kept hold of Darius' hand as he followed Jarred and Madeline to the front door. "I'll lock up after you."

"Jarred." Darius hesitated then took a deep breath. "The man Harnoop saw speaking to the American jogger is a security guard. Harnoop witnessed him throw the jogger off the cliff but feared telling you for obvious reasons."

"That explains his nervousness when we spoke. There are two men on the other security team who have the strength to carry out such a cold-blooded act. Stay close to Simon for now, I'll be in touch."

CHAPTER TWENTY-TWO

Darius tried to quell her unease as Simon closed then locked the front door. By telling Jarred about the murderer, she'd put the Sherpa at risk. She hoped her intuition wouldn't let her down.

Simon leaned against the door, his gaze intent. "Do you have any injuries I don't know about? Did Alistair or Vijay hurt you?"

"No, what about your knuckles? They look raw and painful."

"Nothing a little TLC won't fix. Let's find somewhere private, so you can tend my injuries and I can do some more research."

"Now! What about the summit?"

"Everyone will be curious to meet the woman on the yacht. We have at least an hour. Plenty of time for kissing." He bent slightly then tossed her over his shoulder.

"Simon!" She clung to his black T-shirt as he marched through the ground floor of the villa, one arm locked around her legs and one hand firmly planted across her bottom.

"Not what I'm looking for. Let's try upstairs."

"Only kissing." She smacked his backside. "I don't want your friends finding us in a compromising position."

"Not a chance, sweet pea." He took the stairs two at a time then paced along a wide hall to a bedroom at the end.

"This is more like it." He lowered her feet to the tiled floor then raised an eyebrow. "What do you think?"

Darius peered at the luxuriously pillowed bed with trepidation. "Very nice, but I don't feel comfortable making out in the owner's bedroom."

"We aren't." He tossed off his shirt then locked the door. "Believe it or not, this is a guest room. And when I say I want to kiss you I mean every inch of your delectable body."

A tremor of anticipation rippled down her spine. "Will it be as thrilling as taking a shower with you?"

He closed the distance between them. "Let's find out." He untied Harnoop's *sulu* then helped her out of his ripped shirt, leaving her in the Frangipani print dress.

Darius pressed closer as Simon traced her nipple through the dress, sending quivers racing over her skin.

He smiled. "This dress is hampering my research." He reached around to unzip it then peeled the fabric down her arms, locking them by her sides. "That's better." He bent, capturing her right nipple between his lips.

"Yes." She clung to his shorts, rubbing against his erection as he licked her nipple.

He sank to his knees, running his fingers over the backs of her calves, under the long dress and up her thighs, then down again, shooting delightful quivers throughout her body. "I thought you wanted to kiss me?"

"Oh, I will." He traced his fingers up the insides of her legs, bunching the dress just below the center of her need, almost buckling her legs, before he reversed direction.

"Going commando, Tink?"

"My...underwear is in the other villa."

"I'm not complaining." He lifted the dress higher, bunching it at her hips, then lowered his gaze. "I'll never get enough of you." He drew the dress down to her ankles then stood and lifted her into his arms, his hazel eyes dark and serious. "When I saw that guy drag you into the bush, I didn't know if I'd make it in time."

She touched a finger to his lips. "You did make it in time, darling, and that's all that matters. Once you catch the hacker, we can go home and put him and this summit behind us."

"Sounds good. Where do you want to go on our first date?"

Her eyes widened. "We're not dating, Simon. That doesn't work for me, remember. We're having a wild, spontaneous affair, which you started by kissing me."

He chuckled. "I'd better do some more kissing then." He laid her on the silk coverlet, among richly colored cushions then came down on top of her. "I see this wild spontaneous affair lasting a very long time, perhaps well into the next century.

She giggled. "You think you're that good a kisser, huh?"

"Damn right." His warm breath tickled her neck. "Tell me when to stop." He nipped her earlobe then layered soft kisses down her neck and across her shoulder.

"Hmm." Darius arched, showing him where he should kiss next.

He ignored her to lay kisses across her other shoulder then down the inside of her arm. He kissed her cheeks, eyelids, forehead, nose and chin, before finally taking her mouth in a drugging, sensual kiss that had her head spinning.

She broke away for much needed air.

Simon took the opportunity to slide down her body, kissing, licking and tormenting her breasts, stomach and each leg, before flipping her over. Darius gasped as his lips touched the back of one knee, then the other, moving slowly up each thigh to leisurely kiss the globes of her bottom. She giggled and squirmed, trying to roll onto her back so she could touch and kiss him.

He held her down to smother the small of her back in slow kisses before moving to her shoulders then neck, his erection pressing between her thighs. Heat engulfed her. She moaned, coming up on her elbows to pushed against him. His answering groans a small victory against his erotic torment.

He flipped her and she found herself staring into blazing green eyes. "If you weren't new to this, I'd have taken you from behind for teasing me with that little stunt."

"From behind?" The idea intrigued her. "Will I like it?"

"Jesus, woman. I'm trying to break you in gently."

Darius groaned. "Meanwhile, I'm dying of frustration here."

He chuckled. "You're about to get a little more frustrated." He slid down her heated skin, then pushed her thighs apart. She barely had time to draw breath before he took her ruthlessly with his mouth. Sensation ripped through her like flaming arrows. She screamed, bucking against his lips, her fingers gripping the coverlet as she soared high and gloriously free.

He began to pull away.

"No, I need you inside me."

"Darius." The gruff appeal sounded pained. "You're probably tender."

"You can't stop, not after that buildup." She rolled over, coming up on her knees to press her bottom against his erection. "Show me."

"Don't move."

She tried not to, delighted with her conquest. He cupped her breasts, nuzzling her neck with his lips as he caressed her sensitive skin and nipples. He traipsed one hand down her abdomen, his fingers sliding through wet curls to rub and circle her desperate, aching flesh. He pushed his fingers into her, thrusting back and forth. She cried out, rubbing against him, begging for fulfilment.

"Lean on your hands, and for God's sake stop me if you're tender."

She quickly obeyed, words were beyond her.

He gripped her hips, pressing slowly inside her. There was some tenderness but the pure, overwhelming pleasure of having him fill her overrode all else. She moaned in gratification.

"You're going to kill me, sweet pea." Simon withdrew then thrust deep, dragging another cry of pleasure from her lips. His thrusts grew faster and deeper, spiraling Darius into a vortex of building sensations, until she hit the pinnacle, screaming her triumph.

Simon withdrew, his roar bringing a smile to her lips as they collapsed on the silken coverlet, the warmth of his ejaculation trapped between them.

Darius lay in a lethargic cocoon of bliss, unable to raise a finger as Simon left her then returned with a warm washer. She managed a contented sigh when he finally drew her into his arms.

"Crazy girl. What am I going to do with you?"

"Love me."

Simon held Darius in his arms as she slept, transfixed by her delicate beauty. She wanted him to love her. Mission accomplished.

He'd almost dozed off himself when a thump on the door jolted him back to earth. "Simon, it's Ryan. Get over to the resort, asap. Professor Nutlan and the chef have disappeared, and your absence is causing quite a stir."

"Shit." Simon rolled off the bed. "Give us a minute, mate."

"Shush." Darius slid off the other side, grabbing her dress and clutching it to her chest. "Now Ryan knows I'm in here with you."

"There was never any doubt." He dragged on his clothes. "Tink, I need you to provide me with an alibi as Bellini."

She shimmied into the dress. "But Harnoop knows who I am, and that probably means Alisi does too."

"It's in their own interests to keep their mouths shut. Other than Alistair and the chef, I doubt anyone else knows your real identity."

She turned for him to zip her up. "What happens if Alistair and Vijay expose me?"

"Then they'd reveal their own scheme and never clear your father. Until Jarred turns them over to the AFP, they've got time to draw out the hacker. He may even convince them to work with us. It may save their lives."

With a frown, Darius finger-combed her long black hair into a braid then met his eyes in the mirror. "You mean..."

"If a terrorist group is behind the hacker, they will do whatever it takes to get the third key and disposing of anyone who gets in their way." He kissed her neck. "Ready?"

"As I'll ever be." She smoothed down the dress then accepted his hand. They ran along the hall and down the stairs. At the bottom, Ryan stood lounging against the wall. He grinned at Darius. "Enjoy your *siesta*?"

"It was very *nice*, thank you."

"Nice." He raised an eyebrow at Simon. "You obviously need some tips, mate."

"When I say *nice*," Darius fluttered her eyelashes at Ryan. "I mean Naughty... Intense... Concerted...and Erotic." She blew Simon a kiss, before sashaying through the foyer to the front door. "Coming, Simon?"

"You bet, sweet pea." Simon held his hands wide and grinned at Ryan. "I guess I don't need any tips after all, *mate.*"

The stunned look on Ryan's face was worth a thousand words. Giving him a two-finger salute, Simon strolled over to Darius and opened the door. "After you."

After closing the door, he took Darius' hand. "Your true colors are coming out, Tink. Everyone believes you a shy little thing, when in actual fact you're the wicked fairy queen."

"I am shy."

"No way. A shy woman wouldn't pretend to be an exotic *senorita* intent on stealing my wallet, or an actress so she could infiltrate a secret cyber summit, or dance on stage wearing a coconut bra and grass skirt. A shy woman wouldn't coerce a guy trying to take things slowly into doing what we've done in the last twelve hours. Not that I'm complaining." He winked at her. "Come on, we'll take the Vesper."

Simon jumped on the motorcycle, relieved to find a key in the ignition. He balanced the bike while Darius hitched her dress then climbed on behind, wrapping her arms around his waist. His gaze fell to one shapely leg, and his mouth dried. Only a fairy queen could have this much power over a mere mortal.

She squeezed his waist. "What are you waiting for?"

"Just admiring the scenery." He switched the key then held in the left brake lever and pushed the starter button. The little machine purred to life and they were off, sweeping along the curved drive and through the open gates. The refreshing breeze helped clear his head, as they rode down the sweeping bends to the resort.

Simon made a point of tooting the tinny horn at several delegates out walking, drawing their surprised attention. Darius played the part of Bellini, waving and laughing as they whizzed past, her long black hair flowing behind.

Simon rocketed in under the portico, deliberately close to Richard Chapman.

The professor jumped back, his expression thunderous. "Damn idiot, watch where you're going."

Releasing the throttle, Simon made a wide circle then pulled up in front of Richard. "Sorry, old man. As the morning session seems to have been postponed, we've been exploring the island." He placed his hand on Darius' bare thigh, unable to resist staking his claim. "Told you I'd have you back in time for lunch, sweetheart."

Sharp nails pinched his waist. "Thank you...darling." She climbed off, smoothed her dress down then flicked her hair back. "Will I see you tonight?"

"You bet." This was too good an opportunity to miss, especially with Richard glowering at him. Simon reached for Darius, bringing her closer. "*Baciami.*"

A soft blush crept into her cheeks. "Say please." She raised a delicate eyebrow then licked her upper lip, sending all his blood south.

"*Per favor, tesoro mia.*"

"I like the sound of that." She leaned over and kissed him. "Catch me later."

It was an effort to drag his eyes from hers, but their audience had grown. Sir William and Marguerite Lémaire stood with Richard, all three looking like they'd like to throttle him.

"Is there a problem, folks?"

Sir William pointed a finger. "I distinctly heard Alistair say staff are off limits."

"You're right, but Bellini is not an employee. She's a guest. As such I accepted her invitation to go for a ride this morning."

Darius pinched his arm.

"I thought you left the island, my dear." Richard's gaze travelled slowly down Darius' figure, raising an instant ferocity in Simon.

She edged closer, linking her fingers to Simon's hand, whether for protection or because she sensed his fury, he couldn't be sure. "A miscommunication, plus Simon offered to teach me how to fly...a kite. That is where we've been all morning. Riding and flying. The heights we reached were astounding."

Simon fought his grin and lost. "Astounding."

"There you are, Simon and Bellini." Alistair strode out of reception. "Professor Nutlan and Vijay have disappeared. You haven't seen either of them, have you?"

Simon raised an eyebrow. "Not recently."

Alistair's imploring eyes gave Simon food for thought. "Professor Nutlan hasn't been seen since last night, and Vijay disappeared after breakfast."

"I can't help you. There is however a security guard looking the worse for wear. I haven't seen him before, but he attacked Bellini this morning, hence my damaged knuckles." Simon held one hand up. "If he crosses my path again, I'll beat the shit out of him a second time." He let his gaze settle on Richard. "And anyone else who thinks to lay a finger on her."

Alistair's shocked eyes had settled on Darius. "I'm so sorry, my dear. This isn't what I wanted."

She smiled. "I'm fine, thanks to Simon. What's happening with your convention, Professor?"

"Our start this morning has been delayed, due to the arrival of a woman on a damaged yacht. We should be ready to kick off after lunch."

221

His gaze dropped to Simon's and Darius' joined hands. "Bellini, it's been suggested you might be willing to share your villa with the stranded lady for a few days?"

"Sure. Where is she now?"

"In the kitchen. Madison offered to fill in for our missing chef, as a way of paying for her accommodation. She's helping Alisi prepare lunch."

"I will introduce myself."

She dropped Simon's hand then ran into reception, leaving him and the others staring after her. She was safe for the moment, so he discreetly studied Marguerite, Richard, Sir William and Alistair. Two of them bore expressions that sent a chill through him. Richard's was lecherous, his half smile lewd. Marguerite's eyes had narrowed to slits, her lips curled in a snarl.

Sir William's and Alistair's lips were compressed. They appeared vexed. No wonder. Two people dead, two missing and two attractive, young women to distract the delegates.

Marguerite's gaze shifted to Simon, her expression undergoing a drastic change. She dipped her chin coyly, pouting her red lips as she peered at him from downcast eyes, like he'd somehow hurt her feelings.

"Simon, *mon cher*, I have been looking for you. May we lunch together?"

"Sure, why not." Simon nodded at the others. "Care to join us gentlemen?"

"No, *mon cher*, I meant..."

"Excellent idea." Sir William cut Marguerite off. "There's a few things I like to ask you about that program you and Alexander Cortez invented."

"I'll answer what I can, but I don't know the third key, which is critical if one wants to operate the program to its full capacity."

"Be that as it may, I would still like to pick your brains and—"

An ear-piercing scream had Simon leaping off the Vesper and sprinting into the foyer. He almost collided with Jarred. They both swung towards the kitchen as another female screamed. Fear like he'd never known tore through Simon's chest. "Tink!"

"Wait!" Jarred shoved him sideways against the reception counter. "God knows what's happening in there. We go in one at a time."

One woman continued to scream hysterically, drawing a crowd behind Simon.

"Darius and Madeline are in there."

Jarred gave him a sharp nod. "I'll go first. Give me five seconds, then follow."

"Fuck." Simon clenched his fists, counting off the seconds. He made it to four then ran through the office. The door to the kitchen swung back and forth. Simon shoved it hard and swept his gaze round the kitchen. The screaming had dropped to sobbing, coming from beyond a half open door.

He ran between two stainless steel counters then eased through the doorway into a short hall, where he found Alisi, tears streaming down her face, peering into what looked like a cool room.

He eased her aside, his gut churning. "What happened?"

Alisi shuddered. "Bellini went into the cool room for fruit juice. We heard her scream." Alisi wiped mucus from her nose. "There was so much blood. It's...everywhere. Madison slipped in it and I freaked out."

"Stay here. Don't let anyone through but security." Simon barely held it together as he entered the dark room. The metallic stench hit him immediately.

"Darius?" His heart hammered against his chest, perspiration coated his forehead as he dragged one foot after the other, terrified of what he would find. Stepping into the cool room, his gaze flicked along aisles of floor to ceiling shelving, crammed with tins and cartons.

Cool air dusted his face and arms, a motor whirled somewhere towards the back. Jarred's hushed, soothing voice, drew Simon to the last aisle. He'd only heard the boss speak this way once, after they found a traumatized Afghani boy, digging through rubble, searching for family. The fact Jarred spoke that way now, chilled Simon to the bone.

Taking deep breaths through his mouth, he stepped into the aisle. A pool of dark liquid covered the concrete floor, seeping in under the shelves on either side. Blood. Way too much for a minor injury. A person or large animal had bled out and, by the sizable smear, something had been dragged through the blood.

His gaze lifted to Jarred, sitting on a carton, cradling Madeline in his arms, her face buried against his neck. Blood streaked her bare legs and arms, soaked her shorts and shirt and hair. "What happened to Madeline?"

"She slipped in the blood and wacked her head. She's not quite with it." Jarred ran a bloodied hand up and down her back. "Everything's okay, Maddie, I've got you."

"Where's..." Simon cleared his throat. "Where's Darius?"

"Beside me." The steel thread in Jarred's voice brought Simon up sharp.

CHAPTER TWENTY-THREE

Simon needed to get to Darius without contaminating evidence. The blood wasn't fresh, so it didn't belong to her, but why wasn't she saying something? He began to process the scene. He'd seen goats tethered by the roadside, which might explain the amount of blood, but not why an animal had been slaughtered in the cool room.

Focus. Most logical explanation, a person had bled out and they had two missing people to choose from. Professor Nutlan and Vijay.

Jarred continued to speak in a low tone, never taking his eyes of Madeline, so Simon stepped warily, his runners sticking one second then sliding the next. The blood became thicker the closer he got to Jarred and Madeline.

"Darius?"

"I'm here," her whisper barely reached his ears. Impatient to see for himself, Simon lengthened his stride then edged around Jarred.

Darius had her arms wrapped around her bent knees. As he stepped closer, she raised her face to reveal trembling lips and haunted eyes. Whatever she'd seen had killed her playful energy. He squatted in front of her and placed his hands around hers. "Talk to me, Tink."

"Vijay…" Her gaze darted to the end of the aisle. "He has a spear in his chest."

Simon glanced along the aisle, his breath hitching when he saw two sandaled feet poking out from between shelving. "Jesus."

Darius shivered. "I couldn't find a pulse. What kind of monster would do this?"

"I'll be back in a minute."

"Take photos," murmured Jarred. "But don't touch him."

225

"Understood." Simon straightened then took out his phone. The volume of voices in the kitchen had grown. Keeping to the edge of the blood, he took three strides.

Vijay sat slumped in a cavity between two tall shelves, saturated from chest to thighs in blood. His huge arms hung slack by his sides and a fishing spear protruded from his chest. By the amount of blood, he didn't die immediately. The speargun lay between Vijay's legs. This was no accident.

Looking up, Simon noticed the gutted carcass of a pig. It hung lopsided, an empty hook on the horizontal bar. "Vijay must have been taking the carcass down when he was shot."

"That's my reading," muttered Jarred. "He must have discovered or witnessed something that got him killed, or Alistair didn't want us speaking to him.

Raised voices had Simon pushing that thought to the back of his mind. He photographed Vijay, the pig and the aisle, making sure he didn't capture Darius, Jarred or Madeline.

Jarred exhaled. "We need to get the ladies out of here." He came to his feet in one fluid motion, keeping Madeline cradled in his arms. "The cyclone is a way off yet. I'll take them to the small villa and get Ryan can keep an eye on them."

"Good idea." Simon squatted in front of Darius. "I'm going to carry you out of here, Tink. I want you to stay at the villa for now."

"Will you come too?"

He scooped her up. "No, I've got to stay here, so the hacker can approach me."

"Be careful." She clung to Simon's shoulders as he stepped carefully through the blood. "Vijay was always nice to me. Do you think Alistair killed him?"

"I wouldn't have thought so, but it's possible." Simon grimaced. There was a more likely possibility, but that would mean the hacker or terrorists were onto Alistair.

They reached the cool room door, where Jarred stood waiting. Talos and Sam had formed a human barrier against curious delegates, staff and two security guards from the other team. The noisy onlookers, who only moments ago had been demanding answers, quietened, some gasping as they parted for Jarred to carry Madeline through. Several gasped again when Simon followed with Darius.

He glanced down and silently cursed the murderer. Darius not only had blood on her hands, but over the dress and her feet.

Alistair pushed his way to the front. "What happened? Who did this?"

An explanation had to be given. Jarred took up the mantle. "There is a dead man in the cool room. This young lady slipped in his blood and wacked her skull fairly hard. Bellini isn't injured, but she *is* traumatized. If you'll excuse us, I'm taking the ladies away from prying eyes."

"Yes, of course."

Simon maneuvered his way after Jarred through the kitchen.

Alistair dogged his heels. "Simon, where are you taking them?"

"To Bellini's villa." Jarred nodded his thanks to Alisi, who held the door open. "As this is the third death in two days, I will leave a security guard with them."

"Yes, yes, that's fine, I'll make sure everyone knows the ladies are not to be bothered." Alistair gently patted Darius' shoulder as he caught Simon's gaze. "There's so much blood, are you certain she's not injured?"

"Yes, just badly shaken."

"Then explain the blood?" demanded Richard Chapman, stomping through the crowded kitchen. "We have a right to know what's going on."

"The chef's body is in the cool room. As it's a crime scene, security will need to handle things, so evidence isn't compromised more than it has been already."

"Vijay is dead?" The color leeched from Alistair's face. "How?"

"Speargun through the chest."

"*C'est horrible*," Marguerite fell against Talos. "*Un accident?*"

"I doubt that." Simon turned his back on them and strode across a small, bamboo enclosed courtyard to an open gate.

Jarred sat in a golf cart, the motor humming, Madeline tucked under his right arm. "Simon, things are coming to a head. Be vigilant and watch your back."

"I will."

Madeline blinked at him. "Hi, Simon."

He glanced around quickly, relieved to find they had no audience. "Madeline, can you do me a favor?"

"Sure."

He placed his precious bundle on the seat. "Don't let her fall out."

"I won't." Madeline linked arms with Darius. "Us girls will stick together like glue."

Jarred rolled his eyes. "I'll catch up with you later. Sam and Talos can deal with any questions for now. You clean up then mingle during lunch. Let me know if you see Nutlan."

"Will do." Simon waited until the golf cart rounded the bend then kicked off his runners and threw them in a trash can. His shirt followed suit. He didn't want anything in his bure with Vijay's blood on it.

Deciding to bypass the main hub, he took a pathway leading down to the cove. Once on the sand he jogged to the water then washed his feet and hands. The small beach was deserted, except for Etera. The waiter stood facing the sea, his head bowed, and his shoulders hunched. He had to be affected by Vijay's death. He could also be working for Alistair. His actions at the bunker had looked furtive.

Simon kicked the water. The summit had become one huge clusterfuck. What he needed was cool, logical thinking. Darius was safe. Jarred would make sure she and Madeline had twenty-four-hour protection.

He paced along the water's edge, processing everything he knew or suspected. Keith Heckle, Vijay and the American had all been murdered. Nutlan was missing, possibly dead. It could mean the hacker was disposing of allies, or people who could identify him.

Harnoop might have duped Identiscan, but only because Alexander Cortez had given the Sherpa a new identity. That was hard to accept, although *if* Alex *was* planning to commit suicide, he'd have known the Sherpa's reputation would be ruined, so possibly a new identity was his way of making rectification.

Keith Heckle's murder raised more questions. The jolly professor didn't have a malicious bone in his body. He had to have seen, heard or remembered something pertinent. He'd certainly seemed agitated yesterday morning.

Simon exhaled. Priority one—get Darius and Madeline off the island. That would be a challenge.

Priority two—take photos of the unidentified security guards then run them through Identiscan. Now that he had a satellite phone, he could do that easily enough, if he came across them.

Priority three—find Nutlan. The professor had to be somewhere on the island.

First thing first. He needed to shower before the luncheon drum sounded. To draw out the hacker, he had to mingle with the other delegates and give the appearance of a self-serving guy, open to the highest bidder.

⤐⤐

Bile rose in Darius' throat. The image of Vijay's lifeless body wouldn't leave her. He may have been working for Alistair, but the chef had always been kind. He'd waved whenever she passed him in the gardens. He'd played the *lali* drums while Alisi and the kitchen girls taught her to dance the *Meke*. He'd even shown a protective side after Professor Chapman had propositioned her. Now Vijay was dead.

She sat on the tiles as the torrent of hot water pelted down, gradually taking the chill out of her body. Her skin stung, raw from scrubbing with the loafer, yet the awful metallic smell still tormented her nasal passages. She'd used a full bottle of shampoo, so there'd be no black henna left in her hair. The smell had to be in her mind, as the water round her feet had been running clear for ages. She bit her lip. Jarred had said Sam and Talos would deal with Vijay when they found him. Had they?

A soft tap sounded on the door. "Darius, it's Madeline. Are you okay?"

"Not really."

"I've brought fresh clothes from your room. They're outside the door."

"Thank you."

"You're welcome. I've made chamomile tea when you're ready."

Chamomile tea. Her grandma had made chamomile tea after her dad had died. Darius rested her forehead on her bent knees, unable to summon the energy to cry or stand. Grandma and Mom and Brianna were having a nice time on Hamilton Island, in the Whitsundays, with no idea they were being monitored day and night. Did Grandma and Brianna like Darren? If she'd gone with them, she'd wouldn't now be faced with the heart-breaking truth of her father's treachery and suicide.

"Why did he do it?" She rolled her head from side to side. "Why go against everything he believed in? Why desert us?"

Blackmail. It was the only explanation. Who would do such a wicked thing to a brilliant, noble man? A hacker and terrorist group who now had Simon in his sights. Alistair was right.

She jerked as a loud triple-knock banged on the door.

"Darius, turn off that shower now." Jarred sounded more frustrated than angry. "You will run the island out of water at this rate."

He probably *would* break down the door.

"Darius!"

"I heard." She reached up and flicked the lever off, then clambered to her feet and out of the shower. "I need to speak to Simon."

"Not happening. He has a job to do. Ryan will be here to protect you." The soles of his shoes slapped the tiles as Jarred paced away.

Damn. She couldn't infiltrate the summit now that she'd run out of black henna and scrubbed off her spray tan. Her gaze fell on the vanity bowl, where the frangipani dress had turned the water red.

The thought of wearing that dress ever again made her gag. "Wait a minute. I don't need to be Bellini, when I can be someone much more powerful." It was risky and needed a bundle of courage, but would certainly bring things to a head, and she did have the Steele Ops Security team at her back.

Frantically, she rubbed herself dry as she plotted. A quick look in the mirror confirmed her skin had definitely lightened, and there was no trace of henna in her hair.

Wrapping the towel around her torso, she unlocked the door then peeked out. The wide hall was empty, murmuring voices coming from the kitchen, and a neat bundle of clothes were at her feet. Madeline had left Darius' blue bikini and matching floor-length beach dress. It wasn't what she'd choose to wear to a secret summit lunch, but they were on a tropical resort, so it wouldn't be out of place.

She twisted her hair into a top-knot then pushed four bobby pins in to hold it. Her sandals would add a couple of inches to her height. If her plan was to work, she'd need Madeline's assistance. The fact the journalist had sabotaged a yacht would indicate she might be open to a little subterfuge, but whether she'd go to the lengths Darius needed was anyone's guess.

She padded barefoot into the kitchen, where Ryan sat on a high stool, his arms crossed, frowning at Madeline as she fried three fish.

Madeline smiled. "Jarred's gone back to the resort. Go relax on the terrace, I'll bring you lunch as soon as Ryan gets off his high horse and makes us a drink."

"I'm not on my high horse, Madeline. You've taken a huge risk by coming to the island. Look what happened to Vijay. No wonder Jarred's like a bear with a toothache."

"I'm fine. The headache is almost gone, and my eyesight is back to normal."

"You ladies are a distraction we don't need." Ryan brushed past Darius then strode onto the terrace, to sit at a table and stare into the shimmering pool.

"Men!" Madeline drummed her fingernails on the counter. "I may be under their protection, but I refuse to sit idly, twirling my thumbs when I could be assisting them. At least by coming here, my enemies can't blow me up or kidnap me."

Darius blew out a breath. "I could do with your assistance."

"Oh?"

"I intend to expose the people responsible for my father's suicide. I believe the hacker is working for a terrorist group and they intend to kidnap Simon. I can't let that happen. Do you think you could distract Ryan for me?"

Madeline stared open-mouthed at her. Not a great start.

"I need help to sneak out of this villa, so I can gatecrash the delegates lunch."

"To do what?" At least Madeline now looked intrigued.

Darius grinned. "I'm going to announce I have the missing key to my father's program and I know the hacker's identity. As an incentive, I'm giving you the scoop."

Interest flared bright in Madeline's eyes. "Do you really know the key and the hacker's identity?"

"I know the key, and I think the hacker could be Richard Chapman, Phillip Nutlan or Alistair Finch. My announcement will put the cat among the pigeons, don't you think?"

Madeline smiled. "Okay, I'm in." She turned off the gas then scooped the fish onto a large plate. "I'll tell Ryan you're having a rest and don't want to be disturbed. If he wants to check on you, I'll offer to do it, but promise me you'll stay close to Simon?"

"Once I crash lunch, he's not going to let me out of his sight."

"That's true." Madeline raised an eyebrow. "Especially in that dress."

Darius frowned at the thigh to ankle slits. "Is it too provocative?"

"No. It's feminine and alluring. It will do nicely, especially with your hair up. You will bring out Simon's protective streak, again." Madeline looked as nonchalant as a Parisian model, standing in a café in *Champs-Élysées.* Not a hair out of place and the essence of sophisticated poise.

"I wish I had your confidence."

"Are you kidding, Darius? You've taken on men with knives, built a fabulous robotic eagle, hid listening devices all over the resort, downloaded data from delegates' computers, and your costumes are fantastic. You're my heroine." Madeline picked up the fish and a bowl of salad. "Go now, I'll keep Ryan occupied."

"Thanks, Madeline." Darius ran through the villa then slipped out the front door. Her private golf cart sat under the carport with its key still in the ignition. She unplugged the charger then jumped in and turned the key. The electric motor hummed. With her heart in her mouth, Darius released the foot brake then pressed on the accelerator. No one came running as she cruised along the drive.

Ironically, the challenge ahead brought a smile to her face. She was about to gatecrash a secret summit lunch without a disguise. "I do seem to come out of my shell when I'm angry, or someone I love is in danger."

As she drove through the gates a brisk wind buffeted the golf cart. The horizon had disappeared behind low slung storm clouds and choppy waves. According to Madeline, they would catch the edge of the cyclone. Darius shuddered at the thought, wondering how much time they had before it hit.

She parked by the staff courtyard, relieved to find it empty. Her plan would blow away in the wind if she ran into any of Simon's friends. Gathering her courage, she ran to the kitchen door, praying her gamble would pay off.

CHAPTER TWENTY-FOUR

"Who are *you?*" Alisi hurried round the counter, a heavy frown between her eyes.

Darius swallowed. Heaven help her, at this rate her heart would jump out of her chest. She darted a quick glance toward the dining room then approached Alisi.

"It's me. Bellini. My real name is Darius Cortez and someone at this summit betrayed my father. I'm here to set things right."

Alisi blinked, her mouth dropping open. "Oh, no, you can't go in there."

"Yes, I can." Darius started forward.

Alisi grabbed her arm. "Miss Darius, you should go back to the villa."

"You've known who I am all along, haven't you?"

"Yes, but we can't protect you if the delegates know your identity."

"Who is 'we'?"

Alisi looked about frantically. "Me, Hans and Etera. Please, you must go back to the villa before any of the delegates see you."

Crossing her arms, Darius assumed a stubborn stance. "Alisi, who are you protecting me from?"

"There are bad people in there." She nodded towards the dining room, where the din of conversation and cutlery reached them. "Vijay was protecting you too." A tear rolled down Alisi's face. "There is much at stake, Miss Darius."

"I know, that's why I have to do this before anyone else dies." Darius drew a deep breath and turned for the door.

"This is not what your father wanted."

Darius spun back to face Alisi. "I beg your pardon?"

Alisi sagged. "Alistair Finch and the owner of this island knew your father. That is why the summit has been held here. They believe one of the delegates pressured your father into using his program for criminal undertakings, which is why he killed himself. Professor Nutlan have been helping them."

"What?" Darius clenched her fingers. "Professor Nutlan was not close to my father."

"Maybe not that you noticed, but he has done much to help and now he is missing."

Darius glanced over her shoulder and flinched. She'd been noticed by a tall, well-built security guard from the other team. His hard gaze pinned her as he made his way around tables. She had no time to lose. "It's too late, Alisi. I have to do this now."

She marched into the dining room. Silence fell as every delegate turned her way. Simon came to his feet, his eye's shards of flint as he watched her approach. She tried to swallow the lump in her throat, but it was a stubborn little blighter. "Good afternoon, ladies and gentlemen. I am Darius Cortez. Professor Alexander Cortez was my father."

A gasp went through the room.

"I believe I have certain information that is pertinent to this summit."

Richard Chapman stood so fast his chair crashed to the floor. "Darius, my dear, you should not be here. This conference is of no concern to you."

"It is if you're discussing the Amethyst Code, as I have the third key. I assume *most* of you would like to know who used my father's program to divert a Navy frigate."

"You know this, *ma chére?*" The French woman sat as stiff as a steel rod beside Simon, who still stood glowering at Darius. If looks could kill, she'd be boiling in a cauldron.

"I do, and I've decided to go public with the whole sordid story."

Most of the delegates began calling out questions.

Sir William rapped his cane on the table, until he had everyone's attention. "Now wait just a minute, young lady. This is a secret summit, so who told you about it, and how did you get on the island?"

"One of your delegates told me about it. Before my father died, he gave me a coded message, which I only discovered recently. He wanted me to expose the person who betrayed him, and a terrorist group, who I assume wanted the Amethyst Code."

Somebody close by spluttered, others began arguing. Simon shook his head, his gaze turning darker.

"Obviously Miss Cortez came in on the yacht." Jarred stood near the bar with his hands on his hips. "I was told the other security team searched it thoroughly."

"They did." The sharp-edged, accented voice came from behind Darius.

She spun to find the tall security guard, standing in the exact pose as Jarred, his ice-blue gaze boring into her. She'd seen him about, but not up close. His eyes had a coolness about them that sent a chill rippling through her.

"Thrown any joggers off the cliff lately?"

The tiniest flicker of his eyes was his only physical reaction. "I have no idea what you're talking about, Miss Cortez." He spoke with a soft drawling American accent.

"*Pardon, ma chére.*" The French woman called out. "How would you know about the American's death? It happened only yesterday."

Darius turned back to the delegates as Marguerite Something-or-other touched Simon's arm. "You were close to Professor Cortez, *mon cher.* Is this little girl really his daughter?"

Darius bristled.

"Yes, but I can guarantee, Darius knows nothing about the Amethyst Code or the hacker or the last key. Her sister is a famous and beautiful ballerina. This is an attempt to gain a moment in the limelight."

That hurt. Darius straightened her shoulders. He might be trying to protect her, but she'd come too far to back down now. "I have no need for fame, Simon. My goal is to expose the truth behind my father's death. I know the key and the hacker's identity."

"Excuse me." Alistair came to his feet then placed a hand on Sir William's shoulder. "Perhaps it would be wise to hear Miss Cortez out then make our own decision?"

"You're right. That would be best, Alistair," answered Sir William.

"Are you mad?" yelled Professor Chapman. "It's a preposterous idea. God knows what sensitive information she's been sitting on."

"Calm down, Richard." Alistair held up a hand for quiet. "I was going to suggest we finish lunch then Sir William and I will speak with Miss Cortez in private."

Voices rose in outrage as arguments broke out at each table. Most delegates wanting to be privy to the conversation, while others deemed the information too sensitive for an open forum. Professor Chapman argued vehemently against it, which in Darius' book, painted him as the hacker.

Simon left his table and paced to her side. "I don't approve of this, but it's done now." He grimaced. "Sir William is waving you over."

"Who exactly is Sir William?"

"He works for Britain's National Cyber Crime Unit, and the woman beside him is Colonel Judith Sutton, a military advisor to the President of the United States. The Japanese man opposite is Itsuki Takahashi. I'm not sure what his role is, but he's high up in Japanese Intelligence."

"What about the French brunette?"

"Marguerite Lémaire, she's a banker, storming her way up the corporate ladder. Brilliant, but I've been told she's a viper and will do whatever it takes to succeed."

"Was Alistair Finch really a professor at Cambridge University?"

"Yes. My research shows he now does consultancy work for cyber fraud agencies all over the world."

She glanced at Simon's table as they passed. Marguerite Lemaire's frosty gaze swept over Darius condescendingly, as if she'd been judged and found inadequate.

Alistair lifted an empty chair from under another table and placed it between his and Sir William's. He nodded at Simon. "As you know each other, why don't you pull up a chair and join us?" His eyes beseeched them both to play along.

"Thank you, I will." Simon gave Darius a grim smile that she had no difficulty interpreting as a warning. For the moment neither of them would expose Alistair.

Adjustments were made so that Simon could slide into a chair on the other side of the table. Once he sat, Etera placed Simon's partly eaten meal in front of him.

With a tight smile, Alisi placed grilled fish and a mango salad in front of Darius.

The Japanese man beside Simon smiled across the table. "I am Itsuki Takahashi. What is it you do in Australia, Miss Cortez?"

"I'm a robotics engineer, specializing in surgical equipment."

"Would you care to explain that to us?"

"Sure. Robotic surgery is used to perform operations with small medical instruments attached to a robotic arm. Surgeons use a computer to control the arm and a narrow tube with a camera attached at the end, called an endoscope. It allows them to view enlarged 3-D images inside the body as surgery is taking place."

"What is the advantage to normal surgery?" asked the American woman.

"Robotic surgery can be performed through small incisions. It's less invasive and the recovery time is much quicker."

"What sort of operations?" asked Sir William.

She looked around the table at each person watching her intently. They weren't interested in robotic surgery, so this small talk was to put her at ease. She hoped they had strong stomachs. "Robotic surgery can be used for gallbladder removal, hysterectomy, mitral valve repair, coronary artery bypass, kidney transplant, the removal of cancerous tissue, radical prostatectomy—"

"I think we get your drift, Darius." Alistair placed his knife and fork on his plate and pushed it forward.

This was going better than she'd hoped. "Would anyone else like to ask me a question about my personal life?"

Alistair's gaze dropped momentarily to the atom charm hanging just above her cleavage. "No need. We know you live with your grandmother and you're involved with an amateur theatre group."

"Did you also know I dabble in costumes and stage makeup? I can change my appearance so that even my mother doesn't recognize me."

He darted a look at Sir William. "No, that's something we didn't know."

"It's how I've been able to move about the resort freely and download data from all your computers."

Itsuki and the American lady almost choked on their food. Simon groaned.

"I call it insurance in case something happens to me."

Itsuki tilted his head. "Miss Cortez, you may have the data, but you cannot get it off the island. The satellite dish has been damaged."

"You obviously don't know about the dish on the main villa's roof, or the surveillance cameras and listening devices dotted about the resort. The listening devices are mine, by the way."

"I think you missed your calling, young lady." The African American on the other side of Simon winked at her. "David Shields, it's a pleasure to meet you, Darius. You should come work for me in Central Intelligence."

"Or for me in Japan," offered Itsuki.

She laughed. "Thank you, but no, I'm actually interested in pursuing my love of robotic toys and drones. You may have noticed my Goshawk flying above the island over the last few days, until security shot it down this morning."

"That was *yours*?" Sir William threw his hands up. "You obviously didn't come in on the yacht this morning, so when did you arrive?"

"Wednesday. I realized anyone who might know something about The Amethyst Code, or the cyber breaches would be invited to this summit along with the usual horde, and so does the hacker."

Alistair's hand flexed on his thigh. "You should have stayed at home, Darius, now you've made yourself a target."

"I was always going to be a target, which is why I've decided to bring things to a head. We're surrounded by security guards and secret service agents. I have more than enough protection."

"Let me assure you, once this gets out, you'll need it." Sir William cackled, so like her father, she lost her train of thought.

As conversation turned to the imminent cyclone, Darius pretended to concentrate on her meal as she gave Sir William a sidelong glance. He was in the right age bracket and of similar height to her father and could have injured his leg falling into a crevice, but why hide from his family? Sir William wore the same style glasses as her father, but his eyes were a different brown, and his facial structure was wrong.

She switched her attention to Alistair. He dressed smartly, didn't wear glasses, and his eyes were gray. The trimmed goatee worked well with his earring and hair tied back in a band. His appearance and dress sense were so opposite her father, she found it hard to believe they'd been friends.

Sir William pulled out a pen and began jotting things down in a notebook as he conversed with David Shields. Each time Sir William stopped to think, he flicked his pen between his fingers, another habit of her father's.

Darius broke out in a cold sweat. She could change her whole appearance, so perhaps her father had too. Contact lenses, plastic surgery, change of style and a British accent. The plastic surgery would be excessive, but not impossible. It would be a brilliant disguise, if not for the fact Sir William worked for Britain's National Cyber Crime Unit, and if alive, her father would never turn his back on his family.

Marguerite's flirty laugh brought Darius' head up with a snap. The French woman had crammed a chair in beside Simon, so close she was almost on his lap. He chuckled at something she whispered in his ear. They *were* flirting. A cruel vice squeezed Darius' heart so tight it risked popping like a balloon.

Simon dipped his head to murmur in Marguerite's ear. She giggled in response.

"Dari, your thoughts are plastered over your face."

She blinked at Sir William. "What did you call me?"

He smiled. "Best not to pin your hopes on Simon Hawke. He's destined for bigger and better things. That young man can have his pick of jobs." He didn't need to say *and women.* Darius got the message loud and clear.

She shot another peek at Simon. He drank his beer then stood, shifting his chair back for Marguerite to stand. They were leaving, together. He didn't even spare Darius a glance as they strolled out to the foyer. The vice around Darius' heart tightened. Simon had to have a good reason for leaving with the French woman so publicly.

"You're doing it again, Dari?"

Her attention snapped back to Sir William. "You called me Dari."

"Yes." He smiled with teeth that looked perfectly aligned. They weren't his own. "I have a daughter your age. She loves sailing."

"Sailing?"

"Yes, or at least she did. I haven't seen her in five years."

Darius forked a piece of fish into her mouth then stared at him, searching for the smallest resemblance to her father. He flicked the pen between his fingers again then tapped it twice on the table edge before dropping it in his shirt pocket. Another ingrained habit of her father's. He caught her eye then tapped his nose. "I'm glad you came to the island, Dari."

Breathing became difficult, her cutlery weighed a ton, the fish in her mouth turned to sawdust. If Sir William was her father then he hadn't been murdered or jumped into the crevice. He'd been alive, living in England with a new identity, while his devastated family mourned him.

Like a rudderless boat, she drifted on a sea of rolling emotions. The only two men she loved with every fiber of her being had turned their backs on her. With a leaden heart, she looked across the room and locked eyes with Talos. His questioning eyes showed concern.

It wasn't her style to make emotional scenes in public. Slinking back to the villa to sob her heart out in privacy was much more to her liking, except...

Darius placed her knife and fork together then turned to Sir William. If he were her father, she had to congratulate him on creating a compelling new identity, but she'd never forgive him for turning his back on their family and ethics. To discover the truth, she'd need to tighten the web.

"I'm going to expose you." It came out as a whisper, but he heard and stiffened.

He darted a glance round the table. "Meet me under the wharf. I will explain."

"Is that what you told Keith and Vijay before you had them killed?"

One eyebrow rose. "What an imagination you've developed, Darius."

Their whispers were drawing attention.

"Please, excuse me." She pushed her chair back and looked around the table. "I'll be right back." She needed to find Simon.

Alistair started to rise, so she put her hand up. "I'm just visiting the bathroom."

He sank down, but not before giving a nod to Jarred and Talos, standing by the bar. They separated, Jarred ambling to the back wall where the toilets were situated, and Talos walking out through reception. The tall guard with the icy gaze followed Talos.

She ignored them and the delegates' stares as she made her way around tables to the ladies' restroom, shutting the outer door firmly behind her.

She ran to the furthest cubicle, kicked off her shoes then climbed on the seat and removed the glass louvers. Getting onto the ledge was awkward thanks to her long dress, but once up she squeezed through, then jumped to the ground, just in time. Heavy footsteps pounded along the path from the drive. She dived under a fern.

It wasn't Talos but six security guards with what looked like machine guns. One man's battered face brought a chilled gasp to her lips. Thankfully the wind and waves masked it. Once the men rounded the corner, she jumped to her feet and ran, using the gardens and hedges to hide her escape.

The path to Simon's bure looked empty, but she couldn't risk using it, as Nick would see her on the monitors, so she kept to the gardens until the very last minute then sprinted to his door. The curtains were open and the bure empty.

"Damn, where'd they go?" She slapped her forehead. "Marguerite's bure." This wasn't looking good, but she'd make no assumptions.

How to get to the other side of the cove without being seen? Her gaze fell on the beach hut where Etera kept snorkels and flippers. "Perfect."

She scrambled through ferns then jumped to the sand below. No one was on the beach, so she lifted her dress and sprinted to the hut. Stripping off her dress, she shoved it under a bench seat then rummaged through a plastic tub for flippers and a snorkel that would fit. A repetitive rat-a-tat-tatting halted her frantic search, but whatever it was stopped. She pulled on the smallest wet suit and hood, tucking all her hair out of sight, then picked up the flippers and snorkel and ran into the water.

She was a good swimmer, so it didn't take long to cross the cove even with the choppy waves hindering her progress.

Leaving the snorkel and flippers under the wharf, she ran up the sand then climbed the bank to the path above. If memory served her right, Marguerite's bure was number eight, and one of the larger bures with a separate bedroom.

It would be a surprise to see Darius in a wetsuit, but Simon needed to know the hacker's identity, before anyone else got killed.

They weren't sitting on the small deck, so she took a deep breath and marched to the front door. The glass slider was slightly open and the room in a shamble. Lamps and chairs knocked over, a huge dent in the wall, cushions everywhere. The back wall shuddered, as something large crashed into it, followed by loud grunts.

Darius ran across the room and peered around the half open door. A huge security guard stood with his back to her, holding a gun to Simon's head. The love of her life kneeled on all fours, minus his shirt and breathing hard.

Darius clamped a hand over her mouth and backed away. She noticed Marguerite's laptop on the counter. Before she could change her mind, she picked it up and crept back to the door.

The man was speaking in a low tone. "You invented the program, so if you don't know the third key, I'll have to ask Professor Cortez's pretty daughter."

"Neither of us have the key, and neither of us know the hacker's identity."

"That's what Professor Heckle told me, before I killed him." The gunman leaned down close to Simon's head. "Will you beg for your life like Professor Heckle?"

"No, you bastard, I won't."

Darius wasn't waiting for the gunman to pull the trigger. She ran forward and smashed the laptop into his face with a resounding whack.

The man bellowed.

Simon surged to his feet, bringing his fist smashing up under the man's chin with a sickening crack.

A spurt of blood hit Darius on her cheek, as the man's eyes rolled back in his head. He crumpled to the floor.

Nausea threatened but then Darius spotted Marguerite minus her dress, crouching by the bed, her breasts bulging out of a strapless bra, eyes wide as she stared at the gunman.

Fury rose in Darius like a tidal wave, threatening to overwhelm her. She stepped back, her fists raised, as her wrath fixed on Simon.

He grimaced, rubbing his shoulder. "Thanks, Darius, your timing is impeccable." He grabbed his T-shirt and dragged it on.

"You bastard-rat. I trusted you. I believed in you."

"Darius, I know this looks bad, but I can explain."

She stared into his frantic green eyes with hazel flecks. Another man she'd trusted, wanting to explain his betrayal. "Go to Hell, it's where you and my father belong." She threw the laptop at him and ran.

"Darius!"

She burst from the bure and leaped the side rail, crashing down through the foliage to the sand, then she sprinted along the beach, tears blurring her vision. She would not let her father or Simon destroy her. She crawled under the wharf, swiping at the tears.

"I'm twice the woman that French tart is."

"Darius!"

Flattening her body to the sand, Darius peeped out. Simon was standing on the sand, looking back along the beach towards the resort.

She wriggled deeper into the shadows then pulled on the snorkel. She heard Simon yelling her name, and that repetitive rat-a-tat-tatting again. Machine guns.

She peeped out again, but Simon had disappeared. There was one place she could go and one person who might help her but getting there wouldn't be easy.

Fitting her feet into the flippers, she rolled into the shallow water then crawled under the wharf until it was deep enough to swim. The flippers and snorkel would help, but once she cleared the wharf, negotiating the reef was going to be a nightmare. Then she'd have to climb through mud and mangroves, before scaling a cliff, above the bone-shattering rocks. If she reached Harnoop, they still faced the six security guards bearing machine guns. They worked for Sir William, who could well be her father and the hacker.

It was a colossal quest, but how else would she save all the innocent people, and the bastard-rat. If the corrupt guards got hold of him, they'd kill him. She had to save the man she loved, even though he'd betrayed her with that French tart. The injustice of it made her growl, earning her a mouth full of water. She choked and splattered her way across the cove, silently repeating a new mantra. *Bastard-rat, bastard-rat, bastard-rat.*

Chapter Twenty-five

"Shit." Simon shoved the gun down the back of his jeans then stormed back into Marguerite's bure. She'd played one of the oldest tricks in the book and he'd fallen for it. Now Darius hated him.

He found Marguerite bending over the unconscious security guard. "Get your fucking dress on. We have bigger problems than reviving that bastard."

"*Mon cher,* I think you are no ordinary computer scientist." She stepped into the dress then wriggled it up over her skimpy underwear. "I am with French Intelligence and have been working undercover as a bank executive."

"Really? This gorilla barges in, primed to beat information out of me, and when that doesn't go to plan, he puts a gun to my head, yet you didn't lift a finger."

"*Oui,* but I knew Jonas wouldn't kill you. He wanted that third key too much. It is a shame about Keith Heckle, he was an amusing man, but we will work together, *oui?*"

"Not even in your wildest dreams. I saw the sadistic gleam in your eyes as I fought the security guard." The man's bulk had been Simon's saving grace, although they'd almost demolished the bure. When the gorilla produced a gun, Simon honestly thought he wouldn't see another day.

He picked up one of Marguerite's scarves and secured the man's hands behind his back then sat on the armchair to send a text to Jarred.

She zipped her dress up. "I have ID."

"Which can be easily forged. No thanks, I'm handing you both over to the Steele Ops Security team. They can determine your identity."

"That would not be wise, *mon cher*, those men could be working for anybody."

"As you two have just proved." Simon shook his head. "I heard machine guns. Do you know anything about that?"

Her eyes widened. "*Non*, but that could indicate a siege, *oui*?"

"Possibly." He snatched another scarf from the bed and tied the guard's ankles.

Marguerite crossed her arms. "So, *petite* Darius is in love with you, and I think you care for her too, *oui*?"

"That's none of your business. Are you working alone?"

"No, I am part of a small collective, interested in finding the hacker and the reason behind Alexander Cortez's suicide."

"How many of you are on the island?"

"A few. I cannot give you names, in case you are interrogated by the wrong people."

Simon grimaced. "I assume the staff are somehow involved, as they didn't question Darius' arrival." He frowned. "What about Vijay and Professor Nutlan?"

"We do not know who killed Vijay, and Phillip Nutlan's disappearance is a mystery. Perhaps he is caught cold feet and took a canoe. Phillip is...how we say...*facilement effrayé*. Easily frightened." She scowled. "I do not want to speak to the Steele Ops team."

"You have no choice." Simon urged her out of the bedroom then shut the door. "If there is a siege, you should stay away from the main hub and, as there's a cyclone brewing, I suggest you go via the beach to the main villa. It's fairly sheltered and sturdy enough to withstand a major storm." He didn't mention the bunker as he didn't trust her.

"I will. How is it you have a phone?"

"Just lucky I guess." He sent a text to Nick to unlock the front door. Then he sent a text the Sam. Jarred might not be able to reply, but Sam would, if all was well. Nothing came back. "Time to alert the Feds." Simon tried ringing Gibbs, when all he got was static, he sent a text.

Need urgent support. 3 dead, 1 missing. Possible hostage situation.

His screen flashed. *Grounded. Cyclone imminent. You're on your own.*

"Fuck."

"What is it, *mon cher*?"

"Don't call me that." He narrowed his eyes. "Who do *you* suspect is the hacker?"

She laughed. "I do not have a crystal ball. However, I know your presence here is a direct result of a request from the British Prime Minister."

Simon narrowed his eyes. "Explain?"

"As a creator of the Amethyst Code, your presence guaranteed the attendance of the hacker and other interested parties, who would want that third key."

"I see." He hated being manipulated, but time was passing and he needed to check on his team mates and Darius. "Stay in the villa until the cyclone passes."

"What will you do?"

"See what's happening at the main hub."

She sniffed. "It is as I thought. You are no ordinary computer scientist."

Choosing not to respond, Simon followed her out of the bure then waited until she'd rounded the curved pathway leading to the next cove. He drew in a deep breath and prayed Darius had gone to the bunker and would hear him out. The devastation in her eyes had driven a dagger into his heart. He looked out to sea and frowned.

"What the fuck?"

Exhaustion dragged at Darius. She struggled to kick against the current to avoid being smashed against the reef. The wetsuit had protected her so far, but she'd have a heap of bruises, if she could negotiate the reef and make it to the mangroves.

Marguerite's scantily clad body and Simon's naked torso kept distracting her. There was only one reason to be in that state of undress, and it wasn't to compare their computer skills. No matter which way she looked at it, Simon would have made love to that woman, if the security guard hadn't interrupted them.

He wasn't the icy blue-eyed guard who'd been in the dining room, but another who'd often given her leering glances. He'd been about to shoot Simon.

She banged her knee on a submerged rock and swallowed another mouthful of salty water. She came up spluttering. Heaven help her, she'd drown at this rate.

The swells were getting higher and purple thunder clouds had amassed overhead with the menacing promise of a violent storm. She washed into another rock, hitting her elbow. "Ouch."

At this rate, she'd never make the mangroves. A flash of white caught her eye. Something was in the water behind her. "Shit." She treaded water, her heart in her throat, her mind a blank. Reef surrounded her. She might have had a chance to escape a shark at low tide, but not high tide.

Wrenching off the snorkel, she frantically searched for a fin among the rising swells. Relief surged as not a shark, but a canoe rose over the waves. She had nowhere to go and no energy left to get her there. Whoever was paddling would hopefully have the strength to lift her aboard.

"There you are. I thought I'd lost you." Simon's harried words and fretful eyes almost undid her, but his concern couldn't wipe out his betrayal.

"Get lost. I have nothing to say to you." Her words, meant to sting, held little weight while she actively clung to the canoe. With the strong current, she'd be swept out to sea if she let go.

"Darius, I never had any intention of betraying you. Before you derailed lunch, Marguerite made me an astounding job offer. It's what I've been waiting for, so I had to feign a believable interest."

"Oh, it was believable all right." She didn't want to hear anymore. "We're done, Simon. I never want to see you again."

"No." He leaned over and hauled her into the canoe. "You *will* hear me out."

With a gasp, she landed on her butt, lying between his legs, her head against his hard stomach. "Bastard-rat." She kicked off the flippers then scrambled into a sitting position, wriggling as far forward as she could. He might have saved her from drowning, but fury flooded every cell as she stared mutinously ahead.

The swells were growing, as was the wind. Simon worked the oar hard for a couple of minutes, ploughing it through the water on both sides, directing the canoe toward the mangroves. She could almost feel the heat of his gaze as he fought the current.

They reached shallower water, which meant rocks and reef, so Darius put aside her anger momentarily to watch out for the reef. Silence ensured as Simon steered the canoe through the rabbit warren and into a narrow estuary. They were safe.

She heard the relief in his exhale, yet she couldn't utter her thanks. The hurt of his betrayal still too fresh and consuming.

"Darius, all I ask is that you hear me out?"

The anguish in his voice rattled her resolve. "Fine but make it quick. Once we're through the mangroves, I have a cliff to climb."

"Over my dead body."

"If you insist. Clobbering you with a rock has a lot of merit."

He sighed. "After you distracted me and every other delegate, Marguerite flirtingly suggested we continue our discussion in the privacy of her bure. She isn't the only delegate who noticed my preoccupation with you. Every person at lunch realized you and Bellini are one and the same. I flirted with Marguerite to protect you."

"Sure you did."

He sighed again. "I needed to hear her out, in case she represented the terrorist group. Once we reached her bure, she made it clear that my employment hinged on us having an affair. I made it very clear I was interested in the job, but not her. There's only one woman I want in my bed, Tink."

"I'm not that naive, Simon. I know what I saw."

"Marguerite chucked a hissy fit and threw a glass of fruit juice at me. Then she apologized and insisted on rinsing out my T-shirt. I stayed in the lounge."

Darius glanced over her shoulder. His T-shirt was wet through, his eyes deadly serious. "Go on."

"When Marguerite came out of the bedroom, she'd taken off her dress. I told her she didn't interest me and to shove the job. That's when the security guard burst in. I didn't betray you, Tink, because I love you."

The sincerity in his eyes sparked hope. She desperately wanted to believe him, because she loved him with all her heart. She swallowed. "I think Sir William is my father."

"What?" Simon stopped paddling.

She told him everything that had passed between her and Sir William. "If I'm right, then he's the hacker, but that doesn't explain his coded message. Unless he's working with Alistair. They're in charge of security. They could be involved with terrorists." Her breath hitched. "They want you to join them and, if you don't, they'll kill you."

"Let's not jump to conclusions. Your father wouldn't condone murder and he'd know there wasn't a snowball's chance in Hell of recruiting me into a terrorist group."

"Sir William called me Dari and did that table tapping thing my father used to do, before putting his pen in his shirt pocket."

"Still—" Simon's gaze snapped to his right. "Professor Nutlan?"

Darius twisted round, her mouth dropping at the bedraggled man struggling toward them through the swampy mangroves. His thin hair stood in dirty clumps, his bow tie askew, his eyes wild, bristles covered his lower face.

He clambered over tree roots than clasped his hands. "Miss Cortez, what are you doing with him? What's happened?"

Simon's eyes narrowed. "She's been here all the time, disguised as Bellini. There's a cyclone coming, and we think the delegates may have been taken hostage. Care to tell us why you're hiding out in a mangrove swamp?"

His surprise apparent by his slack jaw and wide eyes, Professor Nutlan darted glances between her and Simon. "It's safer here than at the resort."

Darius frowned. "Do you know anything about Vijay's death?"

"Vijay's dead?" Professor Nutlan's shoulders sagged. "How?"

"He was...found with a fishing spear through his chest."

"Good Lord, they're closing in on us. I knew this was a bad idea."

Simon jumped out of the canoe into waist deep water. "What's a bad idea?"

"There is a group of people, which includes Alistair Finch and Sir William. They believe Alexander Cortez was blackmailed into working for a terrorist group, which ended with his death. At first, I resisted their requests to help. I know my limitations and I'm no hero, but I knew Alexander wouldn't turn traitor, unless...his family were threatened. He'd have done anything to keep them safe."

Everything he said was true or had been once upon a time. Darius gulped down her grief. "Is Sir William my father?"

"Good God, whatever gave you that idea. Sir William has been around for years. He's with Britain's National Cyber Crime Unit."

"But he does things my father used to do, and he called me Dari."

Professor Nutlan huffed. "Even I know your father called you Dari. These people targeted you, because they knew you would draw Simon Hawke into the game."

"Are you freaking kidding me?" If Simon died, it would be her fault.

Professor Nutlan's eyes hardened. "Your father is dead, Darius. I don't know if he killed himself or was murdered. My job has been to monitor Richard Chapman and Keith Heckle for the last four years."

Simon had stood in silence, his eyes narrowed as he watched Nutlan. He dragged the canoe further into the mangroves then lifted Darius out, placing her on a tangled mass of mangrove roots. He turned back to Nutlan. "Why do they want me here?"

"You present the biggest target. It's common knowledge you helped Alexander create the Amethyst Code. You would know the first two passwords, and probably created a back door. They fear terrorists will entice you into working for them."

Nutlan sneered. "If they haven't already. If you refuse, you'll likely meet a nasty end, just like the American jogger, Keith Heckle and… Vijay." His lips thinned. "If these people or the terrorists realize you two are close, they will use Darius to blackmail you into doing what they want."

Darius gasped. "What about the hacker?"

"My dear, I doubt there is a hacker. These people engineered the summit to bring all the important players to one place. An isolated island where they hope to snare a member of a small, well-organized terrorist group. And, they did it with the approval of governments all over the world."

"No!" Her fearful eyes met Simon's. "This can't be happening. If you die…"

"Shit." Simon caught her to his chest. "It's happening all right. The two of us are integral to both sides' success, which makes us expendable in the eyes of the world's intelligence agencies."

Darius shivered in his arms. "You're not exactly filling me with optimism."

The fact she tried to make light of it, filled Simon with pride. He looked over the canoe at Nutlan. "What do you know of Alistair Finch?"

"I believe he and Alexander were what you might call friendly rivals."

"Hmm." Simon studied the cliff top, barely distinguishable against the sky. "Darius noticed six security guards with automatic rifles at the resort and, when I was on the beach, I heard gunfire."

"Dear God." Nutlan scrunched his hair in two clumps. "I have provisions enough to last another day."

Simon blinked as rain drops struck his face. "It's too dangerous to stay here."

Nutlan turned horrified eyes on Simon. "We can't take the canoe out into that turbulence. We'll be swamped by waves and torn to shreds on the reef."

Darius lifted her head from Simon's chest. "We can climb the cliff face. Harnoop does it all the time."

"Don't be absurd, Miss Cortez. That's suicidal." Nutlan looked about mulishly.

"As is staying here." Simon considered the cliff face above them. If they didn't lose their footing on the slippery surfaces, they risked the brewing tempest blowing them onto rocks. "You can stay if you want, Phillip, or you can help us find another way up. Wanna be a hero and save a bunch of innocent people?"

"That, young man, would take a team of trained soldiers."

"Luckily we've got one. Are you coming?"

Simon's gaze caught on a wad of palm fronds nestled among the mangroves. They offered scant protection against rain, let alone a cyclone.

Rolling his eyes, he eased Darius back onto her perch then tied the canoe to a tree. Whether it remained there or ended up washed out to sea wasn't his concern. He could see Nutlan was in a quandary, as he kept glancing between the sea, the sky, and the cliff, which really did look daunting. "I'll go first."

Thankful Darius wore a wetsuit, he lifted her back into the water then held her hand as he waded through the waist deep water, using mangrove roots to keep his balance against the current. As they neared the rocks, breaking waves sent a backwash knocking them every which way.

It became a battle to keep Darius on her feet. Nutlan wasn't doing any better, crying out every time he lost his footing. If it weren't for the eerie wind haunting the mangroves, Simon would have told him to shut his trap.

After an eternity, they made it to the base of the cliff which became another battle. The rocks were slippery, sharp and cumbersome. Simon peered up the cliff face and deflated. Even with the rock-climbing anchors, the wind and sheeting rain would make it a treacherous climb.

"Forget the cliff, we'll take the rocks around the headland to the east coast then find another way up."

"If there is one." Nutlan leaned against a boulder, breathing hard, his glasses skewwhiff, wet clothes clinging to his thin frame. He looked like the increasingly wild wind might pick him up at any second and hurl him through the sky.

Darius squeezed Simon's fingers. "My father may have been manipulated by evil people. And others might think to manipulate us but promise me you won't antagonize them. I don't want you hurt.

"I'll do my best." His heart lurched at the concern in her eyes.

They steadily worked their way over the rock formations and around the headland to the east side of the island. The wind and crashing waves weren't as harsh this side of the island. Still, Simon hugged the cliff face, until he found a narrow crevice, wide enough to enter. They climbed a crumbly dirt track which bore evidence of recent use. Flattened grass, dislodged rocks and large shoeprints reached all the way to the top. Behind the first row of trees, they wandered into an empty campsite.

Nutlan collapsed on a fallen tree trunk. "That is something I never wish to repeat."

"Me either, but we're alive." Darius sank onto the log beside him.

Simon grimaced. "Let's see if we can figure out who has been camping here?" He ducked inside the tent, where two bedrolls lay side by side. At the head of each was a green waterproof duffle bag. Inside he found socks, men's jocks, bottled water, cigarettes and protein bars. Taking three bottles of water and a handful of protein bars, he strode back to Darius and Nutlan. "We need to maintain our hydration and keep moving."

"I don't have the energy to take another step." Nutlan hunched over his knees, still breathing hard.

"You'd better find it." Simon looked about. "The men in this camp will be involved in the takeover. If they come back, our asses are fried, especially as I've beaten one up."

"Come on, Professor, on your feet." Darius took several swigs of water then bit into her protein bar. "Harnoop lives near here. He'll help us."

Simon certainly hoped so. He overtook Darius then led the way along a flattened trail to the edge of the golf course. Fifty feet to his left stood a shed and beside it a neat bure with a brood of hens shut underneath. The bure and shed blocked the golf course surveillance camera.

Simon stepped onto the narrow porch then tried the door. It creaked when he pressed it open. Unable to detect any sound, he ducked his head inside, his gaze darting about a darkened sitting area.

Darius squeezed past him. "I'm freezing. Maybe Alisi has some clothes I can borrow."

"Miss Darius."

"Argh." She jumped back, colliding with Simon's chest.

"Damn it, Tink." He lifted her aside, shielding her as he faced a curtained doorway.

The Sherpa stepped through, a pick-ax in his hand, his eyes darting from Simon to Darius, who shoved her way past. "I so glad to see you are safe, Miss Darius."

"Harnoop, we think the resort's been taken over by the British security guards."

"You are right, Miss Darius. Alisi and my unborn child are in danger. This is the only weapon I could find." He waved the pick-ax. "We must rescue them."

"Hold your horses." Simon stepped further into the room so Nutlan could enter then he closed the door and turned to Harnoop again. "What's your part in all this?"

"Professor Cortez sent me here five years ago. I am the greenskeeper. I need to rescue Alisi."

Frustration ate at Simon. "No one is going anywhere until I get some answers. I know you, Alisi and the other staff have a part to play in this summit. What is it?"

"We are supposed to watch Miss Darius and assist Sir William and Professor Finch to monitor the delegates. That is all."

"You knew who I was all the time." Darius put her hand on Simon's arm, her touch instantly calming him. She smiled at the Sherpa. "Harnoop, who gave you those orders?"

He shuffled from foot to foot, not meeting their eyes. "The people who wish to apprehend the terrorist who compromised your father."

Simon frowned. "Sir William and Alistair Finch?"

Harnoop's gaze darted to Professor Nutlan. "And others."

Nutlan grunted. "I didn't realize all the staff were in on it."

The tension went out of the Sherpa. He met Simon's gaze with one of relief. "The French lady and the tall American security guard are also part of it."

"American?" Darius' eyes widened. "Has he got icy blue eyes?"

"Yes. His name is Adam Garcia. He never mixed with the staff, but Vijay told me the American was a Navy Seal, and now works freelance."

A noticeable shiver ran through Darius. She looked up at Simon. "He's probably strong enough to throw a man off the cliff, and drown Professor Heckle."

Simon raised an eyebrow. "He could be working for anybody. We need to find out what's happening at the resort, and if there's any casualties."

Darius eyes lit. "We need to create a distraction, something to deflect attention while I send in one of my remote-control butterflies."

"Wait!" Nutlan shrugged off a small backpack then pulled out a large zip lock plastic bag. "I have one of your butterflies and the gadget you use to control it. It's fascinating the way your mind works, Miss Cortez, so like your father. All we need is your laptop and we can see for ourselves what's going on at the—"

Darius snatched the bag. "Where did you get these?"

"I witnessed you pick up a large Monarch butterfly then place it in a hibiscus tree. Out of curiosity, I approached the tree and discovered an ultra-light, beautifully made toy, with a miniature camera in the underbody. I then searched your room at the villa and found another butterfly, along with a controller."

You're a godsend, Professor."

Simon exhaled. "The butterfly could come in handy, but if we can get to the bunker, the surveillance cameras will show us what's happening at the resort. I'll send Nick and Ryan a text. Hopefully they haven't been captured and are in lockdown. I've tried to ring Gibbs but can't get through. I'll text him just in case things don't go our way."

Darius frowned. "What about Jarred, or Sam and Talos?"

"They're not replying."

"I could wait here with the greenskeeper?" Nutlan looked at Simon hopefully.

"No, Professor." Darius clasped her hands and began pacing. "I need you to be a hero and collect my costume from Simon's bure then take it to the main villa." She looked to the Sherpa. "Harnoop, you hide in the staff courtyard then wait for us to join you. If Alisi comes out, bring her to the bunker, but don't rescue anyone unless it's safe."

She met Simon's gaze. "If we create enough of a distraction, there are six ex-SAS soldiers on the island who will come to the rescue?"

"I like this plan." Harnoop nodded vigorously.

Simon raised an eyebrow, disgruntled at how easily Darius had snatched the reins, yet he couldn't fault her thinking.

"A hero, you say?" Nutlan stuck out his thin chest. "Perhaps you should tell us what you have in mind, young lady."

CHAPTER TWENTY-SIX

Having Darius and Marguerite in a confined space, glaring daggers at each other wasn't making Simon's task any easier. The darkening sky and teaming rain gave him poor visibility. Gusting winds made matters worse, blocking outdoor cameras with palm fronds being shafted back and forth.

Two cameras weren't transmitting, probably cast to the ground by the ravaging storm. The pool's day beds had been hurled against shrubs or into the pool, their mattresses long gone. Weather shields had been dropped around the dining room—which wouldn't stand up against a cyclone—and the reception area had debris littered across the tiles. He combed the wall of monitors. "Where's Talos and Garcia?"

"Fucked if I know," muttered Nick. "I've accounted for everyone except them." He caught Simon's eye. "Ryan and our female guest are on their way here. Harnoop should be about ready to create a distraction. Nutlan is hiding in a reception cupboard waiting for Darius' signal."

"Bring up the dining room." Darius slid onto the chair beside Simon and plugged in her earphones. The shirt and trousers Harnoop had lent her where saturated, sticking like a second skin. Madeline would bring a dry change of clothes.

Simon pressed the key and instantly the wall monitor showed the surveillance camera's view of the resort's dining room and occupants.

Sitting on the other side of Nick, Marguerite placed her hand on his arm. "I see we are missing the big Australian and the American security guards. This is bad, *oui*?"

Nick removed her hand. "It's not good."

"With luck they're together," muttered Simon. He'd verified Garcia's identity through Identiscan, the minute he'd reached the sealed room. The ex-Navy Seal worked for an American security firm with ties to the Secret Service.

Simon zoomed in on Sam then Jarred. Both men had their hands tied behind their backs. Jarred kept blinking.

"What's wrong with his eyes?" Darius leaned closer.

Simon grabbed a pen and paper. "It's Morse Code. He says... restroom."

"He wants to use the bathroom." Marguerite rolled her eyes. "Really?"

"No, it's...he wants us to come through the ladies' restroom."

"Nonsense." She scoffed. "There is no external door. Only a monkey could fit through the high windows."

Nick glanced at Simon. "A monkey or Darius. It's how she escaped after you and Marguerite left the dining room together." He didn't need to add 'fucking idiot'. Simon could read it in his eyes. He glanced at Darius, who had the earphones plugged into his satellite phone and was speaking quietly to Nutlan and Harnoop.

Viewing the playback had shown Darius' distress and driven a knife into Simon's chest. He had no idea if she believed him or intended to run at the first opportunity. He wouldn't give her up.

He'd also viewed the hostage take-over, unsurprised to discover the man who'd attacked Darius, another stranger and four British security guards had an agenda of their own. If Adam Garcia had gone undercover, his absence didn't bode well.

"What's Alisi up to?" Simon zoomed in on the manageress, sitting next to Alistair Finch. They appeared to be having a whispered argument.

"Check this out." Nick pointed.

A huge orange and black butterfly fluttered in from reception, its wingspan wider than his two hands, a piece of paper dangling below its belly. The butterfly hovered over the hostages until one guard jumped up and caught the paper, ripping it from the butterfly. The reception door swung closed. Simon grinned. "You're a genius, Tink."

"I hope he can read." She chuckled, her eyes fixed on the iPad in front of her, as she guided the toggle controlling the butterfly. It hovered high above the hostages. "Thank you for releasing it, Professor, now hide in the cool room."

"Bullshit." Marguerite sneered. "You cannot tell me this *petite* blonde is controlling the butterfly."

Simon smirked. "This clever blonde is a robotics' engineer, and yes, the butterfly is entirely under her control." He pulled the keyboard closer. "We need to free those hostages and find out who is in charge of the gunmen. But first..."

Simon booted up the central computer then reached for the hard-drive he'd fixed behind one of the wall monitors. He plugged it in then flexed his fingers. "This won't take long."

Once the screen opened, he typed in the fifty-digit key he'd never used. It was his back door into the program he and Alexander Cortez created. A key no person or machine could change but him. It bypassed Professor Cortez's password.

Keeping the Amethyst Code on his hard drive was an oversight Alistair Finch would live to regret, as Simon intended to destroy it once and for all. He shouldn't jump to conclusions. Professor Cortez could have sent the program to Alistair for safe keeping, and it didn't mean Alistair was the hacker, but the odds were climbing.

The screen flickered then up came the words *Amethyst Code*.

"Ooh-la-la." Marguerite clasped her hands. "You have the master program, *oui?*"

"Yes." Simon wiped perspiration from his forehead, as an electrical storm, sound effects and all, erupted across the screen, sending Nick and Marguerite lurching back.

Simon chuckled. He'd had fun creating that introduction. The screen flashed red then asked for the second level password. Aware Darius had pulled out the earplugs and had her eyes fixed on his monitor, Simon typed in the seventy-digit key and hit enter. A beautiful fairy with golden tresses and big blue eyes flitted back and forth across the screen, waving her wand.

Two more steps and there would be no trace left of the Amethyst Code, if all went according to plan. He selected Mission Control.

"It is asking for the third password." Marguerite was almost hyperventilating.

Taking a deep breath, he turned to Darius. "Would you do the honors, sweet pea?"

She moistened her lips. "How long have you known?"

"I didn't, not for sure, but it makes the most sense."

"I could be wrong. Dad often challenged me to invent passwords, but the last time we played the game, he asked me to retype it, twice. And I remember him asking me to retype the same password on a couple of occasions." She landed the butterfly on a beam, high above the hostages, the camera showing almost the entire dining room. Placing the controller on the desk, she leaned across Simon and typed, twenty-two keys, some symbols, some numbers and some letters, in upper and lower case. "It's a cryptogram which when deciphered spells..." She put her lips to Simon's ear and whispered, "Tinkerbell loves Simon." She hit enter.

A soft alarm sounded, then an amethyst gem appeared, growing larger and larger.

"You've done it." Marguerite squealed. "*Magnifique.*"

Grinning, Simon brought up the tool bar, clicked on Insert, then clicked on Captain Hook. A flashing message appeared. *Do you really want the treasure buried?* Simon hit YES and sat back.

Darius and Marguerite gasped as big black cracks appeared in the Amethyst Gem. The beautiful fairy flitted across the screen, waved her wand and the gem disintegrated, leaving a blank screen.

Marguerite squealed. "What is happening?"

"I destroyed the Amethyst Code. Darius and I are no longer any use to terrorists, which also means intelligence agencies won't come after us either." He gave Marguerite a salute. "My work here is done."

Marguerite sputtered. "You imbecile, what have you done?"

"What Professor Cortez and I should have done years ago. Let me show you to your accommodation." He drew the gun from his pants and waved her out of the room.

Standing, Nick chuckled. "I didn't see that coming. Way to go, buddy."

Marguerite glared at Simon before stalking into the hall.

He picked up a battery-operated lamp then paced to a door further along the hall. The small room contained two bunks, a portable toilet and good supply of bottled water and snack bars. "If you're legit, you'll be released after the cyclone." Simon handed Marguerite the lamp then pulled the door closed. He locked it and turned to find Nick and Darius behind him, each holding softly glowing lamps.

Nick considered the door. "If she can pick locks, it probably won't hold her for long." With a shrug, he strode to the external door and slid the bolt open. "I'll leave this unlocked for the boys and hostages, if they make it here."

"Good idea." Simon waited until Nick sealed the computer room, then led the way up the internal stairs, removing the key in the top door. He doubted Marguerite would lock them out, but it was easier to remove temptation.

They'd almost reached the front door when it opened, spilling Ryan and Madeline into the foyer. The force of the wind threw Simon back against Darius and Nick.

Ryan forced the door shut. "It's turning into a ripper of a storm." He shook water off his head. "Madeline brought dry clothes for her and Darius, but is there anything downstairs that will fit me?"

Nick's lips twitched. "Yes, as long as you like Frangipani print."

"Ryan will look sweet in flowers." Madeline hugged Darius. "You did well, sweetie."

"Thanks."

"Madeline, you'll need this key." Simon passed her the bunker door key. "I've locked Marguerite in one of the storerooms, where she is to stay until Jarred interviews her. She insists she's with the French Secret Service, but I have my doubts."

Nick stepped forward and gave her the key card. "Seal yourself in the computer room and don't opened the door for anyone but us."

"Okay."

Ryan passed his phone to Simon. "Jarred sent a text you need to see."

"Oh." Simon opened the message. "Mission aborted. Get S & D to safety."

Ryan grimaced. "Any news on the cyclone?"

"Latest forecast still has us copping the edge of it." He exhaled, his gaze resting on Darius. "You can't come with us, Tink. Stay in the computer room with Madeline and wait for us or Gibbs to arrive. As long as the generator doesn't fail, you can watch the monitors and see what's happening."

She narrowed her eyes. "What are you going to do?"

"Go ahead with our plan and hope for the best. We never leave a man behind."

She put her hands on her hips, her eyes flashing with fury. "I'll stay for now."

He passed her the phone. "Text Gibbs, if we don't come back." Simon longed to hold her in his arms, but her stiff posture and clenched jaw held him back. "I love you, Tink."

Tears filled her eyes. "I'm not happy. If you get killed, I'll never forgive you."

"I'd never forgive myself if they got their hands on you, Darius." Going on instinct, he grabbed her, kissed her hard then set her against the wall.

Nick opened the front door, his face set as Simon passed. Without a word, Ryan followed, wrenching the door closed behind them. Nothing could convey what each of them were feeling. They all had family who would be devastated by their deaths, yet leaving Jarred, Sam and Talos to face what amounted to a terrorist group, wasn't on the cards.

They ran through the torrential rain, taking the road, as it gave them some shelter from the furious squall and flying debris. Staying on their feet had never been so hard. They pushed on, reaching the resort as the sabotaged satellite dish hit the road behind them, slamming into the staff quarters.

"Move!" yelled Ryan.

Nick took the lead, diving to the ground, then slithering along under shrubbery as palms swayed recklessly above them.

There were no external guards, so they crawled to the back of the dining room, where the kitchen and amenity blocks were situated. It wasn't hard to spot the window Darius escaped through, which was definitely too narrow for them.

"I don't get it," shouted Ryan. "Why would Jarred tell us to come this way?"

Simon went to shake his head then stopped. "He wants us to leave him a gun?"

"Here." Nick handed over his gun then linked his fingers. "I'll give you a leg up."

Simon sprang to the ledge, reaching his arm in as far as possible, to gingerly place the Glock on the cistern. He landed softly on the earth beside Ryan then pulled out the gun he'd taken from the security guard. "Where's Talos when you need him?"

261

A wad of wet mulch hit Simon on the head. He looked up to see Talos leaning out from the thatched roof. He signaled them to silence and to throw up the gun, which he caught then put out of sight. Almost immediately, he signaled them towards the kitchen.

Hidden by shrubs, Simon, Nick and Ryan crawled along the base of the wall to the kitchen door. It opened when Simon tried the handle.

They crept in and closed the door. The overpowering stench of ammonia hit Simon like a blast of toxic gas. The boys or staff must have cleaned the cool room floor. No wonder the kitchen didn't have a guard.

"Speargun." Ryan coughed, pointing to the primed weapon lying on a stainless-steel bench. "You take it." He dropped low then crawled across the kitchen.

A draft of wind hit Simon's head. He looked up to see Talos' peering through a man-hole. He gave them the thumbs up, before swinging down, landing on the bench without a sound. "I'll warn Jarred we're about to interrupt the party. You boys ready?"

"Yes," whispered Simon. "We've left a gun in the ladies' bathroom."

Talos nodded. "I'll let Jarred know it's there. The old Morse Code is getting a work out today. Wait for my signal." He reached up, gripped the edges of the manhole then hauled his body into the roof cavity. Talos' strength never ceased to amaze Simon.

A couple of minutes passed then Simon heard distinctive thumps on the ceiling. Anyone who didn't understand Morse Code or wasn't paying attention, would think something had come loose and was banging in the wind.

Talos appeared in the manhole, he fisted then spread the fingers of one hand twice. They set their watches for ten minutes then Talos disappeared.

Simon dropped to all fours and crawled to the office door. Nick had the dining room door cracked with one eye to the gap, a fish-gutting knife in his hand. Ryan crouched beside a counter, his Glock held ready.

After two minutes, Simon tapped his watch face then held up eight fingers. Nick and Ryan nodded their understanding.

At the five-minute mark, Nick gave the thumbs up.

Simon and Ryan crawled through to the reception desk. Cane chairs were overturned, and the howling wind drove sheets of rain and plant matter into the foyer. The dining room doors remained closed. More than likely there'd be a guard on the other side.

Simon's watch showed three minutes. He was in the process of wiping grit out of his stinging eyes when Ryan tapped his shoulder and pointed. He edged around the counter to see an extremely rotund, Fijian woman lumbering into the foyer.

"Fuck, Darius is still in contact with Harnoop and Nutlan."

Ryan grimaced. "You did say we were going ahead with the plan."

"My plan, not hers." He'd ring Darius' neck if they made it out of this alive.

The Fijian pushed against the dining room doors then stumbled, almost falling on her face. "Cyclone coming!" Her high-pitched, voice definitely sounded panicked. "Why you men standing there with guns? We need to go to bunker quick smart or we be blown into ocean."

Simon glanced at Ryan. This might actually work.

"Get over here, lady, and shut your mouth." The British accent had to belong to one of the security guards, as Simon didn't recognise it.

He clicked the safety off the speargun and followed Ryan along the wall, counting down the seconds.

A heavy crash was their signal go. Talos must have dropped through the roof.

Simon dived left. Ryan darted right, firing at a bunch of security guards pointing their guns at Talos, as he wrestled with a huge guard on the raised dais. The guards lunged for doorways or behind overturned tables.

Ryan scooted behind the bar as a volley of bullets sprayed the mirrored glass, bringing it shattering down on top of him.

Two guards sheltering in doorways held their guns on Talos and the guard while the others continued to unload a barrage of bullets at the bar.

The hostages were flat on their bellies, screaming. Simon had taken cover behind another overturned table. He used the pandemonium to check on the delegates, staff and Fijian woman. She was under the next table, her massive ass sticking out like a damn beacon. A guard was sneaking up on her with an automatic rifle.

Simon fired, the spear hitting the guard in the thigh, propelling him off his feet and into a screaming heap. Simon lunged behind a thick pole as bullets sprayed his way.

The door to the kitchen slammed open, bringing with it a volley of bullets from Nick. A section of roof lifted off, allowing in a squall so strong, tables and chairs went hurtling across the floor.

Talos hammered his opponent's head into the dais then leaped over the bar and took cover with Ryan. The way the bullets were splintering the bar it wouldn't protect them much longer.

Simon snatched up a machine gun from beside the guy he'd speared, who continued to scream blue murder, competing with the hostages screams, gunfire, ferocious wind and torrential rain.

Simon writhed along the parquetry floor towards the hostages. Using the overturned tables as a shield, he sprayed the far wall with bullets. Confusion was the best way to deal with these bastards. With luck they would think they were surrounded.

He risked a quick look and spied Alisi crawl in to the female's restroom. A minute later she crawled out then squeezed beside Jarred, shoving something behind his back.

The gun wouldn't do any good if the Colonel couldn't use it.

Simon pulled out his flick knife and threw it at them. It landed short but didn't attract the closest guard, still firing at the bar from behind a pole.

Simon cursed. Nick had run out of bullets. The guards would soon realize that too. He cursed again as the Fijian woman crawled out from her hiding place and picked up the knife. She dropped it in Alisi's lap then clambered to her feet, blocking Jarred and Alisi from view.

The guards came to their feet warily, the nearest waving his hand for the Fijian woman to sit down. Most of the hostages lay flat on the floor or curled into balls with their hands over their heads. Movement caught Simon's eye.

Harnoop darted out of the men's room and dragged Alisi back inside.

Simon's mind blanked. If Harnoop wasn't inside the silicon body suit, then who was masquerading as the voluptuous Fijian? A chill spread through his body.

The Fijian stood her ground, so the guard roared at her to sit down against the wall. Frustration ate at Simon. He couldn't get off a clear shot.

The guard roared again.

She gave him the bird.

"Fat bitch." The guard moved so fast, Simon could only stare in horror, as the woman he loved was shot in the stomach.

"No!" He sprayed the guard and one in a doorway with bullets.

Jarred leaped to his feet, shooting two other guards. Instantly hostages surged to their feet, screaming hysterically as they ran into restrooms or the kitchen.

CHAPTER TWENTY-SEVEN

"Darius!" Simon dragged the dead guard off her and dropped to his knees. He couldn't detect a pulse through the silicone, so dragged off a thick arm sleeve. "What the...." He fell back on his heels, his heart pounding as he stared at the hairy arm.

It's not Tink.

This had to be what winning the lottery felt like. He found a pulse, surprised to detect one. Whoever it was could be bleeding to death. He tore the dress apart searching for the bullet entry.

Jarred and Talos were securing the guards as Sam calmed delegates and staff.

The bullet had entered through the thick silicon stomach, but its trajectory suggested it had gone towards the occupant's chest. He rolled the man onto his front as Ryan knelt beside him.

"Bloody hell." Ryan shook his head. "What was she thinking?"

"It's not Darius."

They unzipped the suit, revealing a thin, pale skinned man. Finding no exit hole, Ryan used his knife to cut the body-suit open, while Simon carefully peeled off the wig and mask.

"Nutlan." Simon blew out a frustrated breath. "Harnoop was supposed to wear the suit. What the hell is Nutlan doing in it?"

"As Harnoop would be desperate to save his wife, I assume Nutlan offered to take his place." Ryan rolled the professor over and winced. "Bullet's gone into his chest. Find me a medical kit."

"Silly old fool." Simon ran into the kitchen, throwing open cupboards until he found the medical box. He raced back to Ryan and Nutlan.

As the team's medic, Ryan was well used to removing bullets and stitching deep wounds. He grimaced. "The bullet is lodged in a rib."

He poured antiseptic solution over the wound, then applied a sterile dressing. "The sooner we evacuate him and the bloke you speared, the better."

Talos squatted beside them. "That could be a while. Best we get everyone to the bunker."

Simon looked at the debris around them. "Is there a golf cart we can use?"

"Ready and waiting." Talos kicked the legs off a narrow table. "We'll use this as a stretcher. Sam, give us a hand."

They lifted Nutlan onto the makeshift stretcher then carried him to the golf cart. The portico offered no shelter from the gust driven rain, but its ferocity had dimmed.

As Talos drove away with Ryan hanging onto Nutlan, Simon turned to Sam. "Are all the gunmen accounted for?"

"Yes. Nick and Jarred took the two who are still alive to the bunker and will interrogate them, then we'll know who they're working for."

Simon grimaced. "I think it has to be Alistair Finch. He had the Amethyst Code."

"I don't think so." Sam kept his gaze on Etera, who had his hands full helping Richard Chapman through the debris. "During the siege, Alistair put his life at risk trying to reason with the guards. That stunt with the butterfly had the guards arguing with each other and the delegates. I couldn't tell who was in charge, but stating you'd joined forces with Darius and planned to destroy the Amethyst Code caused a major ruckus."

Simon frowned. "My Identiscan program verified Alistair's identity, but...if he's the mastermind behind this summit then he could well be part of a terrorist cell?"

"If you're right, he's fooled a lot of people."

"I didn't see Adam Garcia, the American security guard."

Sam grimaced. "That's because Talos found him badly beaten on the edge of the golf course this morning. Garcia discovered a campsite, so passed the info onto Vijay to report, then went back to stake it out."

"What happened?"

"Guards he didn't recognize ambushed him, gave him a serious beating, then tossed him down the mountain. Garcia managed to grab a tree root before he went over the cliff, which is the only reason he's alive. After what's just happened, I suspect Vijay passed the info onto the wrong people. They killed him then went after Garcia."

"Where's Garcia now?"

"I stashed him in the boathouse for safe keeping. I'll move him to the bunker. You wanna come with me?"

"No, I need to speak to Sir William."

"Watch your back." Sam sprinted out into the torrential rain.

"No time like the present!" Sir William limped out of the foyer. "I'm happy to speak with you, dear boy, but first we should ask Darius to join us." Sir William held a gun pointed at Simon.

"What's with the gun?"

"It's a precaution. Along with Alistair and a select few, I've been seeking the person who took the Amethyst Code. You, my boy, have always been the prime suspect. Now, we know you seduced Darius into aiding you."

Simon stiffened. "Neither of us ever had the Amethyst Code. We put that on the note to save the hostages. You need to look closer to home. Try asking your friend, Alistair Finch."

Sir William laughed. "Alistair is the only person who believed you innocent. He started this enquiry. No, you can't wriggle out of it now, my boy. Shall we ask Dari to join us." He pointed the tip of his walking stick at a large Monarch butterfly hovering above them. "I suspect she's within hearing distance. Do join us, Dari, darling."

A huff of disgust reached Simon. He spun round as a utility cupboard creaked open.

Darius stepped out, wearing black T-shirt and tights. "Oh, look, it's the two people I detest most in the world. My father and his brilliant student, two double-crossing traitors, who'll do whatever it takes to get what they want."

Simon's gut clenched. She hadn't believed him. "Darius, this isn't your father, and I didn't betray you. I love you."

Sir William scoffed. "That's very touching, Simon, but all I'm interested in is the third password, so the two of you will accompany me to a seaplane arriving in five minutes. Otherwise I will shoot Darius."

Her big blue eyes widened. "You'd shoot your own daughter, knowing she has the third password. I don't think so."

Sir William's sadistic laugh chilled Simon. "You do have a fantastic imagination Dari, but your father did jump into that crevice. I assume to protect his family from me."

Her face lost all color. "If that's true, then you're part of a terrorist group. You had the American killed and Vijay and Professor Heckle?"

"Sadly, Lex Boyd and Keith Heckle became liabilities. As for Vijay and Adam Garcia, they discovered my extra men, so we had to get rid of them." He pointed the gun at Darius. "The password?"

Simon clenched his fists. He couldn't make a move without Darius being shot.

Her eyes welled with tears. "I'll only give it to you, if you let Simon go."

Fear clutched at Simon. Sir William would shoot Darius without blinking an eye. He took a step forward, drawing Sir William's aim. "The password is useless. I've destroyed the master file. Any copies will self-destruct within the month."

"You're lying." Sir William's knuckles whitened on the cane and gun.

"It's true." Marguerite staggered into the foyer, resembling a drowned rat who'd been spat out of a garden mulcher. "Mr. Supercomputer Man had the Amethyst Code, and his *petite* girlfriend had the third password. I witnessed them destroy the program in a bunker under the big villa."

"It's unfortunate you didn't stop him, Marguerite." Sir William grabbed Darius, pressing his gun to her chest. "No heroics, Simon. I'm taking Dari with me as insurance, but we shall be in touch. If you value her life, you will keep your mouth shut, and do as we ask. I'm sure a man of your brilliance can recreate the Amethyst Code."

A tidal wave of terror washed over Simon. By Darius' blank gaze, she'd gone into shock. With luck Madeline would still be manning the cameras. He needed to gain enough time for the boys to return. "I'll come with you willingly, if you leave Darius here unharmed."

"That is the mistake we made with Alexander Cortez. No, you shall stay here, and if you wish to keep your pretty little girlfriend unharmed, you'll do exactly as we say." He smirked at Marguerite. "Thank you for dispatching Vijay. That was impressive work with the speargun."

"*Merci beaucoup.*" Although drenched, Marguerite stood utterly composed as she held a gun on Simon. "Our *rendezvous* did not end the way the chef expected.

Simon glanced about furtively. "It's madness to fly in this weather." He took another step toward Darius, but she held up her hand.

"Please do as they say, Simon. I do believe you and I trust you. I was just trying to keep you safe by saying those horrible things about you."

He swallowed down his rage, a hot head would get her killed. What he needed was logical thinking and his mates near the wharf with high powered rifles. "I'll do whatever they want."

"Good." Sir William and Marguerite backed out of the foyer, pulling Darius with them. Once they were out of sight, Simon tore through the kitchen then courtyard, leaping over fronds and what was left of the bamboo screen. He hit the road running, ignoring the devastation on both sides as he sprinted up the road.

He reached the bend as Jarred, Talos and Alistair came hurtling round in a golf cart. They skidded to a halt.

"What's happened?" called Jarred.

"Sir William and Marguerite have taken Darius. They plan to use her to force me to recreate the Amethyst Code. We have to stop them. They're flying out in a seaplane."

"It's already landed. That's why we came down." All three men jumped out of the golf cart and ran with Simon to the beach.

They took cover behind the snorkel hut and watched as Sir William hobbled as fast as he could along the wharf. Marguerite kept shoving Darius with the gun. It was too dangerous for Talos to take a shot.

"I'll kill that bastard," muttered Alistair. "We thought the traitor might be Richard Chapman or, at a far reach, Keith Heckle. Never once did I suspect Sir William."

Simon glanced at him. "Keith Heckle was in on it too, and the American they threw off the cliff. Marguerite killed Vijay. They know I destroyed the Amethyst Code and they're using Darius to persuade me to recreate it."

Alistair's eyes widened. "Good Lord, Simon, you installed a back door in the program. I'm very proud of you. Now we need to save my Dari."

Momentarily stunned, Simon sat back on his heels and stared at Alistair. "Nice to see you alive, Alexander, but if anything happens to Darius, I'll kill you."

"Have faith, my boy, Dari is far smarter than most people give her credit. She will come up with a plan, she has to." His anxious eyes locked on Simon. "I faked my death to protect my family. I've been working as part of an undercover operation to expose my traitor and the terrorist organization who recruited me. I'm not proud of what I did, but at the time I had no choice. Since my death, I've been rectifying things and following your career. I realized you and your Steele Ops friends were my best way of protecting Darius."

"Why couldn't you let me or your family know you were alive?"

"You could have been in on it. They got to me. They could have got to you too. I only let my wife know the truth after I'd been dead five months. She insisted I create another alias so we could be together, at least for part of each year. A year ago, I approached the British and Australian Secret Service. They agreed to grant me immunity for the capture of the terrorists. The seaplane will be tracked. Wherever it lands, the Secret Service will be waiting. They've promised Darius will come to no harm."

"Fuck you, Alex. I'm not taking that chance. It's too dangerous to take off in this wind." Simon launched to his feet and sprinted along the sand. The seaplane had been tied to the pylon but was bobbing about recklessly.

The pilot helped Sir William into the front seat then tried to hold the plane steady as Darius then Marguerite climbed in the back.

Shit. Simon leaped onto the wharf then pounded along the boards, breathing hard, pushing himself to go faster, swearing as the pilot sliced through the holding line then climbed into the plane. The propeller began to rotate, and the plane moved away from the wharf, rocking dangerously.

"Darius!" Simon roared her name as he reached the end of the wharf, deflating as the plane picked up speed. "Fuck." He doubled over, clutching his knees, gasping for oxygen. Jarred thundered along the wharf, stopping beside him to stare helplessly at the plane as it lifted off the sea.

"Fuck you." Simon roared his pain again.

"Hold on!" Jarred put a hand up to block the rain. "One of the doors is open."

Simon straightened. "Holy shit, Darius is climbing out on the float." A gust of wind hit the seaplane, knocking it sideways. She slipped, dangling by one arm. "Christ, she's going to get smashed."

Jarred gripped Simon's shoulder. "Talos has gone for a boat. If she falls, we'll find her."

"Before or after she drowns?" Simon flinched as another gust slammed Darius against the float. She wouldn't be able to hang on much longer. A hand reached out of the plane. Darius knocked it away.

Alexander reached Simon and Jarred, holding his side as he gasped for air. "What's she doing?"

"She's gonna jump." Simon tore off his shoes then jeans and shirt and dived into the choppy water. The plane flew in a wide circle as Marguerite leaned out, stretching her hand toward Darius.

It was small comfort they needed her alive. Simon kept swimming, praying she wouldn't land on the reef and that he'd make it in time. She managed to straddle the float, releasing the door to cling to the support strut.

The plane was almost overhead and losing altitude. They were going to land again, then force her back inside. "Look for the deep water, Tink." He kept swimming and watching.

The plane dipped to the right and Darius swung her legs over and jumped, feet first, dropping like a miniature torpedo into the churning ocean.

He'd never get to her in time. Simon put on speed, his heart fit to explode as he ploughed through the waves. He could hear a motor in the distance, but if she'd lost consciousness, Talos would never make it. The plane flew over again then dipped sharply to the left, just as another gust hit its right side. The plane flipped then nose-dived into the ocean.

Darius popped up on a rising swell, gasping and choking, floundering to stay above the waves.

"Yes." Elation infested Simon, infusing his body with much needed energy. He swam on, never letting her out of his sight.

She washed off a swell, into his arms. "Simon, my father died to protect us."

"Alistair is your father, Tink." He kept them afloat by treading water.

"What?" She pushed away, treading water herself.

"Your father faked his death. For the last year he's worked as part of an undercover operation to expose the terrorists who conscripted him."

"Alistair is my father? Are you sure?"

"Yes, sweetheart. He had to invent a new identity to protect you."

"What am I going to tell my mother?"

"She knows. Darren Turner is another alias your father used."

"Oh my God." As they rose on a swell, she looked about frantically. "Where'd the plane go?"

"To the bottom of the ocean with any luck."

A motor grew louder. He could see Talos behind the wheel of a runabout. Ryan and Nick leaned over the sides, searching. Simon waved, groaning with relief when they waved back. Exhaustion pulled at every muscle.

Darius frowned. "They've got scuba gear on."

"The boys would have dived for you, Tink. They know what you mean to me."

She washed against him, then clung to his shoulders, her eyes glassy, her lips trembling. "Simon, I'm going to need time to come to terms with everything."

"That's fine, Tink, just remember I love you and I won't give up on us. Ever."

Epilogue

"Professor Nutlan is somewhat of a hero?" Madeline took a sip of her wine. "I hear he's convalescing at Colonel Judith Sutton's house in Hawaii."

Simon nodded. "Nutlan's life has been turned around, since he took a bullet for the good guys."

"So, he really didn't know Alexander Cortez was alive?"

"Nope. Nutlan thought he was helping Alistair and Sir William discover the truth. He still has no idea Alistair is Alexander." Simon wondered how long he had to wait before tracking down Darius. He turned the sausages then lowered the gas on the barbecue. "I'm amazed the Feds sent you in on that yacht. Is there something I don't know?"

She raised an eyebrow. "Like what?"

"You don't work for the Feds, do you?"

She laughed so hard tears came to her eyes. "I'm a nosy journalist, Simon. I just happened to be in the right place at the right time, and Zachary Gibbs was desperate."

"You saved our bacon. Thanks." He gazed across his parents' back lawn, at his nephews and Nick's son, chasing each other with water pistols under the watchful eyes of their parents. Jen waddled around the table, helping his mother and Nonna arrange the banquet of salads made even trickier today as Madeline and the Steele Op's wives had contributed their own dishes to the feast.

Talos had one arm around Jane and held their baby daughter, Ella, in the other, while they watched their eldest little girl jump on the mini trampoline.

Madeline waved a hand in front of his face. "I asked where Ryan is today?"

"He's taken leave to visit his sister. She lives on an island off Queensland."

"I'm surprised he didn't wait until after your birthday." She narrowed her eyes. "Unless he had a good reason to miss it." Madeline had her hair up in a ponytail and wore a shirt tied at her midriff and cutoff jeans, making her appear much younger. Her eyebrows lifted. "There is a good reason, isn't there?"

"A rumor about a shipwreck has surfaced. It's drawn treasure hunters and undesirables and there's been some trouble. Ryan took Adam Garcia with him."

She frowned. "The ex-Seal who got beaten up on the island?"

"Yes, Garcia was recuperating at Ryan's apartment. He jumped at the chance to see the Great Barrier Reef."

Jarred wandered over and handed Simon a beer. "I received a call from Ryan this morning. He's been doing some diving on a reef off the island. Yesterday a boat tried to mow him down. Last week the local museum was broken into and two old timers had their homes ransacked. Ryan said there have been other incidents in past weeks which has the local cop pulling his hair out."

"You knew this and didn't tell me?" Madeline glared at Jarred.

"Ryan asked me to keep a lid on it until he did some investigating." Jarred's lips twitched. "There's one treasure hunter in particular he has his eye on."

"Hmm," Madeline raised an eyebrow. "I could do with a holiday on the reef. Who knows, I might even uncover a story worth...."

Simon frowned at Madeline, who seemed lost in another world as she stared across the garden.

"Excuse me." She handed Jarred her glass then ran across to Jane and Talos, where she took possession of Ella. The bright-eyed baby smiled with delight.

Jarred exhaled. "I can't figure that woman out and, God help me, I'd like to throw her husband under a bus. I told him we have a fishing expedition planned and the fucking moron asked me to take Madeline with us."

"Jesus, that won't go down well with the boys."

"I'm thinking of sticking her on the island with Ryan's sister and Adam Garcia. Madeline can nose around to her heart's content while we can go fishing."

Grinning, Simon turned the sausages again. "Any news on Alexander Cortez?"

"It's been decided he will remain dead and Francine will marry Alistair Finch. They intend to spend half the year on their catamaran sailing about the Whitsundays and the other half in their small villa on an island in the Lau Archipelago."

"You're kidding. Alexander Cortez owns the small villa?"

"Alistair Finch! Over the last ten years, he and the island's owner have made millions from their cyber security firm. It's why he initially created Alistair's identity. Incidentally, Alistair asked Gibbs to pass on a message to you."

"Oh."

"He sent Vijay to deal with a person of mutual interest four years ago, so don't waste your life seeking revenge." Jarred grimaced. "Gibbs also informed me the bodies of Sir William, Marguerite Lémaire and their pilot have been recovered. The guards we captured gave up the rest of their terrorist friends who have now been arrested."

"Excellent. What of Richard Chapman?"

"He wasn't involved. His only crime is being a cheating, sleazy bastard. I believe Alistair has taken care of that too. Mrs. Chapman filed for a divorce."

"The day is improving by the second." There was only one more thing Simon could wish for.

Jarred's lips twitched. "Our PM sent his personal thanks, along with those of our allies. I foresee plenty of work for us on the horizon."

"Good to know." Simon waved at his tiny niece. "Thanks for your help with the house, Jarred. I had no idea settlement could go through that quickly. I'm now the proud owner of a two-story Federation in Warrawee."

"No problem."

"I never really appreciated family." Simon's gaze settled on Sam, smiling indulgently at his wife, Kallie. Nick stood with an amused expression, listening intently to whatever his wife, Ava was saying. Both women were rubbing their bellies, almost protectively. He'd known Ava was expecting twins, she even had a pronounced pod, but it seemed Kallie might be in the family way as well.

Simon glanced at Jarred. "I actually felt sorry for the boys when they got married, but they're to be envied. Don't get me wrong, boss, I look forward to our fishing trips and the occasional game of golf and our gym workouts, but I want what they've got."

"Hell, at this rate, I'll be the only single man standing." Jarred's eyes were trained on Madeline, dancing barefoot in circles with Ella.

The doorbell chimed. Simon narrowed his eyes as his mother and three sisters dropped what they were doing to rush into the house, almost knocking a tray of steak out of his father's hands. They were up to something.

"Did Inspector Gibbs have any news on Madeline's attackers?"

Jarred shook his head. "The car was stolen. We could have a lead, thanks to something Alistair Finch let slip. I want you to dig around Madeline's family, she doesn't seem to have a lot to do with them and look into her husband's business partner. I think—"

"Simon!" His mother's overly cheery voice was a warning to bolt for the closest exit. Unfortunately, this was *his* birthday. "No, not today." There was only one woman he wanted. He'd said he'd give Darius time. Other than a text saying she was with her family, she hadn't contacted him.

"Simon, there's a very pretty young lady here for lunch."

He closed his eyes and groaned. "Mamma, you promised."

"It doesn't count if she's loved you for years." The voice he'd craved to hear sent a ripple of awareness over his skin. He spun round.

And there she was, his beautiful, golden-haired fairy, wearing a soft blue dress with an extraordinarily large white bow at her waist.

She smiled. "Happy birthday, Simon. I wanted to buy you a gift, but I couldn't think of anything you need more than me."

"Is that so?" He laughed, loving the wicked glint in her eyes.

"Yes. However, I come with a warning. If you accept me, you must promise to love and cherish me for the rest of our lives."

Simon's mother, Nonna and three sisters gaped. They might be forever introducing him to single women, but none had taken this extraordinary approach.

With eyes only for the gorgeous woman in front of him, Simon clasped both her hands. "As you own my heart already, that's a promise I can easily make, and if this is a marriage proposal, I accept."

A round of gasps drowned out her reply, but he read it in her sparkling eyes and on her smiling lips. She came into his arms and into his kiss.

Simon eased back, surprised to find his family and friends had discreetly moved out of hearing and were being seated by his sisters, who kept darting curious glances across the terrace. "How's your family?"

"They're good. Grandma and Brianna are still on the island with my parents. It's still weird seeing Alistair but knowing it's Dad, but it's wonderful having him back." Her lips twitched. "Do you know the legend of the Phoenix?"

Simon frowned. "At the end of life, it's consumed by fire."

She smacked his arm lightly. "It builds a pyre nest of branches and aromatic spices *then* it's consumed by fire. A few days later the phoenix is reborn from the ashes. I should have guessed Phoenix was my father, but it didn't sink in until he gave me a black gambling chip. It was my way to recognize him when we met face to face." She looked across to the crowd of interested spectators. "Curiosity is killing your family and I'm also looking forward to meeting them."

He laughed. "You know my mates, so I'll introduce you to the Steele Ops wives."

"No need. Madeline did it yesterday, when we all met for lunch. How do you think they found out about your birthday barbecue?"

He laughed. "You never cease to surprise me. On a serious note, it's *your* birthday in three days, so I thought you might like to pick out the furniture for a two-story Federation house I bought in Warrawee. It's got a massive Liquid Amber in the front garden, a cute balconette, and is very close to your grandmother's house. There's also a huge garage where you can build your robotic toys and drones."

"You bought my house." She wiped a tear away. "Thank you, but you can keep your Mustang in the garage. Jarred offered me my own workshop in the new Steele Security and Special Operations building. I'm your new Robotics and Intelligence Engineer."

"Is that so, *bella ragazza*? Anything else I should know?"

"I love you, Simon." She smiled her glorious smile. "So very much."

Happiness and gratification cloaked him in a cocoon of warm glory. Later, he'd take her home, where he intended to savor every inch of her in the privacy of their room with the small balconette.

His lips twitched. "I really should open my present." He pulled the white ribbon, letting it float to the grass at their feet. "I love you, Tink." He drew her into his arms, kissing her deeply and leisurely to the cheers and whistles of his family and friends.

ABOUT THE AUTHOR

 **Erin Moira O'Hara** grew up in the Blue Mountains of Australia, with a garden backing onto native bushland, hidden caves and fabulous lookouts. Weekends were spent exploring, climbing trees and creating secret bases. Her love of reading began with visits to the local library, where she became absorbed in a world of intrigue, fantasy and action-packed adventures. The moment Erin read her first romance; she recognised the importance of finding the right man to share her life. She now lives with him close to the largest saltwater lake in Australia. Their home overlooks bushland and is surrounded by an abundance of bird life and an ever-growing garden.

Erin's writing encompasses everything she loves—intrigue, suspense, passion and romance.

If you would like to know more, please visit:
http://www.erinmoiraohara.com

www.ingramcontent.com/pod-product-compliance
Lightning Source LLC
Chambersburg PA
CBHW031943130726
47905CB00002BA/481